CATALYST

TALES OF A WITCH'S FAMILIAR
BOOK ONE

ALBA LOCKWOOD

To my family who believed in me even when this felt like a distant dream.

And for anyone who has ever looked at a cat and thought "what an easy life you have."

CONTENTS

CHAPTER 1

CLAWDIA

*T*he small clock hand ticked another warning.

Mary will be here soon. You'd better hurry, I told the witch rushing around the room, a dark blur picking things from shelves and bringing them to the table.

We were in the garage where Winnie, my witch, had set up her workshop. It was soundproof and spell-proof, the inside invisible to human eyes. Which was a terrible tragedy for humans, because it was a lovely space.

Winnie had decorated it in bright pinks and deep purples and furnished it with antique wooden cabinets, bookshelves, and a large desk.

"I know, I know." She took a book off the shelf and returned to the desk where I was sitting. "This one is another big one. Are you ready?"

Of course. I narrowed my eyes. *Why have we been doing so many spells recently?*

I didn't mind, of course. I'd have done anything for Winnie, despite my fatigue from the last spell a few days ago. That had been an invisibility charm we'd needed to "test." But I wasn't told why.

She flipped the book open to the page, and I sneezed as the dust swirled into the air. When I reopened my eyes, Winnie was holding a finger on the line she needed, her dark skin a contrast to the yellowed pages.

I followed the words. A spell for bottled magic.

Winnie placed a jar opposite me on the desk.

What is this for? Why do you need bottled magic?

"No time to explain." She blew a red curl away from her face and bit her lip as she concentrated on the words in front of her.

I huffed, thinking that, if this were so important, she should have done it earlier. But I kept that to myself and went silent.

Winnie mumbled under her breath, her eyes shut and her fists clenched. My fur prickled as the spell activated. Magic bled from me; like a tug from my core, power seeped out from my pores in thin clouds and moved in slow, glowing rivulets to the jar before rushing inside like a waterfall and intertwining with the magic Winnie pulled from herself.

My heart raced as a small adrenaline rush surged through me—not my own, but an echoed feeling through the bond between my witch and me. As the jar got fuller, my own exhaustion caused my legs to give way, and I lay down.

Winnie whimpered when she cut the spell. Closing the lid on the jar, she grinned widely at me. "Oh, Clawdia, you're so amazing. Every time, I think I'm asking too much of you, but you give me so much power. You're the best familiar in the world. I'm so lucky to have you."

I preened at the praise, exuding my shy pleasure and embarrassment. She stroked my whole body from head to tail, and I purred.

You know I'd do anything for you, Win, I told her.

"I know. You're a gift."

My tail rose in a question mark as I cuddled closer,

rubbing my head against her long nails and then over to the jar in her other hand. I stared at it curiously, a feline trait I've indulged in this life.

What is this jar of magic for?

"Oh, nothing important. Anyway, I need to get ready." She floated out of the room, taking the jar with her.

Nothing important? Why would she need bottled magic if it wasn't important? Do witches usually carry extra just in case? In case of what, though? Do they run out?

I'd only been with Winnie for two years, and there was a lot to learn about witches.

Get ready for what? I asked as I hopped down from the desk, my paws touching the cold stone floor. My claws splayed as I stretched. I followed her slowly to her bedroom upstairs, enjoying the rhythmic sound of my tip-tapping as I walked. *I thought you were spending the day with Mary.*

The wardrobe doors were open, and she'd thrown her clothes across the floor. My witch stood in only her under-garments as she stared at her options. I jumped onto her bed and made myself comfortable in the messy quilt.

"I have to get this right. It's important that I make the right impression," she muttered to herself as she trawled through her clothes.

I huffed. Exasperated with her ignoring my questions, I drawled, *Why would you need to impress Mary with an outfit? She has seen you naked.*

"You shouldn't stop trying to impress a partner, Clawds. If you do, then the relationship dies."

I checked the clock on the bedside table, and the glowing green numbers suggested that Mary would be arriving any moment while Winnie stood swaying in her underwear. Mary wouldn't like that. *I think she'd be more impressed if you were dressed at all.*

Winnie gasped, covering herself dramatically with a

blouse she had pulled out. "Are you saying you think I look better with my clothes on?"

I wouldn't know. You aren't my type. I sniffed distastefully and looked at her with one eye. Another feline talent I had picked up.

She laughed. "No, I know your type. He's next door." She twirled toward me and posed. "What do you think about this?"

The outfit was just as good as the ones she had before. The pencil skirt was black and hit below the knees. She had paired it with a summery orange blouse that complimented her dark skin. Her heels were low and reminded me of the kind I used to wear.

You look beautiful, Winnie. Are you going to a job interview?

"Of a sort." She turned back to admire herself in the mirror.

You already have a job.

She rolled her eyes. "Maybe I want a new one."

I narrowed my eyes in response. *Why wouldn't you just tell me that? You're being awfully secretive lately.*

She looked at me, expressionless, and moved to sit with me on the bed. When I began purring at her nails scratching my chin, she smiled brightly.

"I just didn't want to get my hopes up. That's all," she said. "I'm not keeping secrets from you, Clawd. I couldn't. You're my familiar. You're my bonded soul for life."

Jingling keys against the front door's lock interrupted my softening. We both tensed. Winnie shot up.

"Oh goddess, I'm not ready!" she whispered urgently. "Go distract her, Clawds."

You know she can't hear me and barely spares me a glance. Just be quick, and she won't get so annoyed.

"Win!" Mary shouted. "I'm here. You ready?"

4

Her footsteps pounded against the floors as she traipsed upstairs, and my ears flattened.

"We're going to be late if you aren't ready," she continued. "I bloody told you to pick your outfit last night."

Winnie's bedroom door flung open, slamming against the door stop on the wall with a bang. I flinched, lying tensely on the bed.

There stood Mary, dressed in striped trousers, a white blouse, and a red blazer. Her neat, slicked-back brown hair showed the shaved sides, but the frown that deepened as she looked at Winnie was not made prettier by the pink lipstick.

She continued her tirade. "I knew you wouldn't be ready on time. You never are."

Winnie tried to interrupt. "That's not fair—"

"You know how important this meeting is. Why are you trying to sabotage our chances? Do you even want this?" Like a bulldozer, she tore around the room, picking things up and putting them down in different places.

"You know I do," Winnie whispered and bowed her head, a sight that always troubled me.

"Well, you're not acting like it. We have to go, Win. Get your stuff. Let's move," Mary snapped, already storming to the door.

"I just have to—"

"Do it. Quickly." She barely spared me a glance as she turned and left the room.

Winnie and I both sighed.

She's always so loud, I said.

I didn't tell Winnie that I thought her girlfriend was controlling and a mean witch. I didn't tell her that Mary's behavior frightened me because it reminded me of my past.

Winnie gave me an apologetic smile. "She is. I'd better go." She picked up her bag. "Are you going to be okay today?"

I'll be fine. I'll probably go next door and bother Charlie.

"Again? Can't you just watch Netflix like a normal familiar?"

He's more entertaining than anything on Netflix. The smirk in my voice couldn't be shown on feline features as I thought about what I had planned for him.

"I'm sure. A man sat in his boxers on a computer, hacking. Sounds thrilling," she said sarcastically. "Your crush on him is cute, Clawds, but you need to be careful. You know how mopey you were when he was with Lydia."

If I had lips, I would have pouted. *I was not mopey.*

But Lydia did distract Charlie from me. So I couldn't spend as much time as I would have liked with him. Which … displeased me.

And Lydia didn't like me, although she respected me as Winnie's familiar. She would talk to Winnie about the intimate side of their relationship, which I thought was very distasteful and not at all interesting.

But I didn't mope.

"You did so mope," Winnie said. "Just promise to behave yourself. You're like a little boy pulling pigtails to get attention."

If you keep saying untrue things, I will simply stop listening.

She ignored my snooty comment and continued. "I'm not saying don't see him. Just see him less. He's human, and liking him will only end badly for you."

It's not like that. I just … like him. His company. I want to have one friend outside of you. Please?

"Winnie!" Mary screamed from downstairs.

We both jumped, having forgotten her in our conversation.

"Shit," Winnie cursed, then threw her bag and coat over her arm and snatched the jar from her desk as she ran out of the room. "Coming!"

I followed less urgently and sat on the bottom step as they

rushed out of the house, collecting things, shutting windows, and locking the back door.

In the background, the TV murmured. A news presenter informed the public that disappearances were on the rise.

"Terrible," Winnie acknowledged.

Mary wasn't interested in the news. She wittered on at Winnie about how orange wasn't an appropriate choice for the meeting.

I didn't understand their relationship, but Winnie said she loved Mary, so I didn't voice my opinion of Mary's cruel tendencies.

When the door slammed behind them with a loud bang, I was glad for the peace.

And also very curious about their meeting.

I thought Winnie enjoyed her work as a retail administrator, but maybe I was wrong. Maybe she didn't share all her desires with me. After all, what could I do about them? I was simply a cat-shaped power bank.

Our conversation about Charlie had soured my mood, but I knew she spoke from a place of love.

The wonderful thing about being a cat was that I could shake emotions from my fur like rainfall. Angry? Not for long. Sad? No. Scared? Never.

I was a mini lion. Prey feared me. I was fierce and beautiful.

Hear me roar.

Vanity, courage, and curiosity seemed to be feline traits I inherited when I became a familiar. I just hoped the sayings about curiosity weren't true.

Since cat emotions were duller and not as long-lasting, I didn't dwell for too long on my conversation with Winnie— not about her obvious secret or about Charlie. I contemplated it for two, maybe three seconds, before I went looking for something to entertain me.

I wandered into the kitchen and headed through the cat flap and into the garden. A deep breath of the fresh, English spring air, wet pavement, and budding flowers soothed my soul. After stepping onto the grass, I paused as I looked up at the fence and then made a leap. I balanced precariously as I walked along, the wood scratching at my paws, until I reached the kitchen rooftop.

Jumping from the fence to the roof in a practiced move, then from the roof into Charlie's bedroom window, which he always kept open, no matter the weather, I gave myself a mental pat on the back. As I landed gracefully on his carpeted floors I announced my perfect score with a triumphant meow.

"Clawdicat, you're here early. Winnie's gone out for the day?" he asked.

His deep, indulgent voice made me immediately happier. I almost felt guilty for what he would find downstairs. Almost.

He was sitting on his bed in nothing but his boxer shorts, casually rubbing a towel over his brown hair.

I stopped for a moment to appreciate the sight. Charlie was a beautiful man. His hair perfectly tousled and wet, his brown eyes shrouded with thick but not unruly brows, and his body as chiseled as a stone monument although I'd never seen him exercise.

Yet another wonderful thing about having the soul of a human and the body of a cat: no one suspected a cat was staring at them appreciatively.

I snapped out of human-mode and meowed, letting him know he was right. Then I hopped onto the bed next to him.

"I just washed these sheets, Clawdia. Get down."

I ignored him as I rolled around and then circled him, rubbing my face against his elbows. I loved the smell of his sheets. Although they smelled of fresh laundry powder today, they usually smelled of him. His aroma was like woods and spice from a deodorant he used, and it drove me to distraction.

A drop of water ran down his body from his hair, past his broad shoulders, and down his back. I licked it before I thought to stop myself.

He jumped. "Ouch. Your tongue fucking hurts, Clawdicat. Get off me."

I meowed an apology and moved around him to sit by his side. He sighed and stroked me firmly, which made me purr.

I rolled to my side so he could stroke my belly, and he muttered, "Soppy cat."

When he stopped and stood, I stared at him through narrowed, pleased eyes as he changed. I had seen him dress and undress the same number of times as I had seen Winnie. I just couldn't tell Charlie what I thought about his choice of outfit. Black jeans, black t-shirt—boring but handsome.

When he turned back to me, he said, "Come on. Off."

I stared at him a while longer, long enough that he got more frustrated.

"Clawdia, I swear—" He didn't finish the thought, though. Instead, he strode out of his room, and I knew just where he was headed.

I huffed my annoyance, but my insides were happy as I dropped off his bed. Knowing what he would find, I raced ahead of him, down the stairs, and into his office so I could see his expression.

He walked in after me, muttering and looking at his phone. When I meowed, he looked up and then around. His mouth dropped open.

"What the fuck?"

I meowed again, letting him know I was the one responsible for the "fuck."

"Clawdia, how in the shitting hell did you do this?"

I lay down on the ripped toilet paper and rolled around in it. As expected, he growled at me. "You shredded all my pissing bog roll, and now you're going to play in it like you've done nothing wrong?"

I meowed. He looked at the ceiling and muttered, "I swear to God."

He pointed at me. "You are a hellcat. I know I've done some fucked-up things, but I don't expect immediate karma like this. I hoped I'd be a slug in my next life to make up for it."

I giggled internally at the thought of him as a slug but stopped when I realized he'd need to die for that to happen. I turned slightly away, as if I was bored with his complaining, and swiped at more paper littering the floor.

He growled and left the room, stomping to the hallway cupboard where the hoover—dreaded contraption—lived.

Knowing what was coming, I jumped onto his desk and stepped on the keyboard of his computer since I liked to make music with the noises the keys made.

Then Charlie angrily tidied up the room with the vacuum, the loud roar making me wish I hadn't bothered with my prank. But I hadn't made it easy for him. The larger sheets needed to be picked up by hand. Cue movie-made evil laugh; Netflix hugely influenced my education in this new life.

I blamed my feline instincts on my urge to bother him, but I also knew it was more than that. Winnie might think I was teasing him like a little boy teases a girl, but actually, I was *testing* him.

I hadn't ever been close to men. My father was the only man I'd spent a lot of time with, and he had a short fuse. He didn't forgive. And he didn't touch me with affection.

Charlie was unlike any man I had ever known. He growled and shouted and cursed, but he always forgave me. I didn't know if it was because he thought I was a stupid, ordinary cat instead of a familiar with a human soul, but it mattered to me that, even when I pushed him, he didn't push back.

After the roar of the evil machine suddenly died and Charlie locked it away again, he strode back into the room, glaring at me. It only made him more handsome.

"You are such an annoying fucking cat. Get off before you break something."

I flicked my tail but moved off the keyboard and sat on the desk instead.

He scratched my chin as he moved around the desk to sit in his chair, and I knew he forgave me, even if he didn't voice it yet.

He typed and got settled into doing some—probably illegal—work. I didn't understand it, the how's and the why's, but surprisingly, my old-fashioned sensibilities didn't stop me from liking a man that was a thief.

Or a hacker, as Winnie called him.

He was the best man I had ever met. I didn't know his reasons, and I couldn't ask him, so I just enjoyed his company.

I meowed, having not had any attention for at least five minutes, and Charlie's gaze swung to meet mine. He rolled his eyes, and I smiled internally because I knew he couldn't stay angry at me.

"Don't fucking do it again, Clawdicat," he told me sternly before he picked me up and placed me on his lap.

While he opened his emails, he stroked my head, and I closed my eyes, loving the attention and the affection.

At that moment, being a cat seemed purrfect.

Then a mechanical chime from Charlie's computer changed everything for both of us.

CHAPTER 2

CHARLIE

*I*t wasn't about the money. Let me get that straight.

I mean, at first, it was. I used to be the go-to guy to find things. Lost items, people, rare prizes, whatever they wanted. I was good at it. Talented beyond all reason. I could find it, anything, and make tons of money for it. Which, at the time, I really needed. There was a thrill I got, which made it addictive. The adventure of seeking, the challenge, was unparalleled.

Problem was, the people paying me weren't good people. Don't get me wrong, some of them were just lost souls like me, some were damned funny, and others had family they protected with their lives.

But there was a reserved sign in the fiery depths of Hell for them when their actions inevitably caught up with them.

Being a hacker, a digital thief, meant I started getting pulled into shit I didn't want to do by people who meant business.

After a struggle, I grew a pair of balls, cleaned my shit up, and changed my life. For the past two years, I've been legally hacking into company software and bank accounts and getting paid to do it.

And I'm so bored.

There wasn't any thrill. No challenge. No camaraderie from a job well done. It was just me, at home, in my office.

Hell, half the reason I let Clawdia get away with the shit she pulled was because it entertained me. Added a bit of variety to the day.

So when an email from a stranger flashed into my inbox, requesting a tour around the world for a ridiculous amount of money, I salivated. It read:

> *Charlie,*
>
> *We are a party of three males requesting that you assist us in our tour around this world. To pay you, we have set a budget of $100,000. We will also pay for all travel, accommodation, and meals on the trip for the four of us. The duration should be longer than one year, and except for a few specific locations, which we can discuss at a later date, we are happy for you to plan our travels. We will arrive tomorrow. We look forward to meeting you.*

It was a scam. A scam I hadn't seen before, but a scam, nonetheless. They probably sucked you in with the promise of money and then asked for you to send something, like a booking deposit, but the opposite.

I stroked Clawdia's head as I sighed and pressed my finger forcefully on the delete key.

"If fucking only, Clawdicat," I muttered. Her purrs were appreciative, rhythmic and softened the twinge of heartbreak.

The same address sent another email when I looked back. The subject line now read "DO NOT DELETE," and the message had this added part:

*We will arrive tomorrow morning, 9 a.m. to be exact, at a
"Pigeon Park." I realize this may not be enough time to
organize accommodation. We assume you have a home and
are happy to stay with you until you have somewhere more
comfortable for us.*

I stared at it for a moment, frozen. Then Clawdia
sneezed, and my brain rebooted.

Who the fuck does this prick think they are? Happy to
stay at my house?

My anger cooled to curiosity when I looked at the location. Whoever emailed me knew I lived in Birmingham and
used the colloquial term for Cathedral Square.

Was this a prank?

I replied:

*I'm not a tour guide, but if you Google locations you want
to travel, there will be links to tour services who can help
you out. Also, lower the price on that offer, or people will
think you want more than guiding.*

My email binged again almost instantly:

*I do not know what google is, but I will request that you
explain when we arrive. We thought the offer to be a
reasonable one and do not require the use of your body in
any other capacity than a guide. Humans are not our type.*

I stumbled at that one. Who's never heard of Google?
Who refers to people as humans?

Aliens, that's who.

I won't lie and pretend it was my first thought. I sat on it
for an hour or two. Assumed it was a crazy person, or a
conman, or one of my old acquaintances.

14

So, I did what I do best. I went digging.

And I got nothing. Sweet fuck all. No name. No alias email. No IP address. Nothing. It was like it was written by magic.

"Magic aliens" was my working theory by lunchtime.

Sandwich in hand and Clawdia following close behind to nibble the ham when I wasn't looking, I sat back at my desk and typed my reply:

> *Okay, I need you to give this to me straight. No games. Are you an alien? I can't find you, and I can find everyone. So, who the fuck are you?*

The Alien/Police/Bad Guy/Conman/Crazy Person replied immediately:

> *Charlie, while all of my party are strangers to your realm, we are not aliens. We are three different paranormal races from three different realms. This will come as a shock to you, but I am asking you to guide us around the human realm. We are curious and rich. What more do you need to know?*

So much. I needed to know so much more because it was so fucking bizarre.

Not an alien, but not from Earth. Not human, but a paranormal race. What the fuck does that even mean?

Was this less sci-fi spaceship-traveling-green-monsters and more fantasy portal-hopping-humanlike-creatures?

Did I even believe they were telling the truth? This could be anyone. Anyone with an agenda. Anyone who wanted to make me look like a dick and have me believe this shit.

My finger hovered over the delete button. I had two options: I could delete the email and continue with my boring-ass job, or I could go along with this ruse and try to discover who or what these people were.

My curiosity and longing for entertainment and challenge won out.

I'd find this prick.

So, I asked:

Why me? There are plenty of actual tour guides. Why do you need me?

The email reply read:

Because it is you I saw.

They saw me? Shit, was I bugged? Being stalked? Watched?

My fingers danced over the keyboard as I typed my reply:

How did you see me? Where?

The ping of the notification, seconds later, made me jump.

Do not worry, Charlie. I saw you in a premonition. I know you are the one we need.

My goosebumps were telling me this was too fucking weird. If this was a prank, then they were really playing into the paranormal race vibe. If this was a crazy person, then they were answering surprisingly logically. And I didn't think any of my past acquaintances would be this mysterious.

Who was this?

I needed to know. They wanted to meet in Pigeon Park, then we'd meet in Pigeon Park.

I replied:

Okay. See you tomorrow.

The reply was instant:

Tomorrow. I hope you have an interesting itinerary planned. We are very curious about mummies.

I laughed, the thrill of a chase making me buoyant, and Clawdia peered up at me questioningly. I scratched her chin and told her, "I'm having visitors tomorrow. Before I let them into my humble abode, I need to check them out."

I closed down my computer and pushed Clawdia off my lap, leaving a cold spot on my legs. She huffed and licked her paw daintily as I rifled through my drawers and picked out a few cameras and listening devices. I grabbed an overall and a high-visibility jacket. Just as I turned to leave the house, Clawdia meowed.

"Go home, Clawdia. I've got stuff to do before tomorrow."

Shutting the front door, I pressed the button on my car keys, and the lights flashed as it unlocked. I drove about ten minutes down the road to Pigeon Park. It would have been five, but the one-way system around town was never kind.

I looked around the square, a small pair of ladders in one hand, my other hand holding a bag of equipment.

The entrance to the cathedral was the most sensible place to wait. Spring showers meant the weather was unpredictable. Sitting on a bench or the grass to wait would likely cause a soggy arse.

I set the cameras in the direction of the cathedral's entrance and also put some on the gates around the square, just in case. No one questioned me as I climbed up and situated my devices. The high-vis made me just as unnoticeable as any other maintenance workers.

I threw keys on the kitchen table as I walked back into the office. Wiggling the mouse, I sat back in my chair as the screen came back to life and I activated all the devices. The picture was clear, the sound even better, which was a relief since I hadn't had to use them for this kind of reconnaissance in years.

I smirked and kicked my shoes off, throwing my feet onto the desk and leaning back into the chair.

I'm going to get you, you fuckers.

* * *

THE NEXT DAY, I woke up excited. It was time to get some answers. I ate my corn flakes and watched *This Morning*. At half eight, Clawdia came into the living room and jumped onto the sofa to sit with me. So distracted by the telly, I didn't look at her. I just stroked her once and continued spooning flakes into my mouth. When something touched my leg and Clawdia meowed, I looked down absently and then again once the picture resonated in my brain. She'd dropped a flower on my lap.

"Er, thanks, Clawdicat. Aren't you supposed to give me a mouse or a bird? What kind of cat catches a fucking flower for someone?" I asked and stroked her head since she looked so proud of herself.

Clawdia meowed and nudged the flower. Sighing, I picked it up and muttered something about being bossed around by a flower-catching cat.

I didn't have a vase, so I popped the flower in a pint glass and clanked it on the kitchen table. Clawdia tilted her head at the glass and then looked at me directly.

I was clearly being told off. "Where do you want it, then?"

She huffed and hopped down before jumping up onto the table. I marveled at the intelligence of the average house cat as she nudged the glass directly to the middle of the table and tapped the flower around so it faced the front door. She looked up at me when she finished, expecting praise.

"Are you satisfied now?" I asked. She meowed, and I rolled my eyes as I headed to the office. Clawdia padded after me.

I sat down and turned on my computer ten minutes before nine. Clawdia jumped up on my lap and rested her chin on the desk, her eyes open just a slit as I opened the cameras and turned on the devices. I waited.

As the clock on the screen turned nine, they appeared outside the cathedral, out of nowhere. Literally out of nowhere. There was a cathedral and people milling around, and then suddenly, there were three paranormal peoples.

And fuck me, they were the most obvious paranormal people in the world. They looked like they'd walked out of a comic con convention.

I physically gasped and leaned away from my screen like the space between my eyes and the image would make it smaller and easier for me to understand.

"The human is late," remarked a super tall and freakishly beautiful bloke with skin like ice, shoulder-length green hair, and bright green eyes. His face was all sharp angles with thin lips and nose to match; even his ears were elongated and pointed. I automatically assumed him to be a kind of elf.

"He's testing us. Allow him time to assure himself of our honesty," a giant, golden, muscular guy spoke next. He looked like a young version of Zeus from the Disney film *Hercules*. His clothing was a gray-laced tunic that covered his chest and tucked into tight leather trousers.

The third and final man was the most unhuman, with

stubby black horns and matching leathery wings and skin. His hair was as red as flames and tied in a topknot. His face was relatively human looking, and his ears were pierced with three small hoops on either side. He looked like a demon. "I don't imagine he was expecting us to be honest."

He wasn't wrong. But how are you supposed to trust someone who openly admits they are a paranormal race? And yet I knew instinctively that they were hiding something from me.

Clawdia meowed at me, bringing me back to the room. I blinked and relaxed into my seat, stroking the cat, my thinking face on. As soon as my back hit the leather cushion of the chair, I realized exactly what I was looking at.

There were three paranormal people, obvious non-humans, chilling in plain view of the public.

I panicked and jumped up from my chair, knocking Clawdia to the floor. "Oh fuck," I yelled as I ran out of the house.

I didn't get in the car. I could get there in an eight-minute dash if people were smart and moved out of the bloody way. Thankfully, they heard the siren of "oh fuck, oh fuck" and let me overtake. The chilly spring air didn't bother me as I quickly built up a sweat and my breathing turned to panting.

They were still there, standing around, waiting for me. I didn't care that they looked pissed off. I needed to hide them before the police or the army or the secret service or someone was called.

"Ah, human! There you are!" the beautiful elf said as I approached. I cringed so hard I shuddered and then coughed because I was really out of breath.

I grabbed a hold of the demon's arm as I bent over and took a deep breath. "Zaide, look, the human is touching me," he whispered playfully.

"I can see that, Sav. It must mean he likes you," the golden giant said with a grin stretched across his face.

"No. No. Quiet. You have to be fucking quiet." I coughed, still trying to inhale. "What were you thinking? Appearing in a busy square without a disguise?"

"I think our human believes us fools," the beautiful elf remarked. He didn't even lower his fucking voice.

"Stop saying the word human! Fuck! Let's hope everyone thinks you're in cosplay. Come on, we need to get out of here before they realize you're the real deal." I tugged on the demon's arm, and he and the others followed me.

It's a wonder I wasn't arrested for looking like the shiftiest fuck ever as I tried to hide my new friends and employers from view. The demon kept chuckling as I dragged him behind me, occasionally pushing them all into alleyways or stopping and pulling them to the ground to hide behind bushes. Not that the bushes covered much of them.

When we got to my street, we ran the rest of the way. Well, I ran. Towering over me, the big bastards walked in strides that matched my running gait.

My fingers shook as I unlocked the front door and pushed them inside. Shutting the door behind me, I sagged in relief and took a deep breath, my eyes closed.

When I opened them again, I saw the three faces of my new paranormal friends looking at me with concern. It was strangely endearing. And fucking weird.

Now that I had them back home, and now I knew they were telling the truth, my mind whirled with the danger they had just placed us all in.

CHAPTER 3

CLAWDIA

*C*harlie's guests were otherworldly.

I was hiding under the lounge chair in the living room when Charlie dragged them all into the house. He slammed the door shut and fell back against it, panting as though the world were chasing him.

I flinched at the loud noise and tried to shake away the fragments of memories that pressed in closer from the edges of my mind. Charlie took deep, gulping breaths, and I copied him, calming almost immediately. When a guest spoke, I froze and looked at them properly. I saw the color of them. The shape. The fact that one had wings. I blinked rapidly. But they were still there.

I'd seen a lot of strange things since I'd been reborn in this time. Dishwashers being one of them. I also lived with a witch, so I saw spells being cast, potions being made, and naked rituals.

Nothing Winnie conjured up could have prepared me for people like this.

"This is your home? It is ... quaint," the beautiful elf said, glancing around.

"What were you thinking? Appearing like that in the center of town! Who knows who's coming after you now?" Charlie shouted, finally getting his breath back. "I'm going to need to fight my way through so many firewalls to check if the government knows you're here," he muttered while walking toward his office.

The creature with wings and horns laughed and said, "Fear not, Charlie the human. We have traveled many times before to many different realms. You won't need to fight any walls on fire. Although why you would need to do that is beyond me."

"That's what you think, but nothing goes unseen in this world. Make yourselves at home. This might take a while."

The green-haired elf lowered himself onto the sofa hesitantly. He bounced slightly, testing it, and then sank into the cushions. He rested his arm on the side to stop the sofa from swallowing him whole. He began, "What Savida said is true, Charlie. My magic cloaks us when we arrive through the portal and disguises us as the most sentient being. Please calm yourself, and perhaps we can talk more about our trip,"

Savida watched his friend with a huge grin, then launched himself onto the sofa next to him. They both bounced, and Savida chuckled as the elf, disgruntled, rearranged himself. There was only a hint of a smile in his eyes that suggested he enjoyed his friend's playfulness.

The third guest walked to sit in the chair I was hiding under. I hadn't studied him properly since he had stayed so quiet, but as soon as I looked at him, I couldn't look away.

He was huge. So tall that his head scraped along the ceiling as he walked toward me. His skin was golden, not a true gold, but closer than human skin could ever be. He had purple lines like veins that raced over his arms and up his neck with one strand reaching to his left eye, which was also the same stunning color. His hair was a bright white and braided to his calves, swinging around his body like a tail. He had large purple eyes, a nose that was flat and wide, big lips, narrow cheekbones, and a square jaw. He was stunning.

A strange feeling enveloped me as the golden god sat in the chair above me. I felt protected. I felt warm. And I had the urge to rub myself all over him and enjoy his large hands petting me as I fell asleep in his lap.

Restrain yourself, Clawdia. You don't know if the otherworldly men have ever seen a cat before. You could frighten them, a sensible voice in my head told me.

I giggled at the thought of them all screaming and running from me and then focused on the white braid that lay on the floor next to me. I clawed it closer to me, intrigued by the small pendant dangling from the tie. It looked like a black stone. There was a faint outline of an engraving, but I couldn't recognize the symbols. I sniffed it and resisted the urge to chew on it. I kept it close so I could continue to breathe in the smell.

I turned my attention back to Charlie, who looked torn. He chewed on his lip and ran a hand through his hair and over his face. "Yes. Okay. Magic. Sure." He walked back to the chairs and sat down. "Introductions would be a good start. How about you start, large golden one?"

Above me, a voice growled his name, "Zaide."

I thought of his name, turning it over in my mind. It suited him somehow.

The room was silent as Charlie waited for Zaide to go on. When he said nothing more, Charlie prompted, "And you are a ...?"

The winged man smiled and nodded encouragingly as the giant above me sighed loudly. "My people were once titans, but now we are nothing but large, magicless, broken beings. We are slaves, as I once was." There was a silence and a tension that made my stomach clench. My heart broke for him. "Does that satisfy my introduction, human?"

"It does." Charlie paused, and his voice softened. "I'm sorry that happened to you. That's fucked."

Zaide grunted a laugh. "So it is."

In the brief pause, I contemplated the term "titan." *Is a titan the same Titans who fathered the classical Greek Gods? Or is that a human myth based on brief interactions with his people?*

Charlie turned his head to the elf, who began his introduction, "I am Daithi, Son of Eriman, and I am faei from Álfheimr. My kind has magic to create illusions and portals. I am also cursed with premonitions."

Faei, as in Fairy?

"Blessed," the winged person interrupted and looked at his friend meaningfully. "He's blessed with premonitions."

"Okayyy." Charlie drew out the word, clearly taking in all the information but not coming to any conclusions. "And who are you?"

"Savida. I am a demon, but I remember nothing before Daithi found me here."

A demon?

My mind conjured pictures of a hellscape, eternal fires, and screams of pain from all who were punished by the winged creatures with pitchforks. That was what I was taught about demons. I shuddered.

But Savida had a kind face with a broad smile and an exuberance that filled the air with energy. He didn't look like any depiction of a demon that I had ever seen.

Perhaps his species had been villainized due to fear of the unknown. Humans are good at that.

I thought about the witch trials, slavery, homosexuality, and disability and how they've been treated throughout the ages. Humans were notorious for killing and villainizing what they didn't understand.

Charlie seemed to have similar thoughts because he said, "A demon. Of course." He ran a hand through his hair before turning to Daithi, "You *found* him here? Wondering the streets of Birmingham?"

"I had a premonition that he was buried in the human realm. So, I came and found him," Daithi told him, his tone emotionless, giving nothing away.

"Buried?" Charlie's eyes flickered between Savida and Daithi. "I don't understand." Savida shuddered, and Daithi glared, saying nothing more about it. I could see the curiosity burning in Charlie's eyes, but he changed the subject, asking Daithi, "So, this isn't your first time here?"

I was getting frustrated with Charlie's line of questioning. *Ask about where they came from!* It was times like this that I wished I could talk to him like I could Winnie.

Daithi shrugged a shoulder and leaned back into the sofa before answering. "No, but I came to find Savida and take him home. We did not look around in case he was in danger."

"Take him home? Where are you from exactly? Where is Álfheimr? You mentioned realms … You appeared out of nowhere …"

Yes! Now we are getting somewhere. I leaned my head on my paws, my ears pointed forward, listening intently.

"There are many realms in one interlinked dimension." Daithi opened his hands, and bright, colorful sparkles jumped into the air to form nine balls. Charlie gasped, and I flinched even as my eyes widened in awe.

"I am from this realm, Álfheimr." A bright green ball came to the forefront and expanded, showing the details of the land, the rivers and lakes, the people roaming around on stone paths and stone homes.

"My people can create portals to the other realms." The illusion focused on one person, who then created a tiny ball of bright pink light. When they stepped into the ball, the focus shifted outward until all the nine colorful balls were visible again, and the pink ball came to the forefront, expanding to show the green person coming through the mini ball surrounded by pink figures. "Myself, Savida, and Zaide have been traveling the realms like this for many years now. Does this clarify things for you?"

"Yep," Charlie squeaked, his face frozen with a look of amazement and confusion. He looked rather constipated, and I could practically hear the cursing and screaming happening in his mind. Grunting to clear his throat, he composed himself and continued, "Thanks for the visual presentation. It was very enlightening."

"You're welcome."

A short silence followed until Charlie asked, "You really want to look around this realm?"

Daithi paused, glancing for a second toward my chair. "Yes. That is why we got in contact with you."

"But why me?" I recognized the suspicion in Charlie's eyes. He often looked at me like that, even when I was behaving myself.

"I told you. Because I saw you."

"Saw me in a premonition?"

Daithi looked at the golden giant residing in the chair above me and, upon getting a signal I couldn't see, told Charlie, "Yes. I was looking for someone and saw you. I believe you will help me find them."

"Okay, that makes more sense. I'm good at finding people." He chewed on his lip thoughtfully. "So, do you want to look around the world, or do you want me to find someone?"

Daithi raised a green brow. "We assumed finding someone would require a certain amount of traveling, so both."

Savida grinned, his excitement glittering in his dark eyes.

"I would like to see mummies. I understand they were buried and unearthed like me."

Charlie smiled at Savida's enthusiasm but replied to Daithi, "That might have been how we look for people before the internet, but now I just tap, tap, tap"—he imitated tapping on his computer keyboard—"and bish, bash, bosh, sorted."

Zaide's gravelly voice shocked the room. "You can find anyone? With tapping? Is it magic?"

"It's … a human's version of magic." He waved his hand, dismissing the poor explanation. "I can find people. I just need to know who you're looking for."

Daithi cleared his throat and glanced quickly at the golden giant above me. "Her name is Margaret."

My heart raced at the sound of the name. I shrank in on myself, curled my tail tight against my body, and dipped my head. But I listened. My feline curiosity peaked, and I was on tenterhooks waiting for more information.

"And?" Charlie prompted. "What's her last name? Address?"

No one replied to him. Savida shuffled uncomfortably, as though even that brief silence was too much for him.

"So, all you have is a first name, and you hope I can fucking find someone with that?" Charlie ran a frustrated hand through his hair and sighed. "If all we have is a first name, we haven't got a hope in hell of finding her my way. You have magic. Can't you find her?"

Daithi raised a green brow. "My premonitions are not so reliable that I can search for such information."

"But reliable enough to come asking for my help?"

Daithi looked unmoved by Charlie's teasing. "I have faith she is near and that we will find her. My visions always come true."

"If you say so." Charlie stood up. "Can you see if a cat will be joining us for lunch? I'm starved and don't want to share."

Rude.

"What is a cat?" Savida asked, resting both elbows on his knees and his head in his hands, the picture of interest.

Charlie grinned at Savida. "I'll show you Clawdia the cat later. She turns up at my house when her owner is out. She lives next door." Savida's wings fluttered, and he grinned widely at Charlie's announcement.

Zaide's voice growled from above me, "Owner? She is a slave?"

I decided there and then that he was my favorite of Charlie's guests. He sounded so concerned that someone locked me away next door. As though he would charge over and rescue me if Charlie told him I was. Swoon.

Charlie shook his head. "She's a cat. A domesticated animal. A pet. She can't survive on her own without her owner. There's no need for your muscles right now, He-Man. When she turns up, you can see her and know that she's treated well." He took a breath and turned to Daithi. "I'm starving. Anybody fancy something to eat?"

"You do not look starved," Zaide pointed out.

"What can we eat?" Savida asked.

"Well, come into the kitchen, and I'll show you."

Savida bounced up from the sofa, and his wings seemed to vibrate as he raced to catch up with Charlie. Daithi stood gracefully and also moved to the kitchen. Zaide sighed, and his braid dragged away from me as he heaved himself from the chair. I found I liked the back of him as much as I liked the front as I watched his braid swing around broad shoulders, a sculpted backside, and powerful legs. And with his absence, so too went those pleasant feelings of safety, calm and joy.

I had taken a step to follow him before I realized what I

was doing. Huffing out a breath, I tried to dispel the strange emotions, the lust and the urges. I was a cat. A familiar. Feelings like that would not help me. It was enough that I liked Charlie. I didn't need feelings for a titan.

I stayed hidden under the chair for a while longer. Sounds of cupboards opening and closing and pots and pans clanging echoed out from the kitchen while I debated following them in and letting Charlie introduce me. I was sure they would be very interested and curious, and I would love the attention. But something held me back. I needed to think.

Charlie's guests weren't human; they were looking for a human. A Margaret. It was big news, and I wanted to share it with my witch, who I knew would love to hear the whole exciting tale.

Creeping out from under the chair, I darted upstairs to Charlie's bedroom, jumped out the window and, after skillfully hopping from the roof to the fence, plopped down on the grass outside my home.

* * *

I DIDN'T GET to tell Winnie until she returned later that evening. I'd eaten some of the food she'd left out and watched another episode of *Call the Midwife* while waiting for her. It reminded me of the good parts of my past life.

To my disappointment, Mary came back with her.

"Hi, Clawd. How were Charlie's visitors? Were they nice to you?" Winnie greeted and sat on the sofa next to me, while Mary continued straight into the kitchen.

It was certainly eventful. How was your day? I knew she wouldn't tell me since she was keeping secrets now, but I gave her the chance to tell me every day, just in case.

"Oh, you know, same as always."

Mary came and sat next to Winnie, putting an arm around her shoulders. She'd just poured herself a glass of wine but didn't offer one to Winnie, despite it being her wine. "I hate when you two talk. I can't hear what the cat is saying, Win. Translate."

"You weren't here a second ago. I'm not going to shout everything Clawdia has to say."

"I'm just saying it's rude. Like whispering."

"It's only rude if we're talking about you, and we weren't."

"Well, I can't verify that since I can only hear what comes out of your mouth. If you weren't talking about me, what were you talking about?"

I wished I could roll my eyes. *It might come as a shock to you, Mary, but the world doesn't revolve around you.* Winnie's lip twitched.

Before Mary noticed Winnie's amusement, she told her, "I was asking how her visit to Charlie's house was today. Charlie was having guests, so Clawds, being the old-fashioned lady she is, took him a flower to put on his table."

Mary rolled her eyes. "Wow. And he still thinks she's a normal cat?"

"He was dating Lydia recently, so she may have told him, but since they split up, probably not."

"Lydia?" Mary hummed thoughtfully. "I wonder if she'll be getting involved in our ..." She looked down at me and chose her word carefully. "... project."

My ears pricked up at the mention of a secret they've kept from me. Winnie shrugged. "She hasn't spoken to me about it. But she's a good witch, and she's ambitious. I imagine we might see her there."

My ears pricked up.

You're going away?

Winnie hadn't spoken to me about it, which told me she

didn't intend to bring me with her. I huffed, upset. What was I supposed to do in the house on my own?

She looked down at me guiltily. "Only for about a week."

When?

"In a few days."

So soon? Were you going to tell me or just go when I wasn't looking?

"No! I was going to tell you, just not so soon. You'll ask questions I can't answer."

Mary interrupted, "You're doing it again."

Oh, bugger off, Mary.

"Clawdia!" Winnie's head whipped to glare at her girl-friend. "Mary, not now."

"Don't 'not now' me. I hate being left out. What is she saying?" Mary snapped.

Winnie took a deep breath and calmly told her, "She's upset because I didn't tell her we're going away."

Mary crossed her arms and raised her eyebrow. "Why would you need to tell her? She's just your familiar. She doesn't get a say in what you do."

"No. That's not—You're so wrong, Mary. Clawdia is my familiar, but she's also my friend and my roommate and has a soul just like yours or mine. She feels and thinks, and she's not a pet. She's entitled to the same treatment from me as any human that I care about. I've explained this to you, but you don't get it. She's not just a cat. I have to think of her, too. That's why not telling her about this ... project ... is killing me. I shouldn't have let you talk me into it."

There was a shocked silence. Winnie wasn't an argumentative person, but she had just stood up for me. Happiness and gratitude overwhelmed me. I was so thankful I had a second chance at life with her by my side. I was also relieved to hear that the secrets between us weren't just hurting me.

Thank you, Winnie.

She gave me a small smile.

Then Mary began, "You told me you wanted this as much as I did. That you wanted to be a part of witch history. Isn't that right? Didn't you say that?"

Winnie sighed. "I did, but—"

"I didn't push you into anything. I wanted to do this, and you came with me."

"I just—"

"And now you're blaming me because your cat is upset you haven't told her anything. Talk about ridiculous." She huffed and moved to the kitchen to refill her glass.

An awkward silence followed. I stood to hop down from the sofa and go to bed. I didn't want to talk anymore.

Before I could leave, Winnie whispered, "I'm sorry. I know I'm keeping secrets and not treating you like I should, but Mary is right. This is something I want to do, and I've been magically sworn not to tell another soul about our project. I promise when it's all over, I'll tell you everything."

I sighed. *Yes. Okay. If it's something you really want to do, then I don't want to stop you. I just don't like the distance between us now.*

"We don't have to be so distant. I'll tell you everything I can, and you can always tell me anything. You didn't tell me about Charlie's guests. Did he like the flower?"

I laughed in my head, remembering his reaction, and begrudgingly told her. *He thought I was a terrible cat for catching him a flower instead of a mouse or a bird. He put it in a pint glass. Silly man.*

She smiled, enjoying my happiness. "You said the guests were interesting. Were they family? Have you discovered more about the mystery that is Charles Bennett?"

Honestly, this has only added to the mystery.

"Really? Do tell."

I didn't know how much I should say, but if anyone knew

about the existence of people from other realms, it was Winnie. *His guests were three giant men.*

"Ooo, tell me more."

Paranormal, otherworldly men.

She waited for me to continue. "Wait, what? You're joking." She shook her head. "Oh my goddess. What a plot twist. How did Charlie know them?"

I told her about him getting emails and that he set up cameras to see who they were. That's why I was so interested to see too. I explained that when they appeared on the camera this morning, Charlie panicked and ran to meet them and dragged them home.

"And what did they look like?"

"What did who look like?" Mary asked, coming back with her glass in hand.

"Clawdia is telling me about Charlie's guests. You'll never guess who they are."

"Prostitutes?"

"No. Otherworlders."

Wait. You knew about them? I asked Winnie, but she ignored me.

"Yeah, okay." Mary rolled her eyes.

"No, seriously. Clawdia wouldn't lie. She's about to tell me what they look like."

"If she's telling the truth, why don't we just knock on the door and see what they look like for ourselves?" She raised her eyebrow and took a swig of her wine. "That familiar of yours must have been a shitty writer in the past, because this reeks of bullshit."

It's not! You couldn't see them if you wanted to because there's one with magic that keeps them disguised from people who they don't want to see their true forms.

"Magic?" Winnie whispered excitedly. Mary coughed, and Winnie told her what I said.

"Magic like us? Like a witch?" Mary asked excitedly.

I don't know. He's not a witch. I didn't see him cast any spells like you do.

"A potion, then?"

I didn't see him when he did it, but I didn't get the impression it was a potion.

"Interesting. Tell us about them, then. What do they really look like?"

They are all huge. Bigger than Charlie. The smallest one has wings that look like stretched leather and are almost the same size as him. He has little stubby horns poking out of his head. He has a huge smile and is so cute that I was surprised when he said he was a—"

"Demon," Winnie gasped.

Yes, how did you know?

"What? A demon? One of the otherworlders is a demon?" Mary was suddenly excited, which made me very wary. Winnie told her what I'd said about them. Mary got up and ran to the bookcase.

No. Not in the Christian sense. He's so happy and seems sweet. I think his species was just written in myths as bad.

Mary returned to the sofa with a book and quickly flipped to a page. "Does he look like this?" She showed me an illustration of a creature that looked like Savida. The drawing looked angry and aggressive but otherwise had his defining features.

Yes. Sort of. He didn't pull that face. Why are you so excited?

Winnie informed Mary of what I said and then responded, "Why wouldn't we be excited, Clawds? There's a creature next door that we've learned about in our studies as witches. What's not to be excited about?" She gave me a brittle smile, and I tilted my head to look at her curiously.

Was that a lie? Was that her lying smile?

Mary stood up suddenly. Winnie looked at her sharply

and glanced at me, then back at her. They were communicating something with their eyes and twitching brows. I didn't know what was going on, but something felt strange. I didn't like it.

Mary turned her quick movement into a slow and exaggerated stretch and yawn. "Wow, that wine has really hit me. I'm suddenly so tired. I think I'll go home."

"I'll see you out," Winnie said and jumped up.

You don't want to know what the others looked like? I was confused and hurt that they'd cut me off halfway through my story. They didn't know about the otherworlders looking for someone named Margaret. How Zaide was my favorite. How beautiful and powerful Daithi was.

"Maybe you can tell us tomorrow." Winnie continued walking to the door, leaving me on the sofa.

I huffed. Still annoyed, and with my fur on end from the strange tension in the air, I went to bed.

Falling into a dream.

A memory.

My past.

CHAPTER 4

MARGARET CLAUDIA

MONDAY 6TH SEPTEMBER 1920

"Where are you going?"

The cruel tone to my father's voice gave me pause as I packed my satchel with my lunch.

When I turned, he was leaning against the doorway, still in his clothes from the day before.

Archibald John Smith used to be a tall and strong man, with a quick smile, a caring nature, dark hair that was thick and clean, and blue eyes that lit up at the sight of me.

But his eyes no longer gazed at me with light, or clarity, or sobriety. His hair was greasy and thinning. His strength and height turned soft and slumped as he stood glaring at me, one hand holding his suspender strap and the other holding a bottle of homebrewed beer.

It was a sight that was becoming all too familiar.

"I'm going to work."

"Work," he scoffed. "What do you know about work?"

I didn't know how to reply. He knew both mother and I

had turned our hands to work while he was at war. A volunteer at the hospital wasn't comparable to the heroic service he'd done for our country, but I did know work. Especially now that I was a student nurse at the Free Hospital.

The tuition cost me the price of the trinkets my well-to-do grandparents had sent me over the years, and since my relationship with them was practically nonexistent, I felt no shame in selling them for my education.

I looked away, playing with the straps of my bag. "Why don't you get to bed, Father? You look tired."

His eyes flashed, and he charged toward me. "Do not think you can tell me what to do, Claudia."

At his approach, I instinctively backed away, suddenly fearful of the man who raised me. I stumbled into the open cupboard door, which slammed shut.

One moment, my father was snarling and storming toward me, and the next, at the bang of the door, he gasped, his eyes clouded as memories took him. He threw himself on the floor and covered his ears. He whimpered, and the panic inside me ebbed.

The doctors said it was shell shock. That many men returning from war were suffering night terrors and that loud noises could send them back to the battlefield.

PEACE WAS the only known cure. Except not even that seemed to help my father. He found his own cure in the bottle.

"What in the world—" Mother came into the kitchen and, having spotted Father on the floor, rushed to him, muttering words of reassurance and stroking him like you might a frightened animal. "It's all right, my love. You are here. With me. You are safe."

With her polka-dot skirt pooled around her as she

kneeled on the tiles next to her husband, Margaret Angela Smith looked every bit the perfect housewife. All evidence of the independence she had, the knowledge and experience she gained from employment with women from all walks of life while he was at war, was gone.

While my parents named me after my mother, and shared her blond hair and bow lips, our similarities ended there. I enjoyed working. I supported the suffragists, protesting for my rights to be an equal, and didn't want a husband. No man had ever appealed to me, and the thought of a marriage night turned my stomach. What's more, a husband would mean he would be my highest priority, and I didn't want to forget all else for a man.

My mother's support of my father in all things meant I'd been forgotten now. Over the past few weeks, my mother did not deflect his verbal jabs at me. Instead, she watched quietly. The comradery we'd built as the women of the house left alone, the trust we'd built to look after each other, disintegrated more with each time she ignored Father's treatment of me.

When his whimpers quietened, she looked up at me sharply and said, "You'd best be on your way now."

I nodded and quickly snatched my satchel from the table and dashed from the house. I closed the door quietly behind me, so as not to further shock my father, and left. After letting out a shaky breath, I tugged my satchel strap over my head and headed to the bus stop.

The walk was quiet since it was still early and many people in the neighborhood were only just rising. Bird song and the rustle of autumn leaves brushing the pavement were my only company as I strolled to the bus stop.

I exchanged pleasantries with other passengers as I walked down the aisle to an empty seat. My uniform, a black dress with a white apron pulling in my waist, drew stares.

I wasn't the most typical of nurses, being so young. With so many men killed at war, many women were turning to a career instead of marriage.

Smiling at the women at the desk as I walked into the London Royal Free Hospital, I wondered about my patients.

Mr. Devlin will need to be discharged this morning.

He'd fallen off his ladder when lighting a streetlamp, and the accident had aggravated a previous injury on his leg. Despite his pain and complaints, he only needed to keep it rested, and he could do that from home.

Mrs. Allsop will need checking and rebandaging.

She'd cut open her hand with a knife when chopping vegetables, and the wound continued to open and bleed when she moved in her sleep.

My small heels tapped along the corridor's wooden floors as I turned into the staff room and dropped my bag off.

"Good morning, Margaret." Sister Martha greeted me with a bland smile, revealing a crooked tooth.

While I hated to think it, Sister Martha perpetuated the stereotype of a suffragist. She was a rotund woman, with shoulders that could carry patients of all sizes without breaking a sweat. She was intelligent and had a lot to teach as my mentor but preferred to shout orders rather than explain.

She also called me Margaret even though I asked to be called Claudia. She knew it bothered me, but I pretended it didn't. "Good morning, Sister. How are you?"

"Very well. I'm just admiring the press of your skirt. Did your mother do that for you?"

I bit back a huff at the attempt to patronize me. "No, I manage the washing of my uniform so she doesn't pick up anything lingering on me from the hospital."

She sniffed. "How ... thorough of you."

I followed her out onto the ward and began my rounds,

pleased to see the improvement of a young boy who had a severe fever.

Every day, I walked around these hardwood floors and looked into the eyes of a thankful patient; I was grateful for this opportunity. Being a student nurse at the Royal Free Hospital was a dream come true for me.

The hospital was renowned for its delivery of free treatment to patients and training female staff. The first to train female doctors. Being surrounded by ambitious and intelligent ladies inspired me. Made me hope for a more liberating future for women.

I would never achieve a university education since I could only afford the tuition for my nursing training because of a small inheritance from my grandmother when she passed. But all the same, I was extremely grateful for the opportunity to become my own person.

I fell into my easy routine: checking patients, assessing new ones, talking to families, and chatting to staff. I paused when, toward the end of my shift, sitting on the last bed of my round was Mrs. Longly, who lived on our street. Her five children were about seven years my junior, and so I used to look after them when she was working.

"Mrs. Longly, what brings you here?" I asked, concern coloring my voice. Although she'd lost two children to the influenza, she hadn't contracted it and had never complained of ill health before.

"Oh, it's nothing serious." She crossed her ankles, knotted her fingers, bit her lip, and refused to look me in the eye. If it wasn't serious, it was certainly embarrassing for her to admit.

I covered her hands with one of my own and waited for her to look at me. "I promise, whatever it is, it's nothing I won't have seen before, but I understand if you'd prefer to see another nurse."

A blush rose on her cheeks, and she looked away again as she said, "I'm expecting."

"Congratulations." I gave her a small smile. "But you're having issues with it?"

"It's different this time. I'm exhausted, lightheaded. I have a headache that won't leave me, I can't pick up the laundry basket without getting out of breath, and Samantha told me I'm unusually pale."

"It could be because you are a little older than the last time you were expecting, but it could also be anemia. We have Dr. Lucy Wills here, who is currently researching it and should be able to confirm if it is and make suggestions to ease your symptoms … If that's all right with you."

"A female doctor?"

"I assure you she's qualified, and her research will be very helpful. You're in safe hands."

"I'm sure." She gave me an exhausted smile and politely said no more on the matter.

I grabbed the attention of a porter, who I asked with a winning smile if he might be so kind to find Dr. Wills to speak to Mrs. Longley. He scowled at me, his limp, graying hair falling into his face as he shook his head and walked off to do as I bid.

When I turned back to Mrs. Longley, she was studying me, a question on her lips which didn't take long to escape. "Claudia, I've been meaning to ask you, how is your father doing?"

"Ah." It wasn't what I was expecting to be asked, but I knew why she did. "He's in good health, but as I'm sure you're experiencing with your husband, he is struggling with things that remind him of his time on the battlefield."

She nodded knowingly. "We had a consultation with a specialist doctor who told us to reduce the noises and triggers for his condition. He also told us that animals keep one's mind occupied and in the present. We are going to get a dog. Perhaps that could work for your father, too."

I pondered that thought long after Dr. Wills interrupted us to assess Mrs. Longley. It distracted me as I finished my rounds and left for home.

Could a pet do what his family couldn't? Would it save him?

As the sun set behind the houses of my street, squinting and daydreaming of a happier father, I almost walked straight into a postbox.

Chuckling sounded from the garden to my right as I dodged the large red object.

"Good evening, Mrs. Lamply." I acknowledged her with a sheepish smile.

Mrs. Lamply was an elderly lady, five doors down from us and the sweetest person alive. "Ah, Claudia dear, how are you?"

"Well, and yourself?"

"Good, good. I'm fine, my hip aches, but otherwise, I'm as strong as an ox. Coming back from the hospital?" She leaned forward on her cane and squinted at me through thick-lensed glasses.

"Yes."

She tutted and shook her head as though it were bad news. "A girl so young and beautiful shouldn't be working. The men have returned. You should look for a husband."

I had the same conversation with someone every day, but I tried to keep the frustration out of my voice as I replied, "Not all have returned with their right mind, Mrs. Lamply. I would rather help many in the hospital than serve one in a home."

"The Lord gave us an angel on earth when he gave us you, Margaret Claudia. You are always trying to save someone." She chuckled.

A lightning bolt hit my mind as I remembered a conversation with another neighbor last week. "Laura mentioned Mittens had more kittens."

If she was surprised at the change of subject, she didn't show it. She tapped her cane and nodded. "That's right. Her third litter."

"Do you have homes for them?" I knew she wouldn't but asked anyway.

"Now, Claudia, don't go getting yourself upset. You know we can't be overrun by cats."

"But killing them is so cruel." I sighed and plucked a leaf from the bush protecting her front garden.

"Crueler for them to live on the streets, unprotected and unwanted. Sometimes it's a mercy."

I bit my lip, my brain and my heart warring over the sentiment, but continued to twirl the leaf in my fingers, not looking up at her. "Simon hasn't killed them yet, has he?"

"No." She drawled the word. "The grandchildren wanted to say goodbye before they go to the farm."

"Why don't you give me one?"

"What do you want with a kitten?" She stared at me suspiciously.

"The doctors have suggested an animal could help Father … settle." She didn't look convinced. "I could pay you." I still had a bit of money from the inheritance, plenty enough for a kitten that would otherwise die.

"Pay?" she gasped.

"Well, yes, they are your kittens after all." I shrugged.

A gleam appeared in her eyes as an idea sparked. "Do you think other people might pay for a kitten for their soldiers?"

"They may if they have heard about the benefit of helping them."

"What a bright idea, Miss Claudia. Saving your father and

a kitten in one day in a single conversation." She patted my cheek. "So enterprising."

As I clutched a squirming black and white fluffy body in my hands, I sent a prayer to God.

Please let this change our lives for the better.

CHAPTER 5

ZAIDE

*T*his journey would change me forever.

Daithi believes I will meet my soul pair during this visit to the human realm. Something that hadn't happened for my species since our souls were ripped apart and tossed across the realms, never to meet again.

It would be a momentous occasion, something Daithi and Savida were excited to see and be a part of. They wanted me to meet the other half of my soul so I could experience the same joy and love they had with each other.

The prospect of it had me sweating with nervous excitement. But I was wary too. I didn't trust my fortune.

I was quiet as Charlie asked questions and Daithi explained. It was something many of our hosts in other realms had also needed. They wanted to know who we were and why we're visiting. Although most of the other species in the interlinked dimensions had long lives and even longer memories, so they knew of each other even if they had met no one outside of their own realm before.

From Charlie's reaction, the human realm seemed to have cast the many races across the realms into myth and legend.

My stomach grumbled at the mention of food, and I followed the others into the kitchen, my braid hitting the back of my legs as I walked. I paused as a curious sense of loss washed over me. A hole in my soul that was filled without my noticing began leaking. My stomach growled again, and I pushed the odd feeling to the back of my mind.

As I stepped through the doorway, I took a seat at the table and watched Charlie mutter as he threw one yellow block and a thin pink square on top of a soft white thing. He covered it with another soft white thing and put it in a contraption that burned lines in it.

Plates clattered to the mats in front of us in no time, and Savida, Daithi and I stared at each other, wondering who among us would be so brave as to try something created so quickly and pulled from packages.

"What are you waiting for? Dig in." Charlie picked up his own meal and took a big bite. The yellow thing had melted and pulled away in long strings, which Charlie attempted to chew through.

The horrified look on Daithi's face echoed mine, but Savida picked up his meal with a curious expression. After a few testing bites, he told us, "Not as bad as the Locus Pie, but not as good as the Ambrosia Biscuits."

With his assessment, I could ignore my stomach no longer, and I, too, bit into the food.

"I didn't take you all for drama queens," Charlie commented, a humorous glint in his eyes as he watched us. "I promise I won't poison you until after I get paid."

His laugh assured me it was a joke.

"What is this delicacy called, Charlie?" Savida asked, his wings flapping excitedly behind him.

He laughed again. "I wouldn't call it a delicacy. It's a ham and cheese toastie."

He pointed out the ingredients, the ham and the cheese

and the toast, but knowing that the thin pink square was meat both confused and repulsed me. Meat should look like meat.

When we had all taken a few bites, Charlie began asking more questions. "So, you're here to find a human named Margaret. I'm assuming you saw her in a vision like you saw me?"

Daithi tilted his head in acknowledgment and lowered his toastie to his plate, answering Charlie, "You are correct to assume that. However, unlike the vision in which I saw you, Margaret felt distant, the vision unclear."

"What does she look like? Were there any distinguishing buildings or features in the dream that I might recognize? Something to help locate her?"

Daithi closed his eyes, no doubt reliving the vision in which he saw her. "She has pale skin, as you do, perhaps even lighter. Her eyes are purple, and she has yellow hair. She looked … young."

"Purple eyes," Charlie mumbled and looked at me. "And young? How young?"

"In my vision, she looked like a child."

Although I had already heard this, my stomach sank.

"What?" Charlie glared. "Not for all the money in the world would I hand a kid over to alien slave traders or pedophiles." Although his eyes were angry and his words accusing, it reassured me of his honor and morality. He was trustworthy. I relaxed my guard slightly, my shoulders falling.

Daithi barely blinked at the accusations. "We don't appreciate the connotations of the word 'alien'. We prefer other-worlders."

Charlie rolled his eyes. "Noted."

"What is a pedophile?" Savida asked.

"Someone that sexually abuses kids."

We all gasped and unanimously denied vehemently. "No."

"Charlie, we are not any of those things. We don't want to harm her," Daithi promised.

Charlie didn't sound convinced. "Then why do you need to find her? Is she in trouble? Buried like Savida was?"

Daithi shook his head. "I did not sense that."

"Then why are you looking for her?"

Daithi paused, searching for the right words. "Because she is important to one of us."

He looked around the table, staring at us as though our faces would spell it out. "Why is she important?"

"Charlie, can you not trust that we mean her no harm and only seek to meet her?" Daithi sighed, exasperation in his voice but not in his expression.

"I think the real question is, why won't you tell me? Is she the love child of one of you? Is this the otherworlder edition of *Long Lost Family*?" He paused, then gasped, "Is she my daughter? In the future? Is this some kind of *Terminator* shit?"

Savida chuckled. "She isn't anyone's daughter."

"Is she the heir to a kingdom? Are you going to help her take back the throne or kill her so you can rule?"

"You do not give up, human," I grumbled.

"And he has an active imagination," Savida added.

Charlie suddenly beamed. "Thank you."

"Do you feel better now that you have emptied yourself of your suspicions?" Daithi asked.

Charlie cringed. "Never say 'emptied yourself' again. That was reason and logic at work, not a case of verbal diarrhea."

"Diarrhea?" Savida interrupted at the sound of an unfamiliar word. He loved learning new things about planets and their people.

"Endless shit."

"That's horrific. That happens?" He pulled a face showing his discomfort.

Charlie looked equally disturbed. "You don't shit?"

"Yes, but not endlessly. Are you cursed?"

"It's not a curse. It's an illness, and you just have to let it flow." Charlie chuckled.

Daithi huffed his disapproval. "Illness that flows. This is a cursed realm."

Charlie waved his hand dismissively. "You keep saying cursed. We don't have curses. You're such drama queens."

"You keep calling us queens when we are not ladies nor rulers." Daithi looked at Savida as though he might know the answers. Savida just shrugged.

Charlie moaned and leaned his head into his hands. "Jesus Christ, this is going to be difficult."

"Jesus? Who is this? Do you speak to spirits, human?" I asked.

While Savida was interested in the people, their language, and their culture, I was interested in their beliefs and their wars.

"Of a sort." Charlie shook his head as though his over-crowded thoughts would fall out of his tiny pink ears and make room for something more important. "Stop fucking distracting me. I need to know more about the Margaret situation before I commit to helping you. I like you weirdos, and I don't get the impression you're evil, but I need to know she'll be safe when we find her."

I sighed. He'd proven he was trustworthy and was looking out for my soul pair. He deserved to know the truth. "Daithi's vision was of a girl, but he heard my voice say the name 'Margaret' and something else. He believes she is my soul pair. I will not go into much detail, but it is unheard of for my race to meet their soul pair. I would die before harm came to her."

He stared at me and must have seen something in my eyes, because he nodded and said, "Okay, I'll help find her."

"Thank you," I whispered. Then I turned to Daithi, "Show him."

"Show me what?"

Daithi nodded. "Margaret."

In a practiced movement I had seen many times before, Daithi waved his hands and, just as he explained the realms, created an image of who we believed to be my soul pair.

Charlie pushed away from the table in a panic. "What the hell?"

"You have been handling everything very well so far. Why are you just now getting overwhelmed?" Daithi asked calmly.

"Because although you've got weird accents, I'm hearing you speak English, so it's easy to pretend that you're just wearing a really good costume." He rubbed the heels of his hands into his eyes. "I'm going to need so much therapy when this is all over."

"Now you are behaving like a queen of drama." Savida's chair squeaked across the floor as he stood. He picked up the mat and the glass of water and placed it on Charlie's head. Then he took the flower from the glass and bowed, presenting it to Charlie, "Your Royal Highness."

Charlie stared speechlessly at Savida.

"He seems to be mentally broken. Perhaps we will need to find a new human to help us search for Margaret," I teased.

Charlie snapped out of his bewilderment and glared at me. "No. I'm not broken. I'll find her." He took the glass and the mat off his head, ignoring Savida's giggling, then muttered, "Bloody otherworlders trying to take my sanity."

He turned back to the table, and the image hovering above portrayed a young human girl standing next to two other humans, a male and a female I assumed to be her parents. They were standing outside a glass building. There were other humans in the background, but they were blurred out, irrelevant.

"Those aren't modern clothes." Charlie raised his hand as though to stroke the material of the humans' coverings. "Are you sure she's still a child?"

"You think this is a vision of the past?"

"Maybe that's why the vision felt distant to you. You've never done that before?"

"No." His eyebrow raised slightly, which was all that showed his surprise at Charlie's suggestion. "Or at least I'm not sure that I have not."

While Daithi pondered the power of his visions, my mind focused elsewhere. "You don't think she is a child?" I asked with hope.

Charlie pointed at the figures. "The woman's dress is touching her ankles. She's wearing a hat. The man has a flat cap and a jacket. That isn't something that anyone would wear these days unless it's fancy dress."

"Do you know when it is?" Savida asked curiously.

"I'm not a fucking historian, so I can't tell you exactly. I don't recognize the building, but it feels like it's in England. It reminds me of the Titanic pictures."

"Titanic?"

Charlie sighed and ran his hands through his hair. "It was a ship that sank in the early 1900s."

"Then you believe it could be 1900s," Daithi concluded. "That was not long ago?"

Charlie was silent a moment before saying in a low voice, "That was over a hundred years ago." He paused again. "I don't know how much you know about humans, but there are very few that live over a hundred years."

My heart sank to my stomach. I shook my head fiercely. "She is not dead. She is not."

"I'm just saying it's unlikely. If she's still alive, she's going to be as wrinkled as a raisin." Charlie pulled a face.

"A raisin?" Savida questioned.

"Literally, it's a dried fruit." Charlie looked at me solemnly. "I'm guessing a soul pair is someone you want a romantic relationship with? But basically, she is going to be past all that, if you catch my meaning."

"I will cherish my soul pair no matter her form," I told him earnestly. I was giving up my search for my family to find her. She would be my everything. Even if it was only for a short while.

"That's very romantic." Charlie said with an expression which made me believe he had a strange taste in his mouth.

Daithi interrupted, "Does this help find her?"

"If I give you a piece of paper, can you print this image onto it?"

"Please. That is not a challenge."

Charlie ran into another room and returned with a white page. He put it in front of Daithi, who, waving his hand again, seemed to drag the image from the air and place it onto the paper. "This will benefit you in finding her?"

"I can upload this onto the internet and do a reverse image search and see what comes up." He saw my frustrated frown and explained further, "It will tell me if there are any other images of them which might give me more details about who they are."

"This will take a long time?" I asked, embarrassingly desperate to find her. Now that I know we could be so close, and that she might not have much more time left.

"Research can sometimes lead to a dead end. I'll see what I can do as quickly as possible, but I can't give you a date and time when you'll meet her."

I looked desperately at Daithi and he answered my

unspoken question, "You will meet her. We will find her. Be patient."

* * *

To lighten the mood, Savida regaled Charlie with stories of our past visits to other realms. Savida had a talent for storytelling. He embellished where needed with funny descriptions and threw himself into acting out the characters.

I was sure Charlie's tiny human brain was fit to bursting as the daylight gave way to the evening. Eventually, he stood from the sofa, stretched and said, "Just in case you have dimensional travel lag and need to sleep soon, let me show you the guest room."

We followed him up the stairs to a room with a large bed in the center. "I changed the sheets last night. Two of you can sleep here and someone else can sleep in my bed and I'll sleep on the sofa bed in the office. Hopefully, no one has any problem with doubling up."

Savida laughed heartily, and Daithi breathed a few chuckles. "There will not be any problem with us sleeping together." Savida grinned.

"I feel like I'm missing something." Charlie's gaze darted to each of our faces.

I hastily told him before he interrogated us again. "Savida and Daithi are partners."

And they were good ones. They balanced each other out. Savida's playfulness lightened Daithi's serious heart, and Daithi's good sense prevented Savida's chaotic recklessness.

"Oh." Charlie looked between them and nodded. "I can see that. Well, in that case, keep the sex noises to a minimum, please."

Savida laughed. "We will do our best."

"Thank you." Charlie looked at me. "I guess you're in my bed. Let me show you."

It looked very similar to the guest room. Neat and organized, with a large bed in the middle. "I do not wish to put you out, Charlie. I will stay in the office bed."

"It's fine. I want to stay in there tonight anyway, so I can get started on uploading that picture and researching."

I paused. "You will do this as we sleep?"

"Well, yeah." He rubbed the back of his head. "You want to find her as soon as possible, right?"

"I'm honored you would lose sleep to help me. Thank you." I laid my hand on his shoulder and squeezed.

"Let's not make a big deal about it. I'm curious too and finding things is a specialty of mine. I like a challenge."

I nodded. "There is great reward in winning a challenge."

"Well, let me grab some clothes and stuff and I'll be out of your way." He moved to the long doors opposite the bed, opened them, and pulled out a few items.

As he was closing the door behind him, I spoke softly and stopped him. "I appreciate your help, Charlie. Know that by finding my soul pair, I will owe you a life debt and you will have my greatest respect and friendship."

Charlie cleared his throat. "I'll do my best for you, Zaide."

"That is all I ask."

With a soft click of the door, he left me in silence. I removed my clothing and shoes, leaving only my undergarments on, and sat cross-legged on the floor. I pulled my sacred stone from the tie in my braid, closed my eyes and inhaled slow breaths and I traced the narrow, carved lines in the stone.

I prayed.

Almighty gods, to you I pray. My life and worship are yours. I continue to thank you for my friends, Savida and Daithi who, by your guidance, saved me from slavery. I am ever grateful that you helped me.

And yet, selfishly, I ask more.

I pray to Riseir, god of life, that our time on Earth be a joyous one. I pray to Hedri, god of love, that you guide me to my soul pair. Finally, I pray to Charos, god of death, that my soul pair has not greeted you as she passed from this life.

But, as I crawled into bed, I had the sinking suspicion that I might be too late.

CHAPTER 6

ZAIDE

*S*omething brushed my foot, and my eyes shot open. A smile stretched across my face as I rolled over in Charlie's bed to see that I wasn't alone. Savida had crept into the room and curled up next to me in the night. He was still sound asleep and wrapped up in his own wings on top of the bedsheets.

It was a rare occurrence and only happened when he felt unsettled.

I stretched, overjoyed to have slept solidly for the first time in many years. Nightmares about my family or my captivity didn't encroach on my peaceful slumber. I sent a quick prayer of thanks to my gods for yet another miracle.

Perhaps it was because I was in the same realm as my soul pair, and that missing part of me was already healing.

I moved to wake Savida when Daithi and Charlie knocked softly and came in.

"I thought I might find him here. I'm not offended my lover sneaked into bed with you, Zaide." Daithi's expression was empty of emotion, but his voice was full of humor.

"I do not snore as you do." I grinned at him teasingly and stretched.

"Okay, so this is normal? He usually sleepwalks?" Charlie asked. "Should I expect to find him in bed with me tomorrow?" Savida sighed deeply and snuggled deeper into his wings. He mumbled something. "Aw, he is kind of cute. Like a giant bat."

"Unless your scars are luminous in the night, he will not bother you," Daithi informed Charlie.

Charlie looked at me. There was an intrigued sparkle in his eye. "Those are scars? They keep glowing in your sleep? That is bloody mental."

"You are more impressed by his scars than my magic?" Daithi raised a green brow.

"Your magic still freaks me out. His scars are cool." He had a thought and then asked, "Why is Savida attracted to glowing scars? Is he like a moth?"

Daithi was silent for a moment before he spoke. "I do not know what a moth is. However, Savida likes to fall asleep with a light."

"He's afraid of the dark?"

"He was in that hole for a very long time, Charlie."

"He was conscious?" We nodded, and Charlie's face distorted with his disgust. "That's fucked up. Did you find who did that to him?"

Daithi shook his head slowly. "We left the human realm a day or so after I found him. I wanted him safe."

"But how did he get there, here?"

"I don't know, Charlie. Perhaps you can help us find that out, too."

Charlie nodded and whispered, "If he needs a nightlight, we can go shopping and get him one. That wouldn't be a problem."

"Shopping?" Savida's eyes suddenly opened, and he

unraveled his wings, setting his arms free. "We are going shopping?"

I guffawed at his excitement, and Daithi's lip curled slightly.

The exclamation and sudden movement startled Charlie, but he grinned at Savida and shrugged. "We can if you fancy it."

"Right now?"

"Yeah, after breakfast, we can go."

He rolled straight out of bed. "I'm ready."

There was a movement on the other side of me. The window material rustled. "Charlie, something is invading your home."

From the material dropped a fluffy, small creature. Everyone was still. Assessing.

I was enraptured. In the puddles of sunbeams, from the gaps in the hanging material, sat a creature with violet eyes that flicked to everyone in the room. Its fur was a white and orange blend, exceptionally thick and shone under the light. Its tail swayed, curling from one side to another like a large feather. At the sight of the creature, calm and peace covered me like a blanket.

When the creature moved toward the bed, Savida screamed and jumped behind Daithi. "What is it?"

The creature stepped back and made an aggressive hiss at the loud noise. I glared at Savida.

Charlie tried to calm the situation. "Calm down, you big fucking girl's blouse. It's Clawdia. The cat from next door I told you about yesterday."

"Look at the creature. She is magnificent," I whispered in awe. "Small but mighty."

The cat stopped hissing and, with her attention solely on me, sat down, huffed, and then began regally licking her paw with her eyes closed. She stopped after five licks with her pebbled tongue and looked at me again. She was showing off for me. I grinned.

Charlie scoffed but also spoke to the cat softly, "And the most annoying thing in the world. Hey, Clawdicat, welcome to the party. These aliens are here for shopping and a good time."

"I am Zaide." It was only right to introduce myself.

"She's a cat. She doesn't understand you. And stop flirting. It's weird."

I ignored him. I sensed a deep understanding in this creature and slowly got out of the bed and moved toward her. She continued to lick her paw as though she was completely unaware of me. I held my hand out close enough for her to see. She paused and hesitantly sniffed it before pushing her head into my large fingers and making a trill sound.

"What is it doing now?" Savida whispered to Charlie fearfully.

"She's purring. It means she's happy." Charlie sighed.

"Are you happy, fierce little cat? We won't hurt you. There is no need to hiss in anger at us," I cooed and stroked her fur.

"I'm starving, so I'm going to put some food on." Charlie walked out the door with Savida at his heel, interrogating him about the morning meals available to him.

"It's interesting," Daithi began. "This cat was resting on Charlie's lap in the vision that began our communication."

I realized that the cat in question had stopped with her happy noise and instead was staring intently at Daithi. There was intelligence in her eyes. Beautiful violet eyes. They flicked to meet mine briefly before she flicked her tail and padded after Charlie to the kitchen.

Charlie told us he was treating us to a traditional English breakfast, and admittedly, it was much more appetizing to look at than the last food. It also tasted pleasant, which was a surprise. While we ate, Savida asked Charlie about shopping in the human realm.

Clawdia batted at my hair while I ate. I swished it back and forth across the carpet until she pounced. Her little claws and teeth were not strong, and the slight stinging in my scalp was worth the frustration I could feel building in her as she tried to hold my hair still underneath her.

When she was tired, she came to the side of my chair, then jumped onto my lap and started sniffing at the food.

"Are you hungry, Little Cat?" I chuckled as she dragged a piece of bacon over with her paw. "Is that safe for her to eat?" I asked Charlie.

He scolded me with his eyes. "You shouldn't let her eat off the plate. It teaches her bad habits. But bacon is fine for her."

"I am so full of English morning meal that I can't move," Savida exclaimed and patted his stomach.

Daithi wiped his mouth. "That was delicious, Charlie. I heartily approve of the English's taste."

"Well, nothing goes better with an English breakfast than a cup of tea and an orange juice. Stay there."

We didn't enjoy the tea or orange juice as much as the morning meal, and our stomachs were so full that even Savida couldn't muster up the energy to do anything other than watch TV. We learned about all the transport humans used, the buildings, the countries, and how creative they were.

Savida asked more questions than Charlie could keep up with. He was so interested in learning. Daithi looked on with a small smile as he watched Savida.

Clawdia sat with us, mostly on my lap, and made her noise of happiness, which settled my longing spirit. If I couldn't find my soul pair, this soft, fierce creature would be a close second.

As though Charlie could hear my thoughts, he turned to me. "Can I talk to you for a second?"

"Of course." Although I was confused about why he asked since he had already begun talking to me.

He stood up from the sofa, and the green pillow behind him fell down, making Clawdia's head jolt toward the motion. I watched him walk toward his office until he turned around and noticed I hadn't moved.

He laughed. "Just move her off you."

Charlie mistakenly believed I hadn't moved because Clawdia was on my lap. I ran a hand through her fur. "Did you not want to speak to me?"

"I do," he replied. "Privately."

"Ah." I looked at the creature staring up at me. "Clawdia cannot join us?"

He sighed and ran a hand through his hair. "Zaide—"

"I will guard the small beast," Savida interrupted cheerfully. "You have been hoarding all her attention, and it's my turn."

I looked back down into violet eyes. I sighed. "Very well."

Elated, Savida clapped his wings and sprang out of his seat next to Daithi toward me.

"Come, fluffy beast. Come play with me," he coaxed in a high-pitched whisper. Clawdia glanced up at me again, as though disbelieving, and I almost laughed. Savida continued, "I am much more fun than Zaide. We can—" He looked at Charlie. "What can we do?"

Charlie smirked and shrugged. "Cats like to chase things. You could get her to follow a piece of string or a tiny light. Or you could just tell her what you want her to play. She is freakishly smart. If she ignores you, it's because she thinks you're stupid."

I smiled and scratched at her chin, proud she was so clever. Then dark hands snatched her from my lap, and I saw

Savida raise her above his head. "We are going to have the grandest time while the human and Zaide talk. We are going to play a game."

She made a crying noise. I stood and looked at Charlie.

"Don't freak out. She's meowing. That is an agreement," Charlie said.

I calmed and nodded, and Charlie began walking to his office again. I cast one look back at Clawdia to ensure she was all right before I followed him inside.

He closed the door behind us and then walked to sit in a wheeled chair behind his desk. I stayed standing. "What is it you wish to talk about?"

"It's about the picture Daithi gave me yesterday."

I stood straighter. I didn't know how long human tracking would take, but I did not expect results so early. "You have news already? You know where she is?"

He sighed and shook his head. "I've identified the building behind them. It's called the Crystal Palace."

He paused, and I spoke, unable to bear the silence, "This is good, is it not? Where is it?"

"It burned down in 1939." His face betrayed his sorrow at telling me this news, but I didn't understand. He continued, "So, at the earliest, it puts us at Margaret being ninety years old."

"That's very old?"

"That age isn't something everyone gets to experience." He sighed.

I raised a fist to my heart as though I could shield it from pain. From disappointment. Again.

"You believe she might have already passed from this world?" I croaked.

Charlie whispered, "I think it's likely."

Silence seemed to emphasize the crack of my heart at the news that we were too late. "But Daithi, he saw her—"

"He saw her past. Maybe that was to tell you something. Maybe not. Surely Daithi has visions that don't mean anything."

"He does," I reluctantly agreed.

"There you go, then—"

I interrupted, "He knew she was my soul pair. Why would he have a vision about my soul pair if I would never find her?"

He shrugged. "I don't know what to tell you. The universe is a fucked-up place."

"This, I know." I paced the small office space, my thoughts racing and my heart crying.

Charlie leaned back in his chair and joined his fingers across his stomach. "Why is this such an important thing? What is a soul pair?"

His question made me pause and turn to him. I trusted him. He took us into his home, listened to our request, and delivered his promise to research Daithi's vision. I had no reason not to tell him my people's secret. Their weakness.

"Charlie, my people do not find happiness or glory or peace anymore. We are slaves. I was extraordinarily lucky to be freed. I am one of few. While I count myself lucky to be free and content, all of us are born without a part of ourselves. Cursed and ripped apart, half our soul gone, flung across the universe, never to be found again. Without our other half, we will never be whole or happy or as powerful as we once were. With holes in our hearts, otherworlders easily turned us into slaves. We offered no resistance."

He gaped at me. "Wait, what do you mean, ripped apart? Like, you were the same person, but then you got split?"

"I do not know the extent of the ripping, as it did not happen to me. It is a story I was told as a child. Yes, we were once powerful beings, but to take our power, the Fates and the gods split us apart." I stared at my hands and the purple glowing scars that laced them. They were a constant reminder that I was powerless. Half.

When I looked up Charlie was glaring at me. "Okay, so you want to find Margaret to get your power back?"

I stepped back as the accusation hit me, and I bumped into the lounge chair. The bang echoed around the room as I collected myself to answer, "No. No, I do not care about the power. I don't even know what power it is." Swallowing, I forced the next words from my mouth. "I ... I want the ... companionship. The ... love. Living with Savida and Daithi has proved that there is such emotion, and I ... want ... that."

I struggled to describe how much I ached for someone to look at me as Savida and Daithi gazed at each other. How I always felt as though I was missing something. How I would pray every day for her. How I would wake up with a name on my lips and snippets of dreams cut too short.

He raised an eyebrow. "Why does it have to be with your soul pair? Why can't you find love with someone else? You ever heard of Tinder?"

"That is not your business." I crossed my arms defensively. I had already given too many of my secrets and didn't wish to display any more vulnerability.

Charlie's brows were high on his face. "I didn't think that was an intrusive question. I take it you're defensive because you were rejected by someone or hurt and don't believe in love without a bound? Some shit like that?"

"I do not enjoy your inquisitive nature," I growled.

"You don't enjoy it when I'm interrogating you. But otherwise, my nature benefits you in finding your soul pair. But why do I have to? 'Love Is All Around,' as Wet Wet Wet would say. Let's get you signed up to Plenty of Fish. They love freaks." He turned to tap at something on his desk, the clicks sounding louder in the quiet office.

Confused and disorientated, I pushed on. "I don't want to

be wet or with fishes. She is the only one I can be with. I—" I took a deep breath and spoke quickly, "I'm not interested."

Charlie paused his tapping. "Sorry?"

"I'm not interested," I repeated.

"I'm lost," Charlie announced, pushing away from his desk.

I closed my eyes and clenched my fists. Taking another breath, I gave him another secret, "Sexually. I am not interested sexually in any other."

When I opened my eyes, Charlie looked at me wide-eyed. "I'll not ask how your race survives, but I want to know another time." He shook his head and collected his thoughts. "I don't think you'll find a ninety-year-old sexually attractive no matter if she's your other half."

"We will have to see when we find her." I refused to believe she was dead. I looked at him, desperation etched into my face. He sighed and nodded.

He stood up and walked to the door, saying, "Come on. I'm sure Clawdia will have marmalized Savida by now, and that'll cheer us up."

We stepped out into the living room to find Savida wearing Clawdia like a hat and massaging Daithi's feet.

"What the fuck is going on here?" Charlie choked out, half laughing, half shocked.

"Master Charlie, you've returned. How can I serve you?" Savida asked, dropping Daithi's foot and walking to Charlie, Clawdia still perched on his head.

"Are you playing weird, kinky games with my neighbor's pussycat on your head?"

Daithi grabbed Savida's hand and turned him back around to face him. "You don't serve anyone but me," he growled and pulled him down for a kiss.

Clawdia jumped down from Savida and padded over to where Charlie and I stood, shocked, confused, and amused.

Charlie bent down to pick her up and whispered, "If he was playing weird, kinky games with you on his head, you can tell me. I'll give him a right good hiding."

"No kinky games, Charlie, I promise. She was my slave master, and I was her slave. She made me do many things. I fluffed pillows, I rearranged the plant on the table and, as you saw, massaged Daithi's feet."

"I'm sure she did." Charlie rolled his eyes and put Clawdia down. "She doesn't seem traumatized, so you're forgiven."

Clawdia meowed, and I smiled. "How could she be a slave master? She is too kind."

Charlie snorted. "Kind? You should have seen what she did to my office the other day."

"She has a healer's spirit," I said and felt the truth in the words.

"You called her fierce." Charlie raised his brow, a smug expression on his face.

"When threatened."

He rolled his eyes again and walked toward the kitchen, Clawdia meowing at his ankles.

I joined my friends on the sofa. "That was a long conversation," Daithi noted.

"Yes." I didn't want to talk about it with them yet. I didn't want to think about the possibility that Charlie was right.

Savida asked, "He has not found your soul pair?"

"Not yet."

Daithi leaned forward and stared at me intently, a lock of green hair falling into his eyes. "I know, Zaide. Charlie is skeptical because he doesn't know my visions. But I know. I know she is yours. You will meet her."

"What if I don't?" I whispered.

"Don't entertain the thought."

We were all quiet as we sat in our own thoughts. Savida

broke it. "I like the human Charlie. He belongs, don't you think?"

"It's a bit early for that, beloved," Daithi told his lover.

"Ah, but I don't think it is. I think he should come home with us after we have found Margaret. He is lonely here."

I glanced at the kitchen and realized that Savida was right. Charlie didn't have anyone. I had just revealed all my secrets to him. He was now as knowledgeable as Savida and Daithi about my situation. I trusted him. When he found Margaret, I would owe him.

I nodded. "He should."

"Zaide will have a brother to play with." Savida laughed. "They already argue so well."

My lip twitched at his antics. "We might be a family, but you are not my parents."

Daithi's eyes sparkled as he said, "This adventure will see you partner with your soul pair. How could we not feel as proud as parents on the eve of a joining ceremony?"

I pouted and folded my arms huffing, playfully. "Stop it."

Savida laughed and opened his mouth to speak when Daithi suddenly collapsed. "Dai?" Savida checked his eyes and said, "A vision."

I nodded and stood to join Charlie in the kitchen, leaving Savida to make his lover comfortable.

Charlie was chopping something, and Clawdia was lying on the counter, watching him. "You are making a midday meal?"

"Yeah. Should be about ten minutes. Why?"

"Daithi has just fallen into a vision. He might be a while."

Charlie looked up from his chopping quickly. "Is he okay? Does he need anything?"

Savida joined us then, the door clanging loudly behind him. "No, he'll be fine. We'll know when he wakes if he needs anything."

"I suppose we should wait for Daithi to wake up before we go out."

Savida agreed with a sad huff. He picked Clawdia up and placed her on his head again. "My slave master will distract me until he rouses from his vision."

* * *

WE WERE in the middle of eating when we heard Daithi yell. Savida jumped up, dropping his cutlery into his bowl, his wings flapping frantically as he rushed to his lover.

Charlie and I chased after him. Charlie was especially alarmed, as he had never seen Daithi's suffering after a vision. Opening the door, Daithi had his head buried in Savida's chest. The demon was stroking his green hair, which was tangled from his panicked awakening.

I bent down beside and said, "Daithi, what did you see?" It worried me, seeing him cling to Savida like that.

Although seemingly emotionless, Daithi loved deeply, and his history showed that his gift caused him more pain as he loved more beings, which was why he only had Savida and me to care about.

Daithi took a deep breath and lifted his head to look at me. His green irises were stark against the now red whites of his eyes. "Savida. In a circle. Screaming."

Charlie paled. "Well, there goes that trip into town tomorrow."

"My visions always come true. It does not matter. It will happen."

Savida's expression did not change. He had no care for his future pain, only the present pain bubbling out from his beloved. He did not stop stroking the green locks as he said, "Am I not a powerful demon? Am I not the best and most loyal lover to a faei seer? Do you think I will fall victim to this circle of evil easily?" He tilted Daithi's head so they were looking into each other's eyes. "I will not be felled. Don't worry about me."

Daithi closed his eyes. "You didn't move. You couldn't. Someone hurts you."

"I'm not afraid. If I cannot save myself, you will save me, as you have saved me before."

"What if I can't save you?" he whispered and flinched as though the thought physically hurt him.

"You will. Did you see to prove otherwise?" Daithi shook his head. "Then I have no doubt, and neither should you. Besides, we don't know when this will happen. It could be years away."

Daithi mumbled, "It will not make it easier for me."

"We do not do easy." Savida gave him a lingering kiss on the forehead.

"So, shopping is back on? You won't end up in a circle screaming if you leave the house?" Charlie asked cautiously.

Savida raised his eyebrows playfully at his lover. "Say we can go. You know I love shopping."

Daithi drew away from Savida's chest, wiped his eyes, and became the stoic faei we all knew. "You must come back."

"I swear on my fire." He pressed a hand to his chest.

Charlie hummed questioningly. "I think you mean heart."

"My fire makes me a demon. Without it, I would be nothing. A shell," he informed Charlie.

Charlie looked at me in confusion.

"It is like a soul," I explained.

"Fire is also power. I don't know my powers since I don't remember my home, but I imagine they are fearsome." Savida said cheerfully.

Charlie chuckled. "If the myths are to be believed, then yeah, I imagine you have badass powers."

"You have myths about demons?" Daithi asked.

"Some people believe that when you die, if you've been a good person, you go to heaven. If you've been bad, you go to hell. Hell is where demons live, and they torture you for all eternity. They do the devil's work, possessing people and making them sin, hurting them."

Savida was noticeably upset. "Demons are bad?"

"Obviously not. Humans just like to blame everyone else for their problems. And since demons don't look as human as other otherworlders, they've probably made them the baddies. At least, that's my theory."

"You're probably right, Charlie," I said.

"Humans like to exaggerate, too. Here, I'll show you a picture of what humans think a demon looks like." He took his phone and, after a few taps with his thumbs, presented us with a picture of a 'demon.'

He wasn't wrong. The creatures had pointed horns and leathery wings, but the pointed teeth, cruel expression, tail, and pitchfork were far from Savida's identity.

"These creatures seem to be based on demons," Daithi said, and Savida sent him a pouty look. "I said 'based.' You are far more attractive."

Charlie raised his brows, then smirked and said, "I don't know. The resemblance is striking."

Savida hissed at him, and I chuckled quietly. He was fitting in nicely with us.

As I watched my friends joke with each other I wished it could stay like this forever. But Daithi's premonitions were never wrong. Something terrible would happen to Savida. It was only a question of when.

CHAPTER 7

CHARLIE

"*I*t's shopping day!" Savida gleefully shouted as he entered the kitchen with Daithi at his heels.

I was just putting juice on the table when Clawdia showed up again.

"Master!" Savida cheered as she curled herself around his chair.

"Little Cat, you look especially fluffy today," Zaide told her as he ran his big golden hand over her. He'd pouted when she went home the night before.

The perkiness of everyone was too much before my morning coffee. Dreams of portals and cats and other-worlders disturbed my sleep last night, and so this morning, I was grumpier than usual.

"Clawdicat, I swear, I'll fucking squash you on purpose if you keep getting in my way," I growled as she twisted around my legs again while I moved to the table. I slammed my plate down, and she jumped onto my lap. "You're just trying to make up for being all over Zaide yesterday. I'm not falling for it, traitor."

"I cannot help if the little cat prefers my praise to your

censure," Zaide replied as he joined me at the table with his own meal.

I stroked her with one hand and picked up my breakfast and stuffed it into my mouth with the other. Around a mouthful of sausage sandwich, I garbled, "Well, she's a glutton for punishment."

I had left a bit of sausage on my plate, and Clawdia clawed it toward her, sniffed it, and then munched it down as if we'd invited her over to join us. I glared as she looked at my sandwich expectantly. "You've had enough, fatty," I told her.

Savida gasped with his knife inches from the butter. "Charlie!"

"What?"

"You should never remark on a female's weight. Even small animals," he remarked, oddly serious.

"That's a universal rule, then?" I laughed as Daithi sat gracefully on the chair opposite me. He didn't look well; his eyes were still bloodshot, and his skin was a little less sparkly and a little sweatier. I didn't want to ask about it, and from the way Savida was catering to him, I assumed it was normal for him to look a bit out of it after a vision.

Savida brought over both his and Daithi's breakfast to the table. He set the plate in front of Daithi, and when the seer looked up to thank him with a small smile, Savida brushed his dark fingers through his lover's green hair and tucked it behind his pointed ear. As he bent to sit down at his own seat, he brushed a small kiss on Daithi's cheek. Daithi's eyelids fluttered closed for a moment to savor the feeling. They both looked up from their plates at the same time to see me watching.

"It's not rude to stare in the human realm?" Daithi remarked coldly.

I chewed and remembered what Zaide had said yesterday

about how their love proved that to him that romantic love exists. It wasn't something I was looking for, but seeing it in front of me did make me curious. "Not every day that I see a faei and a demon loving on each other at my dining table. I'm interested; when did this happen?" I waved my hand between the two of them.

"You are asking for our love story?" Savida asked eagerly.

I almost regretted asking, but I was curious to know how two different species, and opposite personalities, were so in love. I nodded, and Savida wolfed down the rest of his breakfast in two bites. He poured his orange juice into his mouth and then gasped when he finished.

He wiped his mouth and, with his wings flapping in excitement, said, "It began when after many, many years of darkness, cold, and silence, suddenly, there was light. I could see. It was painful but welcome, and with the light came a beautiful face."

Although I already knew Savida had been conscious while underground, I was fucking horrified to hear him say it himself. Somehow, that made it more real. "How did you survive that?"

Savida's eyes glazed slightly, but he shook himself, brushing off the memories. "It takes a lot to kill a demon. But let us not dwell on unpleasant things. This is a love story." He smiled brightly at Daithi. "I gazed at the beautiful face shading me from the blinding light, and two tears fell from his eyes. They splashed me. I remembered being so very confused. I asked if he was hurt, although my throat and voice were sore from disuse. He shook his head and reached down to pull me out. As I climbed, I felt the wind for the first time in a long while, and my wings fluttered. I had almost forgotten I had them. Had anything." He reached behind him to stroke the leathery ends of horns.

"And I stretched them, wide and long, when I came out of

74

the hole, but they couldn't hold me up. My legs were shaky, too. But the faei kneeled down, even though he was wearing very expensive clothing, and draped a cloak around my shoulders. He whispered, 'You are safe with me now, Savida. Let me take you back to my home.'" Daithi squeezed his hand.

There was only a brief pause before Savida continued, his voice wavering with emotions, "I had not heard my name in so long that it shocked me to hear it. I was so grateful to my hero that I'd let him do anything, take me anywhere, so I nodded. He bathed, fed, and looked after me for months. We grew close, and I learned my beautiful hero was also funny and smart and needed me as much as I needed him. We were perfect for each other from the start." He smiled at Daithi, love shining in his eyes. "It is quite the romantic tale, yes?"

I coughed and ran my hand through Clawdia's fur, who seemed as shell-shocked as me. "It's definitely something."

He smirked. "You wish you had a story like ours, yes?"

I nodded robotically. "Yep. You caught me. I'm super jealous."

He crossed his arms smugly and looked at his lover. "Not all creatures are as blessed as we are. But maybe you will find a love like ours someday, Charlie."

"Here's hoping," I said agreeably, although I had no desire for the love of my life to walk my way.

Zaide interrupted, "When are we leaving to explore your town, Charlie?"

I gave him a grateful half-smile. "When everyone's ready."

"I am ready," Savida announced.

I looked pointedly at his wings and horns. "You don't look human to me."

"I will disguise them before you leave," Daithi said quietly.

Savida looked at him in shock. "You are not coming with us?"

"I am still drained from yesterday's vision." He looked at me solemnly. "Do not fear, Charlie. I have enough energy to cloak them until you return." And suddenly, I wasn't sitting at the table with three otherworlders, just one faei and two humans. "This will do?"

I gaped at Zaide, who was now a large human man with tanned skin. His purple eyes and his white hair were still present and made him recognizable. "Are we ordinary like you, Charlie?" he asked, his lips turned up in a wide smile.

I scoffed. "I'm not ordinary. I'll have you know I was voted most attractive in my year at school."

Zaide glanced at Savida, recognizable by his red hair, gray eyes, and dark skin, which was now a human shade. He grinned widely and bowed toward me. "Ah, so sorry, your handsomeness. We didn't realize you were rated so highly. Our mistake."

They both looked like models. The bastards. "For fuck's sake, Daithi. You couldn't have just stuck a bag over their heads?"

Daithi raised a green brow. "Savida's wings would have been visible. I thought you desired them to look human."

"You know humans come in all shapes and sizes. They don't both have to look like they've just walked out of a bloody photoshoot. Jesus Christ." I huffed and ran a hand through my hair.

Zaide immediately asked, "Who is Jesus Christ? A spirit you pray to?"

I sighed. "I'll take you to a church." Clawdia hopped off my lap, walked to the backdoor, and turned and meowed at me. "All right, Clawdia's going home. See you later, Clawdi-cat," I said. There were disappointed sighs and halfhearted whispered goodbyes from my guests as I opened the door and watched as she jumped onto the fence separating our gardens.

* * *

WAVING goodbye to Daithi at the front door, Savida, Zaide, and I left home and ventured into the town center. We were walking since the sun was shining and there weren't any rain clouds in the sky. I also wasn't sure how they'd feel about the car.

As it was a weekend, town teemed with people, so my new friends had the chance to truly observe the variety of humans in this realm. Tall, small, and all sizes in between. Shades of white, cream, brown. Facial features that were various shapes and lengths. Eyes that were shades of blue, green, gray, and brown. Hair that was of any length and any color.

"Look there, Charlie. That female has green hair. Do you think she is a relation of the faei?" Savida pointed out a girl sitting on a bench. She wore all black, from her dress to her boots, and her hair sat in two bunches on her head.

"She probably dyes it. It's not her natural color." But his question raised another one for me. "Are there relations of the other races here?"

The myths about demons and faei and titans had already confirmed that they'd been here in the past, but I didn't think of what that could mean for humans.

I'd forgotten the classic human adage: If you can't beat it, fuck it. Of course there would be descendants.

Zaide answered since Savida had already skipped ahead to stare through the window of a shop. "Undoubtedly. Daithi said that before the fall of the titans, many realms visited the human one, sometimes in passing to another realm."

Savida distracted me and waved us over, practically jumping on the spot. "Charlie, that person is so wrinkled." He cooed as he pointed through the window to an old man looking at a pot. "He. is. Adorable."

I chuckled, having visions of the scene from *Despicable Me* where the little girl is hugging the fluffy unicorn. "Don't let him hear you say that. And no, you can't keep him."

He pouted playfully and took off again. I turned to Zaide. "He's like a child."

"He doesn't remember his childhood, and his trauma has left him with a thirst for pleasure."

"Oh, yeah." I watched Savida peering down an alleyway as though it were the most fascinating, interesting, mysterious place instead of a spot for shops to hide their rubbish bins.

"Do you think Margaret will be like that old man?" Zaide asked quietly.

I bit my lip, debating whether honesty was the best policy. Sighing, I said, "If she's alive, she'd be older."

"Oh." He nodded with furrowed brows. "He looked very fragile."

I knew what he was thinking. "I'll do my best to find her, but I can't promise how quick that will be." He nodded again, and we continued to walk in silence. Breaking the ice and appeasing my curiosity, I said, "So, there could be supernatural people, like in the myths: vampires, shapeshifters, witches, gods."

Zaide stared down at me. "I don't know about the other beings you named—perhaps we have different names for them—but the gods are not myths."

Arriving at the cathedral where they first appeared, I ushered them inside, and we sat at the back on a bench with them on either side of me.

"This is a sacred place," Zaide whispered. I looked at him to see his eyes wide as he stared at the statues, the paintings, and the stain-glass windows.

"If you say so," I muttered.

Savida turned to whisper to me, "Titans are very pious.

78

Their gods created the life pool so generations could continue to be born after the fall. Zaide prays every day."

I nodded silently but didn't understand what he was going on about with "life pools." I didn't know what else to say or do other than let Zaide feel connected to a greater being, or purpose, in these old brick walls.

"What are they doing, Charlie?" Zaide pointed to a corner at the front.

"They're lighting candles. They do it usually in memory of someone they've lost."

Zaide nodded and then stood, walked to the candle tray, where tiny flames flickered, and took a candle from the box. He lit it as he had seen the people do, putting the wick against the flame of another candle, and placed it in the candle tray, the other candles flickering with the movement. He stared at it for a long moment.

"I wonder if my fire looks like flames," Savida mused, oddly serious.

I gave him a concerned frown. "Well, if it's inside you, I guess we'll never know."

But then I supposed if I didn't know what a heart looked like, I would wonder if it looked like the symbol we draw.

Zaide rejoined us, and we stood to leave. As Savida raced ahead of us, I turned to him and asked, "Who did you light a candle for?"

"My family. My mother and father, my brother, and my three sisters."

* * *

WHAT FELT LIKE AN ETERNITY LATER, Zaide and I sat down at a cafe. Savida's endless energy and enthusiasm had worn us out, and I needed a break from him. Savida, however, was determined to carry on. He left a dozen bags with us at the table and then darted off, buzzing to continue his search for human rubbish.

"You know, we have a saying here. 'Shop until you drop.' I never understood it until now. I didn't think anyone could shop until they dropped, because if you were shit tired, surely you'd just go home and order online instead of fucking fainting like a startled goat. But I get it now. This is me fucking dropping," I ranted as I squeezed ketchup onto my burger and chips with a satisfying squirt.

I handed Zaide the hot sauce since he had been complaining about food being bland. But I wasn't going to tell him how much to add. I considered it an experiment of sorts.

"You will get used to this. Savida enjoys shopping," Zaide told me as he sprinkled half a bottle on his burger.

I gave him a look in response to his comment. "Get used to it? I don't think I'll be showing him any more shopping centers on Earth. Fucking ever."

I took a big bite of my burger and moaned at how good it tasted. Shopping with a demon was hungry work.

Zaide chuckled. "I doubt that will stop him." He also took a bite of his food, and the slight widening of his eyes, which pulled the scar tight across his brow, told me he could taste the hot sauce. He swallowed and continued, "But I meant when we travel to other realms. Savida is just the same, so you will have to get used to it. That or join in."

I stopped, my mouth open and my burger awaiting arrival to my face hole. I stared at the seemingly normal human across the table from me and asked, "I'm coming with you?" A tomato fell from my bun onto my plate with a splat, spraying ketchup up onto my hands. I was so focused on Zaide I didn't even notice. "When I've found Margaret and you've done your sightseeing, I'm coming with you?"

"Of course," he answered easily, as though I should have

figured that out already. Warmth spread in my chest at the thought that they wanted me to stay with them.

Don't embarrass yourself by blushing, Charlie. This isn't school. You haven't just been asked on a date.

He looked up, seeing that I was dumbstruck, and lowered his burger to the plate before continuing seriously, "Daithi, Savida and I all agree that you fit with us. We enjoy your company, and we'd like you to come with us on our adventures. Whether we find Margaret or not. Whether she is alive or not. Regardless of the outcome of our search for my soul pair, I am glad to have met you and to call you my friend."

In a typical, self-sabotaging way, my mouth blurted, "I wouldn't be much use without human technology."

I hadn't entertained the thought of going with them. I didn't think it was an option. But now that Zaide had suggested it, I was suddenly planning to sell my house and belongings and portal into the unknown, because what else was I going to do for the rest of my life now that I knew there was so much more than this world? Rot behind a computer? Be alone forever with nothing but a cat for company? Yeah ... fuck no.

"You are our friend now. You don't need a purpose to be with us," Zaide assured me and polished off his burger. "And if we cannot find Margaret with your human technology, we will need to plan our journey around the human realm."

I took a bite and chewed slowly, thinking. "Planning a journey like that could take a while."

Zaide shrugged. "We will be happy to rest for a while. We have been traveling for many years."

I tilted my head, curious. "Just traveling, or searching for something like you are now?"

"Isn't everyone who travels searching for something?" He looked away from me.

"That's a politician's answer."

He sighed. "My family."

"The ones you lit the candle for?"

He nodded. "My siblings and I were all taken as slaves on the same day. I don't know what became of them. We traveled back to Tartarus to see if my parents were still there, but they weren't. I want to find them all and free them."

Tartarus? Like Hell?

But I didn't ask; it wasn't important when I could see the pain in his eyes as he thought about his family. "That's... I don't know what that is. 'Sad,' 'fucked-up,' and 'brave' are the words that come to mind."

"I will take them." The side of his mouth quirked up. "Does it bother you that our travels will be in search of them?"

"No. They deserve to be free. I want to help you find them."

"Then you agree you'll be joining us?"

"I'll need to think about it." I was silent a moment before I shook my head, grinned, and stood up. "Right, I'm going to get the bill and go to the little boy's room before we find our demon."

When I returned from the toilet, I paid for the meal, and we left the restaurant in search of Savida. He said he'd stay in the shop until we came back to retrieve him. This shop, however, had three floors.

"I'm betting he's in men's clothing, staring at shirts and wondering how he'll be able to squeeze his wings through cuts he puts in the back," I declared. My find-it superpowers were kicking in.

Zaide laughed. "It is a good bet. Unfortunately, I have the knowledge and experience to bet that he is currently in the home department observing lamps."

"You might win this one," I lied. I knew exactly where Savida was. Zaide wouldn't win this bet. "He was after a nightlight so he didn't have to crawl into bed with your glowing arse."

"It is not my arse that glows, but my scars."

"Either way, it's weird."

"Only to you, dull human."

"Dull? That's harsh."

As we dodged and weaved through the crowds of people in the men's wear department, I noticed a flash of red hair.

"There he is. Men's section. I fucking knew it!" I laughed and pointed in the direction I'd seen him. "Savida!" I called, and he turned to face us, a big grin on his face and his hands full of clothes.

Someone jostled us as we made our way over to him, and I looked down for a second—just a second—and when I looked up, Savida wasn't there anymore.

"Sav?" I called.

"Where has he gone now?" Zaide huffed and brushed his hand down his front in annoyance. "I do not enjoy how densely populated your town is, Charlie."

I put my hand up. "No. Shut up. Something is wrong."

"What do you mean?"

"I don't know where he is." I started to panic.

Frantically looking left and right, I pushed through crowds of people. As much as I hoped he would jump out at me, I knew I could always find something, and the feeling that told me he was in the men's section was now empty. Wrong.

"Yes, but we will find him again. He probably found something bright and followed it. He has little impulse control. There was this time—"

I interrupted him, "No, Zaide, I'm being serious. I don't know where he is."

He paused, confusion written all over his face. "I don't understand."

"Look, I've always been able to find stuff. When I know people, I find them more easily. I knew he'd be in men's wear because I could feel him there. I can't explain it. But now I can't feel him, and he's fucking disappeared, and Daithi is going to murder us if his vision comes true," I explained hurriedly. I could feel in my gut that something was wrong. I knew it.

I started moving again, searching the aisles, Zaide following closely behind, and soon I found a pile of clothes. The same clothes Savida held in his hands only moments ago.

"No," Zaide whispered. He picked up a shirt from the pile. "He wouldn't have just dropped them, Charlie."

"I know."

We were silent for a second. "What are we going to do?" Zaide asked. "This is going to kill Daithi."

"We're going to need help. Maybe Daithi can track him magically?" I didn't look at Zaide for an answer. I just started moving toward the exit. "Come on, we need to get back. Now."

CHAPTER 8

CLAWDIA

*I*t was my fault. It was all my fault.

When Charlie, Zaide and Savida left to go into the town center, I went home. I could tell Daithi wasn't a fan of mine, and sitting around with him would have made us both uncomfortable.

I jumped down onto my garden fence and noticed there were bags of something in the garden. Something that hadn't been there this morning. It could only mean that Winnie was home. I dashed through the cat flap and into the kitchen, where my witch stood typing furiously on her phone. She had been missing this morning, and I was pleased to see her home.

Winnie! You're home! I greeted her happily. *Where have you been? What are those bags outside?*

Winnie grimaced at me, "Oh, you know, this thing Mary and I have been doing. Just setting stuff up."

Ah, yes. The mysterious thing. Are you ever going to tell me?

"I'm sworn not to tell another soul, Clawds." She sighed.

Sworn. Witches had powerful magic triggered by words. If she'd sworn her secrecy, bad things would happen to her if she broke her silence. And since our lives depended on each other, bad things would also happen to me. I was suddenly more understanding and thankful she had more self-control than I did.

I'm sorry I pushed.

"It's okay. You weren't to know." She shrugged and then put on a smile. I couldn't tell if it was because she was unhappy in her situation and trying to lighten the mood, or if she was about to lie. "So, you've been next door. What are Charlie's aliens up to today?" Then she laughed. "Charlie's aliens. I love it."

They went shopping today. All except Daithi. He didn't look well. So, I came home to have a snack and watch more Netflix.

She turned away from me and opened the cupboard full of cups. "Daithi is the demon?"

No. I stopped short of telling her his name. I had a feeling in the pit of my stomach that something strange was going on.

She pulled out her phone and sent a quick message before she turned back to look at me, grinning. It looked alien on her face, and her eyes were emotionless. It made me wary. "What's the demon's name?"

Why are you so curious about him in particular?

"I'm interested in a creature I've read about. Sue me," she huffed and folded her arms across her chest. "I don't understand why you won't tell me his name. It's not a big deal."

Because you are acting strangely.

"You don't trust me."

I trust you with my life. You're my entire world. But I don't trust Mary. I don't trust this mysterious project. And I don't trust your single-focused interest on just one of Charlie's guests.

"I can't believe you, Clawds. The one time I'm asking you to help me, and you're treating me as though I'm a stranger."

You are acting like one. I thought about all the extra magic

86

we had been doing. How it had drained me, but I still did it. And now she was saying I do nothing for her.

She was silent for a moment. "I just need his name. Please."

I don't think I should tell you.

"Fine." She stormed away from me, opened the back door, and slammed it behind her as she went into the garden.

My stomach sank. Winnie and I had never had an argument like that before, and for a second, I contemplated whether I was wrong to keep something so trivial from my witch.

Surely his name couldn't hurt anyone.

I moved to the cat flap, my soul hurting with the need to make it better, but stopped. I wasn't wrong. Winnie had been acting strangely, and while I understood she couldn't tell me anything about this mysterious project, I didn't see why she would have such a strange reaction to Savida. I shook my head. A cat's brain wasn't made for feats of logic, and so I hid and licked my wounds rather than contemplate the problem at hand. Or paw.

* * *

After a nap under the chair, I woke up when a hand touched me. I tensed and then calmed, realizing it was Winnie. I opened my eyes to see her big brown ones staring back at me. They shimmered with unshed tears.

"I'm sorry," she whispered. "This project is really weighing on me, and I'm taking it out on you. Forgive me?"

I sighed, my heart relieved to let go of the distance between us. *Of course I forgive you.*

"Thank you. I really don't want this thing to come between us." She stopped stroking me and pulled away. "I've made you a snack if you still want it."

A snack? What kind of snack?

"It's bacon."

Wow! Yes, please. I darted out from under the chair and stretched on my way to the kitchen. Winnie placed the bowl in front of me, and I shoved my head in without thought or hesitation. Bacon to my cat tongue was pure heaven. Bacon was life.

But I realized a few bites in that the bacon smelled funny. It was subtle but definitely there. It didn't taste any different.

I looked up to question Winnie—my witch, my sister, my life—and read the guilt on her face and the emotion eating at her soul.

What have you done? I asked, panicked. *Winnie, is this bacon magicked?*

"No. No." Her voice pitched higher, and her fingers twitched. At least, I thought they twitched. A cloud descended over me, and I realized it wasn't a cloud. My eyesight was blurring.

Winnie? Winnie! My eyes. I can't see. What have you done? Why have you done this?

"Your eyes? The spell didn't say anything—"

I heard her panicked mutterings as I tilted to the side, my paws spread to catch me.

"Clawds? Clawds!" Winnie picked me up, and I heard her whispering, "Oh fuck. Oh shit. What have I done?" She lay me down on what I assumed to be the sofa. "Okay, okay, it's going to be okay. Oh god, Clawds. I'm so sorry."

Breathing became difficult, and I cried out, *Why, Winnie? I can't move. Please, help me, I can't move. I can't see. I can't breathe. Help.*

I heard her sob. "I'm so sorry. You don't need to apologize. This is all my fault. I'm going to make it better." Her magic pushed against me, and my tail twitched, my eyes blinked, and my lungs filled. Relief flooded me, but I still couldn't move.

There was a sudden bang as the front door slammed open. Winnie and I both jumped, and she haphazardly wiped tears from under her eyes.

Mary fought her way into the house, panting and dragging something behind her. My eyes took in her bedraggled appearance. Her hair was matted with mud, and huge sections of her usually slicked-back ponytail were now hanging around her face. Her makeup seemed to have melted away, leaving her face a red, blotchy mess. Her clothing had also been ripped. The black pleated skirt was torn in a zig zag slit up the side and revealed the silk underskirt. Her vest top looked undamaged but, like her hair and face, was covered in mud.

"Next time, you get to retrieve the demon," Mary growled at Winnie and continued heaving and pulling something toward the garden.

Demon? I thought dazedly. She retrieved a demon? My brain clapped, and two thoughts became entwined, and I knew exactly what was happening. As she heaved past me, I saw what she had caught in a large magical net—Savida.

He was struggling. Black wings flapping, his enormous body rolling and pulling and squirming. I almost felt sorry for Mary, who was being battered as she tried to pull him along. His eyes met mine for a moment, and he stilled, his face confused. He mouthed my name, and I meowed pitifully. I could only flick my tail, even as I tried my hardest to move, willed my body to work, pushed my energy to my paws, and pulled magic from my witch.

Winnie didn't notice. She was questioning Mary. "You look awful. What happened?"

"Your tracking spell worked, even without his name. He was in the men's wear section, holding a bunch of clothes. When

Charlie and the other one called, I captured him and wrapped us in an invisibility spell. I had him spelled to sleep, but it wore off too early, so the last ten minutes back were a struggle. It was lucky we thought to bring the extra magic, because I didn't have enough magic reserves for four spells at once."

"I'm so sorry. I should have gone instead."

"We needed you here to deal with your familiar. She can't get help this way."

I managed a small hiss. *You are not the person I thought you were.* Winnie magicked my bacon so I wouldn't see or know what she and Mary planned and get help. She knew how I would feel about this. She heard the venom in my thoughts and winced, her eyes filling with tears.

My anger bubbled under my skin, forcing my fur to stand on end. I wasn't concerned about Winnie's feelings. Only her betrayal. And that pain was feeding into my energy. My paw twitched at the thought of biting and scratching Mary. The evil witch.

Mary stopped to open the back door and stared at Winnie. "Have you been crying?"

"No." Winnie looked away swiftly, but Mary grabbed her face and squeezed her cheeks between her finger and thumb.

"Winnie, I can see your face. What the fuck are you crying about? Have you seen the state of me? Have you seen what I've been through to get this far? You haven't got anything to cry about, and you can't back out now, so don't even think about it."

"No, it's not that. It's nothing. I'm fine." She wasn't looking her in the eye.

"You can't use the 'I'm fine' trick. I'm female too. If you're crying over that damned cat—"

Winnie interrupted on a sob. "She won't forgive me for this, Mary. We shouldn't have done this."

No, you shouldn't have.

Savida interrupted, suddenly sucking in a breath and screaming, "Let me go. Let me out, you evil Lagworms!"

"Thanks, Win. You distracted me enough that my fucking silent spell broke." She pulled the net out into the garden, with Winnie following, wringing her hands. I tried to follow. I pushed with all my power, and my paws moved. With only determination and a broken heart, I crawled toward the garden.

"You will pay for your crimes! When my friends find me, you will be sorry!" I heard Savida yell.

Mary spat viciously. "Shut up. No one is coming for you. They won't find you."

"Not find me? I'm in the garden next to Charlie's. He will find me."

Mary laughed. "It will already be too late for you by then. We'll have taken your fire and left."

"My fire? Why would a human need my fire? You have a soul of your own."

"You don't need to know the answer to that."

I was regaining my energy, my body responding to my commands but not quickly enough to jump next door and hope that someone could save Savida. As I pulled myself onto the patio, I took in the scene in front of me.

Savida was now lying in a large salt circle on the grass with a pentagram design also drawn with salt inside it. A casting circle for difficult and dangerous spells was used to contain and protect the outside from the experiment inside. I went cold.

I'd heard the words they'd been saying as I dragged my disabled body toward them, but I hadn't taken them in. Now that I had seen the circle, I knew they were going to take his soul. His fire. For a mysterious witch project.

And I had led them straight to him. His eyes met mine again. I meowed and tried to move toward him.

"Why does the cat struggle to move? What have you done to Clawdia?"

His concern for me shamed me further. I wanted so badly to save him.

Please. Please, Win. You need to stop. You'll hurt him. Kill him.

"I can't stop now," she whispered. "It's too late."

No. You can stop this. You can save him. I'll forgive you. It will be okay, but only if you stop her. Please.

"I can't."

Mary interrupted our whispered argument. "Win, I need you to hold these spells while I get the box."

"Okay," she agreed easily.

Savida continued to shout, "What have you done to Clawdia? You would harm a being smaller than you? You are evil."

I felt the sting of hurt in Winnie as his words shook her. "I—I haven't hurt her. She'll be okay. Please be quiet."

He scoffed. "I should just await my death in calm silence? Is that what you would do?"

"Please. I don't want to spell you, but I will," she replied more firmly.

No, Winnie. Leave him alone. I hissed and moved toward her, but I walked into an invisible wall. I fell backward. Confused and slightly dazed, I looked at Winnie, whose hand was outstretched toward me, but her body and eyes remained focused on the alien in the circle.

Another lance of pain ran through me at yet another betrayal of the person who guided me in this new world and new body. I growled my anger and shouted at her. *You've changed, Winnie! You used to be a good person. Now you're as bad as Mary. You're going to kill someone today. You're a murderer.*

"He's not a someone. He's a demon."

You're dehumanizing him because he doesn't look human. But he enjoys shopping, and he has a male lover, and he is a positive person despite the horrible things that happened to him. Please. Please, Winnie. I don't want you to be another horrible thing that happens to him.

"Who are you talking to? Is it your spirit? Is it telling you to let me free? You should listen to it, human."

"I'm not just human. I'm a witch, and we have a power that others don't. And I can't free you. I need to be a part of this. It's my way in. Please understand."

"A witch? You have power? Like magic?" ever quizzical Savida asked.

Mary opened the door and walked back into the garden. "Okay, I have the box. Let's get this done and get going before his friends really do come for him."

"I'm sorry," Winnie whispered, but I didn't know which of us she was apologizing to when she cast a quick and almost unnoticeable spell. One of silence. On both myself and Savida.

Realizing he could no longer speak, he struggled against the net which held him captive. I did the same, desperately trying to find my way out of my invisible box. I was screaming at Winnie in my mind. But apparently, the spell had done more than silence my voice. It had silenced my mind and our bond.

Mary began chanting, and Savida struggled again. She approached the circle, and suddenly, it lit up, the lines of salt glowing red, highlighting the being inside. She put her hands out toward it, and the light around the edge of the circle became solid. The circle became a dome, and Mary placed her hands against it. She gasped, her muddy hair and clothes flew outward, and she grinned. She looked at Winnie with her excited eyes, and with a nod of her head, she indicated it was time for Winnie to join.

Winnie approached with far less eagerness than Mary had, but that did not forgive her for the actions she took.

"Can you feel it, Win? Can you feel the power of his fire? It's amazing."

She nodded and nervously licked her lips. "Let's just get this over with."

Power pulled from us, myself and Winnie, as she chanted. It wasn't like other times where she had cast a spell or made a potion and pulled from our reserve. This time, it hurt. I felt complicit. I was helping to cause him pain, to kill him, and that made it even more painful. I whimpered silently and curled into myself, helpless to do anything but watch.

The dome light turned to a darker red, and inside, Savida went still, his mouth open in a silent scream and his back arched. And then he collapsed; his head and body dropped to the grass and bounced as he lost consciousness.

The light in the dome dimmed and then ran out from the salt lines to crawl up Savida's limp body, converging on the center of his chest. It shimmered and became flame-like, floating in mid-air like a lantern on water. The dome remained solid until the witches took their hands off it, and it faded out.

Mary quickly grabbed the glass box, which had been next to her, and plopped the open side over the flame still dancing above Savida's body. Turning it over slowly, she got the lid on it before it could escape.

With the lid snapped shut, Mary gasped and then cheered, waving the box around and twirling. "We did it, Win! We really did it! The fire of a demon is ours!" She skipped to my owner and smacked a kiss on her lips. "That was so amazing. Well done. We couldn't have done it without your extra boost."

She squealed and twirled again. "I can't believe it! I'm going to call them right now and let them know we'll be leaving soon." She danced past me into the kitchen, still holding the glowing box.

I glared at Winnie, who stared at Savida's limp form. Her body seemed frozen, as though if someone touched her, she'd shatter. A thin pink line was in place of her usual full lips and happy smile as her jaw clenched and she swallowed.

Her actions had taken a toll on her, but she was trying not to show it. I didn't have any sympathy.

After a few long moments, she turned to look at me, and with her dead eyes, she blinked and said, "I'll set you free when we leave. We'll be gone for a while. I'll make sure someone comes round to feed you."

No apology. No compassion. But also no elation. She knew it was wrong but found herself too deep and too committed to stop. She had crossed a line that had no return. Our relationship would never be the same, and I wouldn't forgive her.

She cast a wind spell, making the salt disperse across the grass, and then cast a levitation spell to move Savida's body into the shed. I saw red. How dare she. After all that she had done and how she had made him suffer, she disrespected his body by hiding it with the garden tools. I hissed soundlessly and clawed and pushed against my invisible cage, fury making me blind.

"Clawdia, stop it. You're going to hurt yourself. Stop."

Oh, now you care.

She heard me. "I've always cared. I know you hate me right now, but I promise, when this is over, I'll explain everything and you'll understand." She had turned off the silent spell, so I hissed again. Winnie continued calmly, which only further riled me. "You need to calm down. I told you, I'll set you free when we are gone."

I didn't reply. I stopped hissing and clawing at the walls. Suddenly exhausted, I lay down but refused to shut my eyes.

I didn't want to let my guard down like I did before and end up even more helpless.

As though she could read my mind, Winnie sighed, stood up, and walked indoors.

A little while later, the front door slammed shut, and I turned toward the sound automatically before realizing I was no longer trapped in the invisible cage. I raced toward the shed, and after fighting with the door, I dragged myself in. Savida lay motionless, tossed carelessly into the corner by the lawnmower.

Cursing witches in my mind, I jumped over tools and crawled through cobwebs to stand on his lap and peer into his face. I was hoping for some sign to tell me whether he was unconscious or dead. His face remained still, but from his nostrils, a slight exhale of air brushed across my face.

It was all the hope I needed and immediately dashed to Charlie's house, praying Daithi would be there, understand me, and help.

Jumping into Charlie's bedroom, I heard silence around the house. And running down the stairs, I found out why. Daithi was asleep on the sofa.

Of all the times to be asleep, I thought angrily. *Your lover is dying, Daithi. Wake up.*

I leaped up onto his prone body and pressed my paw into his face. I jumped. I jumped again. I meowed and meowed and jumped and he still wouldn't wake. Desperately, I aimed my claws at a place I knew would get any male's attention and every other male's sympathy when the door slammed open and Charlie and Zaide ran in.

CHAPTER 9

ZAIDE

"*C*lawdicat, what the fuck are you doing? Were you about to claw Daithi's balls?" Charlie stepped back as though to take the scene in. Then shook his head in what I believed to be the human brain reshuffle motion. "Get off him. We need him."

Clawdia meowed, dodging the shooing hands of Charlie.

I looked at Daithi's still body and knew. Panic left my body in a sigh. "He is in another vision, Charlie. He cannot help us look for Savida until he wakes," I informed him, shutting the door behind us.

Now standing on the back of the sofa as Charlie leaned over to peer at Daithi's face, Clawdia tried to paw at him, but he ignored her. "What? How can you tell? He looks like he's asleep."

"Daithi is usually a light sleeper. He would certainly wake if a creature jumped on him." I approached them as Charlie stood and sat on the arm of the chair.

With Charlie ignoring her, Clawdia walked, balancing precariously, over to me. She meowed, her violet eyes begging for something, but I didn't know what. "You are very vocal today, Little Cat. What are you trying to say?"

She meowed once more.

Charlie huffed impatiently. "She's being needy. Probably bored out of her fucking brain staring at Daithi all day."

I was happy to oblige her needs, and so I picked her up and cuddled her close to my chest, her soft fur brushing my chin.

Charlie continued, "What are we supposed to do now? I can't find Savida without divine intervention or a magic faei, and neither are looking likely right now."

Clawdia meowed and squirmed in my grip.

I understood his panic. Only moments ago, my heart pounded with the anxiety that Savida was going to come to harm. But panic was not useful while we could do nothing. "Calm, Charlie. Daithi may see the information we need to find Savida as we speak. We can only wait." I stroked Clawdia, trying to soothe her agitation, and my hand came away dirty. "What have you been up to, Little Cat? Why are you covered in filth?"

She meowed an answer.

Charlie came closer to look at her fur. "It looks like cobwebs and ... salt? Is that salt? What the fuck have you been doing? Visiting the basement witches?"

She meowed three times.

"She clearly has much that she wishes to tell us about her journey," I noted.

"She'll have to wait." We turned, surprised at the sound of the voice, to see Daithi awake and pulling himself into an upright position. He looked at us with one green raised eyebrow and asked, "Where's Savida?"

The blood drained from my face, and Charlie tensed next to me. I placed Clawdia on the floor carefully. She meowed three times in protest and clawed at my trousers.

"He is missing. We think your vision has come true, and we need to find him," I said, bracing myself for his reaction.

"No," Daithi whispered. "No."

"I'm so sorry, Daithi," Charlie mumbled.

"What happened? Did you see who took him?"

I began, "We left him to shop—"

Daithi surged up off the sofa and shouted in my face. "You left him? After my vision warned us of this?"

"We were tired—" I tried to explain but knew there was no explaining why we failed him. Failed them both.

"Tired? You knew he would be in danger. You should have been watching him!"

I lowered my head and nodded, feeling truly ashamed.

Charlie interrupted, "We're not trying to make excuses, and we know you're angry with us, but we need you to help find him."

"I won't need your assistance." He closed his eyes and began searching for Savida through their bond.

Charlie, however, didn't know that and asked, "What is he doing?"

"He is bonded to Savida and can search for him through that bond. It shouldn't take long," I whispered.

Daithi opened his eyes, and pain poured from them in a single tear. "I can't find him."

We were silent for a moment. "He isn't in the human realm any longer?" I asked, confused.

Daithi shook his head and closed his eyes. "I could still find him if he had been portaled away."

"He could be hidden with magic," I suggested.

"Or dead."

I shook my head. "You would know in your soul if he were dead. I refuse to believe that was his fate. We will find him." I took a breath. "Your vision. What was it?"

"I have already informed you of it. Savida was lying in a circle and screaming."

"Not that one. The one you just woke up from."

Daithi paused, thinking, and then waved his hand in dismissal. "It wasn't anything about Savida. There was a female calling for a taxi, another with bags. They discussed the arrangements for a person in the home while they were away. I believe it was a clue about Margaret."

Clawdia meowed and jumped onto the side table.

"About Margaret? How do you know?" Charlie asked. Clawdia nibbled on his finger, which rested on the table. Then meowed again when he pulled them away.

"I assume she is the person they are making care arrangements for."

Although my friend was missing, I couldn't stop myself from still wanting to meet her, no matter how old or incapable she was. "Did you hear where the house was?"

He looked at me incredulously. "You would leave to retrieve your soul pair while I am missing my mate?"

"No. It is important information to have. As soon as we have found Savida, I will go to her." It was partly true.

Daithi glared. "Then I will hold the information until then."

"Hold on," Charlie said. "There's no need to be like that. Tell me the address. If it's too far, we'll go when Savida is safe, but if it's around the corner, then it would be stupid to wait while we have no leads on Savida and don't know where to begin. You've assumed your vision is about Margaret, but it could have been about Savida. It's worth checking out."

Daithi contemplated that. "All right. The address was 37 Listerly Lane."

Charlie's mouth dropped open.

Clawdia meowed.

"Well, how far is it? You know this place?" I asked.

Clawdia meowed.

Charlie swallowed and looked at Clawdia. "This house is 36 Listerly Lane."

"She is next door?"

Clawdia meowed.

Charlie broke. "Clawdia, for fuck's sake will you stop meowing. Can't you see we're having a crisis here?" he roared.

She hissed at him and pushed the lamp off the table. Charlie cursed as it smashed, and she dashed toward the office.

"What is she doing now? Clawdia, I swear to God, I don't have the fucking time or energy for your shit right now, so fuck off home." Charlie stormed after her.

"Charlie, don't curse at her," I chastised. "Perhaps she was trying to tell us something." She'd certainly been trying to get our attention since we walked in.

"She's a pissing cat. She doesn't think like that," he growled as he swung the office door wide to show the back of Clawdia's fluffy form sat on the desk.

As she turned her head to look at us, she held some kind of small, colorful stick in her mouth. A stick that had been sticking out of Charlie's computer. She dropped off the desk and when Charlie gasped, realizing what she had stolen, she ran out of the office and toward the kitchen.

We chased after her, only to see her lithe body slip between the ajar window and dash into the garden.

Charlie shouted, "You thieving little rat! Come back here right now, Clawdia. Drop it. Drop it." He opened the back door and stormed to the fence where Clawdia perched, waiting for him to catch up.

"I don't know why you are so irate, Charlie. We need to go to her home to find out why Daithi saw it and she is only trying to hurry us along. She is quite the clever little cat."

"Because she's being a bitch about it by taking my memory stick." He glared at her, and she seemed to glare back. Or maybe the setting sun was affecting her eyes. Charlie continued, "She isn't as smart as you think, Zaide. I mean, she's smart for a cat, but she's not human smart."

She growled. Then jumped to the other side of the fence. Despite everything, I laughed. I enjoyed that such a small creature gave Charlie so much grief.

"Fuck's sake," he muttered and heaved himself over the fence.

"Perhaps you shouldn't speak ill of her, Charlie. She doesn't seem to like it," I teased and waited for his reply.

And waited. Eventually, he said, "Guys. I think you should get over here."

What was it? Margaret? Would I find her here? Was she alone? Hurt? Dying? Or did Daithi's vision relate to Savida? Was I about to find my friend and savior in a position that I could have saved him from?

Dread filled me, and I immediately jumped the fence with Daithi not far behind. "What is it?"

"Something weird has happened here." Charlie was standing in the middle of the grass with a puzzled expression.

I looked around but couldn't see anything wrong. "What? What do you mean? I see nothing unusual."

"It's not something I can see." He shuddered and rolled his shoulders. "It's something I feel."

Daithi moved toward him, frowning. "He is right. This land is scarred by magic. What kind, I cannot tell."

Clawdia was at the door of a wooden building and dropped the plastic. She meowed and looked at us, then looked at the building and looked back at us.

"You might have been right about her wanting to show us something," Charlie muttered as we moved to follow her.

Darkness was coming faster as the sun dipped below the houses, and my scars glowed as we entered the dim building.

My eyes took a moment to adjust, and I held my breath, awaiting the revelation of … something … maybe a someone. Clawdia meowed again, impatient, and then I noticed what she was sitting in front of.

"My love!" Daithi exclaimed,

Knocking me out of the way, he flung himself toward the body of my friend lying haphazardly in the corner of this forgotten shack. His wings were bent at an odd angle, and I couldn't see his chest moving. I feared the worst.

"Oh fuck," Charlie breathed. "Is he—"

"His fire. His fire is gone." Daithi was panting, his body shaking with emotion. "I swore I'd save him. Always look after him. I've failed him." My heart broke with him.

I tried to comfort him. "You haven't failed him. Daithi—"

I reached out a hand to him, but Daithi growled, "Get away from us. You should have been with him today. You might have been able to prevent this."

I bowed my head. "I'm sorry."

"I don't want your apologies. I want him back."

Charlie shook his head and put his hands up as though he could stop our words. "What happened to him? How is his fire missing?"

Daithi quietly admitted, "I don't know." Clawdia meowed, and his gaze fixed on her. "But she does."

Charlie looked at her and then looked back at Daithi. "She can't tell us, though. She's a cat."

Daithi stood up then, brushing the dust from his clothing. "I could help her communicate with us. Give her the illusion of a mouth and a voice. She could tell us what happened."

"Wait. There are so many things wrong with that." Charlie paced and ran a hand through his hair. "She might not even think in human terms. Whatever she says might be incomprehensible. She might not be able to use the illusion to speak at all because a cat has never spoken before."

"The faei are gifted with illusion, but not as you understand it. To you, it is a trick, not real, and baffling. But illusion is creation. Temporarily. It is real. She will not need to use the illusion, because it will recreate her and give her a voice as though she had never been without."

"Isn't that cruel?" Charlie stopped, his brows furrowed and lips tight. "To give her a voice and then take it away."

"We don't have time to discuss the moral implications of giving a creature a voice. Every second we waste discussing this is another second Savida's fire is in the wrong hands. It could be hidden or used or destroyed. Time is of the essence," Daithi wailed.

I stared at the little cat as her head turned, following the conversation. My heart raced, and a wrongfulness stirred in my gut. "This will not hurt her?"

"It should not hurt the creature. As you know, magic affects things differently. I cannot guarantee her safety. But we need to know what she saw." Daithi begged, "Please, Zaide, you owe me this."

I inhaled sharply at the blow. It was a reminder that I'd failed him and Savida today. They rescued me. I owed them a debt. And so, I needed to rescue Savida by whatever means necessary.

I don't want to hurt Clawdia.

I closed my eyes and gave the choice to the Fates. "She is her own being and smart enough to guide us to him. I think she should decide her destiny." I kneeled down, and Clawdia immediately trotted over to me, placing her head in my large hand and nuzzling it. "What do you think, fierce Little Cat? Do you want to tell us what happened?" She meowed. "If you do, go to Daithi. If you don't, go to Charlie."

She walked over to Daithi and sat herself at his feet,

staring up at him. I swallowed my bad feeling and respected her decision. I nodded to Daithi, and he nodded back.

A bright light emerged from him; it was as blinding as it was beautiful. I couldn't look away. The light enveloped Clawdia and then flashed, making both Charlie and I flinch away, dizzily. Daithi moaned, and I heard him hit the floor. I winced at the thought of him hitting the tools scattered around but was helpless to do anything. Stunned motionless, I watched the magic's effect on Clawdia.

She had fallen to her side, and as the light dimmed, it became like fluid, slithering in patterns across her small body. Her front legs suddenly jolted inward, and her back legs grew outward. Her tail completely folded into her body; her claws receded too. Then all the fluffy white fur drew into her skin, except atop her head, where it grew long in honeyed blond tresses.

This is wrong. This shouldn't be happening. He was going to give her a voice.

But I could not stop it. Daithi remained on the dirty wooden floor, unconscious, and his magic had taken on a life on its own.

Clawdia's small mouth opened in a soundless scream, and my heart lurched. Dropping to my knees, I shuffled toward her. "I'm sorry, Little Cat. I'm so sorry."

Her body kept growing, and I hugged her tight against me as the magic continued to do the impossible. Her ears moved, shrank, and turned into ones similar to the ones Charlie donned on his head. The features of the feline softened—her eyes became smaller, her nose buttoned out slightly, her mouth developed pouty red lips, and her teeth changed from fierce and deadly to blunt.

The cloud of light faded, and I could see Charlie peering toward us, trying to figure out what had happened.

He gasped when he saw her. "What the fuck?" I said

nothing in response. "Seriously, Zaide, this is the most fucked up thing I've ever seen in my life. You are holding a naked girl that used to be my neighbor's cat."

I nodded slowly as I looked across the body of the human female in wonder. "I don't think Daithi's illusion went as he expected."

Her head pressed into my chest, so I could feel her breathing, but her hair shrouded her face, and her body shook from the exertion of the change. My hands stayed tight around her, my breathing still hard as shock overtook me.

"No shit, Sherlock." He fell to his knees next to me, and his hands hovered over her, unsure if he should touch, before he pressed the heels of his hands into his eyes and groaned. "A cat turned human is the last thing we need right now. Is she going to shit in my garden? She won't know how to use a toilet, so she'll probably just shit in my garden, and I don't think I'll be able to get over that visual."

"Charlie, you are panicking," I acknowledged, feeling distant from my own emotions.

He took a deep breath and lowered his shaking hands to look at me. "Zaide, this. Is. Fucked. Up."

"You are correct. But perhaps we should dwell on this later. First, let us get everyone home."

He ran a hand through his hair and sighed. "Okay. Pass me Clawdia, and you get the guys."

"Clawdia," I repeated and looked down at the human in my arms. I brushed the hair out of her face to look at perfect features. Glowing, unblemished skin, pink plump lips, a small nose.

Attraction.

I'd never felt it before, but as I gazed at her face and brushed her soft skin, I felt a longing. The urge to brush my lips across her forehead, her cheeks, her lips filled me, pushing out an old pain in my soul.

But I can't be attracted to anyone that isn't my soul pair.

"Margaret?" I whispered, pulling her up. I rested her head on my shoulder so I could look at her properly.

I could see a similarity between the child Daithi saw and the female in my arms, but I didn't know if it was just wistful thinking.

Charlie heard my whisper and frowned as he stared at her. "She can't be. Can she?"

"Charlie, you've just witnessed her turn from a cat to a human. I would think anything is possible."

He paused and then looked at her, studying. "She does look like the little girl in the picture, but how did she end up as a cat for the last hundred years?"

"That is just one of the many things we can ask her when she has recovered from her trauma." I gathered her closer to my chest and stood up. "Be careful with her, my friend," I told Charlie as I placed her gently in his arms, the protective instinct that I felt for her as a cat still present. Charlie nodded but stared at her with an odd expression on his face. "Charlie?"

He shook his head. "Yeah, okay, I'm going. I'll try going through Winnie's house. I'll leave the doors open for you."

"You don't think she is home?"

"Daithi saw her get in a taxi, remember?"

Ah, yes. He thought the vision was related to Margaret. And here we turned a cat into a female that looks like her and makes me feel. It has to be her.

As Charlie left, I bent next to the body of Savida, gently folded his wings into place, then heaved him into my arms and draped him over my shoulder. His chest rose and fell against my back, and it tricked me into hoping that Clawdia or Margaret—whoever she was—would have some answers about what happened to him. I bent again and heaved Daithi up and over my other shoulder.

As I moved from Winnie's house to Charlie's, the cover of darkness hid the suspicious positioning of my friends, and I placed them both gently on their bed, tucking them in and turning on the nightlight we had purchased earlier.

"I'm sorry this happened to you, my friend. I promise we will find your fire and those responsible for your pain will suffer," I whispered.

Charlie came in. "I've put her in my bed and popped bedding on the floor for you." I nodded and continued to stare at Savida. "He's going to be okay, right? His fire just gives him his gifts, right? He's not dead. I can see him breathing."

I sighed. "He is alive, but without his fire, he will not live. But it's been a long day. Let us deal with the problems when Daithi is awake and once we ourselves have rested."

"Okay. Yeah." He ran a hand through his hair and sighed. "I have a feeling I'm going to need a good night's sleep to deal with tomorrow's shit. Night, Zaide," he said and left the room to trudge down the stairs to the office.

"Goodnight, Charlie," I replied and glanced back at Savida and Daithi before shutting the door behind me.

In Charlie's room, a naked human female lay slumbering in the bed. I paused to take in the sight. Margaret. It had to be her. My soul pair. I'd felt connected to her when she was a cat, and I was not any less enthralled now. Charlie had tucked her into the sheets and swept her hair away from her face.

I wouldn't have thought about doing that.

Nerves suddenly overtook me. I had never been with a female. I didn't know what they needed or wanted. So focused on finding my soul pair, I hadn't considered what to do with her when I found her. Failure and shame washed over me. I did not deserve her.

I was a slave.

Lost in memories, it startled me when a soft snore erupted from her. I shook my head as Charlie liked to do to clear his mind.

You are not just a slave. I told myself. *You are a protector. And this stunning creature will need your protection. She will be scared.* With my mind settled slightly, I resolved to sleep and think no more about it.

I said my prayers, thanking the gods for blessing me with her, and then drifted into slumber quickly, the hardship of the day taking its toll.

When I woke in the morning, I felt better than ever before. My heart was steady, my spirit was calm, and my mind had yet to think of the day's problems.

I stretched and yawned but soon realized a part of my body was stretching without my permission. Looking down, I saw the covers tenting around my hips. I gasped, the sound squeezing through unused vocal cords and forced an embarrassing squeak from my body.

My penis is erect.

I have an erect penis.

A huge smile spread across my face as elation flooded me. I wanted so badly to touch it. To experience the joy my kind had not in so long. I lifted myself to look at the human who was the other half of my soul and the reason for my morning glee.

Her eyelids fluttered open.

Then she screamed.

CHAPTER 10

MARGARET CLAUDIA

THURSDAY 14TH APRIL 1921

I was tired. Exhaustion turned my pallor paler and caused my feet to drag heavily through the ward. Even dressing had been an arduous task. The blooming of bright yellow daffodils and the blue and purple crocus all seemed to have lost their sparkle as I walked to the hospital.

Pitiful. Weak. Useless.

My father's words echoed in my head. Like nails down a blackboard, they had the power to make me wince at the memory even as I escaped him at work.

His cruelty hadn't ebbed in the months since I came home with a kitten. Or should I say, his cruelty to me hadn't ebbed, since both my mother and Duchess, the cat, saw only the best of my father.

In fact, there seemed to be a steady increase in malice. His every interaction with me was now just a barrage of insults, judgments, and threats, and I was starting to feel the effects.

It tainted my sleep with nightmares, and I felt no joy at

waking the next morning. My soul felt heavier. Beaten down. When I tried to ignore his words, to tell myself something positive to counteract him, it became harder and harder to believe the good. Despite my efforts, a part of me was absorbing the words he spat.

I tried to understand that it wasn't really him but the drink and that he had demons from the war that were hurting him and causing him to lash out, but understanding a person's viewpoint didn't stop the damage they caused.

Standing in front of the mirror in the nurse's room, I tapped my cheeks, trying to return some color to them. My violet eyes seemed duller even as I flashed myself a forced smile. Sighing, I straightened my gown.

Ugly. So ugly that you were right to send yourself to nursing school. No man would want you.

I closed my eyes and took a deep breath. His voice and my poisoned thoughts shouldn't be able to follow me here. I couldn't escape it at home, but the hospital was my safe space.

I did my rounds, checking my patients with a quiet demeanor and a small smile. Each one asked if I was all right, to which I forced a laugh and said, "You're the patient. I'm supposed to ask you that."

Even your patients think you are incapable of helping them.

His voice seemed louder today, booming in my ears instead of whispering in my mind. I didn't understand why, but it distracted me. Depressed me. Even chatting with my colleagues at lunchtime didn't cheer me up.

Toward the end of the day, Sister Martha called in that deep voice she had, "Margaret! We need you. Come here."

I sighed at her use of my first name but dashed down the ward to find a small gathering of people at the entrance. "What is it?"

Sister Martha pointed at a bed, directing the porters

where to place the patient. Doctor Adams stood hovering to the side, waiting to examine the patient.

Heaves and moans from the porters echoed around the hall as they placed her on the bed. She screamed.

I gasped.

The poor woman's entire body was red and swollen. Her eyes were so inflamed they couldn't open, already turning from red to purple. Her nose was at an unnatural angle, and blood dripped from her lips.

The porters pulled the curtain shut behind us and their footsteps echoed across the wooden floors as they left.

"Who is she? What happened to her? An accident?" I whispered to Maureen, another nurse called in to assist.

"Mrs. Jenkins. I think she's been beaten," Maureen told me.

"By whom?" I hissed.

"Her husband." Maureen gave me a sad smile. "Claims he was just correcting her, as is a husband's right."

Anger incensed me, and I clenched my fists. "To the point of a hospital visit?"

I watched as the doctor examined Mrs. Jenkins, pressing on her stomach, which caused a yelp of pain and a moan.

"Where is he now?" I asked, my blood boiling.

"He left her here and told her that if she lived, he expected dinner on the table tomorrow night." She lowered her voice and continued, "It's incidents like this that make me glad I'm unattached."

"I agree. What an evil man."

Sister Martha was standing behind us, listening. She hissed, "Now is not the time for your suffragist views. She needs help."

"We await your instruction, Sister," Maureen said amiably while anger stirred in my gut.

Doctor Adams's voice drew our attention. "Can you tell me where it hurts the most, Mrs. Jenkins?"

"My stomach," she moaned, her voice wavering and croaky.

My heart broke for her.

He nodded. "Anywhere else?"

"My back and legs."

"Can you roll onto your side so I can take a look?"

She whimpered and choked on a sob as she rolled, biting her bleeding lip to hold in the sound of her suffering.

The dark brown stains on her shirt gave me a clue to what we would see, but it didn't prepare me for the reality. Doctor Adams eased her shirt up to see deep, bloody lashes across her skin. The kind made from a belt. There were even imprints of the buckle in deep gouges.

Maureen covered her mouth, and I closed my eyes to the tears filling behind my lids.

They popped open as the doctor turned to address us. "Nurses, can you assist Mrs. Jenkins into her patient gown, clean and sew her lacerations, and apply a cold compress to her swellings? I'll be back to see how she is getting on in an hour or two."

He stepped away from the bed, his face grave, and motioned for Sister Martha to follow him as he walked to the end of the ward.

"Mrs. Jenkins? My name is Claudia, and this is Maureen. We'll be the nurses looking after you."

She nodded, tears streaming down her face, but said nothing.

"I'll get cold compresses," Maureen muttered and walked away.

I collected cleaning and stitching supplies and went back to my patient.

"This might sting a bit," I warned as I began cleaning the

wounds.

She flinched and gave a sharp, bitter laugh. She looked as though she wanted to say something, but she bit her lip and closed her eyes.

Maureen returned and started applying the compresses to her face, under her stomach, and legs. Then she helped me clean and sew her open cuts on her back and legs. I glanced up to see her eyes flickering to the clock on the wall.

"Everything all right?" I asked quietly.

Maureen looked guilty. "It's nothing."

She doesn't want to tell you. You're untrustworthy. Useless.

Shocked at hearing my father's voice after it being so absent during this crisis, I hesitated. But then I ignored it and asked, "Are you sure?"

She sighed. "I promised my sister that I would look after her children this evening."

"Ah." I popped the cotton buds on the tray next to me. "You can leave if you need to. I can stay with Mrs. Jenkins until Doctor Adams comes back."

"I don't want to burden you."

She doesn't trust you to leave a patient with you. Pathetic.

"It's not a burden. You'd do the same for me. I'm sure Mrs. Jenkins and I will grow to be great friends as I heal her up."

"Thank you. I'll let Sister Martha know, and if I can see another nurse, I'll send her to help you." She stood up and pushed her red curls away from her face. "Mrs. Jenkins, I wish you the best with your recovery and I'll stop by tomorrow to see how you are."

Mrs. Jenkins opened her eyes and gave her a pained smile, which Maureen returned, and then opened and closed the curtain.

I turned when I heard the sigh from Mrs. Jenkins, and I raised my eyebrow in question. "I ... hate that," she groaned.

"What do you hate?"

She coughed. "Mrs. Jenkins."

My brows furrowed in confusion for a moment. Until I understood and nodded. "I can't say I blame you. What's your given name?"

"Lucia."

"A beautiful name for a beautiful lady."

She barked a laugh and then groaned in pain. "Not. Now. No." She was breathless and wheezing, which wasn't a good sign.

"Let's get you up and into your hospital gown."

I did my best to gently remove her shirt and skirt and schooled my expression so she couldn't see my anger and upset at the sight of her bruised and battered body. Her abdomen looked particularly distended and colorful. She whimpered and flinched, and tears continued to stream from her swollen eyes.

"I'm sorry." I whispered, my heart clenching at the sight of her crying.

Her brown eyes met mine, and I saw the understanding and pain in them.

"You're … a beautiful girl," she wheezed. "And simply being in your presence … lessens my pain. You are right to nurse. To stay away from men. They do nothing but take. Take beauty and damage it."

Her chest was rattling with every inhale as I tied the gown and settled her into the bed. "Lucia, I'm going to find the doctor. I don't like the sound of your chest."

I turned to leave, but she grasped my wrist with surprising strength. "No. Don't go."

"I won't be long," I promised.

"No. Stay. Please. Doctor said…he'd come back." She could clearly see the indecision in my gaze, because she added, "I don't want…to be alone."

I couldn't refuse her, so I nodded and positioned her upright in the bed, adding pillows behind her from the surrounding beds and replacing the cold compresses to her skin.

"Tell me...about yourself. Distract me."

For the next thirty minutes, I sat in the chair next to the bed, holding her hand, and wittered on about myself. I told her how I became interested in nursing, the suffragist rallies I had attended, the books I was reading, and the even the gossip in the hospital.

She was engaged in my stories, appropriately adding comment and displaying emotive reactions, but her breathing worsened, and my worry increased.

"Claudia, I'm going to be sick," she groaned, interrupting me, and I leapt to my feet, grabbed a bucket, and placed it under her bent head. I pulled her hair out of her face as she heaved.

It came out red.

Blood.

"Lucia. I must insist that I find the doctor. You're vomiting blood and that can be very serious."

She couldn't respond on account of the liquid she was spewing from her mouth. Shivers wracked her slight frame, and sweat beaded on her brow. I couldn't wait for a decision from her. I raced into the corridor and shouted at the first member of staff I saw to find Doctor Adams and bring him to Mrs. Jenkins.

I dashed back to her, lifting my skirts in sweaty palms to run.

She was crying again. "Please."

I didn't know for what she begged, but guilt battered me anyway. I apologized and stroked her hair, whipped her brow and her lips with a damp cloth.

"Don't. Leave," she gasped.

"I won't leave you now. Someone will get the doctor, and he will see you right."

Her eyes were cloudy with pain, and I saw the doubt, the fear, but she nodded and bent her head over the bucket again. I muttered reassuring babble on repeat, to rouse her spirit, calm her worry, and give her something to hold on to. But with every passing second, I could feel her pulse weaken in the wrist I held.

When the doctor finally arrived, I updated him rapidly. He nodded. "We must make Mrs. Jenkins as comfortable as we can."

I paled. I knew what that meant.

She was dying.

Her husband had beaten her to death.

"Mrs. Jenkins, I can give you some morphine for the pain, if that's all right with you."

She glanced at me. I gave her a small smile and a nod, which seemed to reassure her, and she nodded at Doctor Adams.

Moments later, he came back holding a needle, and I held her hand as he injected it into her left arm.

"That will ease the pain, Mrs. Jenkins." He looked at me. "I trust you'll stay with her until she's asleep."

I nodded stiffly, and he left. I turned to Lucia with a smile fixed on my face. "You should feel the effects soon."

"I know … what he meant," she whispered in a croak. "It's all right. I don't want … to be in pain … any longer. This is … for the best."

My lip trembled as I blinked back tears. I patted her hand, awed by her bravery and saddened by her statement. "I will be here," I told her simply, trying to keep the emotion from my voice.

"Thank you," she replied.

She died forty minutes later as I counted the last beats of her pulse.

* * *

"You're late. Only whores return so late to their homes. Are you a whore, daughter?"

After the evening I'd endured, the last thing I wanted was to come home to find my father sitting in the armchair under candlelight with a bottle in his hand.

"Hello, Father." Emotionally drained and my soul bruised, I couldn't listen to his insults. I acknowledged him but walked past the living area to the stairs.

I heard him clink his bottle on the table loudly before I heard his boots stomping toward me. His hand gripped my wrist, pulling it from the banister of the stairs and tugging me back down. I stumbled, using my other hand to balance against the wall, and gasped at the pain in my wrist.

"Don't you walk away from me when I'm asking you a question," he spat. "This is my house, and I don't want a whore living under my roof. Where have you been?"

"At the h-hospital." I replied, stammering as my heart galloped in my chest.

"Liar," he shouted, and my ears rang.

"I'm not. Y-you can speak to my w-ward Sister and c-check. I was staying with a p-patient until she p-passed." I was shaking now. The fury in his eyes frightened me like he never had before.

"You let a patient die? What kind of useless nurse are you?" He scoffed and finally let go of my wrist.

"I didn't—" I began, but immediately stopped.

Did I let her die?

I could hear her struggling to breathe. I wanted to get the doctor, but she wanted me to stay with her. Could Doctor

Adams have done something if I had called for him sooner? Could I have done more? Was it my fault she died?

The thought took my breath away, and I placed a hand on my chest.

As if sensing my vulnerability, he pounced. "Who was she?"

I shook my head, not supposed to discuss patients outside of the hospital.

He didn't like me denying him; he reached up, grabbed a handful of my hair, and pulled, dragging me down so he could stand domineeringly over me.

"Tell me," he growled.

"Mrs. Jenkins." I whimpered.

He paused, stiffening. "You killed Mr. Jenkins' wife? You stupid, useless, pathetic creature," he roared and pushed backward so I landed painfully against the stairs.

I didn't understand why he cared about Mr. or Mrs. Jenkins, but I couldn't decipher anything with the ringing in my ears and the pain echoing across my body.

Shock set into me like frost on an autumn bloom. Before tonight, my father had never laid a hand on me in violence. I didn't expect him to actually hurt me, despite all the previous insults and threats. Some part of me hoped that deep down, he still loved me enough not to cross that boundary, but that hope was now squashed.

"You don't know what you've done," he ranted. "Punishment. You need to be punished for this. You can't get away with this."

"P-punished? But I didn't—" I whimpered and cowered as he stormed closer to me. Gripping my hair again, he stomped past me on the staircase, dragging me up behind him. "Father, I didn't kill her. I s-stayed with her—" I gripped the base of my hair so I couldn't feel the tug so much and kept close to him as I protested my innocence.

Outside of my bedroom, he suddenly stopped and turned to face me. He let go of my hair and slapped me, hard, across the face.

It seemed to echo in the following silence, and my eyes swam with tears as, like lightning, the pain quickly followed.

I cupped my face and stumbled back in shock. He grabbed my arm, wrenching it from my face, and growled, "Don't you dare talk back to me. I know what you are. You're a murderer. And this is your retribution."

He pulled me and shoved me backward into my room, where I landed on the rug on my back. He slammed the door closed, the shock rattling my mirror, and I heard a lock sliding across my door.

There wasn't a lock on the outside of my door this morning before I left for work. Was this premeditated? Was Mrs. Jenkins just an excuse to hurt me?

I jumped up and raced to the door. I twisted the knob only to find exactly as I thought. Locked.

My jaw ached, my head hurt, and I was so confused and frightened and upset that I thought I could scream with all the emotions crowding my head.

I undressed slowly and saw Duchess from my window, roaming the garden, her tail curling from side to side as she lazily walked through the grass. At that moment, I was so envious of her. She had my father's love, her freedom, and the carelessness of all human emotions and problems.

Being human was particularly difficult on bad days.

I curled up in my bed, tears leaking from my closed eyes and dampening my pillow, and prayed to God that this punishment ended soon.

Little did I know, I would only leave this house once more before I died.

CHAPTER 11

CLAWDIA

Oh lord above, I ache. What happened?
    The last thing I remembered was an excruciating pain shocking every inch of my body. From my nose to my tail.

Behind my eyelids, I could glimpse the sunlight beaming, and I clenched my eyes tighter to block out the light.

It's so bright. Where am I?

My eyes blinked open, wide and bewildered. When I saw two big purple eyes staring back at me, I panicked. I heard a human scream and was shocked to feel it come from me, vibrations echoing through my throat and out of very human lips, which I covered with very human hands.

No. No. No. This cannot be happening.

I scrambled back from the edge of the bed, long, furless arms and legs flailing. The feel of the material against my skin scratched me like the graze of a thousand needles, and I whimpered as I tried to untangle myself from the bedsheets.

I fell. My body hit the carpeted floor, which scratched even more than the bedsheets, and I let out a huff of pain.

Please, Lord, I don't want to be human again. Please let this be a vivid nightmare. I can't go back to that life.

Everything had a bright white aura around it, and my head throbbed in time with my racing heart. Taking a deep breath, I tried to calm myself and focus.

From this angle, I recognized where I was. I knew this carpet because I often rolled around on it. I knew that ceiling because there was a water stain on it. The space under the bed I lay next to was my hiding space when Charlie was cross with me. This was his room.

I'm in his room, but I'm human?

The two states couldn't coexist. I was human in the 1920s. I was a cat, a familiar, when I first climbed into this room and met Charlie.

Suddenly, I remembered what happened; Winnie drugged me, and Mary dragged Savida home. They hurt him by performing a spell to take something from him. I gathered the others to find him and then consented to a spell so I could tell all I knew. It all came to me in a bright, colorful flash of pictures, and I sighed in relief.

I wasn't human in my lifetime again. Somehow, Daithi had turned me from a cat to human.

Overwhelmed, nauseous, and confused, I sat up and tugged the sheet dangling from the bed over my naked body. I glimpsed something in the corner of the room and did a double take.

In the mirror, I saw myself.

I stared back at the gaunt reflection. My hair was wild and tangled in a honey cloud around my shoulders. Dark circles swallowed my eyes. Violet and wide-open with shock and fear, they were identical to the expression I wore moments before my death.

I spiraled into memories of the frightened girl I used to be. I remembered the fear of hearing his footsteps, the turn of a lock, and his laugh. The pain of his fists and feet crashing into me, breaking more than just bone, but hope, heart and spirit. I remembered the color of the bruises. The smell of his breath. The longing to die.

I saw Margaret Claudia Smith, daughter of a war hero turned abusive drunk, a nurse turned victim. And I hated her. She was weak and fearful, and she was dead.

Dead. Dead. Dead.

I crumpled into myself, shuddering and panting and unable to catch my breath. I closed my eyes, hoping the over-whelming sensations around me would dull. Hot tears skated down my face, tasting of salt on my trembling lips.

"Little Cat, calm yourself," a voice said softly. I remembered the purple eyes. Zaide was here. I opened my eyes to see him reaching for me, and I automatically retreated from his grasp. Which gave me a better view of his whole body.

His golden skin was unlike the tan a human could get as it almost glittered in the small strips of light let in by the curtains. Deep purple scars, the same color as his eyes, glowed and pulsed across his broad, chiseled chest. They littered his body, some leading up to his neck and to just below his right eye. Some leading down, down—I stopped. My eyes went wide as I looked at the largest erection I had ever witnessed.

I squeaked and snapped my gaze back up to meet his eyes, and I realized I was so distracted I hadn't noticed him approaching again. He grasped my shaking hands, and I jolted.

Suddenly, I fell into the feeling of his rough palms against my soft skin. The room quieted. I could hear our heartbeats, both hurried but calming. I lost my fear in the patterns and swirls of his purple irises. My breathing settled. I felt more myself. Less frightened. I continued to take deep breaths, focusing on the feeling of safety.

I startled when Charlie and Daithi charged into the room, my screaming having gathered the attention of the others in the house.

"Jesus Christ," Charlie exclaimed and covered his eyes. "For fuck's sake, Zaide. Put your bloody dick away. Now isn't the time for a boner." Zaide grimaced and covered his hips with the sheet lying on the floor where he slept. "Why the hell are you naked anyway?"

"That's how I sleep," he replied with a furrowed brow.

Daithi coughed delicately. "I don't think Zaide meant anything sinister."

"Say that to the monster under the sheet," Charlie hissed.

Zaide's face paled as understanding hit him. "I would never."

I squeaked when I attempted to talk, and all eyes turned to me. Charlie handed me a glass of water from the bedside table. I thanked him with a small smile and tipped the entire contents down my throat. The cold rushing down my neck, quenching my thirst, was a sensation I didn't realize I had missed until that moment.

"What did you do to me?" I croaked. My hand went to my throat, and I massaged my disused voice box.

"It seems I have turned you human," Daithi said calmly.

I was suddenly furious. He spoke to me as though I didn't already know that. Like I was just a stupid cat. I hissed. Or I did the human equivalent. "I can see that. But thank you kindly for informing me of what is most obvious."

"You're posh," Charlie stated with a puzzled expression, which had me tightening my lips to stop a chuckle from escaping.

Mood swings were not something I missed.

I ignored him and turned my attention back to Daithi. "You were only supposed to make me talk, not turn me human. Turn me back," I demanded.

"We will. As soon as you tell us what happened to Savida," Daithi agreed, and I was so relieved I sighed and sagged. I noticed from the corner of my eye that Zaide's fist clenched.

"It's a long story, but I'll tell you." I looked carefully at Daithi and noticed the tiredness etched into his face. I sympathized. "Is he okay? He was breathing when I got to him. You have saved him, haven't you?" There was silence, and I swallowed hard. "He's dead?"

Daithi turned away from us. "It is, as you said, a long story. And complicated. I will know more when you have divulged what you witnessed."

My stomach embarrassed me, growling loudly as though Clawdia the cat now resided in my belly.

Charlie grinned. "Maybe we should feed you before we talk." I hugged my midriff with my shaking hands and nodded meekly. "Full English? You liked it as a cat."

"That sounds wonderful. Thank you."

I then realized I was talking to Charlie. I was saying words to the man I had been stalking since I became a familiar. "Charlie," I said for absolutely no reason other than I could. The downside to that was that everyone else could hear me, too.

"Yeah?" he asked.

"Nothing." I shook my head.

He narrowed his eyes. "Do you remember—?"

I laughed. "Being a cat? Yes, Charlie. I remember it all." I couldn't wait to tell him everything that had been going through my mind, ask him questions, and get to know him as a person.

But for that, I'll have to stay human. Can I do that? Don't I want to be a cat again?

He blushed, something I had never seen before, and ran a nervous hand through his hair. "Fuck."

I coughed out a little laugh. I turned to Zaide, who hadn't

taken his eyes off me. "Can you help me get up? I don't know how steady I'll be on my feet."

"Of course. Charlie, do you have something to give Clawdia to cover herself?" I hadn't realized until that moment that I wore a tangled sheet that barely covered me. I tucked it more securely around myself, and Zaide did the same with his sheet.

"Sure. Two seconds," Charlie said and rummaged around in the chest of drawers behind him.

I looked up at the big purple eyes. He stood gracefully, reminding me of a roman warrior with the white sheet around his waist and the scars covering his golden skin. He reached down and gripped my elbows, pulling me to my feet with ease.

Chills ran up my arms at his touch. There was something both exciting and calming about it. It was addictive. I wondered if he felt the same, because he stared for a long moment when I reached my full height on wobbly legs.

"Here you go," Charlie said cheerfully, passing me a pair of drawstring jogging bottoms and a t-shirt. "Zaide, you can change in the bathroom."

I thanked him. Daithi turned on his heel and left swiftly, and Charlie seemed to have to tug Zaide out with him.

I dropped my sheet, sat on the edge of the bed, and quickly grabbed the bottoms to pull my legs into. The top was more difficult since I had used my energy on the bottoms, but after a quick battle that made my arms ache I got it on.

I stumbled out of the room, pointedly ignoring the mirror.

* * *

I DOVE INTO MY BREAKFAST, making groans and moans as the flavors danced in my mouth and memories swirled in my head. Overwhelmed with sensation, a tear escaped my eye even as I continued shoveling food into my mouth as though I hadn't eaten in the past two years.

The stares of the men sitting at the table unsettled me, but I didn't acknowledge them as my cutlery clattered and scraped against my plate.

Zaide opened his mouth to say something, but Daithi glared and interrupted, "Savida first." Zaide's lips tightened, but he nodded, and Daithi turned to me. "What happened to Savida last evening? How did he end up in the shed on your property with his fire missing?"

Daithi waited until I was three quarters of the way through my breakfast to begin the inquisition. I couldn't blame him since he was clearly anxious, and I tried to push down my irritation at being interrupted. I swallowed. "Winnie and Mary took it."

"What?" Charlie gasped.

Zaide asked, "Who is Mary?"

"How? Humans can't do such things." Daithi's calm facade was cracking, and his anger showed through.

Intimidated, I replied with a nervous tremble in my voice, "They are witches. They have the same lifetime as humans, but more power. Mary is Winnie's girlfriend. I am Winnie's familiar."

"Witches. Next door. Fuck me." Charlie scrubbed his face and pressed his palms into his eyes.

Zaide said firmly, "Explain witches."

"They can cast spells, make potions, and scry for lost things and information. They are like you, Daithi." I glanced at him but immediately looked away again when I saw his granite-like face. "But on a much smaller scale," I explained.

"What is a familiar?" Zaide asked.

127

I rushed to explain, my tongue tripping over itself to pour out this information, finally able to purge myself of secrets I held for two years. "I'm a human soul in the form of a cat. Winnie performed a very powerful spell two years ago, which brought my soul here and tied our lives together. If she dies, so do I because she's my link to the world. I can talk to her telepathically. We can share emotions and power between us. I'm an extra power bank if she needs it for a spell."

"Human soul ..." Charlie hummed thoughtfully.

Daithi interrupted again, "And these witches took Savida's fire?"

"Yes, they took it. Winnie created a large salt circle in the garden, and Mary had gone to the shops to capture him. She caught him and pulled him home in a large magical net. He fought but couldn't get free," I finished, sadly thinking of the horrified look he had on his face when he realized he wouldn't be saved in time.

"If I had known humans had this ability, I would never have brought him here," Daithi hissed at Zaide. Zaide straightened but said nothing.

Charlie wondered aloud, "How did she know to go to the shops?"

I sighed and whispered, "I told Winnie that you'd gone."

Daithi slammed his hands on the table, rattling the plates and glasses, and shouted, "You were complicit in this?"

My breath stuttered as flashes of my past rose to the forefront of my mind. I bowed my head, and my hands turned to fists in my lap. When Zaide's hand covered mine and squeezed in support, a feeling of safety trickled through me, but it wasn't enough to combat Daithi's ire.

I gulped. "No. I didn't know what they were going to do. I wouldn't wish that on anyone, let alone Savida."

"But it was you that told the witches he was here and when he would be unguarded," he growled.

Feeling like less than a worm, I closed my eyes and whispered, "Yes. I'm so terribly sorry. I tried to stop her once I knew, but she wouldn't listen."

"I have heard enough." His voice was low, his words spaced out and full of intention. "You are going to help us get his fire back, or I will kill you in order to exact revenge on the witch who stole my lover from me."

"Daithi—" Zaide protested.

I interrupted with a shudder and a quick nod. "Of course. Anything I can do."

"Wait." Charlie held up a hand and looked at Daithi questioningly. "We can get it back? He won't die without it?"

Daithi huffed and pushed his chair back as he stood. With his hands behind his back, he paced as he lectured. "Demon fire is among one of the most sought-after magics across the realms. Demons are often hunted, and their fire stolen. A demon without fire is useless. It lives, but it does not. Savida's fire is likely intended for use in a powerful spell, and should that happen, he will be lost to us forever. If we can rescue his fire before this happens, we can restore it to him."

"Time is of the essence, then," Charlie concluded.

Daithi nodded and looked at me with hatred flaring in his eyes. "Do you know where they are right now?"

I shook my head quickly. "No. They left immediately after they got his fire."

Charlie leaned forward, focusing. "Daithi, your vision. You said they were getting a taxi. Do you remember the other address?"

It only took him a moment to recall. "78 Acre Drive."

Charlie got his phone out and a moment later told us, "There are a lot of Acre Drive's in England, but there is one twenty minutes from here. If she got a taxi, I can only assume it was for a quick journey."

Daithi looked at me again and asked, "Do you know what is there?" The words rolled around his mouth as though they couldn't land properly, with his distaste for me also being juggled.

I tried not to let him know how much he frightened me. How much his anger and hatred reminded my soul of past fears. I shook my head again. "Winnie swore not to tell another soul about this project she and Mary were working on. It's a magical promise which has repercussions if broken, so she didn't tell me anything."

"A project?" Charlie repeated.

I nodded. "Yes. That's what I assume they need Savida's fire for." I hesitated, but cat-like curiosity had me asking, "What can fire do?"

"That's none of your concern, cat," Daithi spat.

I flinched, and Zaide squeezed my fist again. He growled, "Do not talk to her in such a manner. She is undeserving."

"She is to blame for Savida's demise!" He pointed, his hand shaking with fury. "And if anything happens to his fire while in the hands of the witches, then she will pay the price for it." He narrowed his eyes on me, and the power of his magic pressed against me. I trembled.

Zaide's hand tightened on me. "Do not threaten her again, or you will find I am less sympathetic to your emotions."

Charlie agreed. "Daithi, I think that's a tad harsh. She was a cat. What was she supposed to do to stop it?"

I rushed to add, "I didn't know their plans. I only knew something was wrong when Winnie magicked my food to stop me from seeing anything that she was doing."

"She magicked your food and disabled you?" Zaide asked, his big purple eyes focused on me.

"Yes. Otherwise, I would have been here jumping on

Daithi earlier." I saw the looks on their faces and wanted to defend Winnie. "She tried to fix it when she felt how scared I was. She was reluctant to hurt Savida, too. Mary controls her. I know it's no excuse but—"

"It is no excuse. My lover lies in a bed upstairs, his fire about to be used in a spell which will remove him from this world and kill his body." Daithi's voice wavered.

I bowed my head and whispered, "I'm sorry."

Charlie spoke after a moment's silence. "We need a plan to find them before it gets to the point of no return." He had a look on his face that I had seen a lot as I sat on his lap as a cat. It told me the cogs in his brain were working at full capacity and he was formulating a plan.

"I think Daithi and I should see if they are still at 78 Acre Drive. And if they aren't there, we can see if they've left any hints about where they have gone. Zaide and Clawdia can go back to Winnie's and search for clues there. We need to know more about witches and about this project. If you can get her laptop to me, I might find something on there."

Zaide nodded. "We can do this," he agreed for me, but I had my reservations about ... well, everything.

Walking. Being human again. Breaking into Winnie's. Feeling. Being alone with a god-like man who looked at me like I hung the moon.

"Can we leave now?" Daithi asked Charlie. He'd stopped pacing and now awaited instruction like a soldier.

Charlie studied Zaide and me for a moment before nodding at Daithi. "We can go as soon as you're ready."

CHAPTER 12

CHARLIE

How is this my life?
Daithi walked up to the guest room to get ready for the day while I sat at the table, observing the craziest situation.

A woman who used to be my neighbor's cat was polishing off the rest of her breakfast like she was still part animal. My winged otherworlder friend was in imminent danger of losing his life. A green-haired faei was losing his sanity as well as his heart.

Thinking of hearts, I turned my attention to Zaide. He was sure this cat-woman was Margaret, his soul pair, and if his monster dick hadn't been up for action this morning, I might have doubted him.

She didn't seem to have the same instant infatuation with him as he did with her, though, which I was both concerned about for his sake and relieved for my own. After all, she was, or had been, my cat. Mine.

I rubbed my head, trying to part the weird possessive thoughts from the problem-solving ones.

This is crazy. I need answers. Who is she? Clawdia the cat or Margaret the human? What do we even call her?

I needed the pieces of the puzzle to fit together, and I knew what piece to start with. "Stay here for two seconds. I just want to grab something to show you."

I ran to my office and slid the photo of Daithi's vision of Margaret into my hand and jogged back. I handed it to her, and she automatically reached for it with sadness on her face.

As she stared down, I took a moment to look at her. She was beautiful. There was something innocent but sexy about her features. Maybe it was the combination of her wide violet eyes and her full red lips. The way her hair made me think of caramel.

"This is me," she mumbled. "Where did you get this?"

I looked at Zaide, whose expression brightened with yet another confirmation that she was his soul pair. Ignoring her question, I pushed for more. "You're sure? This girl's name is Margaret, isn't it?"

"Of course I'm sure. I recognize myself and my family. My name was Margaret Claudia Smith." She handed me the photo back, which I found strange.

"That's why Winnie called you Clawdia? Because it's a play on your middle name?"

"Margaret was also my mother's name, so everyone called me Claudia. Winnie added the *w* because she liked the cat pun, but with a *u* or a *w*, it doesn't sound any different."

Zaide asked, "So you won't be changing how it's spelled now you are human?"

"I don't plan on staying human for long." She shrugged, unaware she was crushing Zaide's hopes and dreams by doing so. "Besides, I like puns, and I don't want to be the Claudia of my past."

"Past." I repeated, rolling the thought around in my head

before I continued my questioning. "This is the Crystal Palace." I pointed at the background of the picture.

She nodded. "That's correct. We were visiting for the Festival of Empire."

"It burned down in 1939."

"Did it? That's a shame. It was a beautiful building." She seemed surprised by the news but not devastated. Perhaps it didn't have as much sentimental value to her.

"When was the Festival of Empire?" I pressed.

She looked at the ceiling as she thought back. "Well, we went for my eleventh birthday so it would be … 1911. May."

I paused. Then took a breath. Opened my mouth. Shut it. Finally, I asked, "You were alive in 1911?"

She didn't hesitate. "I was. Didn't that picture already prove that?"

"I have so many questions." I released a shaky breath and ran a hand through my hair. The hits just kept fucking coming. I should've been getting used to it, but each strange revelation had the same impact as the last.

"I'm sure you do," she said agreeably.

I couldn't believe the polite young lady in front of me was the same soul who ripped up my toilet rolls and drove me crazy. I couldn't align those two personalities. She was a complete mystery. A very interesting and attractive mystery. One I couldn't wait to unravel. Discover the secrets of her past.

"How did you become a familiar over a hundred years in the future? Why do you still look so young?"

She folded her hands in her lap, looking regal until I noticed the tension in her hands as they clutched each other for support. "A familiar is a human soul. To be a soul, you have to—"

"Die," I finished and then gasped. "You died?"

"I died." She coughed and rubbed her neck.

"How? When? Young? Is that why—"

Daithi came back downstairs. "Charlie, I am ready to leave when you are."

I choked on my questions, almost pained to put a stopper on my curiosity. Turning to look at him, I saw the redness around his eyes and sighed. "Yep. Let's get going." He nodded and turned to the front door. "We'll be back later. Remember to go next door and get clues and her laptop," I said to Claudia and Zaide before grabbing my car keys from the kitchen counter and following Daithi out of the house.

* * *

IN THE FIRST ten minutes of the drive to the house where the witches went with Savida's fire, Daithi was deathly quiet. He sat in my passenger seat with his hands knotted together and his body stiff and unmoving, his face turned to the window. His body language screamed "unapproachable." Thankfully, that vibe had never intimidated me or stopped me from questioning someone.

At a junction, I turned the radio down and said, "You okay, Daithi?" He looked at me pointedly. "I'm just making sure. You had a big evening. Savida aside, you turned a cat into a human. Surely that's got to have an effect. Maybe you've got a killer headache. A magic hangover."

He was silent a moment before saying, "Thank you for your concern, Charlie. I am fine." And then he turned the radio up again.

I turned it off completely. "You know, we're really big on looking after our mental health over here. We have a saying; 'it's okay to not be okay.'"

He narrowed his eyes at me. "You believe I am telling you lies about my mental state?"

I shrugged, my seatbelt scratching at my neck. "I'm not

okay after everything that has happened. This is a complete mind fuck. So, I don't think it's unreasonable to believe that someone closer to Savida would feel a range of emotions. Ones that may mess with your head."

"I do not have time for emotions," he scoffed and turned his head back to the window.

"There's always time. Now's a good example."

He still didn't look at me. "I need to focus on getting Savida's fire back. I cannot consider what I feel now or how I will feel if I fail."

"So, we're going to pretend you aren't exhausted. You aren't grieving, anxious, and panicked? That you don't blame me and Zaide for losing him in the first place? That you aren't angry you came to the human realm to find Margaret? Sorry, Clawdia."

The ticking of my indicator worsened the silence as I turned right into a road. We weren't far away.

Daithi sighed and then reluctantly agreed with my observation. "Yes."

"Right. Just so I know we're on the same page."

He paused, and I could feel him stare at me. "Where I am from, it is not okay to not be okay. I do not vocalize my problems. How is it you can still hear them?"

"Finder of all things, Daithi. Even repressed emotion." I quirked a smile in his direction. "Just do me a favor and try to talk to Zaide. He is still your friend and wants to help."

As we pulled up to the house, Daithi huffed. "I will think on it."

I didn't acknowledge him. I was now focused on the next task. Getting into the house and finding more information about where Winnie and Mary had gone. "Right," I started, "we are totally winging this. Let's see how it goes."

"Is that wise?" Daithi hissed.

It was too late to stop me. I hoped Lady Luck was with me as I jumped out of the car and strolled casually to the door. I knocked. Daithi approached behind me. We waited. I knocked again. We waited again.

"Charlie, I don't think anyone is inside."

I gave him a sideways glare. "You don't say. Right, I'm going to break in. Can you cover us with some kind of illusion while I work?"

"Of course," he replied. I ran to the car, opened the glove box, and retrieved my trusty tools. "How do you know how to do this?" Daithi asked.

"Misspent youth," I quipped. "A guy I used to work with showed me how to break any lock. I'm rusty, but it's not something you forget." It took me five minutes, and then the door swung open. "Ta-da." We stepped over the threshold, and the smell of potpourri stung my nostrils. Grimacing, I said, "Let's split up and look for something that tells us about whoever lives here."

"She is female," Daithi said drolly as he looked around an entirely pink living room.

"No kidding." I wandered around the kitchen and found letters lying on the counter. I picked up one addressed to Deborah Delaney. "All right, Debs. Why did our witch thieves come see you?"

"She is also a witch thief."

"You might be right." I tossed the letters back on the table and turned as he came into the kitchen.

"I am right. I can feel a small magical signature in this home."

I immediately straightened. "She's here?"

"No. Her magic and use of it in this house has left an imprint on it." He opened cupboards at random. I wasn't sure if he was being nosey or if he was searching for the magic.

"Right. We just need to find out where she's gone, if she's with Winnie and Mary, and if not, if she knows where they are." Spotting a calendar on the wall, I wandered over. I poked my finger at the date. It read, "Delivery?"

A delivery of demon fire? I wondered.

"Hello!" a voice called. "Hello!"

I crouched instinctively. "Who the fuck is that?" I hissed at Daithi, who also crouched, like it was his fault. "Fuck!"

"Hello!" the voice called again. And then it whistled. I frowned. "Hello!"

"Wait!" I stood up and walked into the utility area to find a parrot sat in a cage.

"Hello!" it greeted.

I sighed and called back to Daithi, "It's okay. It's just a parrot."

"You're certain it's not a familiar?"

That's a good point. No. No, I'm not certain.

"Fuck. It could be." I considered it again. "How can you tell?"

"If it is, then we must hurry, Charlie. It could be communicating with its master now."

"Shit, you're right. Go upstairs and see if you can find anything witch-related that can help us learn more about their project. I'll sweep here."

As he walked away with a nod, I ignored the one-word parrot and continued my search for personal details. Her life as a human was my expertise and where I knew I could hurt a person if need be.

I found her laptop in the dining room/study. Helpfully, she had a piece of paper with a list of her passwords in her desk drawer. Witch4life. It made me cringe as I typed it in and loaded up her bookmarked website. I looked through her emails but, as a typical middle-aged lady, she had given her email address to thousands of websites that now spammed her inbox and made searching for anything relevant impossible.

I made a note of her information to log in at home, where I wouldn't be rushed. Then I tried to log in to her bank account, but without the answers to her security questions, I couldn't view any of her recent purchases. I pieced together some of her information from the letters on the counter and set up an alert for any new purchases and their location.

I was still typing on my phone when Daithi came downstairs. "Any luck?" I asked.

"Luck was not in her possession, but I found a bookcase, which seems very useful."

He suddenly had my full attention. "You found books on witches?"

"No. However, the bookcase is interesting. I think you should see it." He turned on his heel, his green hair flipped behind him.

I got up from the desk and followed him to the stairs, muttering, "What could be so interesting about a fucking bookcase? We don't have time to admire woodwork, Daithi. We've got bitch witches to find."

He was looking down at me from the top. His lip twitched. "It is not the woodwork that has me intrigued."

I followed him into the master bedroom, which was decorated similarly to the entire house, with pinks and soft furnishings. The bookcase was floor to ceiling and covered the entire wall opposite the bed. Made of a dark wood, it had thick shelves that were all linear; it *was* some nice woodwork. And books lined every shelf.

"Shit me, Debs. Get yourself a referral for therapy; you've got an addiction."

"Reading is not common?"

I shrugged and touched a book on the shelf. A romance. It demanded that I pick it up and take it home. It wasn't a calling I'd had from a book before. But I trusted my instincts and pulled it from the shelf.

"Not so much now that you can just watch a story on Netflix." Daithi raised a brow at me and looked at my new possession. I shrugged. "It wants me." I looked back at the shelves. "So, other than Debs being a book hoarder, what's interesting about it?"

"Can you not see it?" he said cryptically.

"See what?" I stepped back and took another look at the shelves. My eyes drifted to a deep line in the wood. "Oh. Wait." I followed the line up to the top of the bookcase. "What the fuck?" Excitement bubbled inside me. "Is this a secret door?"

"I believe so."

"Daithi, this is so fucking cool," I breathed.

I could feel the amusement in his voice. "I'm glad you are so enthused about this."

"Enthused? I'm fucking buzzing. I'll get one built as soon as all this shit is over. Witch bitches shouldn't get all the fun things." I moved a book to find a doorknob. The wood groaned as I twisted the handle and pulled it open. I grinned back at Daithi. "Come on, then. Let's go investigate the secret room."

Stepping into the room made me immediately on edge. Like walking into custard, the air had a thick quality and tasted like alcohol and regret. I could smell sickness and hospital and salty tears. And worst of all, I felt like it had dragged all the positivity from me. Like there was a dementor sucking out all the happiness.

"Can you feel that?" I asked Daithi. He nodded but said nothing.

After a few seconds, the feeling vanished as though it had never been there at all, and I shrugged off the experience.

The room itself was actually really disappointing. If I were going to install a secret room, I wouldn't make it look as fucking hippy dippy as this one. Bloody crystals everywhere. A salt lamp. A bohemian wall tapestry. Deb had completely let me down with the decor. Sighing sadly at the lack of skulls or blood, I walked to a table and shelves holding books and other interesting things.

"The magic signature is far stronger in here. She probably casts in here."

I nodded, took out my phone, and started taking pictures. Daithi picked up a leather-bound book and flicked it open. "It looks like a spell book. Perhaps this could be useful."

"Fuck it, then. We'll bring it with us and hope she doesn't notice it's gone."

"It would be helpful if we could also find something that could explain the history of witches and their abilities."

"Witches for Dummies." I gravitated to a cupboard containing lots of little vials and jars, some full of unknown ingredients, some empty. At the bottom of the shelf was a dusty pile of more leather-bound books. I ran my hand over the top one, clearing the dust before picking it up and flicking through a few pages. Smug elation flooded my body as it always did when I found something. "Ask and you shall receive." I grinned and waved the book. "Right, let's get the fuck out of here before we set off a trap and have to wait for Harrison Ford to rescue us."

* * *

THE CAR RIDE home felt lighter than the ride there. Daithi didn't sit as stiffly, even if he was clinging to the books as though they held Savida's fire in their pages.

We sat in optimistic silence for a little while before Daithi said, "I am not angry with you for losing Savida. You had known us for a mere handful of days before this happened. You did not know the seriousness of my vision and would not have had the authority to stop Savida from wandering off. Zaide has been with us for a long time. We rescued him. He knew. And he let it happen."

I processed that. I was glad he didn't blame me. The last thing I needed was to be on the shit list of a magical being, but I didn't think he was being entirely fair. "You say that as though he handed Savida over to the witches. He didn't."

"No. His soul pair did that for him," he scoffed.

"She's been more betrayed by her owner than we have been by her. She wasn't to know." He said nothing in response, so I continued. "Zaide knew your vision was serious and that Savida would wander, but it's not his job to babysit. And you said yourself that once you've seen a vision, it always happens. So even if Zaide had followed Savida around all day, the result would have still been the same, but maybe Zaide would have also gotten hurt."

"I know this, Charlie."

"I don't think you're angry with me or Zaide or Clawdia. You're angry with Savida for being so careless, and you're angry with the witches for taking and hurting him, but you're mostly angry with fate, or your weird magic, which showed you a vision that you can't do anything to change. However, those people and that entity aren't here for you to yell at, so you're taking it out on us. But we are on your side. We're going to do everything in our power to ensure that Savida's fire comes home to him. We are your friends, so stop pushing everyone away by playing the blame game. Don't create cracks in your relationships, because it might not be easy to fix when this is all over."

He was a rude bastard to Clawdia and Zaide at breakfast,

so I was relieved to get this off my chest. Zaide allowed Daithi to talk down to him, blame him, place more guilt on his oversized shoulders because he knew his friend was grieving. But I wouldn't let him get away with being an arsehole.

I was the arsehole in my house. No one could take that title from me.

As we continued homeward, the skies darkened, and the pitter patter of rain against the glass became heavier. Having checked the forecast a few days ago, I knew what we were in for. Thunder and lightning. I put the accelerator down and hoped we'd make it home before the show started.

We were five minutes from home when he finally replied. "You are right. I am angry. Mostly at my visions. I see things which cannot be altered. When it is about someone dear to me, it is torture. Savida would tell me I am blessed. Yet I have always believed it was a curse."

The sky clapped. A flash lit up the gray horizon in the distance. "I don't believe in blessings or curses. I think you get what you work for. In your case, I think you let your magic or fate or whatever control you. You fall into visions. They give you information that leads you to your next adventure, putting you on the set path. Maybe I'm just talking out of my arse here, but maybe you need to make it work for you more. Have you ever tried to induce a vision? Tried to get specific information?"

I took my eyes off the road for a second to gauge his reaction. He was staring at me as though I had just handed him the secrets of the universe. Heat rose into my cheeks.

"I have always tried to avoid my visions. It's not an experience I enjoy."

"I think your magic takes you for a ride, hence how you tried to make a cat talk and ended up turning it human. And hey, going for a ride is fine if you like where it's taking you.

But you should be able to trust that when you want to know something, see something, it'll do as it's told. Maybe if you can figure out how to make that happen, you'll be less angry with at least one person."

"Who?"

"Yourself."

CHAPTER 13

ZAIDE

I *have found my soul pair.*

Elation filled me, and it had yet to dissipate. She was here. My soul pair.

A slave had done the impossible and met his soul's other half. I had regained something I had never thought I would. I was so excited to see what we could accomplish. The stories of whole titans were legendary. With our new power, we could find my family and rescue them from slavery.

And to be on such an adventure with such a beautiful creature … the thought electrified me with energy, and I felt full, happy. It was a sensation I wanted to last as long as possible.

But she had awoken in a state of panic and fear this morning. I had been so consumed by my happiness, achieving my goal, and finding my soul pair, that I hadn't contemplated how she would feel about being human. She asked to be turned back. She didn't want to look at herself in the mirror.

She was so different from the fierce little cat I had met

only days previously. This human female was polite and uncomfortable. It did not, however, stop my obsession.

As she spoke of what she had witnessed and the betrayal of her witch, the movement of her lips, the sound of her soft voice, and the continuous shaking of her hands distracted me. I stared in complete fascination. I listened to her story and found no fault on her part for the events which lead to Savida's missing fire, so when Daithi began spitting venom at her, I defended her. But I also felt guilty. It was difficult to argue with him when I shared responsibility for Savida's demise.

After Charlie and Daithi left, Clawdia went to the bathroom to clean up. I hovered in the hallway, pacing with too much energy.

A noise made me freeze, and I peeked my head into the guest room. The window was open, causing the curtain to smack into the wall with each gust of the wind. I didn't shut it, knowing Savida would want to feel the breeze across his skin.

I perched on the side of the bed and watched the slight rise and fall of Savida's chest.

He was my first friend. The first person I spoke to after he and Daithi freed me from my slaver. He was a light, an energy that kept us all buoyant.

I touched the dark skin of his hand gently. "I'm sorry I was not in time to protect you, my friend. We will fix this. I swear it."

"Zaide?" I heard my name called by a hypnotic, soft voice. I turned my gaze to the doorway, where my future stood.

Her attention turned to my friend, and she joined me on the other side of his bed. She picked up his wrist and felt his pulse. She prodded him lightly in places that would have made him jump and laugh were he not fireless. My heart squeezed.

"It's like a coma?" she asked softly when she finished her ministrations. I didn't know exactly what that was, but I nodded. "They say some people in comas can still hear."

I blinked and looked down at Savida. "He can?"

"Maybe."

"I will need to talk to him often, then, so he doesn't get bored."

She laughed lightly and placed a hand on his chest. "Hello, Savida. I'm Clawdia. We've already met, but I was a cat then." I smiled at the memory of him wearing her as a hat. "We're going to do my best to save you. I'm so sorry this happened. I'm so sorry."

I covered her hand with my own and said, "Daithi is wrong to blame you. You don't need to apologize."

She gave me a small, appreciative smile but said nothing more on the subject. She sighed. "I used to hate this part."

Her comment confused me and asked, "What part is that?"

"Not being able to help anymore. The part where we wait." She seemed lost in her memories as she stared at her hands. "I was a trainee nurse."

"You were a healer?"

"Of a sort."

"That is a wonderful occupation," I told her, awe in my voice.

She shrugged. "It is when you can help. It isn't when you can't."

I shook my head and stood. "But that is where you are wrong, Little Cat. You can help. Right now, we must search your witch's house for things to help Charlie find them."

She nodded.

We walked to the back garden, and I assisted Clawdia as she attempted to jump over the fence. The back door to

Winnie and Clawdia's home was still slightly ajar, and we slipped in quickly.

Clawdia led me around her home, moving gracefully from the kitchen to the living room in silence.

I opened my mouth. I closed it. Trying to find the words to tell her she was my soul pair was difficult. While I was trying to find the words, she was also quiet, her head filled with thoughts. I wanted to know them.

"You are quiet," I noted. "You aren't glad to have another being to talk to?"

She blinked. "I keep forgetting that I can, to be honest with you."

"I always want your honesty."

She whispered, "Everything looks smaller."

I smiled. "That may be because you have changed from a small, fierce creature to a human. You will adjust to it quickly."

"I don't think I want to."

I stopped moving. "What do you mean?"

She continued to look around the living area. "I enjoyed being a cat. It was simpler." She stroked the material of the sofa as she passed and shuddered as I stood open-mouthed.

"Were you not originally human? You hated it even then?" I asked when I finally arranged my thoughts.

She paused and ducked her head before replying quietly. "I didn't. Until I did. And then I was thankful I died."

Thankful for death? What suffering caused a person to be thankful for the end of their life?

I worried then. Worried that telling her she was my soul pair would make her angry or upset. That it wouldn't be a joyous discovery, but a cage. I worried that my selfishness and desire for her to stay human and to stay with me would ruin her, hurt her further.

I clenched my hand into a fist and took a deep breath. "You do not want to be human," I repeated for clarification.

"That's right." She nodded vigorously.

"You will ask Daithi to turn you back into a cat?" I pressed.

She turned to face me. "Yes, but only after I help rescue Savida and stop Winnie from becoming a murderer."

"I see." I paused. "And you will miss nothing about being human? Talking? Food?"

"I may. But after living with everything dulled as a cat, it's almost worse being human again and being pushed into so much sensation. It's too much." She sat on the sofa and bit her lip. I sensed there was more that she wasn't saying.

I frowned, and my heart ached. "That sounds uncomfortable."

"It is painful."

I was a useless soul pair to not have noticed my other half was in pain throughout our entire interaction. I gritted my teeth and growled, "I'm sorry."

She looked at me with a kind of worried confusion. "It isn't your fault. Please don't apologize."

I offered her a small smile and moved to sit next to her on the sofa. "What did you enjoy most about being a cat?"

"Well, other than the smaller emotional range. I liked my tail. My glorious fur. And bothering Charlie." She had a cheeky grin on her face, which hinted at the fierceness I had seen in her animal form.

"You like bothering Charlie?" I asked, echoing her smile.

I was not prepared for the rush of color that moved from her neck to her cheeks. She coughed. "Um, yes."

I tilted my head curiously. "Because you dislike him and want him to suffer?"

"No!" she gasped.

"Because you like him and enjoy teasing him?" I pressed.

She stared open-mouthed, then her lips pressed into a thin line. "Maybe," she said reluctantly.

A strange mix of emotions hit me all at once. I was glad she liked Charlie. Charlie was my friend, and I didn't want her being spiteful to him. I was also worried because her blush suggested she liked him as more than a friend.

She likes Charlie. Is attracted to him.

Having a soul pair is more complicated than I expected.

The instant attraction seemed to be one-sided. She was uncomfortable and didn't want to be in a form in which we can communicate. And she was interested in another. Our situation looked more dismal with every hour.

It is only a problem if she wants only Charlie, a voice whispered in my head.

It was an interesting suggestion, and I was so eager to please her I would allow her anything as long as I got some small part of her time. Her affection.

It was not the time to dwell on such things when everything was still so new. I trusted my gods and knew they wouldn't lead me astray. Not after all they had given me. This was just another challenge to overcome.

Making a small coughing noise, she looked away and changed the subject. "I can't see Winnie's laptop down here. I think we should check her room."

I followed her up the stairs, but since she was wearing clothing that was not suited to her slight frame, I could not admire her figure. She had to hold on to the trousers and flick her legs so as not to tread on the bottoms. I sighed.

"I do not have a tail," I remarked absently as we trudged.

As we reached the top of the stairs, she turned to me, grinning. My breathing faltered for a moment. "I have noticed," she said in the same teasing tone. I wanted to hear it forever.

I continued, staring earnestly into her violet eyes, "I do, however, have hair as long as a tail." She gave me a curious look, unsure of where I was going with this line of conversation. "In my culture, we keep our hair long and braided as a symbol of strength and honor. When we suffer dark times, we hold on to our hair because it is all that is our own."

"That's ... tragically sweet."

"My point is, while you don't have your own tail, perhaps holding on to my hair might offer you some comfort."

I reached behind me and pulled the white braid over my shoulder. She stared at me. "Do not feel pressured to. It is something my people do when they are feeling vulnerable. I don't want you to feel pained as a human and thought perhaps giving you things you enjoyed about your cat form might help you. I can also offer to comb your hair to keep it glorious. And you can continue to bother Charlie. Although Charlie might have something to say about that," I rambled nervously.

She was quiet as she continued to stare at me. I resisted the urge to look away. Finally, she said, "Thank you. I appreciate all that."

My smile rose on my face as hope rose in my heart. "You will hold my hair?"

Color flooded her cheeks, but she nodded and gave me a sweet smile. "Maybe not now, but I will if I need it. For as long as I am human." It was a stark reminder that she wanted to be a cat again, but I refused to let that bother me. I wouldn't tell her she was my soul pair, that had already become attached to her. She would hold my hair and let me comb and braid hers, as a mate should.

Perhaps she would come to want to stay human with me, not because I need her to, not out of duty, but because she had fallen in love with me. I beamed my joy at the thought.

The sound of keys in the door had us both freezing.

I looked at Clawdia wide-eyed, and she quickly grabbed my hand and tugged me into a small room. Shrouded in darkness, there was only a blue light coming from a large box on the wall, which made a droning sound. A "boiler," I recalled from Charlie's tour of his own home. She closed the door behind us.

Squashed into the tiny area, I was suddenly very close to my soul pair. Her hand, small and dainty with long fingers and soft skin, was still in mine. She had taken my hand. No one had ever done that.

My scars glowed in the darkness, so I could see Clawdia staring up at me, her expression a mix of awe and fear. I rubbed my thumb across the smooth skin of her wrist, trying to comfort her. I relished in the feel of the small, ridged lines of her veins. It told me she was alive. She was real. I loved her nearness, the warmth of her body pressed against mine.

She shuddered, and her breath hitched against my chest.

I breathed her in. The smell of the soap she used to wash her hair, her body—it was a spicy scent that didn't suit her but still drove me wild with lust.

But my desire wasn't yet controllable, as I hadn't experienced it before, and I tilted my hips slightly away from her so as not to alarm her. My backside moved something behind me, which clattered against the wall. We both gasped.

"Clawdia?" a voice called.

I assessed my soul pair for signs that she recognized the voice, but with her brow furrowed, I could tell she did not.

We waited, breathing quietly so we could catch the sounds of the stranger as they moved about the house.

There were four loud taps of a metallic object against another metallic object. "Clawdia! Food!" the stranger shouted again.

When Clawdia's stomach rumbled, I had to restrain my laugh as she glared down at herself and then at me.

After a few long minutes, the front door closed, and we let out a sigh of relief. We waited a few moments more before I whispered, "Let us be quick with our mission and get back to Charlie's."

We opened the cupboard door and marched straight into Winnie's bedroom. Sighing, I turned my head to survey the room. "That square on the bed. Is that what we seek?"

She blinked quickly and then exclaimed, "Oh, yes! That's her laptop. At least we've succeeded in one task." She contemplated the wardrobe. "I think I'm going to change into something of Winnie's too while we are here."

I quirked my eyebrow. "You will feel more comfortable?"

"Yes. These jogging bottoms keep falling down."

I nodded. "I will continue to search while you try on clothing. Take extra, as I'm sure you'll need it."

"Try the garage. That's her witch room," she called after me.

I wandered downstairs, into the kitchen, and out into the garage. Similar to her bedroom, the room was colorful and decorative. Along the walls were large bookshelves holding trinkets, jars, statues, and, of course, some books.

I picked one that had a different cover off the shelf—it smelled older and didn't have a picture on the front. Brown, soft to the touch with raised sections spelling the title. I ran a hand over the smooth sides and then flipped it open to see the contents. I stopped when I saw the word "familiar."

"Here you are." I turned to Clawdia's soft voice. Clawdia was wearing female clothing, and my mind was suddenly blank. She followed my gaze to her body. "Is it all right?"

"You look wonderful," I breathed. Her body was now highlighted with a dress that clung to her body. The bodice was a soft blue and splattered with white and yellow flowers. A white-frilled neckline drew my attention to her collar-bones and slim neck. She was simply enchanting.

"Thank you." She gave me a small smile, and her cheeks turned a lovely shade of pink. She cleared her throat. "Have you found something?"

I returned my gaze to the book in my hands and nodded. "Yes, I think so."

"What is it?"

"A book. It says something about familiars. I thought we could learn more about how you came to be a cat for a witch."

"That's a good idea. I'd be interested to know." Then she sighed. "It's disappointing we have found nothing to suggest what the mysterious project is."

I sighed and then had another thought. "Her habits didn't change? She wasn't researching something unusual?"

Clawdia considered that. "She started reading a book about Scandinavian myths a few weeks ago, which was unusual."

"Myths are not part of her interest?"

Clawdia shrugged. "I've never seen her take any interest in myths before. But I've only been with her for two years."

I nodded. "We will take this book with us in case Charlie finds it relevant."

By the time we had gathered our books and the laptop, the weather outside had turned the sky dark prematurely, and there was a hum in the air which warned of something. Rain began pouring down from the clouds above, flooding the ground.

Clawdia looked at the window. "We should get back before it gets too heavy."

Suddenly, there was a flash of light in the sky. Followed by a roar. Clawdia jumped and gripped onto my hair so hard that I started, and she let go just as quickly. "I'm so sorry. I guess I'm a little skittish still."

I gave her a reassuring smile and opened the back door. The rain pelted at the paving and splashed on my shoes as I stepped out onto the patio. I reached behind me, holding the books and laptop in a plastic bag in my right hand and taking Clawdia's with my left.

We dashed to the fence. Rain seeped into my clothes and skin, and soon we were drenched. Clawdia seemed to retain her cat-like agility, especially when motivated by a flashing sky, harsh rain, and loud thunder, as she jumped the fence without my assistance. She received the bag of stolen goods when I dangled it over the fence, then dashed into the house.

Quickly doing the same, I ran into Charlie's home to find my soul pair waiting for me. The sight of her stopped my heart.

Her hair had turned to strings, heavy and dark with rain. So heavy that it dripped, dripped, dripped down from her forehead, along her nose, over her lips. Another drop fell down the side of her neck, past her collar, to a place hidden by material … material that no longer covered but emphasized her body, clinging to her skin. I saw the outline of her breasts, waist, hips, and thighs.

Instantly aroused, I huffed out my frustrations.

I need to find a way to control my desires; otherwise, I will scare her away.

That couldn't happen. I needed her too much.

She shivered.

"Come, Little Cat. Let us get out of these wet clothes." I realized after I said it what it sounded like, but she didn't look disturbed or upset. Just cold, tired, and confused. "I will braid your hair, and then you can rest," I told her softly.

A little while later, we sat on Charlie's bed, wrapped in new, warmer clothing, and Clawdia was showing me how the hair dryer worked. When I figured out how to control the machine, I moved onto my knees behind her and began drying her hair, running my fingers through the strands as warm air blew across them. In the corner of the room, our images reflected in the mirror. Our eyes met.

We looked perfect together. A compliment and contradiction. I was large and frightening, with my scars covering my body, and she was small and soft. I had white hair, and she had white skin dotted with brown marks. I had gold skin with purple scars, while she had gold hair. Our purple eyes were slightly different shades, but I could see the same pain and fear in hers that I felt after Daithi and Savida freed me.

She looked down at her hands. She had taken something else from Winnie's house, a picture—Winnie and Clawdia the cat.

My poor Little Cat, I thought. *Abandoned. Betrayed. Grieving. And so troubled to be human again.*

I vowed to do everything I could to make her happy. To give her the family she lost when Winnie abandoned her.

When her hair was dry, I took a comb and gently brushed it through.

Her voice startled me. "It will not be the same again, will it?" she asked softly.

She turned to look at me, her eyes pleading. I sighed and shook my head. "No, Little Cat."

Her eyes filled, and she turned back around, her shoulders drooping as she stared down at her picture. I braided her hair and whispered, "You will struggle through this change, Little Cat, but you will not be alone. And when you feel you have nothing left to hold on to, you can hold my hair."

We said nothing more. I finished her braid and moved off the bed to let her get settled into it. I could see how drained she was as she crawled under the sheets and curled up. Outside, the storm raged. As her eyes fluttered shut, a semblance of peace smoothed her features, and she fell asleep.

I watched her breathe for a little while, relishing because she was real, alive, and well. I had found my soul pair. But for how long would I have her?

CHAPTER 14

CHARLIE

"*L*ook at this haul!" I exclaimed, walking into my office with four boxes of pizza, bottles of pop, and, of course, potato wedges and garlic bread. Daithi and Zaide sat squished together on the loveseat, yet they still formed a chasm of cold air and pissed-off vibes between them.

I continued in my celebratory tone, "Well done, lads. We'll have Savida back in no time." I passed them a box each and a bottle, then I raised my bottle in the air and announced grandly, "A feast in our honor!"

On my desk were the books and laptop we'd taken from Debs and Winnie's houses. All the items I needed to not only find the witches, but also get ahead of them.

I picked up the witch beginner guide and threw it at Daithi. "This one is for you. We need to know more about their magic. What they can do." He nodded and stood up, holding his food, drink, and book. "Where are you going? You don't have to do it now," I said.

"I have much to think about and would rather be alone," he told me softly. "Thank you for your help today."

When the door closed behind him with a soft click, I looked at Zaide, who stared after him. "Faei, am I right?" I rolled my eyes and dug into my pizza.

With the hand not feeding my face, I turned my computer on. We listened in companionable silence to the whirring and beeping as it warmed up.

I stared at my titan friend, chewing on a slice. He was nibbling dispassionately with his gaze fixed on my very boring carpet. "So, you're quiet. I thought you'd be jumping for joy. You've found your soul pair."

Zaide sighed. "I also have a lot to think about."

I reached for another slice of pizza. "You're going to leave me too?" Zaide shook his head. "This thinking is all to do with the lady upstairs?" He nodded. "She didn't take the soul pair thing well?"

"I didn't tell her," he said gruffly.

My login screen finally appeared. I wiped my crumby hands on my jeans and typed in my password. "Why not?"

He murmured, "She wants to be a cat again."

I picked my slice up and took a bite while my computer logged in. "So?" I mumbled around a blob of stringy cheese.

"She hates being human. She liked being a cat, and we have forced her to be human again." He paused and looked up at me. The heartbreak in his eyes stopped me dead as I continued my battle with the cheese. "I think something terrible happened to her as a human."

A strange, confused emotion ran through me. On the one hand, I was glad she would change back. I hadn't had a chance to miss my little Clawdicat yet, so it was easy to separate the two in my mind, but I knew I would miss her if she stayed human.

On the other hand, I was sad. Sad for her, sad for Zaide, and sad for me, because I fancied her as Clawdia the human. I was curious about her life, both her human past and her

159

cat life. I wanted to know how she saw me when she was strolling four legged around my house and knocking shit over. Just a human to annoy, or Charlie the hottie next door?

I shook off my emotions and nodded. "She's young. I mean, in those days, it probably wasn't so uncommon to die young, what with the war and the Spanish flu and the fact that penicillin hadn't been invented yet. But if she's skittish, it could be something else."

Zaide nodded and frowned. "She said it is painful for her. Being human."

"In what way? Emotionally? Physically?"

"Both, I think. She said the sensations are too over-whelming."

I twisted the cap on my pop and took a big gulp. The burp that followed was legendary, even if Zaide looked horrified. I shrugged and continued, "I suppose that makes sense. Humans have more emotional capacity than cats. And although their hearing and sense of smell is better, our eyes can see color, both long and short distances, and we have more receptors to read pain or pleasure, taste or touch." I leaned back in my chair, thinking. "We can try to limit sensory overload. Ask her what is too much."

"That might want to make her stay human?"

"It'll make her more comfortable." I sighed and turned my head to my computer. Using the pictures on my phone, I attempted to log in to Deb's accounts.

The screen turned black.

"Fuck!"

"What is it?"

"Fucking computer just died."

"It is dead?"

The screen turned back on as I rebooted it. "It's back on. Don't worry." He went quiet again, and I looked over my screen to see him chewing through dried, cold cheese. "There's something else, isn't there? Just say it."

"It is a rather ... personal ... dilemma."

And I knew exactly what he was going to ask me. I moaned. "Oh, God. No. I won't deal with titan pubescence." I threw him the romance book I took from Debs, suddenly realizing why I picked it up. "Read that. Maybe it will help."

His skin flushed rose gold. "Thank you. I do not want to scare her away with my—"

"Monster dick?" I nodded. "Yeah, I saw it this morning. Couldn't miss it when you turned and almost poked my eye out with it. If I wasn't so confident, I might feel very inadequate right now."

"I'm too big?"

I gritted my teeth, turned my attention to my computer again, and tried to sound easygoing. I'm not sure I succeeded. "That's a debate you and Clawdia can have when the time comes."

Zaide tilted his head slightly and looked curiously at me, his eyes boring holes in the side of my head as I logged in again. "You are dealing well with all of this? You aren't feeling overwhelmed?"

I laughed. "I passed overwhelmed a few days ago."

"How is it you are calm, then?"

"I guess all those resilience workshops I took while I was in foster care really paid off," I said without thinking and chuckled. "Fuck," I cursed when my computer died again.

"I'm unfamiliar with that term."

I started checking the cables. Having paid a fortune only a year ago for a new one, it shouldn't be dying.

Stupid fucking technology.

I answered him absentmindedly, "Resilience? It means you bounce back—"

"No. Foster care. What is that?"

I tried rebooting again and heard the beep of it switching on. Sitting back down, I ran my hand through my hair and sighed as I answered. "It's for kids that don't have parents or have bad ones. They get taken out of their homes and placed with foster families that look after them until their parents can take them again or until they are old enough to look after themselves or get adopted."

"That is an ... interesting concept. You have bad parents?"

I sighed, knowing I would have to explain. "No. They adopted me when I was a baby, but then they died in a car accident, so I went into foster care. I was naughty and grieving, so I didn't get adopted again. I just traveled from family to family every few years."

Zaide looked horrified. "Charlie, I am sorry you experienced that."

I gave him a smile. "Don't be sorry. Nothing you could do about it."

"It does not sound like an enjoyable way to grow up."

That coming from someone who was a slave made me feel like shit, but I shrugged. "Eh, other people had it worse. It was what it was."

"So, you are used to change and are therefore dealing with this situation calmly," he summarized.

"It seems so." I logged on for the third time. And the third time was the charm, because using the pictures on my phone of Deb's passwords, I could log into her bank account.

I looked through her recent purchases, but since it had only been a day since she left, nothing was showing yet. There was a huge drop in the available funds that she had, so I knew she was spending the money. I just had to wait until an alert let me know where and what she was doing in real time. I opened Winnie's laptop, and since her passwords were all autosaved, I did the same in half the time.

I mentally high-fived myself and took another swig of my

drink, the gassy bubbles celebrating my genius on my tongue.

I'd forgotten Zaide was in the room until he spoke again. "You aren't upset your cat is gone?"

"What?" His question jolted me out of my thoughts and back into the room to see the earnestness of his big purple eyes. "She wasn't my cat. She was Winnie's. I might have shared her, but I rarely commit to anything," I told him honestly but still avoided the truth of my feelings about her. Telling him that would only get me killed via big gold hands.

"Because you don't want to make attachments?"

I half expected him to don a pair of glasses and pull out a notebook with all these questions. I replied, "No, I make attachments. I just know that they are short-term ones."

"You don't want long-term attachments?"

I sighed and ran my hands through my hair. "Nothing lasts forever, Zaide. Life, emotion, situations, they are all temporary. Why get attached and lose it all?"

"Is that not part of life?"

"Only if you let it be." I shrugged.

"Perhaps you lost too much as a child to want attachments as an adult."

"All right, Dr. Phil. Thanks for the diagnosis." I coughed out a laugh. I knew he meant well, but I didn't want the unsolicited advice. I didn't need it.

Zaide picked up on my "fuck off" vibes. "I do not want to upset you, Charlie. I want to help you."

I gave him a pointed look. "This isn't helping. It's making me wish I had alcohol in the house."

He sighed. "Clawdia was yours first. I am not giving her up, but I acknowledge that you also have a bond with her."

"Yeah, maybe that was true when she was a cat, but she's human now. She's someone I don't know. And I don't feel anything for her other than my interest in her life in the 1900s," I lied.

"She likes you. You were one of her favorite things about being a cat."

Elation lit me up from the inside.

She liked me. She loved being with me as a cat.

Come to think of it, she knew me. She knew all my secrets. Had seen my highs and lows. She was probably the only soul close to me. But I didn't know her. Not at all. And I wouldn't get to know her. Because she wanted to be a cat again, and that was going to mess with my head.

I feigned my indifference, however, and shrugged. "I liked her too. As a cat."

"You may like her as a human too when you realize what she is like."

"I might." I already lusted after her. "But I wouldn't get between you both."

"That's not—"

Incessant beeping interrupted us. I looked at my computer screen and clicked on the alert. The location. I checked again.

"Got you," I whispered.

"The witches?" Zaide asked excitedly. I grinned at him but said nothing as adrenaline flooded me and I ran out of my office.

Dashing into the living room, I saw Daithi asleep with the book he took from Deb's house open and face down on his chest.

I shook him awake. "Daithi, I found her. I found her."

Daithi woke up blearily, asking, "Found who?" Then he shot up. "The witch?"

"Yeah, the witch."

"Well, where is she?"

"Sweden."

"Sweden?" Daithi asked, the hope in his eyes fucking killed me. For all we knew, it was already too late. "Where is that?"

"It's a different country. I bet Winnie and Mary are with her. They've probably boarded a flight and gone."

"Then we must also go." He stood.

I rubbed my hands together. "You can portal us there?"

He sagged and shook his head. "I would need to have seen the place."

"I can show you a picture."

I turned back to my office to print one off, but he grabbed my arm. "No, seen in my visions or my own eyes. A picture does not give me the connection I need."

"Fuck." I grimaced. "It's going to take me a little time to sort stuff out if we are getting there via plane. We'll need ID for you guys and Clawdia, and then I can book the flights and get a hotel."

"How long will that take?" Desperation began leaking into his voice.

I tried to mentally calculate, but there were too many variables. I shrugged and said, "A few hours? More? I'll need to ask my contact."

He nodded and his green hair fell into his eyes. "What about Savida?"

"He has to come with us?" I groaned.

"The sooner we can get his fire back to him, the better."

I had a sneaking suspicion it was so Savida's body would still be near him but decided not to question it and leave him be. "All right. Fuck. How are we going to transport a body?" I exclaimed, running a hand through my hair. I took a breath. "Right, I'm going to do a bit of research and figure this out."

I ran out of the room, hope filling me. I was bouncing with anticipation and knew just who to contact about IDs.

A deep, familiar voice filled the speakers of my phone, and I smiled. "Hello, Adam speaking. Can I help you?"

"Hi, Adam. It's Charlie Bennett. How've you been?" I chuckled slightly. I hadn't contacted Adam in years, not since I cut ties with the criminal world. He was like me in that he didn't want to be a bad guy but didn't have other options. He used to say that when he had enough money to go legal, he would. But skills are valuable, and when people know you, there's no real way of getting out of the business.

Shock colored his voice. "Well, I never. Charlie Bennett. What the fuck you calling me for?" He knew I wasn't calling for a friendly catch up.

"Would you believe I miss the sound of your voice?" I joked and laughed again.

He sighed. "What kind of trouble have you got yourself in now?"

"You wouldn't believe me if I told you."

"Well, you have my attention." I heard a seat groaning as he sat down and the rustle of papers.

"Okay. I need three passports. I can email you a picture and a name for the one, but the others don't matter what name or what picture you use."

He paused, and there was scribbling. "Right. And how soon do you need them?"

"Now."

He coughed. "Yeah, that's not a cheap ask. You got the money?"

"However much you need. It's ready to go as soon as you tell me this is done."

"All righty then."

I rubbed my neck nervously. "Um, before you go, I don't suppose you know how to get a body on a plane to Sweden?"

"Boy, that is the most fucked-up thing I've ever been

166

asked." I heard his grin on the other side of the phone. "Lucky for you, I know a guy."

I sighed, relieved. "You're a fucking legend, Adam. Thanks for this."

"Right, I'll text you this guy's number now and let you know when I've got your passports ready." I opened my mouth to thank him again and sign off, but he continued, his tone a little sadder. "Oh, and Charlie, I don't know if you heard, but Arthur Cartwright went missing last week. Presumed dead. Just thought I'd let you know."

I gasped. "Artie? What the fuck happened?"

"Nothing, as far as I know. He just disappeared. Don't know if it was due to a job going wrong or if it's all this other shit about people randomly disappearing."

I sat down on my desk, shocked. "Artie was careful. He wouldn't have—"

"I know. Whatever is causing these disappearances, I think it got him."

"It?"

"People are talking about alien abductions. That aliens are the only way there could be mass abductions like this."

Adam wasn't a conspiracy theorist. "Who's saying this?"

"Everyone. Witnesses have seen flashes of blue light before someone disappeared." He paused.

Aliens? Blue flashes?

"Anyway, I thought you should know."

The mystery of it tugged at me. I wanted to find out the truth, but I had other priorities.

I shook my head free of thoughts and said, "Yeah, thanks for telling me. And for the quick order."

"I'll be in touch when they're ready. You look after yourself, Charlie. Try to stay out of trouble."

"I'll try," I told him. But I had a feeling it was already too late for that.

CHAPTER 15

CLAWDIA

*W*ithin a few hours, myself, Charlie, Daithi and Zaide were driving to the airport, where we would board an airplane. Charlie was the only one of us who was familiar with that form of transport.

Zaide whispered to me that many other realms traveled by sea or magic, and at that moment in time, I wanted to travel like someone from another world too. Planes were frightening. In my day, we only used them for war.

I clenched my fists at my sides as the car sped to our destination. The smell of the artificial air freshener in the car made my stomach roll as I stared out the window. Houses, streets, and shops passed by too quickly for me to process, and I closed my eyes to shut them out.

I wish Winnie was here.

A tiny whimper escaped my lips. She couldn't help me now. Once my guide in this new century, new life, new body, she had set me adrift. I had no one.

I have Charlie. I have Zaide.

I did have them. But Charlie was, understandably, busy trying to get us to the right place to save Savida, and I also got the impression he was uncomfortable with me as a human.

And while Zaide had been nothing but attentive and kind, I didn't know him. He didn't know me. I was comfortable with him, but he didn't understand why living in this form was so difficult for me, and I didn't have the energy to tell him.

Why did you have to do this, Winnie?

I worried we would be too late to save Savida. Too late to save Winnie from herself. I wanted to do both with everything in me, but it felt like walking underwater trying to get my body to work with me. I'd forgotten how overwhelming being human was.

A large hand on my thigh made me jump back to the present. I relaxed slightly, realizing it was Zaide, and something inside me settled.

He didn't acknowledge his movement, nor did he draw attention to how I was struggling. He just let me know he was there. My gaze moved over his face softly. He was so kind.

My hearing tuned in as he'd been asking Charlie questions about airplanes to reassure all of us. Charlie gave us a basic understanding of the machine and gave him the statistics of the likelihood of an accident, which calmed everyone down considerably.

In the port of air travel, as Zaide called it, I gasped at the amount of people, the bright lights, the size of the building, the shops, the plane. Seeing things on a TV with cat eyes and seeing them in real life were wildly different experiences. The natural indifference I had as a cat protected me from feelings of shock, fear, intrigue, and worry—all feelings that battered me to the rhythm of my quickened heartbeat as a human.

There are so many people. So many things, I thought. I was overwhelmed with the images my brain was processing, and I supposed that since my human brain was dormant for so long, it was struggling to keep up.

"Savida will be sorry he missed such an exciting port," Zaide said as we walked with our luggage to the check-in desks.

Charlie laughed. "Tax free too, so it's cheaper than anywhere else."

"We will forget to tell him that when we come home."

Savida was in a coffin. He'd gotten collected by a funeral director and taken to the airport separate from us. Daithi spelled him to look human and seem dead to human eyes. Charlie assured us it would be very disrespectful to look into a closed casket but asked him to spell Savida, just in case.

In the queue to check in, I started to feel unwell. The voices on the overhead speaker sounded so close they could have been shouting directly into my ears. The lights seemed to blur and swirl around me. I could smell coffee from the café, and the metallic taste in my mouth made my stomach churn.

"Daithi, you guys definitely look like you do in your passports, right?" Charlie whispered.

Daithi scoffed. "Yes."

"Just checking."

"This line is taking a long time," he muttered angrily. "Why is it taking so long?"

"If I had to guess, I'd say the check-in agent is new. See how they've got a supervisor hanging over them?"

Charlie was right. As we were called forward and handed our passports over the gentleman, Fred, he explained that he was new to his role and asked for us to be patient with him. Unfortunately, Daithi had little patience as we waited ten minutes while the man clicked on his computer.

When a frown appeared on Fred's face, a cold sweat

broke out across my whole body. I looked at Charlie in a panic. "Don't worry, deep breaths," he whispered and stroked my hair.

The agent looked over the computer with a sheepish grin. "I'm afraid I'm having trouble. Just let me check with my supervisor." He disappeared to speak with the woman who had been helping him earlier and I tried to take deep, steadying breaths.

"Charlie, what is happening?" Daithi growled.

"Nothing to worry about. Just be patient." His tone was as calm and relaxed as his body as he leaned against the desk. With his sunglasses on his head, he looked like a movie star. Not that I would ever tell him that.

Fred and his supervisor came back to the desk, and she sat down, with him observing. She picked up our passports, asked each of us our date of birth, and did some more typing. When she finally smiled and handed us our passports back, it had been twenty minutes, and I let out an enormous sigh of relief. "Sorry about that, folks. Problem with the system. Thanks for your patience, and have a great flight."

We loaded up our luggage, and after we tied labels around them, they moved down a conveyer to a hole in the wall and disappeared.

But our bad luck didn't end there.

"Right, we'll have to be quick getting through security because we've only got an hour and a half until our flight," Charlie announced as we marched up the stairs to security.

Charlie didn't go into detail but told us it was to check that we had nothing in our hand luggage that could hurt people. He explained the process and that we had to make sure we didn't have any metal on us.

I walked on my unsteady legs through the scanner, which thankfully didn't beep, and they waved me on to wait for our shoes and coats. I sent a small prayer of thanks to God for looking after me, while my stomach gurgled.

Zaide reached me first, and I grabbed hold of his hair as a wave of dizziness passed over me.

"Little Cat, are you well?"

I nodded slightly, breathing deeply and staring at the floor as though communicating to it my desire to stay upright.

Daithi joined us on the other side. "This is a primitive form of security. I've never been robbed of my footwear in my life." I was so shocked he had spoken to us, even if it was just to complain, that I stared at him. "Where is Charlie?" he growled, then muttered as someone pushed past him. "Wretched place."

Zaide collected our items and turned. As the tallest of us, he scanned the area for our lost member. "He is in the larger box in a strange position."

"What?" I cried.

"Don't worry, Little Cat. He doesn't seem to be in any pain." Zaide's hand stroked my back.

We waited. I wrung my hands as anxiety wracked me. Ten minutes later, Charlie emerged from the crowd. He was scowling as he stomped over to us, and it reminded me of how annoyed he would get with me when I teased him as a cat.

"I swear to God, this process has never taken this long. It's bloody typical that when I'm trying to do something more important than a holiday in Spain, I get fucking searched." He huffed out a frustrated breath and ran a hand through his hair. "Come on."

We followed the moving crowd toward even brighter lights. That's when the smells hit me. Sweet and sickly perfume permeated the air and lingered in my nose when I tried to hold my breath. I gasped when someone moved in front of me and sprayed me. I inhaled it. It hit the back of my throat, and I coughed and coughed. Zaide took my hand and pulled me away as my eyes streamed and my stomach rolled.

We escaped the perfumed hell and entered an arena of people. The smell of food from restaurants and the heat from so many bodies made me flush.

"For fuck's sake!" Charlie exclaimed as he stared at a large screen. "The flight's delayed." He turned around to face us and noticed me. "What's up?"

"The flight is delayed?" Daithi repeated.

"I do not think she is well." Zaide was stroking my back. I was calmer but still felt ill.

"That would explain the green tone to her skin. Do you need to go to the toilet? It might make you feel better to get it all out."

I shook my head sharply and instantly regretted it when my stomach clenched, my eyes blurred, and I moaned deep in my throat. Blindly, I reached out for something to steady myself and clasped Zaide's braid. He wrapped his arm around me, and I sagged against his firm chest, knowing he'd hold me steady.

Charlie put his hand on my forehead. "You're warm." He stared at me, concern etched into his face. "Okay, she's not all right. Let's find seats somewhere and then get her to the toilet."

"I'm fine," I protested weakly. I'd always hated being babied. Nursing someone was *my* job, and I hated being the patient.

They guided me toward Wetherspoons as I still clung onto Zaide's hair. I waddled as though my feet didn't belong to me or as if I were walking on custard. They placed me in a seat, and I sank into it gratefully, placing my head on the table.

"Should we not be boarding the plane?" Daithi asked, getting more irritated by the second.

Charlie sighed. "No, the flight is delayed by an hour. We have to wait. Sit."

"Little Cat, what ails you?" Zaide's hand smoothed my hair.

"I feel sick, faint, and dizzy, and I think I have a headache coming on," I listed in a mumble.

Charlie replied, "It could be anxiety, a stomach bug, or migraines. Have you suffered from migraines before?"

Rolling my eyes hurt. "I've been a cat for two years. I didn't have any migraines."

"Do you want some paracetamol? I can go get some from Boots?"

"What is that?" Zaide asked.

"It's a painkiller."

"No, I'll be fine." I sat up reluctantly. "I need to go to the bathroom, though."

Charlie looked at my face, assessing me quickly before nodding. "I'll walk you there and go to the shops. You guys order some food for us all."

He heaved me up out of the chair and walked me, with a little more wobbling, to the ladies' bathroom. When he let me go outside the door, I shuffled my way to the first open stall and collapsed on the closed seat. I took a few calming breaths before my stomach lurched and my breakfast did a somersault. I dropped from the seat to the floor and slammed opened the lid. When my stomach rolled again, this time like a storm making chaotic waves that crashed against the beach, I lost my breakfast in the bowl, and tears squeezed from my eyes.

I heard Charlie's voice from a distance but couldn't make out what he said since I heaved. My stomach tried to empty again, only to have nothing left.

174

There was a knock on my stall door, and a female voice said, "Clawdia, is that you? There's a man called Charlie outside waiting for you. Do you … Is he … If you're in trouble, I can help you, just let me know."

I turned my head in the door's direction, the storm in my stomach quieting but leaving a steady ache. The lady confused me.

In trouble how? With what?

And then I saw a poster on the door giving numbers to help women that were being trafficked. A word I had only heard on TV and didn't think was real. I certainly didn't expect someone to think I was in that kind of trouble.

"Clawdia, are you all right? Did you hear me?"

My voice cracked as I answered, "I'm all right, thank you. Can you please let him in? I think I need help."

"Of course." I heard her footsteps and then the creak of the door. "She's asking for you."

"Clawdia, you okay, baby?" Charlie's voice boomed.

Baby? I thought in confusion but warmed at the term of endearment. I blamed it on my stomach bug.

"I'm … I'm sick. Charlie, I can't go. I can't even move." It was all too much. Tears started pouring from me, and I sobbed. "I hate this." And I did. I hated feeling overwhelmed and ill. I hated being sick. I hated looking at my body and being reminded of how weak and pathetic I was. I wanted to be strong. I wanted to be helpful and save Savida and Winnie, but it was so hard.

"Aw, Clawdia, baby, please don't cry. Open the door. I've got some water and some pills that should make you feel better." I unlocked the door, and he crouched when he saw I was on the floor. My lips were trembling as I bit back sobs and blinked tears away. His eyes were soft as he stared at me. "Come on. Let's get back to the others and get you some medicine."

I crawled toward him and threw my arms around his neck. "I want to go home."

"You don't want to go home, Clawdicat. There's nothing there for you now. Home is with us, and I promise we're going to keep you safe," he whispered to me.

I felt safe in his arms, hearing him call me Clawdicat again and promise that my new home was with him. Tears filled my eyes again, and I trembled with the emotion.

I moaned softly as he lifted me up and helped me walk to the sink. He washed my hands like I was a child, and I didn't even mind because everything ached too much to be independent. I could feel the stares of other women in the bathroom, but I didn't acknowledge them.

Zaide stood up when we approached the table. "Little Cat, you look awful. Are you okay?"

Daithi didn't glance up from his meal. I sighed as I sat down. "I'm okay."

"Nibble on this and then take these tablets with some water," Charlie instructed as he handed me some toast and some tablets.

I nibbled my toast obediently, and Daithi finally looked up. "When will we be traveling? We've been waiting in this port for a long time," he asked Charlie in his usual calm manner. But I saw a flash of something in his eyes and knew it was a facade.

"That's what this part is about, Daithi. We have to wait until they call us for boarding. We won't miss the flight, so don't worry about that."

"We are a day behind the witches. They could have done anything with Savida's fire by now." His fist clenched, but his face remained emotionless. I wished I could be emotionless. Stronger. Daithi had lost his loved one, and he was coping. He wasn't sobbing and throwing up.

"They could have, but we won't know until we get there. I

know being patient is hard right now, but things are out of our control until we are there, so take a deep breath and keep your cool."

I swallowed my last piece of toast. I wanted to ask Charlie how to take the tablets, but embarrassment rose from my past as a nurse, and my pride couldn't face him knowing more about medicine than me.

I'd seen Winnie take them by filling her mouth halfway with water, popping the tablets in, and swallowing.

I tried and succeeded with minimal water damage to my clothing or the table. Charlie stared at me with his lips locked tightly together and laughter in his eyes. Sighing, I promised myself to be a better human while I was still one so I didn't continually embarrass myself on the trip. And a less emotional human, too. Although I wasn't so confident in that promise.

There was another announcement made and blasted around the arena on speakers, but this time, Charlie reacted. "That's us. Everyone, finish your meals, and let's go."

When we finally got on the plane later than expected, Charlie sat me in the middle seat between to him and Zaide. Daithi sat on the other side of the plane, the aisle separating us.

I held on to Zaide's hair as the plane rolled forward and then blasted into the sky. I closed my eyes tight and resisted the urge to scream.

This isn't scary. Every modern person does this and doesn't die. Be braver. Be stronger.

Charlie's hand squeezed mine reassuringly. Or at least, it would have been reassuring if we weren't ridiculously high in a metal box. I cursed myself.

Zaide clenched the armrests, the only sign that he was also afraid, and I wished I had my tail to offer to him.

As the plane leveled out, so did my heartbeat. I spent a lot of the flight twisting the end of Zaide's braid into different shapes. Zaide, Daithi and Charlie were all reading books they had gathered from the witches' houses, and I briefly wondered why I didn't get a book to read.

Do they think I can't?

"What are you reading?" I whispered to Charlie.

He jumped slightly and then turned to me with a smile. "It's a 'witches for beginners' book that we got from Deb's house."

"Why don't I have one to read?"

"I didn't realize you wanted one."

"I want to help, Charlie."

"Clawdia, you were just sick. You don't have to prove anything to me."

"I'm not—"

"Yes, you are. You want to be helpful, but you need to listen to your body. You're not okay. Let us handle stuff until you're used to being human again." He smiled. "Or somewhat used to it."

I understood what he was saying but felt slightly put out by his "let the men handle this" attitude. I used to be a nurse. Until my father imprisoned me, I was independent, earned money, and had a career. I used to order grown men as I helped them, and it upset me that he thought I was too weak to help now. But that was just my pride speaking.

Charlie was right. I wasn't myself, I wasn't coping, and I needed to get a hold of myself before I could help anyone else.

"You called me Clawdicat earlier," I noted, and he looked away. Back at his book.

He nodded, still not looking at me. "I did."

"Why am I Clawdia now?"

He replied thoughtlessly, quickly, "You're making a big deal out of nothing. It's just a name."

I knew he was trying to dismiss me, but it felt important that I voiced my preferences. "I would rather you call me Clawdicat. You did when I was a cat."

He sighed. "You aren't a cat anymore, Clawdia."

"No, I'm not." I tilted my head so I could see his expression. When he looked up at me, I asked, "Are you upset about that? Did you prefer me as a cat?"

A range of emotions flashed across his face too quickly for me to decipher. "No. God, what a fucking trap this question is. Look. It's not that I prefer you as a cat. It's that I knew you as a cat. I don't know Clawdia the human, and so I can't pretend there's familiarity when there isn't."

"Oh." It made sense, but it still crushed me knowing that he preferred the other me. I understood why. Even I preferred Clawdicat to Clawdia. But understanding didn't make it hurt any less. Tears welled in my eyes, and I blinked them away rapidly.

He continued, looking back at his book again. "Don't take that the wrong way. It's day two of being a human, and I understand you're overwhelmed and don't want to stay this way. I get it. Being human is fucking awful. Inevitably, I'm going to get to know Clawdia the human while we are getting Savida's fire back. But if you're going to revert to Clawdicat, then I don't want to reconcile the two of you in my head. Do you get that? I won't be able to look at you as a cat without seeing you as you are now."

"I understand." I did. I couldn't imagine how confusing it must be for him to have a treasured pet suddenly turn human. Not only that, but be a human from a different decade, with a history, fears, opinions.

For me, if I didn't have the overwhelming sensations and the crippling fear, being human, talking to Charlie, and being with him like this would have been a dream come true for Clawdicat. But he was right. When I saved Savida from

Winnie, I'd go back to being a cat, her familiar. We'd go back to normal, being a family, sisters.

And that would mean I couldn't speak to Charlie anymore. If he took the otherworlders around the world, I probably wouldn't see him again, either.

I turned my head away to look in Zaide's direction and let one lone tear fall down my face as I mourned how our lives used to be and how they never would be the same again.

CHAPTER 16

MARGARET CLAUDIA

FRIDAY 24TH JUNE 1921

I reread the words which officially ended my life as I knew it.

Miss Margaret Claudia Smith
You have not attended your scheduled shifts at the Free
Hospital, nor your mandatory academic lessons, for five
consecutive weeks. Both the lessons and the practical
nursing experience are a part of your nursing training.
Since you have ignored all our efforts to communicate with
you, you are being released from the nursing training
programme at the Free Hospital, effective immediately.
We will not refund your tuition for the last year as per the
terms and conditions of the course.
Wishing you all the best with your future,
The Free Hospital Nurse Training Team

Heavy footsteps stomped ominously toward my door,

bringing me out of the trance of staring at the black ink. I sucked in a sharp, short breath, fear making me dizzy as blood drained from my face.

He isn't supposed to come back today. It's too early. I must have done something. Something must have happened. Why is he—

I couldn't allow myself to be distracted with panic. I quickly hid the letter behind the pillow of my armchair, wiped my eyes, and held my breath as I waited.

I heard the clatter of keys against my door as metal scratched at wood and then slid into the lock. At the click of the key, I started shaking. The door swung open, and I tried to hide it, tying my fingers together and tensing my body in anticipation. My father entered the room. His shadow cast on the wall from my dim candle drew him as the monster he was.

My eyes focused on his clenched fists and narrowed gaze. His eyes looked at me with the same disgust I had for myself.

How had I allowed myself to get into this situation?

"Get ready for dinner," he growled, and I heard the slight slur, saw his eyelids close in a slow blink. I knew he had been drinking, and my stomach clenched as even more fear swarmed like a wasp's nest inside me.

"Sir?" my voice quaked and croaked from misuse. They did not invite me to dinner anymore. They did not feed me often.

"Don't question me!" he roared. "And don't make me ask you again."

I bowed my head and studied my red, raw fingernails. "Yes, sir," I said meekly, the fight beaten out of me. I was concerned about this invite but soul weary and knew what a refusal would cause me.

"Dress well. We have an important guest."

My stomach flipped, but I said nothing further.

Still recovering from Father's earlier visit, I moved slowly, ignoring the pain which pulsed across my whole body, and quickly lit a few more candles. The dress I chose was a beautiful forget-me-not blue with yellow detailing on the top. It bagged around my chest and was tied with a belt just below my hips. Both fashionable and convenient, as it covered the bones now jutting from under my thin, pale skin and brushed just above my ankles, hiding the bruises littering my body.

Washing my face, I stared back at the gaunt reflection in the mirror. Dark circles swallowed my eyes. Ten weeks of imprisonment and abuse dulled the vibrant violet color.

When I was ready, I stood staring at the door.

Neither my mother nor father had allowed me to leave my room unless to wash or use the outhouse. I cringed as I placed my hand on the cold metal knob. Twisting it, I took a deep breath and opened my door. I winced at the creakiness and paused, waiting for … something. Someone to stop me. Mother, to guide me to the washroom. Father, to shove me back into my room. But nothing happened. The house was silent.

I tiptoed to the stairs, my heart pounding, my eyes scanning furiously and my body awaiting attacks. Creeping downstairs, I could feel cuts reopening along my back, the material of my dress rubbing against the wounds. I prayed I didn't bleed through. Father really would kill me.

And on the stairs, I stopped. My breathing hitched. Because I realized that the thought of Father killing me didn't scare me like it should have.

"Claudia," Mother hissed when she spotted me motionless on the stairs. I knew then that the guest wasn't there; they didn't have to be on their best behavior. I swallowed hard, released the tight grasp I had on the stair rail, and continued walking down to the dining room.

I didn't look them in the eyes as I stepped into the room.

"Good evening, Father. Mother." My voice quaked slightly. I clasped my hands to stop them shaking.

"Sit, Claudia." He nodded at the dining chair opposite him, and I did as I was bid, wincing slightly at the feel of hard wood against my tender skin. "I have good news," he said calmly. He wasn't looking at me. He took a graceful sip of his drink. It set my heart racing even faster.

"Sir?"

He turned his icy gaze on me suddenly, and I froze, a breath caught in my lungs. "You aren't smiling. I'm giving you good news. You should be smiling."

My stomach clenched in fear, and my lips stuttered. "Forgive me." I etched a brittle smile on my face. "What is the good news?"

"You're to be married."

I gasped, and my heart started racing. "Marriage?" I squeaked. Shock held me rigid.

Marriage. My heart turned itself inside out at the thought, having always longed for something ... else ... someone else. Someone I had never met. Meanwhile, my mind was soaring with possibilities, whispering reassurances to my heart. I could escape here. Escape my parents. This house. My room. Maybe go back to nursing. I'd find myself again. Learn to be unafraid. I'd be more independent. Try to help others who suffered as I have.

But I'd be married.

Perhaps that man didn't want an independent wife. A wife with a career or hobby. Maybe he wouldn't be kind at all. Perhaps I was just swapping one prison for another. Perhaps I'd break with another kind of abuse, one my father doesn't do.

I shuddered.

"It's about time you made yourself useful. You need a husband," my father continued.

I nodded agreeably, my mind still swirling even as my heart felt more and more removed. Cold crept over me, and I jumped at the sound of a knock at the front door.

"Margaret, if you will," Father addressed Mother, who immediately stood and walked to the door.

When Mother closed the dining room door behind her with a quiet click, Father turned back to me. "You are not interested in who your marriage partner is?"

I swallowed. "Of course I am, Father."

"He is a good friend of mine." My stomach dropped. Any friend of Father's could not be a kind man. "His name is Darren Jenkins." My world swirled. The thoughts in my brain drained away like dirty water in a sink.

Darren Jenkins. The same man who beat his wife to death only ten weeks ago. A woman I tried to help. But ultimately failed.

Is this my punishment?

"He's in the market for a bride and likes them pliable and … well, for lack of a better word, broken."

I heard the words but didn't process them. "Broken" echoed around my empty head. I felt nothing. Cold seeped into my skin and creeped around my bones, making them hard, brittle, aching.

"He's had wives in the past that have let him down. But you'll understand the consequences of letting him down. And letting me down."

A soft knock at the dining room door sounded, but it didn't open. Mother would not enter with our guest until Father told her to. She knew better.

Father, in a flurry of movement, pounced over the table, knocking cutlery and plates to the floor with a clatter. He grabbed my face with a large hand and turned my gaze from the door to meet his, so close I could smell the wine on his breath. I tried to pull away, an instinctual movement I hadn't filtered quickly enough, because his grip on my cheeks tightened, and rage flashed in his eyes. I held still and waited.

"It is important that you do not ruin this dinner with womanly weakness. You will be agreeable and silent. Do you understand?"

"Yes, sir," I whispered through squished cheeks and tried to force back the nausea rising in my throat.

"Good girl," he muttered and let go of my face. I immediately dropped my head to stare at my hands again. Leaning back to his side of the table, his gaze was like the brush of a lit candle against my skin as he studied me. "At least now you have more color in your cheeks. I'd hate him to think he was getting a sickly wife." He paused and looked at the surrounding mess. "Clean this up."

His gaze left my face, and I quickly rearranged the cutlery and plates; I welcomed the distraction from thoughts of what was to come. Finishing, I sat back in my chair and closed my eyes, wishing I could hide. Be invisible. Non-existent.

"Come in!" he called cheerfully, and I heard his shoes thump against the floor as he walked to the door.

I opened my eyes when I heard the door open with a creak. Mother walked in, a huge smile on her face. Behind her was a tall, broad man. The dim light shrouded his features. All I could see were perfect white teeth in a grin as he greeted my father.

When his gaze met mine, my heart leaped out of my chest.

"And this is Claudia." I heard my father speak, but it sounded so distant, as though he were whispering in the next room. All I could hear was the roar of blood in my ears and the screams of instinct demanding I run.

I stood, a practiced action which helped me while I continued to struggle with the panic flooding me. My heart continued its strange jumping as though it were literally trying to leave my body to escape.

I reached a hand to our guest, my future husband—although my stomach revolted at that thought—and looked at his chest as he approached. He was well dressed and handsome, but I knew he was a monster like my father. I also knew not to look monsters in the eye.

When his hand picked up mine and his lips kissed the back, a shock of lightning coursed through my veins. I almost pulled away. My body begged me to. My heart cried. Something was tugging on me. On something inside me, which was reticent to leave. A scream bubbled up in my throat at the unknown, frightening feelings stirring panic beyond anything I had ever experienced.

When his gaze rose from my hand to meet my eyes, he smiled, probably feeling the fear leaking through my hands in a cold sweat. His eyes were black. They say the eyes are the window to the soul. He didn't have one. My hands started shaking.

"Claudia, I'm so very excited to finally meet you. I know you are going to make me an extremely lucky man."

Bile raced up my throat, and a sheen of sweat glittered on my forehead in my attempt to stop the vomit from spewing onto the table. He let go of my hand, and the awful pulling sensation stopped. A modicum of relief washed through me, but my panic still raged, my heart still desperate for escape.

We sat down, and Mother walked to the kitchen to get the dishes she had prepared. I felt out of my body as Father and Mr. Jenkins made small talk, Father asking about his business and common acquaintances. I heard the words, but they didn't feel like English. I was a caged animal being traded.

I came back to myself at the succulent smell of freshly

cooked food arising from the plates placed along the middle of the table.

"Help yourself." Mother smiled, took a serving spoon, and began placing food on my father's plate.

I didn't move until they had all gotten something on their plates, and then I spooned vegetables and meat and gravy onto mine. I could feel their gaze. Eating so much was going against my father's ideal behavior. There would be comments, but I couldn't bring myself to care. I hadn't eaten this well in ages, and my future was bleak; I was going to enjoy my food.

"Claudia. Control yourself," my mother hissed.

Mr. Jenkins grinned at me. "Let the girl eat, Margaret. I like a woman with an appetite."

With that, my appetite scattered. Like sand slowly rolling around in my mouth, I swallowed hard and glared at my meal.

Duchess, our cat, wandered into the dining room, having smelled the food. She twirled herself around my father's legs as he sat at the table, trilling happily. His eyes softened, and somewhere behind them, an ember of the man he used to be flickered, and my chest ached. He couldn't be that man for me anymore. The war broke him. And the drink remade him into a monster.

Distracted by the cat, I didn't realize someone had asked me a question. My eyes widened. "I'm sorry. What did you say?"

"Is she hard of hearing?" Mr. Jenkins remarked with an evil smirk.

My father glared. "No. Just stupid."

Mr. Jenkins grinned and continued to stare at me as he said, "I can work with that."

I tensed my aching body to resist the shudder trying to wrack me. I looked back at my plate and ate more food.

Mother spoke up. "We asked how soon you'd like the wedding."

I choked on a spud. My mother squealed as I almost sprayed her with gravy. Humiliation colored my cheeks as I grasped the napkin and covered my mouth, struggling to control my coughing.

Mr. Jenkins's lip turned up in disgust. "It seems her stupidity translates to her inability to eat, too."

"I'm so sorry." My mother flapped, her gaze flitting from him to me. "Claudia, apologize," she growled.

Having got my coughing under control, I muttered, "I can't apologize enough," from behind my napkin, my head bowed.

"I believe we shocked her by talking so early about the wedding. Perhaps my bride and I should discuss this between ourselves. Get to know each other."

My head shot up to stare at the suggestion. Mr. Jenkins was staring right at me with a cruel smirk, making my skin itch and my heart rattle its cage.

"An excellent idea. Come, Margaret, let's leave these two."

Fear gripped me as I watched my parents leave the room. I'd never feared them leaving me before. But I recognized a predator. He was the worse evil. I could feel it.

When we were alone, I chanced a glance at him. It shocked me when I saw smoke curling around his body like a snake. I blinked.

My heart raced and cried out for me to escape this man. I froze as he stood, pushing back his chair and coming around the table to stand over me. He offered me a hand, clearly desiring I stand too, but I didn't want to touch him. His touch was draining. But I couldn't see a way to not touch him.

Reluctantly, I placed my hand in his, and the same horrible sensations washed over me. His hand was like touching ice. So cold it burned. It seeped into my palm, into my veins, sending streaks of fire along them where it reached something inside me and pulled.

I gasped and tried to let go, but he held me tight, his fingers squeezing mine. And when his eyes, black soulless eyes, met mine, they flashed yellow.

A scream caught in my throat, and he grinned. He let my hand go and breath I hadn't known I was holding escaped my trembling lips. I stepped back.

"Such power," he muttered as I collected myself. With his eyes back to normal, he tilted his head as he studied me. "But are you worth the money?"

"Pardon?" I squeaked, genuinely confused about the question. He acted as though nothing had happened. As though I hadn't just seen his eyes change color.

I am hallucinating. Perhaps Father has damaged my mind. Perhaps I really am broken. I couldn't have seen—

He interrupted my shell-shocked thoughts with a mocking grin. "I'm sorry, I thought you knew."

"Your father has been borrowing money from me. Hard to drink that much without spending a farthing or two. But see, he doesn't have the money to pay me back. So, generous gent that I am, I compromised, and for my money, I've got a new bride."

I must have been in shock, because I felt nothing at his announcement. I felt nothing at the thought of being sold off like cattle. Nothing.

He circled me. "I think you'll be perfect for what I have planned. Might even last longer than the others." He smacked my backside, making me jump. He chuckled.

Frozen in place, I didn't move as he stepped even closer to me and leaned down to rest his lips on the shell of my ear. "I will have so much fun breaking you in," he whispered darkly.

I knew he would. My mind went dark, and my body turned to stone—it was too much. I knew little about intercourse except what I'd heard from my married friends. I knew some of them liked it. Some of them did not. Some of them tolerated it. But I knew this man wouldn't be kind. Whatever could be pleasurable, he would make painful. He would make me suffer, and then I would die.

The door opened, letting light into the room, and I sought it out like a moth to flames.

Mother swanned in with a gleeful smile. "Well, I hope you've both had time to discuss the matter of your marriage. If we left you alone any longer, it wouldn't be decent."

"Thank you for thinking of my bride's reputation, Margaret."

"I hope you're pleased," Father exclaimed cheerfully.

"I think she'll do nicely." Darren smacked my bottom again. My heart stuttered.

"Well, I'm glad we've got that sorted. Margaret will arrange everything and let you know."

"Right. Well, I'll see you at the courthouse, bride." He squeezed my bum hard. I whimpered but remained frozen in place.

As our guest left the house, I didn't partake in pleasantries. I remained stuck to the spot. I shut my eyes as though I could disappear inside my head. By the time the front door had shut, I hadn't got a hold of my panic.

Father interrupted my thoughts when he returned to me, still motionless in the dining room, smirking. "You look frightened, dear. Pray tell, why?"

"I—I can't m-marry him, Father." My tongue was like lead in my mouth as I stuttered my pathetic protest.

He raised one dark brow and smiled almost sympathetically. My stomach turned. "You will, and there's nothing you can do to prevent it," he whispered.

Sudden brazen bravery flooded me, and I announced, "I'll run away."

"Run away?" He looked shocked at the thought, as though it hadn't occurred to him I would rather risk homelessness than rape and murder. "My daughter, a beggar, or worse, a prostitute," he growled, prowling toward me, and I stepped backward, hitting into the wall.

"I'd sooner see you dead." He took my arm and pulled sharply.

I gasped and screamed as a lightning bolt of pain ran through my arm and my shoulder pulled out of its socket. He pulled me up the stairs and threw me into my room. I fell onto the wooden floor, clutching my arm and whimpering.

My lip split when he slapped me. He kicked me, and my rib cracked. He punched me, and my world went dark.

I came to moments later, and pain echoed through my whole throbbing body. Each tiny movement, a blink or a breath, caused a tsunami of fire to sweep over me.

"Stupid girl. Look what you made me do! Now we'll not get the money until you've healed!" my father roared with anger and kicked at the furniture. My mirror fell from the dresser and smashed.

With tears running down my face and clouding my eyes, my father was blurry as he spoke the last words I would ever hear from him. "You'll stay in this room until your wedding. You won't eat or drink or relieve yourself with dignity. Maybe you'll be more agreeable after you've experienced the humiliation of defecating in a drawer."

I cried out as he slammed the door and bolted the lock.

I dragged my sore body to rest against the door. And when I heard my mother's soft footsteps, I called out, "Mother. Let me out. Please."

"No, Claudia. You must marry Mr. Jenkins. We need the money."

I collapsed against the door, crying and taking shuddering breaths. "Mother. Mother, no. Mother, please. I can't. He's evil. He'll kill me."

"Don't be silly. Now, I need to go to the courthouse and book the service. I'll be back."

"Momma, I promise not to run away. Please let me out. Please." But she was already walking away, her shoes tapping against the wooden stairs. I banged my hand against the door. Sobbing, I shouted, "Please!"

My heart broke at the sound of the front door closing, and then I was alone. Very alone. Feelings I had been controlling, hiding, came bursting through the barriers I had thrown against them over the years. Despair, betrayal, fear, longing, and jealousy flooded my mind and weighed heavily on my body.

I crawled to my bed.

The pain in my arm and shoulder pulsed a dull ache, and I tried not to disturb its position as I got into bed and fell asleep. It stopped me from thinking and feeling. It gave me peace.

As I drifted into nothing, I wondered whether death was this peaceful.

CHAPTER 17

ZAIDE

*S*he positioned her pussy so his cock slid inside her slick, hot depths, and he forgot everything, even his own name. His hands caressed the velvety skin of her ass and shoved her down upon his hardness.

"Oh, God!" Her hair flung wildly, whipping the silken strands across his face. Her channel gripped his cock, squeezing it so powerfully that it felt like a hand milked him.

Grabbing her head, he pulled her back to his lips, drawing upon the nectar of her mouth. She ground down upon him, whimpering, shaking with need. His blood boiled, and his engorged flesh screamed for release. Her tongue darted swiftly between their joined lips, and then she sucked his lower lip into her mouth. It was too much. Her fervent kiss threw him over the edge. His cock swelled more. With a loud groan, he stiffened as his sperm gushed into her.

I slammed the book shut as I panted, my body aching almost as much as the character in the story.

How is this supposed to help? I cursed Charlie in my head and raced to the bathroom, which was thankfully empty.

I turned the shower on, hurriedly tore my clothes off, and dived into the rainfall. Taking deep breaths, I calmed my racing heart, and my body relaxed in the spray. Everything except my cock.

I gripped my shaft and groaned at the pleasure. I imagined I wasn't alone in the shower. That my hand was smaller, more delicate, and didn't fully reach around the circumference of my member. I moaned, my eyes closed, as I moved my hand up and down, finding a rhythm which kept me on edge as my mind continued to fantasize.

Another small and delicate hand caressed my chest and followed my scars to my arms, my hands. She placed them on a perfect body—small, pert breasts, a narrow waist, curved hips, and finally to a warm, wet haven between her thighs. As my finger dipped into her center, I imagined her breathy moan, and my whole body shuddered as pleasure wracked me. I opened my eyes as my hand tightened on my shaft and my release shot from me in long, thick ropes.

I sighed, feeling completely drained as I leaned against the shower wall and relived the moment in my mind.

That is what I have been missing. It is a pleasure unlike anything.

I looked down at my flaccid member, glad I now knew how to defeat the monster.

A fleeting pleasure.

But with the person who was the other half of my soul, who I wanted to build memories of intimacy, respect, and love with. Memories that would last a lifetime. I couldn't wait to share that pleasure with Clawdia.

She is not ready. I reminded myself.

But I will ready myself. I will study how to pleasure her and how to control myself. I will be confident and sure so she will be comfortable.

There was a knock at the door, which startled me into knocking my brow on the showerhead. "Zaide?" Clawdia's voice rang out, and my soul jumped toward her, a smile spreading across my face just from hearing her gentle tone. "Are you in there?"

"One moment, Little Cat." I hurriedly washed my body, hopped out of the shower, wrapped a towel around me, and opened the door, eager to see her.

She stared up at me in shock. "That was quick."

"I didn't want to keep you waiting, Little Cat." She blushed, trying not to look at my bare, dripping chest. I moved past her. "It is all yours."

The door slammed after she zoomed past me. I did a little celebratory dance as I walked back to the bedroom to dress.

She blushed. She finds me attractive. She might not feel our connection as strongly as I do yet, but she desires me.

Feeling excited about the future, I left my room, which I was sharing with Charlie, and moved to the kitchen.

Charlie had rented us an apartment close to the airport. It had three bedrooms and one bathroom. The kitchen and living area combined in the center of the four other rooms.

It was not as comfortable as Charlie's home or as colorful as Winnie's, with pale walls and stiff beds, but for our temporary stay, it would do. Having gotten in so late, we'd all collapsed into bed and didn't speak about our plans, but now that we were here, I wanted to know where the witches were and how we planned to get Savida's fire back.

In the kitchen, I found Charlie drinking tea at the table. His disheveled hair and the bruises beneath his eyes indicated he hadn't slept as the rest of us had. He nodded at me but continued to search on his laptop for something.

Daithi was preparing himself something to eat and also didn't look as though he had slept well. He'd dressed and looked showered and clean, but there was a dimness to his usually luminous skin, and his green hair lacked luster.

He nodded at Charlie, sat down, and ate his food in silence. He was not speaking to Clawdia or myself unless it was to complain. My frustration grew each time my friend blamed me for something I could not have stopped. Not only that, but he was making Clawdia, who was already anxious enough, feel even more unwelcome. Since I was trying to convince her to stay human with me, this was not helpful.

"Where is Savida?" I asked as I found myself a bowl and filled it with cereal as Daithi had.

Charlie sighed and rubbed his face as he looked away from his computer to me. "We went to the funeral director's this morning and brought him back."

"He's here?" I asked, surprised. "You've been busy this morning." I looked at them again, understanding why they looked so tired. Not only had they not slept long, they also would have used a portal to bring Savida back here. That was a tiring journey and use of magic.

Charlie shrugged and looked at Daithi. "Unsurprisingly, neither of us could sleep for long."

The sound of bare feet padding into the room drew my attention as Clawdia walked into the kitchen. Her hair was still in the messy braid I had put it in the day before, but otherwise, she was dressed in fresh clothing and looked clean and lovely. I smiled. "Are you hungry, Little Cat?"

She gave me a small smile in response and nodded. I pulled her chair out for her and pushed it in once she sat. Her eyes darted around, a blush on her face as I placed the bowl of cereal I hadn't begun eating in front of her and urged her to eat.

In my mind, I saw a checklist. Already ticked: offer braid as comfort, comb and braid her hair, make her blush. I added a tick for my newest success—feed soul pair. I wasn't entirely sure this was the best way to make my Little Cat fall in love with me, but I cherished each slight gesture as a sign of our growing bond.

I retrieved the brush we had packed and untangled the tie

at the bottom of her braid, then gently combed through her hair. She gave me an odd look but didn't stop me. She continued to eat her breakfast as I rebraided her hair.

Charlie watched us with an unreadable expression. He then cleared his throat and said, "How are you feeling this morning, Clawdia?"

Her expression fell slightly at the sound of her name. She swallowed and gave him a thin smile. "I'm much better, thank you. I'm ready to be more helpful."

I stared between them, uncertain why their attitudes toward each other seemed colder despite the warm words.

A familiar beep sounded from Charlie's computer. He looked down, suddenly alert.

"Charlie?" Daithi asked.

"I've got a new location on the witches. They're in a place called Eskilstuna. They bought a coffee at a cake shop about an hour ago. I have no idea why they would be there, but we can see where that leads us. It'll only take forty-five minutes to get there if the traffic is good, and we might catch up with them. I've got an alert set on my phone if they use the credit card again anywhere else."

* * *

WE SET off in the rented vehicle Charlie procured at the port of air travel. The journey was quick, and soon we were exiting the vehicle and wandering through the town to a coffee shop called Mocca Deli.

Before entering, Charlie motioned us to hide behind a pillar and asked Daithi, "Can you make me look like a Swedish police officer?" Daithi gave him a look which informed him that he could do so easily, if only he knew what one was. "Shit. Two seconds," he muttered and tapped on his phone before showing him his desired disguise.

Daithi closed his eyes, focused for a moment, and moved the surrounding magic into the shape Charlie wanted. "There."

Charlie smiled his thanks and pointed to a bench. "Stay there. I'll be back soon."

We did as he bid us and sat down on the edge of the fountain. Savida would have loved seeing the picturesque town. I could imagine him running down the street and exclaiming over the shape of the old buildings, the river, and the pink blossoms. I sighed.

Clawdia wriggled in her seat. I looked at her, an eyebrow raised in question. She looked around and then whispered, "Winnie is here?"

"That is what Charlie said." I didn't know why she was whispering. If her witch was here, the only one safe from her would be Clawdia. And I was glad about that.

"I don't think she's here anymore," she whispered.

"Why do you say that?" I whispered back.

She shrugged. "I can't feel her close by."

Daithi heard our whispering and, like a volcano bubbling over, exploded, "You can feel that she is near you? Why did you not say something sooner? We could have already moved on. Stupid animal."

I reacted calmly but hugged her tighter to me as she curled in on herself. "She let us know as soon as she could. We've only been here a few moments."

Daithi growled low in a tone that I had never heard before. "She is deliberately sabotaging us in order to spare her witch."

Clawdia protested weakly, "I'm not sabotaging anything. I've just told you I don't think she's here, haven't I?"

"Too late. Again." He sneered, and she flinched as though his expression caused her physical pain. Perhaps it did. She warned me that her emotions hurt her. "We are wasting time being here. Savida's fire could be in danger of being lost to us right at this moment. I won't let you and your love for your witch take away the life of my demon."

I tightened my grip on her as she spoke. "You're right. I do love her, but I know she's done wrong. I am trying to help, I promise."

He ignored me and continued to intimidate Clawdia. "The witches need to die for their sins against Savida."

"Not Winnie." I hissed back at him. "Not when it jeopardizes the life of my—of Clawdia. They are bonded." We were attracting attention. Passersby were watching us carefully and whispering to their companions.

He scoffed. "That could be a lie to ensure she isn't punished in Winnie's place."

Clawdia stood, her hands shaking, and my arm around her fell to the bench. "I'm sorry Savida's fire is gone, but that doesn't give you the right to take it out on me. I haven't lied or sabotaged anything, and I will not sit here and let you talk to me like this." She stormed away, down the street.

I turned back to my friend and growled at him. "Stop this behavior before you do something you regret. I will take your slander and hateful remarks, but she is innocent in this. You leave her alone." I took off after my soul pair.

"I didn't think you were one to be ruled by your cock, Zaide," I heard him call after me, but I brushed off his remark.

I couldn't see Clawdia in the crowd, but I continued to walk up the road, hoping to see a glint of her rose gold hair. When I saw nothing, I circled back, believing I might have missed her. "Clawdia!" I called. I received no answer.

When I heard a muffled scream, I knew in my heart it was her.

I rushed toward the sound, my blood pumping, ready to

defeat the monster that would seek to harm her. I turned down a street to see the flash of her golden braid as she was being dragged into an alleyway by a large male in black clothing.

"Clawdia!" I shouted as I sprinted around the corner, pushing pedestrians who stood paralyzed with shock and concern out of the way.

Four males stood facing away from me, surrounded by brick. A dead end. They had nowhere to go.

"Hurry," one said to another.

Clawdia struggled and screamed against the hands of the middle man holding her. Fury ignited in my gut, a kind of anger I hadn't had since I was a slave.

"Put her down and leave with your life," I roared.

They turned their heads to look at me, and their eyes gave away their secrets. I sensed magic covering them. They were otherworlders. I didn't know what kind, as they were all disguised as human, like me.

Why are otherworlders kidnapping my soul pair?

"Deal with him," one said and turned back around.

The swell of magic in the air gave away their intentions. They were creating a portal.

They are escaping to another realm with my soul pair.

With a roar, my fists crashed into the nose of one man who charged toward me. The shadows rejoiced. Blood spurted, and I heard the familiar crunch of breaking bones. Debilitated, he fell to the floor.

He didn't have time to use any magic he possessed.

The next male rushed me as I stepped over his fallen comrade. I wanted to toy with him. I wanted him to feel fear and experience the truest defeat. A flash of blue made my heart stop. The portal was forming, and I would soon lose them.

I dodged the attacks and raced past him. Pulling the man

holding Clawdia away from the forming portal, I separated his grip on her and swung her behind me.

"Zaide!" she gasped and hid her head in the dip of my spine. She was trembling, and I tried hard not to growl in fury and frighten her further.

"Why?" I picked up the male creating the portal—I assumed he was faei—and threw him against the wall. The portal stopped growing but glowed like a swirling moon between two buildings. "Why did you try to take her?" I shouted.

Is someone trying to stop me from bonding to my soul pair? Is it just coincidence? Unlucky circumstance?

Unfortunately, I had forgotten how fragile other beings were. In the fall, he hit his head against the cobbled ground. The bleeding skull and unconsciousness told me I wouldn't be getting my question answered.

I turned to the two conscious beings and glared. "Why did you try to take her? What are you?"

"We were only following orders. Please." The second attacker hovered over the first, crouched in a bloody puddle.

The one who'd taken her stood to the side, glaring. I could see him considering the situation, plotting whether he could complete his job. I didn't know his powers, if he had any, and decided not to chance it.

Keeping Clawdia behind me, I walked along the furthest wall, away from the attackers, not turning my back on them until we were safely out of the alleyway.

I sighed and wrapped my arms around my trembling soul pair. "It's okay, Little Cat. You're safe." Her knees folded, and I picked her up and continued walking back the way we came, stroking her back reassuringly.

My eyes still roamed the streets for danger; my blood still raged with fear, anger, and adrenaline. Humans had their phones out, recording the spectacle, but they scattered as I stormed back to the coffee shop.

"There you are," Charlie called, jogging over when he saw us approaching. He spotted Clawdia shaking in my arms and asked, "What happened?"

"Otherworlders tried to take her. But she is safe now." I couldn't go into more detail without my anger rising. We moved away from the crowd before I asked, "What of the witches?"

"Okay, the bad news is that she isn't there anymore." Daithi clenched his fists, but Charlie continued, "The good news is that Winnie asked about a tourist spot about fifteen minutes from here. If we go now, we might catch them."

By the time we approached the car, Clawdia's breathing had settled into a calmer rhythm, but her shuddering and her temperature had only increased. "Zaide. Put me down please. I feel sick."

I did as I was bid and placed her on the ground in time for her to moan, bend over, and lose the contents of her stomach. I gathered the strands of hair that had escaped her braid and rubbed her back, whispering soft nothings. My heart continued to ache as she moaned and cried.

When she was done, Charlie tipped a bottle of water over our shoes, washing away the sick, before we crawled into the backseats. I wrapped my arms around her, and she leaned into me, still shaking and exhausted, with a stream of tears and snot pouring from her.

I will not allow her to be taken from me again, I vowed.

CHAPTER 18

CLAWDIA

*T*issues sat uselessly in my hands until Zaide opened them and carefully wiped my face, drying the tears. He pressed a kiss to my forehead and hugged me tightly, but shame pierced my heart.

Still so weak. Still as pathetic as you were 100 years ago. My father's voice sounded in my ears, and I flinched.

Logically, I knew I was in shock. The cold seeping into my bones, my teeth rattling, my whole body shaking. My mind whirled.

Why? Why would someone try to take me? Where were they trying to take me?

As if being human wasn't bad enough, I had to watch for kidnapping attempts too? I didn't think when watching *Taken* between licking my toes that I'd ever be in a position to pray for my own Liam Neeson.

What would have happened if Zaide hadn't found me?

Daithi huffed. "I know you said Earth doesn't have curses, Charlie, but evil has followed all this."

I whimpered, agreeing with him for once. "I am cursed," I whispered.

"You are not. You are my fierce little cat," Zaide replied.

I shook my head, and tears flooded my eyes. He was wrong. He didn't know the real me. "I'm not a cat. Just a—" I sobbed. "—a pathetic girl."

He tightened his arms around me and growled gently, nuzzling my hair. "Do not speak about yourself in such a manner. You are getting worked up again." He placed my hand back on his chest and began breathing deeply, encouraging me to copy him.

I closed my eyes. I could feel his chest raising and falling under my hand, under my cheek. Soft breaths tickled my face as he inhaled and exhaled. My racing heart slowed to a less hectic pace as my breathing followed his steady rhythm. I could smell the car air freshener and the leather of the seats, but also the smell of Zaide. A natural woodland scent that calmed me but also aroused my interest. I nuzzled against him.

He is so sweet.

The giant beast of a man easily took out two attackers and didn't work up a sweat. Yet I wasn't afraid of him. He looked like an avenging god as he charged toward us. His fury ignited hope in my heart, and I struggled in the arms of my captor to get to him.

In Zaide's arms, I felt protected. And it was a feeling I knew I could get addicted to.

His fingers brushed over my cheeks, and I opened my eyes to see devotion and desire stared back at me in his gaze. I saw a flash of red and noticed that his knuckles were bleeding.

"Oh." I sat upright and grabbed his hands. "Oh no, you're bleeding."

He chuckled softly. "That is to be expected after a fight, Little Cat."

My body automatically responded to the sight of a

bleeding man. I found the bottle of water Charlie had used to wash the sick off our shoes, and using the last drops of that, I poured it onto a tissue. Taking one of his large hands, I cleaned his wound.

It surprised me that his blood was red since his scars were purple, but I didn't ask him for the details. I looked up at him and said, "I have no antiseptic to clean them with and nothing to wrap them in."

He stopped me with another kiss to my forehead and whispered, "Thank you, Little Cat."

The reverence in his voice made me uncomfortable, and I sighed. "I haven't really done—"

He interrupted with another whisper. A secret. "No one has ever cleaned my wounds. As a fighter slave, I can't tell you how much I wished for someone to do what you have just done."

My heart broke, and I stared up at him, knowing how vulnerable that admission made him. I nodded and brought his hands to my mouth. I kissed them both and whispered, "Thank you for saving me."

"I will always save you, Little Cat," he whispered back, and somehow, I knew he would. It wasn't a false promise. He would fight for me like no one else ever had, and my eyes filled again.

"What's the diagnosis, doc?" Charlie interrupted our intimate moment.

I turned to meet his gaze in the rearview mirror. "He'll live."

He nodded. "Are we not going to discuss the kidnapping attempt? By otherworlders? I thought otherworlders coming here was rare. Is that why so many people are going missing?"

"Humans are going missing?" Zaide asked.

"Apparently so. Masses. My contact mentioned it yesterday. Said that there are theories about aliens after blue flashes."

I recalled watching recent news stories about missing people. Winnie was always angry rather than sympathetic. Said that no one was doing anything to prevent it. I brushed it off before, but now I found her comment curious.

Did she know what was causing it? That it was otherworlders? Was her attack on Savida revenge?

We were all quiet, lost in our thoughts, when we finally parked in the middle of a forest with very little around us.

Zaide looked around, confused. "Where are we?"

"This must be the wrong place," Daithi told Charlie. "There is nothing here."

"This is the place they were talking about," Charlie said as he got out of the car. Daithi did the same.

"She is closer than before," I said, searching for my connection to Winnie. It was stronger, and I knew she was close, but I couldn't gauge how far exactly. I huffed at my uselessness and, as if reading my thoughts, Zaide gave me another squeeze.

He opened the car door and pulled me out, still keeping me close to him.

"Is she getting closer or farther away?" Daithi asked.

I hesitated, trying to feel if the bond was wavering in any kind of direction. Finally, I shook my head and said, "She doesn't seem to be moving."

We were silent for a moment until Charlie, who had been looking around, pointed. "What's that over there?"

We looked over to see stairs leading to a rock. There were a few other people over there, touching the rock, taking pictures and selfies.

"Let us go and see," Daithi demanded and began walking over.

We climbed the stairs and reached a platform which

offered a view of the rock. Daithi waited impatiently at the top. He glared and said, "There is nothing here but this silly rock. I cannot sense magic or feel Savida's fire. Clawdia must be mistaken. They are not here."

"I'm not mistaken—" I started, but Charlie interrupted.

"I don't know why, but Winnie was here an hour ago, and that could mean something. Something to do with their project. Let's see if we can figure this out, and then I'll check their account to see where they've gone next."

I sighed and turned my attention to the rock. It had an interesting carving on it. I didn't recognize the images, but it seemed to tell a story. At my side, Zaide traced the lines, gazing at it. I watched him as he followed the carving from one end to the other.

"Charlie—" Daithi started again, getting frustrated. I was losing my patience with him, but he intimidated me enough that I wouldn't say anything. I had already stood up for myself enough for one day.

Charlie interrupted sharply, "Daithi. No matter what, we will find them today. They are going to be sleeping in a hotel somewhere tonight, and I promise I'm going to know where that is. Trust me."

"It might be too late by then," Daithi shouted.

I muttered, "It could be too late already."

As his glare turned to me, Zaide read aloud from a sign. "Ramsund Carvings. The Norse hero Sigurd—" He stopped and turned to us. "This was in a story from the book we took from Winnie's house. I was reading it on the plane. Clawdia told me Winnie began her interest in these myths only a few weeks ago, which coincides with her beginning this project."

Zaide's announcement didn't satisfy Daithi. "All that means is that we are on the right path. It is not the location of Savida's fire."

"This is a good thing." Charlie eyeballed him. "We aren't

going to find it that easy, and you're in for disappointment if you think we are. All we can do for now is follow the clues. That's what this is. A clue."

Daithi nodded sharply, acknowledging Charlie's frustration with him, and said nothing more.

Charlie continued, "We are assuming they need his fire for this project. But why would they need to see this rock to use his fire? We're missing something." He paced and ran a hand through his hair. "Remind me what his fire can do?"

Daithi replied quickly, enjoying the opportunity to be useful, "Anything. It is pure energy. It can heal, it can create, it can do anything when correctly channeled."

Charlie turned to Zaide and asked, "And the story? What was it about?"

"A dragon and a slayer. The slayer killed the dragon and gained gifts and treasures from its defeat."

"It's fiction?"

I understood what he meant. He thought demons weren't real until he met Savida and knew they were based on his race. Daithi answered confidently, "I haven't ever visited a realm of dragons, but that doesn't mean they don't exist."

Suddenly, I could feel her—Winnie. She was all right. She seemed excited. She was so close her feelings blurred into mine, and I gasped her name.

Alarmed, Zaide asked, "Little Cat, what is wrong?"

"She's here," I said, turning to where I could feel her, and pointed. "There."

Coming out of the tree line, Winnie and Mary walked back toward their car. They looked happy. Both in shorts and strappy tops, they had their arms linked as they chatted.

As though they didn't abandon me. As though they didn't steal the fire from Savida and leave him for dead in a shed. I was angry, but I was also glad she was all right.

"Wait!" Charlie yelled and ran toward them. We followed, my pulse pumping in my throat.

Winnie is here! Our bond screamed gleefully at our closeness.

But I needed to find out if it was too late to stop her from becoming a murderer. And I needed to decide what I would do if she already was.

We approached them; the gravel crunching under our shoes. Winnie and Mary turned to face us; Winnie looked unnerved, but Mary didn't seem fazed.

"Is there something wrong, officer?" Mary asked. Winnie looked curiously at me, and I twitched under her gaze. She could feel our bond, and I knew she didn't understand why or how it was coming from a human.

From the flash of confusion, Charlie had clearly forgotten that Daithi cloaked him as a law enforcer, but he worked with it. "Yes, actually there is. You have something that belongs to a friend of ours."

Winnie looked away from me and frowned at Charlie. She replied, "I can't imagine what that would be. We haven't been in the country very long."

Daithi jumped in. "You stole it in the UK. We want it back. Now."

Her eyes widened as she realized what we meant. Mary sneered. "No. Consider your friend dead."

I stepped forward. "Winnie, please. If you give it back, this will all be forgiven, and we can go home."

Mary glared and asked, "Forgiven?"

"Clawdia?" Winnie gasped. She looked at the others in horror when I nodded. "You turned my familiar into a human? Do you know what you've done?"

Daithi lost his temper and screamed, "Give us the fire you stole, witch! Now. Or die."

Neither witch took his threats seriously and ignored him.

"How did you turn her human?" She looked at us with fresh eyes, and when she realized, she whispered, "the other-worlders."

Suddenly, Daithi attacked with an illusion, but somehow anticipating such a move, Mary escaped the trap. Winnie sank inches into the ground, surrounded in a transparent box, the air taken from her lungs.

I felt her panic, and my terror doubled.

Daithi smiled smugly, while I struggled for breath. I dropped to the gravel, gasping.

Mary laughed. "You can't kill Winnie without killing her familiar, too."

Daithi answered immediately, "That is an acceptable loss."

My heart dropped at the announcement. I knew he blamed me. I knew he hated me, but I didn't think he'd want me dead.

Zaide dropped to the ground to gather me close and growled, "That is not an option."

I gasped, trying to pull air into my lungs, but despite being in the open air, I suffered as my witch did. My heart rate increased as I observed the madness, the anger on Daithi's face.

"Stop. You're killing her!" Zaide shouted.

"She deserves death," he hissed, glaring at Winnie.

Charlie held his hand out to Daithi, looking worried. "Clawdia doesn't deserve that. Stop. We'll find another way."

Mary laughed. "Rebellion in the ranks? You should know it's too late for your friend. I delivered his fire last night."

"Delivered where? For what?" Daithi questioned.

She smirked, and I realized she had tricked us into under-estimating our enemy and blinded us from seeing what would ordinarily be obvious; Mary had been whispering a spell. Zaide stood up to prepare himself for an attack but, in doing so, gave her what she wanted.

She dragged him into a cage that formed around Charlie and Daithi, separating me from them. Thankfully, in trapping them together, Daithi's magic reflected off the walls of the cage. His illusion broke, and it freed Winnie from the trap.

I sucked in air desperately. I heard Zaide and Charlie let out a sigh of relief, and I looked over at their caged bodies. Zaide reached a hand to me, and we both flinched when the magic cage shocked him.

As Winnie sat up and gained her breath back, Mary laughed again. "Whatever you are, you're weak." I knew how much that would hurt Daithi. He thought himself so much higher than witches, yet he'd just been caged by one.

Winnie moved over to me and stroked a hand down my face as I lay still on the ground, panting. "I'm so sorry. This must be so horrible for you."

She didn't mean suddenly being suffocated. Although that was horrible, too. She knew my past. She knew why I was a familiar. How I came to be. How I hated being human, being reminded of my past.

Tears welled in my eyes at her kindness, and yet I was still so angry. It was strange to have such conflicting feelings, but they were familiar ones, having felt the same about my father. Angry, betrayed, hurt, but also just wanting love.

If you had just left Savida alone, this wouldn't be happening, I thought, but she didn't hear me. Somehow, we'd broken our telepathic connection. I wasn't sure if she'd done that on purpose or if it was a symptom of my being human, but regardless, it was another crack in my shattered heart.

Zaide shouted from his cage, "Break your bond with her so she doesn't have to suffer your pain."

Winnie looked shocked at the thought. "Break my bond? She would die. She is only alive now because I formed a connection with her soul."

"A soul gone before their time." Mary smiled cruelly, and I shuddered at the memories of my past.

Winnie ignored her and continued, "Besides, it is being human that's hurting her far more than my bond with her is."

"Poor little thing topped herself the first time. Who's to say she won't do it again?" Mary pouted mockingly. Shame caused my face to burn red. She'd just told Charlie and Zaide my darkest secret. I whimpered and looked at them to see them staring at me, heartbreak in their eyes.

"That's enough, Mary."

The other witch huffed, turned on her heel, and got into the driver's seat of the car while Winnie stayed with me for a moment. "Come with us. I'll find some way to change you back." She whispered, "This is killing you. I can see it."

Being human *was* hard.

I was overwhelmed and confused. Daithi was being cruel, and someone had just tried to kidnap me. But it wasn't killing me. I wouldn't let it. Not again. I was going to be braver, stronger, deserving of Zaide's devotion. I was going to impress Charlie, save Savida, and make Daithi like me. Winnie wouldn't be a murderer.

A plan formed in my mind, and so I didn't reply. It didn't help me argue with her, since I needed her to think all I wanted was to be a cat again.

I turned to look at Charlie, Zaide, and Daithi. Zaide gave me a pleading look that prayed I would choose them.

Winnie saw my gaze and continued, "They were going to kill you, Clawds. They are just using you to get to me. I know you're angry with me, but I don't want you in danger, and I don't want you in pain. Come with me, little sister, and I can try to turn you back."

I nodded and stared at them, hoping they could read my intentions in my eyes.

For all my goals, I needed to be with the witches. And

after Daithi's attack on me, they'd believe my loyalties lay with them. I could get them the information they needed to save Savida. I wouldn't be pathetic or useless.

I stood on shaky legs and walked toward the car.

"Clawdia, no. Please, stay! Please!" Zaide shouted desperately. A part of my heart cracked at the sound of his sorrow. I didn't want to cause that. My body wanted to turn around and burrow into his chest.

But that would save no one.

CHAPTER 19

CHARLIE

*W*hat an absolute shit show that was. We were down one demon and one cat-turned-human familiar, and I was pretty sure the friendship of the remaining two otherworlders was about to implode.

After the car carrying the witches and Clawdia left, the magical cage we were in disappeared. None of the other tourists milling about seemed to have noticed the commotion, which was one bit of luck I appreciated.

We got into the car hoping to chase them but, of course, couldn't find them. After using so much magic, Daithi was drained. Angry and frustrated, he stared out the window.

Zaide looked at me with his heartbroken eyes and said, "I think I know already, but what does 'topped herself' mean?"

I whispered softly and honestly, "It means she killed herself."

And that was fucking devastating. That Clawdia was so desperate or depressed in a time when mental health wasn't a thing that she took her own life, only to become a familiar 100 years in the future. I was heartbroken for her and suddenly understood all the panic attacks, the sensory over-load, the self-hatred. I could tell Zaide understood, too.

Now I was full of regret.

Why the fuck didn't I apologize about last night?

It had been a long day of traveling. I was tired, and having gotten so close to her while she was ill, looking after her, made me want her to stay human even if I lost my furry companion.

But now I knew how complicated being human was for her.

I didn't get to hear the full story. I'd barely talked to her about her life at all before they had stolen her from us. Was it being stolen if you chose to leave? She might have walked away, but with all the confusion, maybe she didn't have the emotional capacity to make the best decision and she was, in fact, coerced and stolen.

Fucking witches.

We drove back to the apartment in a silence as cold as Frosty's snowy balls.

When we stepped into the living room, I addressed the argument that was about to start. "Look, I know some serious shit just went down, but let's just remember we are all friends, and we need to work together if we want to get Clawdia and Savida's fire back. Okay?"

Zaide whirled on his feet. His white braid whipped around him, and his scars pulsated with his anger. Spittle hit my skin as he roared, "It is not okay, Charlie. My soul pair is gone. Taken by the witches because she feared death by Daithi's hands."

I took a deep breath and checked my body. I was pretty sure I hadn't shit myself. If anything was going to do it, it would be a titan screaming at me.

He pointed a finger at Daithi, who stood casually against

the breakfast bar as though he hadn't said it was an acceptable loss to kill Clawdia along with Winnie.

Daithi, uncharacteristically, rolled his eyes. "I was calling the witch's bluff. I would not kill your soul pair. Even if she has been sabotaging us in order to get back to her witch."

"That was taking it too far," I told him. Watching Clawdia drop to the ground, gasping for breath, was horrible. My heart lurched, and I'd wanted to save her, protect her.

But it was the grieving faei who was the perpetrator, and I didn't think he would go that far. I glared. If Mary hadn't cast her spell and trapped us, he might have killed them both.

Neither Zaide nor Daithi paid me any attention as they prowled toward each other like cats with their hackles raised. Their fight was with each other, and it had been brewing since Savida disappeared.

"She has not been sabotaging us," Zaide insisted. "She might have wanted to be a cat again and to be with her witch, but she wouldn't have—"

Daithi hissed, "You cannot know that for sure; you have only just met her, and you cannot judge her true character."

"She is my soul pair. She is the other half of my soul, and it is not a dishonorable one," Zaide roared, and the glass of water on the table quaked, tiny ripples moved across the surface. Like the sign of a T-Rex coming in *Jurassic Park*. Only it wasn't a T-Rex; it was a far more pissed-off titan.

The quiet that descended was a welcome one, and I hoped the argument had ended. But of course, Daithi had to open his fucking mouth and ruin it. "Maybe she is not dishonorable. Maybe she is. What I can tell you is that, with all her hysterics and drama, she is as useless as wet wood. I suppose in that, you are both well suited."

Oooooo, burn.

I cursed the little voice in my head that was thriving on

the chaos and eating popcorn like it was a spectator sport. Zaide didn't deserve that.

Zaide gasped, and I saw the hurt puncture his confidence. His shoulders slumped. The problem with arguing with a friend is that they know where to hit you with their words, and the betrayal of that can be worse than any physical jab. "Neither of us is useless. She told us where Winnie was. I—"

"Yes, you saved her from a threat. Well done. That is the first useful thing you've done in years. But you rescued *her*. You have not put nearly the same amount of effort into rescuing Savida." Daithi continued his assault. "My love is lying fireless, Zaide. Have you forgotten Savida already? Your mind is so taken up with thoughts of your soul pair that perhaps you don't remember your friend. I will be the first to tell him of your treachery when he is reunited with his fire."

Zaide scoffed. "I hope he can hear you right now. It would disgust him. You're hateful."

"I am hateful! I'm hateful because he is gone, and your soul pair is to blame!" he screamed.

"My soul pair is an innocent caught up in this confusing situation because you cannot control your temper or your magic. It is no wonder since you walked away from the teaching of your people," Zaide growled.

Daithi's expression crumbled even more so, and I didn't think that was possible. He placed his hand out and shut his eyes. "Don't. Don't, Zaide," he whispered. My curiosity peaked at the mention of Daithi's past and his reaction to it, but I didn't think it was the right time to ask questions.

Zaide approached him slowly, his voice low and angry. "I warned you once already today to leave her alone. Yet you tried to kill her." He shook his head slowly, fury holding his body stiff. "And I have already fought to defend her once today. Shall I ensure you are bloodied and unconscious as her attempted kidnappers were for attempting to hurt my soul pair?"

Ooooooo, nice.

I didn't know Zaide had it in him. He towered over Daithi, looked down on him with a sneer on his face. His arms relaxed at his side, but I could tell he was ready. He said he was a slave, but now I wondered what they made him to do.

Manual labor? He has the strength for it. Security? He has the glare down perfect. I can't imagine him as a docile captive serving his master. Underground fighter?

I almost brushed it off as my overactive imagination. But as I stared at him, I saw the shadow of a darkness cross his face. A shadow I'd seen on many men capable of many horrific things. As the finder of all things, I knew I'd hit the nail on the head. I wondered then just how much he was hiding beneath his calm, religious exterior.

Daithi started at Zaide, his eyes glowing and his hair bristling under the exhales of Zaide's flaring nostrils, not intimidated at all. Daithi scoffed, "You are welcome to try. My magic is faster than your fists, and you wouldn't get to touch me before I suffocate you like I did your soul pair."

Zaide's purple scars and eyes flashed dangerously, and I knew he was about to strike. I interrupted them before they came to blows. "Whoa! Guys, what the fuck did I say about friendship?"

I jumped between them, pushing them apart and hoping I didn't get a walloping in Daithi's place. They separated easily, and I knew deep down they didn't want to fight. They did care about each other. "You want to lose each other as well as your loves? Then fucking carry on."

Daithi moved backward and collapsed on a dining table chair. Zaide moved backward to lean his hulking mass against the back of the sofa, his arms crossed.

I continued, "If you want a plan to fix all of this, then let's talk, but I won't hang around watching you tear emotional chunks out of each other. Or real chunks either."

Tear emotional chunks. I'm a fucking poet.

Daithi's hands muffled his words as he moaned, "He isn't gone. I'd know. The witch might have delivered his fire, but it has not been extinguished."

I softened my voice. "That might be true, but we can't know for sure. What we do know is that Clawdia is Zaide's soul pair, and they should be together."

She should be with me. I saw her first. She was mine first.

But jealousy, like Daithi's anger, wouldn't get us anywhere, so I turned my attention back to the argument.

"I can't give up on him." Daithi sat back in his chair, folding his arms stubbornly, the hint of a pout forming on his lips.

I sighed. "I'm not saying you have to, but for fuck's sake, listen to logic. We have no clue who the witches delivered the fire to. There hasn't been a payment into their account for it. Nothing shows they are leaving soon, so I can only assume their job here isn't done. We need to get more information from them, and we need to get Clawdia back."

He shouted, "She is not the priority!" I almost expected him to stomp his foot like a fucking child, but he saw my glare and wisely stopped talking.

My temper, which was usually calm, flared to life. "She is while we have no information on Savida's fire!" I shouted back. I was suddenly angry at his selfishness, the single-minded arrogance. "You don't get to call the fucking shots around here when you don't have the first clue about how to get your demon back. Unless you're going to fall into a vision that tells us exactly where his fire is, you can shut the fuck up."

As soon as I popped the *p* on "up," Daithi dropped. His

eyes rolled back in his head, and the sound of his body hitting the floor was like the bang of a drum punctuating my last sentence.

I stared at my hands in wonder. "Zaide? Mate? Did you just see that? I'm a fucking superhero."

Zaide sighed and began rearranging Daithi's prone limbs to a more comfortable position. "You are not a superhero, Charlie. It is by coincidence that he has fallen into a vision. I was too furious to see the signs, the anxiousness and the twitching. And I was too late to catch him." He sighed heavily as he straightened. "What is becoming of us?"

"Well, I can't say I expected that, but it stopped you guys fighting, so that's a plus."

Zaide crossed his arms and huffed. "If we were fighting, he would be dead."

I laughed. "Big talk from the muscled, religious other-worlder. I'd have put my money on the magic elf ruining relationships left, right, and center so he can't get hurt like this again."

He eyed me curiously. "You are a very astute human. I don't believe it's a common trait of your kind."

"Are you saying I'm special? Because I might blush." I walked to the kitchen table.

"Just making my own observations."

"Well, look at us observing shit together. Makes my heart glow with happiness. It's the start of a true friendship." When Zaide came to sit with me at the table, I asked, "Are we just going to leave him there?" I eyed Daithi's body lying next to the other chair.

"He deserves to lie on the floor for being a Lagworm," Zaide huffed.

"What's that?"

"An animal that survives by eating his own waste." He grinned, and I chuckled.

"A shit-eating animal. Nice."

* * *

AN HOUR LATER, we sat on the sofa with snacks we had bought at a shop down the road from our hotel. I was munching my way through a packet of Revels like the wild-card that I am, while Zaide chose the respectable Maltesers. Daithi still lay prostrate on the floor by the table. The telly was on, but it was background noise.

I was too busy thinking about the mystery of our situation to be distracted by SpongeBob Fucking SquarePants.

"I can't wrap my head around all of this," I started.

Zaide didn't take his eyes off the screen. "I think the premise is that the yellow sponge creature is a cheerful fool who lives underwater and gets into trouble, but I admit I am struggling to understand it all, too."

I barked a laugh. "Not the show, you idiot."

"Ah, you mean the situation." He looked at me, silently prompting me to continue my thoughts.

"Clawdia is Winnie's familiar. She is also your soul pair. You guys come looking for her. Clawdia's witch steals Savi-da's fire for a project to do with this Norse legend."

"That is an accurate summary. What is your point?"

"What are the chances that Clawdia's soul pair was trav-eling with a demon? The very thing her witch needed for this project?"

He shrugged. "It is obvious fate and the gods have much to do with our path."

"I don't believe in fate or gods or predestined paths," I told him, waving a Revel around as I spoke. "But I also don't believe in coincidence."

"Those are contradictory statements."

"Zaide, I don't have time to be debating my philosophical beliefs. Can't you see I'm on the cusp of a breakthrough?"

"Ah, I apologize, Charlie. Please continue to extol your genius."

I grinned at his sarcasm and nodded graciously. "My point is, Clawdia seems to be at the center of it all but isn't actually involved."

"I agree." He threw a Malteser in the air and opened his mouth to catch it.

"Maybe that's because we haven't figured out exactly what her connection to this is. Maybe she has a Norse heritage? Maybe she's the descendant of the hero Sigurd. Maybe her past life before the 1900s was in a small village where she was raised by dragons. Maybe—"

"Charlie, you are getting carried away."

I sighed, my imagination deflated like a punctured wheel, and my tangent rolled to a stop. "The thing is, we don't know enough about her to find out how she's connected to the issues rather than being the catalyst. And I think answers lie in her past as a human."

We sat in silence as we let that idea ruminate in our minds.

Note to self: Ruminate. Great word. Must use more.

Zaide sighed and threw another Maltester in the air. He caught it in his mouth because he's a talented bastard and said quietly, "Well, we may not have the opportunity to ask now."

I frowned at him. "What do you mean? As soon as Daithi is awake from his vision, we're going to find her and bring her back."

He shook his head. "She might be a cat again."

"You think it's going to be that easy? Witches need spells. Words. Not just intention like Daithi. They aren't going to have a spell to help her."

"Oh."

"What does that mean?"

He sighed. "I don't know. I am glad she will be human, but I'm also sad she will not be getting what she wants, what she needs."

"She needs you, too. She just doesn't know it yet." My mouth said the words he needed to hear, but my mind didn't want to admit it.

He nodded. "Yes, our bond is not complete. It's why she is so conflicted."

"How do you complete the bond?" I asked curiously. I should have known better, because he blushed, and I put my hands up in surrender. "Okay, yep, I get it. I don't want to know."

He chuckled and then sighed. "Until then, her bond with her witch will be most prevalent and she will long to be with her, as they were."

I hummed thoughtfully. "Zaide, you said Clawdia was the other half of your soul, right? That means, before her past life as a human, she must have been a whole titan with your other half."

He nodded. "That's correct."

"Well, if I'd been stripped of power, then made so power-less in my human life that I killed myself, I'd probably prefer the life that gave me a part of that power back."

"You are right, Charlie. She feels the echoes of her past, and her bond with the witch has reconnected her with magic. It is understandable, her preference." His purple eyes lit up with understanding. But it didn't help us solve any more mysteries.

We sat in companionable silence as we munched more snacks.

"So, you kicked arse today. I have to say, although you're built for it, I didn't see that coming."

He looked at me sharply. "You do not think I am capable of or desire to protect my soul pair?"

I choked on a Revel. "No. God, no. You're more than capable, that's clear. You ... were a fighter?"

He nodded but said nothing else about his time as a slave. It probably didn't bring up good memories, and I felt like a worm for mentioning it. He sighed and told me earnestly. "I'm sorry if I alarmed you."

I gave a startled laugh. "It's okay. I was actually feeling a bit constipated from the traveling, but you've sorted me right out." I laughed again; however, my humor was wasted on my audience.

"Constipated?"

"The opposite of diarrhea."

"You cannot shit?" I laughed at the horror on his face. "Charlie, you said there weren't curses, but I don't believe you. That is a curse." He tilted his head back to stare at the ceiling. A small clunk sounded as the charm on the end of his braid hit the floor. "We are cursed."

And thinking about all the bad things that had happened, I agreed with him.

* * *

We fell asleep there, our heads tilted back, our snores making a symphony, our legs stretched out on the coffee table in front of the sofa. It's also where we woke up when Daithi shouted, "I know where she is!"

We jolted to awareness and turned to see him sitting up and rubbing a sore shoulder. I didn't have to look at Zaide to see his smugness.

"Who?" I asked. "Clawdia?"

He nodded. "And the witches."

"Okay, where?"

Daithi closed his eyes. "It's a hotel near to the coffeehouse we visited today. It's called Best Western Plaza Hotel."

"I'll go get her," I said.

"You do not want me to come with you?" Zaide asked curiously.

"I'm going to be far stealthier without a golden giant following me around." I headed toward the door, keys in hand and adrenaline increasing production inside me. "You stay here, rest, and read. We need to know more about their practice, abilities, and familiars to get an advantage." With a hand on the handle, I turned to look at them both. "And for fuck's sake, please don't kill each other while I'm gone."

CHAPTER 20

CLAWDIA

*W*innie sat in the back of the car with me, holding my hand. I could feel her concern through our bond, and it was nice to know she still cared. Genuinely cared.

As we drove away, I saw Charlie, Daithi, and Zaide still locked in their cage, staring after us. Leaving them was hard. Surprisingly so. I didn't realize how much I cared for Zaide and Charlie until I no longer felt Zaide's protective air or saw Charlie's cheeky smile.

Mary turned the radio down and finally spoke, "What the fuck happened, Winnie? How is your familiar human?"

"That's a good question," Winnie replied. She squeezed my hand and peered at me behind long eyelashes. "Do you feel comfortable answering it?"

"I don't know what happened exactly." I sighed, sagging into the seat, and pulled my hand from Winnie's to bury my face in them. "There was a glowing light that came from Daithi," I said without thinking. "And then I was asleep and woke up human."

When I heard myself say the words again in my head, I

gasped. I told them his name. His powers. I could have put him in danger, just like I did when I told Winnie about Savida.

Why should I care if he's in danger? He almost killed me. He was happy to sacrifice me.

I shook my head. I was so angry with Daithi, and more than angry, I was hurt, physically and emotionally. But I would not let my anger dictate my actions. I wouldn't knowingly endanger him or the others. I swallowed and swore to myself I'd be more careful. Exhaustion and a near-death experience were not an excuse.

Mary, of course, leaped on the information. "Daithi is the one who has the magic? The one who made his friends look different?"

Winnie interrupted, saving me from a response, "They haven't ... touched you or anything?"

Touched me? I had flashes of the trafficking poster in the airport bathroom. *She thinks they are hurting me?* Her concern was heartwarming, but it upset me that she assumed they were evil just because they were different.

"No!" I exclaimed, then hesitated before continuing, "They aren't bad people. One of them combs my hair and holds me when I am stressed." I opened my mouth to tell her more of the many kind things Zaide has done in the short time that I have known him. How he lets me hold his hair. How he rescued me from kidnappers only hours ago and promised to always save me.

I wanted to talk to her like I used to, like we were sisters. But everything had changed. And just because I was feeling vulnerable and tired didn't mean I had forgiven her. On the contrary. She had a lot of making up to do when this was all over. I wasn't here to gossip about my adventures. I was here for information to feed back to the others so they could save Savida.

Get information, get it to the others, save Savida. Then I can figure out how to be a cat again and how to repair the broken trust between Winnie and me.

She sighed, relaxing into the leather seat. "Good. I would have felt really guilty about leaving them with you if they had mistreated you."

"The magical one almost killed you both." Mary reminded us with her eyebrows raised, her eyes staring back at us through the rearview mirror.

"I didn't consider the risk that you would get hurt because of me." Winnie closed her eyes, regret etched into her features. "I shouldn't have left you alone. They turned you human to hurt me."

You shouldn't have started dating Mary. You shouldn't have started this project. You shouldn't have drugged me, stolen Savida's fire, and started this whole mess. My bitterness poisoned my thoughts, but I wouldn't let them spill out and ruin my plans. I took a deep breath.

"Daithi is grieving for his lover. He has been ... unpleasant but not cruel. The others have been really kind," I insisted, not mentioning their names even though they knew one was Charlie.

Mary rolled her eyes. "If they were nice, it was only to get information out of you about us."

No, they are good people. Unlike you. It was then that I realized I was talking to Mary. Mary, who had treated me like an unimportant pet. Who had just revealed my most painful and shameful secret and laughed as she did.

I gritted my teeth against all the nasty things I wanted to say. Past and present.

Ignoring her, I looked at Winnie, crossing my arms and raising my brows. "Are you being kind to get information from me about them?"

Winnie's mouth dropped open, and hurt flickered in her

eyes. "Clawdia, you're my familiar, and I love you. I'm worried about you."

Blinking back tears, I glanced up at the roof of the car and my lips pursed. I wanted to trust her. Believe in her. Feel the love she'd shown me for the last two years. But she hurt me when she was the only person in the world who wouldn't.

She continued, "I won't ask anything more about them if that's what it takes to get you to trust me again. I'm so sorry."

I shook my head. "You aren't sorry."

"I am."

I whispered, "No, you're sorry you got caught. You are not sorry for doing what you did, and you aren't trying to fix it."

"You don't understand. I can't stop now," she whispered. Her brown eyes pleaded with me, but I couldn't understand what she couldn't tell me. I shook my head in disappointment.

She sighed. "I will make it up to you. When this is all over, I'll explain why this had to happen, and you'll understand. And I'll help you turn back." I was quiet. I wanted her to believe that returning to my feline form was the sole reason I was with her. "If that's what you want."

"You can't want her to stay this way! A familiar isn't supposed to be a human," Mary exclaimed.

"I won't do anything she doesn't want," Winnie said firmly, not taking her eyes off me. "She's had enough of that already."

Memories flashed in one long, horrific second, and I relived everything that had brought me to this moment. The power taken from me. My independence stripped. I lost my life. My entire world gone and then turned upside down when I arrived as Winnie's familiar. My human body became a memory, but the trauma of my past still followed me.

Only for it to happen all over again when a faei accidentally turned me human.

Nothing that happened was within my control, and the powerlessness of the situation only made me feel more useless. Just like my father believed I was.

My lips trembled, and with a quick intake of breath, I started crying. Winnie stroked my hair and made comforting noises, and eventually, I could stop the heaving sobs.

This is the first time you've chosen to do something. You're finding out information to report to the others. Pull yourself together, and prove everyone wrong. You can do this.

"Think about it. You don't need to decide now," she said. I nodded and pulled out of her arms, wiping away my tears. She continued, "If you want to be a cat again, we'll find a way to turn you back. We've got a huge gathering of witches here for an event, so we can talk to them and see if they have any ideas about how to turn you back. We could even try using the fire."

My ears pricked up.

An event. Lots of witches. Lots of fire?

I replayed her words in my head.

Use the fire to turn me back?

The very thought that a demon would lose his fire to turn me back turned my stomach. That someone's friend, lover, sibling, or parent would die because of me was horrifying.

Mary and Winnie didn't view Savida as a person. They didn't see the fire as anything but a source of power to be harvested. Just something to be used. It made me wonder whether my ability as a familiar, how I supported their magic, put me in the same category as demons. I protested, "I don't—"

Mary interrupted, "Win, look, I don't think you should promise anything you might not be able to do."

"What do you mean?"

231

"I'm just saying that they have planned this event for many, many years, and this collection of fire has taken years and years to reap. I don't think the witch council is going to let you use the fire to fix your familiar."

Winnie twisted her fingers and looked down. "They might," she said slowly, hesitantly, like even she didn't believe her own words.

"She's not as important as the other stuff we have going on," Mary said sternly and glared at Winnie through the rearview mirror.

Winnie shook her head in denial, her red curls bouncing. "There isn't anything more important than Clawdia."

My heart swelled at the exclamation, but actions spoke louder than words. I knew that when push had come to shove, she hadn't chosen me.

She continued, "And it never hurts to ask. Even if we can't use the fire, we can find another way. Maybe capture those guys and force them to turn her back." I frowned and shook my head. I didn't want Daithi, Zaide and Charlie to end up like Savida. Winnie noticed my unhappiness and said, "I wouldn't hurt them, but if it turns you back, wouldn't that make you happy?"

I stayed silent. It wouldn't make me happy.

"We can't afford to use any extra energy, Win. We're going to need to put almost all our magic into the reservoir. You can't promise to fix her."

We were all quiet for a moment. The only sound was ticking of the indicator as we turned into a hotel car park. Pulling the handbrake and turning off the car, Mary turned to us and waved us out. "I'm going to call Debbie."

Winnie led me to the lift in the lobby, which took us to her room. The door clicked shut behind us, and the sound echoed in the silence. I sighed and sat on the bed, unsure of what to do now. I still didn't know why she was doing this or where Savida's fire was, so I kept up the ruse.

Winnie whispered, "Are you really okay?"

I shrugged. "I hate being human again, but they didn't hurt me. They just want their friend back."

"I want to ask you about them." She saw my narrowed eyes and continued, "I won't, though."

She threw her bag on the bed, and I asked, "Why are you doing this? Is this ... project ... something you really want?"

She sighed. "There's a lot you don't know about me, Clawd, but trust me when I tell you I need this."

"But why?"

She sat on a chair by the desk and mirror and began taking off her shoes as she spoke. "You know, growing up black isn't easy. You're on the fringes of society even if everyone pretends you're not. Being a black lesbian, that's even worse. You're in your own bubble, watching from the outside. When I found my father, he told me I had witch blood. At first, I didn't want it. I didn't want to be even more different. He gave me books and a contact for someone who could teach me, and when he died, I got in touch with them.

"I found a community that didn't care about my skin or my sexual preferences. They cared about power, and that was something I could work on. Did you know I am the third witch in my coven to call a familiar? It takes an awful lot of magic, practice, and sacrifices. I poured myself into casting to make sure I could excel in this community. I was finally successful when I got you, and that was proof to a lot of the senior coven members that I was ready to learn more. Be part of something bigger. When I met Mary, her enthusiasm lit a fire in me. I need this now. I need to prove myself."

I shook my head, confused. As far as I could tell, she had done nothing of worth as a witch. Even my existence was to show off to the others. "Prove yourself to be what? A monster? Because you are taking the lives of innocent beings and using them for something. Can't you see that it's wrong?"

"You think I'm a monster?" I could feel her hurt and rejoiced. It meant I could still save her. Still convince her to stop this.

"Savida didn't deserve what you did to him." I turned my nose up and looked away from her so she could see the depths of my disgust and the disappointment.

She was silent for a moment before she whispered, "You are so beautiful, Clawdia. I always thought you would be."

Then she whispered something, and when my eyes got heavy, I knew she'd spelled me to sleep. I wasn't surprised.

* * *

IT FELT like only minutes later when I woke up, but the room was significantly darker. I heard the door open, then footsteps and voices. I was sleepy and disoriented. Too disorientated to feel ready for interaction.

"This is her?" I heard, and my bleary eyes caught sight of a tall woman with blond hair tied in a neat bun on her head. She had a deep voice and a sturdy body. Alertness flashed through me, and adrenaline began pumping around my body. I sat up quickly and assessed the situation.

"This is my familiar, Clawdia. Clawdia, this is Debbie. She's going to see if she can help us," Winnie said, coming around to the side of the woman. I noticed the difference in her words; there wasn't any certainty or promise in them anymore.

"You are usually a cat, are you not?" Debbie asked. I nodded. "How is it you are human?"

"I don't know," I lied.

"Don't lie to me, or I will spell the truth from you," she

sneered, her calm facade falling away to reveal an ugly, desperate woman.

She pulled a book from her handbag, turning to a dog-eared page. "Did the male who changed you look similar to this?"

She showed me a picture of someone very similar to Daithi, except they had different hair and eye color. I couldn't let her spell me, or I wouldn't be able to control what I told her. I needed to be honest, but not completely. Hesitantly, I nodded.

She turned to Winnie. "It is as I suspected. A faei. They are a powerful and ancient race that has visited our world throughout the ages. You could not see the group's true forms because the faei can create impenetrable glamours which disguise them. Faei cause a lot of upheaval. If we have a faei looking for the fire, we can expect they will try very hard to stop our event and may even succeed. You will need to stop them however you can."

I almost felt proud they were so concerned the guys were going to crash their event and take back Savida's fire. I laughed to myself.

Be afraid. Daithi is going to make you suffer.

"Stop them? How?" Winnie asked.

"By whatever means necessary," Debbie insisted. "This event has been centuries in the making and is essential to our survival now. We can't afford to have any threats."

"The quickest way to get rid of them would be to give back the fire of their demon friend," Winnie noted hesitantly.

The tall lady seemed to grow, and her voice deepened even more. "For centuries, witches have been summoning demons, capturing them, and burying them in the earth for this moment. Witches who knew they wouldn't be alive to see this. They wouldn't get to witness the rising of a legend. But they persevered, and because of their efforts, we have reaped enough fire for our mission." She paused in her rant to lower her voice to a threatening whisper. "I will not be handing over any of the hard-earned fire to otherworlder terrorists. Do I make myself clear?"

Winnie's voice quivered when she replied, "Yes, mam."

"Good." She shrank to her normally large size, and her tone was cheery again. I remained frozen on the bed, watching, listening, trying not to tremble in fear at the terrifying lady in front of me. "I will need you and Mary to sort out this problem for me. I can call more witches to add their power to the reservoir, and you can add anything you can spare after you've dispatched the faei."

"What about the others?" Winnie asked.

Debbie turned to me, and I stiffened under her icy gaze. "The other two males are not faei, are they?" I shook my head. "Do you know what they are?" I shook my head again, promising to keep Charlie and Zaide safe from her.

She tilted her head as she stared at me. "Someone broke into my house a few days ago. My casting room was discovered, and the bad luck curse I used to punish such fools has been activated." She narrowed her eyes. "I don't suppose you know anything about that either, do you?"

I shook my head.

She cursed Charlie and Daithi with bad luck?

"Why are you protecting them, familiar? Your loyalty should be to your witch. In the old days, we'd have separated you from her and killed you for your treachery."

Winnie gasped and jumped to my defense. I didn't know if that was to protect me or to protect herself. I wasn't sure what breaking a familiar bond did to a witch, but I didn't think it was pleasant. "She knows nothing about it, Deb. We won't need to be separated."

She eyed us both suspiciously. "I have a book on the

subject if you change your mind. I think she needs to be properly punished, Winnie."

Thinking quickly, Winnie added, "Perhaps the faei has cast a spell on her, making her silent. I can't punish her for that."

"Very well. She is your familiar. Do as you see fit." I flinched as she glared at me. "However, if she causes any more upheaval, I will separate you, and there will be nothing you can do to stop me. As for this spell of silence ..." She grabbed my arm and squeezed tightly.

I made a noise of protest and tried to move out of her grip, but Winnie held me, too. Debbie's eyes were closed, and I could suddenly feel her magic spreading through me, rifling through my brain, seeking answers. It hurt. It was a violation. My body revolted as I struggled underneath her. Fury flooded me and I tried to push her magic out, to no avail. I was so tired of being a victim, of being taken advantage of, of being out of control.

The witch opened her eyes, let go of my arm abruptly, and hummed. "Human and titan. That's what the other two are."

Winnie's eyes shuttered over her emotions, and she turned to Debbie. "What do you want me to do with them?"

Debbie considered that for a moment. "If a human goes missing, you might get yourself in trouble with the police, and that will take more time and magic to fix than we can spare. I suggest you erase his memory and kill the titan. See if there is anything harvestable from his corpse for a potion." I felt sick at the picture she painted.

Not going to happen.

Winnie nodded, but it was not enough for her leader.

"Swear it to me."

"When I see the faei and titan, I will kill them. When I see the human, I'll erase his memory." There was a subtle glow coming from her chest. "By magic of old, it will be done."

Debbie smiled when she saw it. "By magic of vow, you are bound. Death is your punishment should you fail," she replied and clapped her hands jubilantly. I flinched. "Well, I'm glad to have gotten that sorted. If successful, you and Mary will be an important part in ensuring this event goes smoothly. Witches years into the future will know your names, and I'm sure that once he has risen, he will want to give you his thanks."

Winnie nodded meekly before asking, "What about Clawdia? Can we help her?" My heart burst with hope and happiness. She hadn't forgotten about me and, despite her fear, asked this terrifying witch to help me. I didn't want to be a cat when I still had a promise to keep, but it was the thought that counted.

I was a little less appreciative when Debbie turned her dark, intense eyes to focus on me. "She seems settled in her new form," she finally said after a period of silence, dismissing me. "I'm afraid there isn't anything we can do for you. You will need to get used to being human."

Nothing they can do? I'll be human forevermore?

"But I—"

"You were a cat, but if you were not meant to be human, you would not be. A faei's magic cannot completely reshape a being. You are human now. A human familiar. Enjoy." And with that, she turned to the door. Before closing it, she peered her head around again and said, "Winnie, I will expect updates on your progress with our terrorists. Do me proud, dear."

The slam of the door had both of us flinching.

Winnie crawled onto the bed beside me. "I'm sorry, Clawd. I really thought she'd be able to help. Now we are in even more trouble."

"It's okay," I whispered. It would be okay because I had information now. I could help. I just had to get back to them. I wouldn't stand by and watch as Winnie killed Daithi and Zaide or erase Charlie's memories.

But now I was left with a horrible conflict inside me. Did I stop my witch from completing her sworn mission, which would lead to both our deaths? Or did I betray the others by allowing my witch to hunt them down? Neither option sat well with me, but I had to do something.

When I heard the soft breath of Winnie next to me sleeping, I took my chance. Slowly, I rolled off the bed and then moved as quietly as a hunting cat to the door of the hotel room. I peeked outside for any sign of Mary or Debbie and then ran to reach the stairs before anyone knew I was gone.

CHAPTER 21

CLAWDIA

*C*reeping from the hotel, I kept close to the building, my eyes scanning the area for anyone who might stop me. The rising sun cast the car park in shadows, which made me more paranoid.

I didn't know how I would get back. I scanned the car park, looking for a taxi or someone who could help, hoping I could get them to take me back to the apartment and get Charlie to pay when I arrived. I decided to walk the way we drove until someone passed me.

Suddenly, someone pulled me back into the shadows of the building, one hand against my mouth and the other wrapped around my waist.

Not again!

I tried to scream and wiggle away.

The man shushed me. "Clawdia, stop."

Charlie! I sagged in his arms. *Thank God.*

Hidden behind a large green bin, he set me down and turned me to face him. He ran his hands up and down my arms. "Are you okay?"

I slapped his chest. "Someone already kidnapped me

yesterday. I didn't need to relive that. Why did you think that was a good idea?" I hissed.

He looked surprised and rubbed his chest. "First, ow, Clawdia. And second, I'm trying to rescue you. This is the thanks I get?"

"Rescue me? No. I'm rescuing myself," I scoffed and crossed my arms.

"What?" His handsome face turned puzzled.

"I've just run away. I'm coming back with you," I informed him.

It was his turn to scoff. "Well, of course you are. Because I'm rescuing you."

I rolled my eyes. "You're being pedantic."

"Big word. Was that on your 'Word of the Day' calendar today?"

The playfulness fell out of my voice as I thought about everything that had happened. "I didn't have anything that happened today on my calendar."

He sighed, matching my seriousness, and took my hand. "Come on, let's get you back to the others. Zaide has been a wreck. He almost killed Daithi for what he did to you."

Awww, that cute golden giant!

I smiled. "He is very protective of me."

"That's an understatement."

Getting into the car, I clicked my seat belt in place and then we were off.

"So, what happened? You're still a human, I notice."

I glared at the side of his head, which was focused on the road. "Yes, I'm sorry to disappoint you, Charlie. Clawdicat might never come back." He threw me a quick glance, an eyebrow raised.

There was a pregnant pause before he shook his head. "I want to know why you think that, but first, I want to apologize. I shouldn't have said what I did about the Clawdicat and

Clawdia debacle. I hurt you when you were already feeling like shit, and that's not okay."

I sighed and sagged into the car seat. "Charlie, you don't have to apologize. I understand. I can't imagine how strange it must be for you."

"See, that's the thing. It is strange, and it's also not. I've been without Clawdicat for a few days now. It might be because I've not been at home and haven't had time, but I haven't missed her. Some part of me has easily accepted that you are one and the same. You are Clawdicat. And I've not been treating you like you are, so I'm sorry."

I didn't know what to say, so I said nothing. The sound of the car engine was the only noise filling the silence.

He knew she was me? What did that mean? He liked Clawdia and Clawdicat?

I was so confused, and referring to myself in third person was making it harder to make sense of it all.

After a little while, I laughed.

"What?" he asked.

"You said you hadn't been treating me like Clawdicat. Then I imagined you trying to shoo me out of a room or tell me to move off something while I'm human. It entertained me."

He laughed too. "I think you'd be more obedient as a human."

"Probably," I agreed.

"Did you ignore me to wind me up?"

I laughed. "Made the days go faster, I suppose."

He chuckled and asked, "Do you remember when you knocked over that statue Lydia bought me for Christmas? That abstract kangaroo one?"

I nodded. "You shouted at me." A playful pout stopped me from grinning.

"I had to. Lydia was watching." He gave me an apologetic

look but then grinned. "But I was so glad you smashed it. It was fucking hideous. Looked like a cock and balls."

I laughed and jumped in my seat. "I knew it! I knew you weren't angry. Your lips were twitching."

Charlie's half grin at my enthusiastic response made a flush rise to my cheeks. "Weird to think you were you and not an annoying house cat."

"They aren't mutually exclusive." I raised a brow and smirked, my confidence rising after completing my self-assigned spy task and remembering my cheeky cat persona.

Bantering with Charlie was everything I'd wanted for the past two years. I loved it. It was exactly as I imagined.

I knew him. I'd spent time with him and replied to everything he'd ever said, but until now, he'd never heard that. And the appreciation I saw in his eyes made me feel amazing.

"Clearly." He chuckled and then frowned. "I felt terrible because you didn't come round for ages after that."

"I couldn't. I was getting too—" I stopped, swallowing the word that almost escaped.

Jealous.

He stared at me funny, clearly curious, but a sizzling sound interrupted his thoughts, and he looked out the window. Smoke rose from the bonnet, and the car suddenly jolted with three coughs, throwing both of us forward. Charlie's arm swung out across my seat to help the seat belt keep me inside the vehicle.

"What happened?" I asked, as the car stopped.

Charlie's eyes were dark and angry. "Fuck!" he shouted and banged the steering wheel. "Why is nothing simple?" He got out of the car and stomped toward the bonnet. Steam erupted as he opened it. He coughed and turned his face away.

"Shit." He looked at where I was hovering by the

passenger door. "You know, I think the guys are right. Maybe we are cursed."

I gasped as I remembered what Debbie had said. "Charlie, you might be."

His brow furrowed. "You don't need to sound so excited about it."

"No. Debbie, the leader witch, was there tonight. She said there was a bad luck curse on anyone who went into her witch space. She asked if I knew anything about it."

"You're fucking joking," he growled.

"No. You really are cursed."

"Fucking witches," he yelled into the forest. I laughed, and he glared. "This isn't funny."

"It is a bit." I smirked.

"How the fuck are we supposed to beat these bitches if luck isn't on my side?" He paced, running his hand through his hair as he often did when he was stressed.

"It must run out at some point." But that was a guess. Surely bad luck was only temporary.

"Really? Because things have only been getting worse." He slammed the bonnet closed and pulled his phone out of his pocket.

"I think my bad luck and your bad luck are different," I remarked wryly.

"And of course. There's no pissing signal," he exclaimed, waving his hands dramatically. Pining me with a stare, he asked, "How do we get rid of bad luck?"

"You get good luck?" I asked because I had no idea, but it made sense.

"Yes!" he said excitedly. "Okay, okay, what gives you good luck?" He tilted his head back and stared at the sky for inspiration. "Clover!" I laughed at his enthusiasm and watched him as he rubbed his hands together and strode determinedly to the edge of the forest. "Come on, finder of all things. Find me a four-leaf clover."

"Good luck, Charlie!" I shouted, hoping it helped.

He scoured the grass and the moss and the mud for ten minutes, using his phone as a torch, before he cheered his victory and ran back to me, holding his prize. "A four-leaf clover." He presented it to me.

I shook my head and got back into the car. "It's your luck. You need it."

He hopped into the driver's seat. "I think we all need it." He turned the key in the ignition and cheered and waved his four-leaf clover when the car growled and sputtered to life.

I just hope his good luck lasted longer than the bad.

* * *

WHEN WE GOT BACK to the apartment, Daithi was sitting in the living room, reading. He put the book down when we entered and turned eagerly. "You found her! The witches?"

"I have her," Charlie told him. "But she 'rescued' herself."

Zaide's door slammed open, and he raced toward me. He spun me around and cuddled me close, sighing like he'd been holding his breath until now. When he set me down, he looked me up and down. "Little Cat! Thank the gods you are all right," he said reverently. "You are all right, aren't you?" He looked me up and down again.

I smiled at his concern. "I'm fine," I assured him.

Daithi stared at me, one brow slightly raised. "They were unsuccessful in changing you back?"

No apology for almost killing me and Winnie. Just a reminder that I was not what I wanted to be.

"They didn't try, and they told me it would be impossible," I told him emotionlessly.

Zaide squeezed my hand in sympathy. "I'm sorry, Little

Cat. I know you don't want to be human. But I am glad to spend more time talking to you, and perhaps you will find happiness." I offered him a shy smile.

Daithi scoffed and raised an accusing brow. "Is that why you are back? To ask me for my help?"

I gritted my teeth. His arrogance had no end. "No, I'm back because I have information you need. I want to save Savida."

"Now's a good time to tell us what you learned, spymaster cat," Charlie said, throwing himself onto the sofa.

"I don't know where to start." I shook my head and sat down. "There's an event happening. I don't know what it is exactly, but it sounded like it's been something the witches have wanted to do for centuries. They have been summoning demons like Savida and burying them on Earth so they could reap them of their fire for this event. Now they finally have enough fire and magic."

There was a gasp around the room. "I found Savida here," Daithi said in shock. "In this world, buried. He was always meant for this horror."

"No," Charlie stopped him in his self-destructive path. "He was always meant to help stop whatever this event is."

"How can he stop anything when he is fireless?"

Charlie sat up and stared at him, his tone serious. "He has a lover who will do anything for him and anything to get him back. He needs you to end this, Daithi."

Daithi's eyes glittered with unshed tears, but he closed his eyes and nodded his thanks to Charlie.

I began again, "They are afraid of you. They know what you are and that you could stop them. They really don't want that to happen. So, they've sworn Winnie with the task of killing you. And Zaide."

"Not me?" Charlie asked, annoyed.

I tried to stop the smile blooming on my face at his

offence of being left off the murder list. "They don't want to get in trouble with the police, so they've decided just to erase your memories."

Charlie scoffed. "Well, that's rude. Bastards."

Daithi glared. "How did they know what I was?"

"The leader witch, Debbie, had a book with a picture of someone of your race," I whispered. "She asked me if it was you who turned me human."

He was furious. His eyes flashed, and there was a stir of magic in the air. "You've given away any advantage we had."

I defended myself even though my knees were shaking and my palms were sweating. "I couldn't tell them nothing!"

"You could have told them we were all humans."

"A human couldn't have done this to me. Besides, they already knew you were all otherworlders from the moment you came to Charlie's."

Daithi wasn't listening. His temper had taken control of him, and he ranted, "You are so selfish. You only want to be a cat again. They couldn't fix you, so you've come crawling back to us."

Fury and confusion and fear sparked in my head. "I went with them to get information, despite the fact you tried to kill me. I promised to help save Savida," I shouted. "I came back to warn you!"

"You came back because you think trading this information is going to make me want to turn you back. Well, my apologies, but thanks to your thoughtlessness, I'm going to be too busy using my magic to save us from your witches. You'll have to make do for now."

It did not surprise me at how dishonest and deceitful he thought I was. It disappointed me, though.

I crossed my arms protectively and held back tears. "I didn't ask you to turn me back. Even though you hate me, I don't want to see you die."

"Your warning is unnecessary and ridiculous. Like a witch would win a fight against a faei," he scoffed, derision on his face.

"They won against a demon," Zaide said softly.

"And there are a lot of witches around for the event. Debbie said she would use their powers too," I added.

Charlie stepped in. "That's why we're here. Stop fighting with everyone, Daithi. We know you're grieving, but if you want to see Savida alive again, you need to work with us."

The fight in Daithi's shoulders left, and he settled deeper into the cushions on the sofa. His eyes shut.

The silence that bounced around the room was uncomfortable.

Even when I try to do right, I'm wrong.

Finally, he spoke, "Forgive me. I realize I am losing my temper, being cruel, and taking my frustrations out on you all. I do not hate you, Clawdia, I do not know you. You have given us this information in order for us to survive and rescue Savida's fire, and I appreciate that."

I didn't trust his apology, so I didn't acknowledge it. I knew as soon as he found something else I said or did offensive, he would strike again.

Zaide moved closer to me on the sofa and asked softly, "Did they say what this event was, Little Cat?"

I swallowed. "Not exactly. Debbie said that if Winnie was to kill you, that witches would remember them until the end of time and that *he* would want to thank them when he rises."

"Who is *he*?" Daithi asked.

I shrugged. "I don't know."

Charlie hummed, considering the puzzle. "They're trying to raise someone from the dead?"

"What has led you to that conclusion?" Zaide asked.

Charlie shrugged and said, "'When he rises' just sounds very *Buffy the Vampire Slayer*."

"Can fire raise the dead?" I asked, horrified at the thought. Zombie movies I watched as a cat flashed in my mind, and I shuddered.

"Yes. It can do anything if you have enough of it. And clearly, they do." Daithi looked a little shell-shocked. "Did they say anything about where they are storing the fire?"

I shook my head. "No, they didn't say."

"We need to get it back before they use it. Did they say anything about the timescale of this event?" Daithi seemed panicked now, his hands twisting in his lap while his face displayed a fraction of emotion, his chest rising and falling quickly.

I sympathized and told him what I knew. "I got the impression that it was soon. Winnie and Mary had been told not to use their magic because they are going to be pouring as much as they can into this reservoir."

Daithi looked horrified. "What are they raising with that much magic?"

"That's what we'll have to figure out," Charlie said.

"How? How do we figure out who they want to raise?"

"I don't know. Maybe there's a witch forum online that I can monitor for information about this event?" Charlie shrugged. "If worse comes to worst, we'll try to grab one and make them talk."

Daithi shook his head, his green hair swinging with the action. "That is very dark for you, Charlie. I don't think it will come to that. Your ways are more underhanded than that."

"I prefer underhanded, but I have experience in both."

Zaide interrupted that thought. "What about the books? Has anything of interest come from there?"

Daithi shook his head. "Nothing I believe to be beneficial. It talks about the steps in learning to cast spells."

Charlie groaned. "If we just had some clue where the

event was going to happen, we could do some digging. Literally. If they've got no body, they can't raise it right?"

"If they are using fire they have collected for centuries and their own magic, I suspect they are going to raise something skeletal. They need the magic to reform the body."

"Okay, I can look into that. There's not much to go on, but maybe something will ring a bell when I see it." He flipped his laptop open, rubbed his eyes, and sighed.

We need a miracle, I thought as I leaned my head back against the sofa and stared at the white ceiling. Sighing, the effects of the worst day ever settled into me like a winter chill, and I rubbed at my temples, trying to massage a headache away.

Zaide was staring at me from across the table. "You are unwell?"

I shook my head. "Just tired."

He nodded slowly, a deep sadness in his purple eyes. "You are tired of being human, are you not, Little Cat?"

It was a feeling I was sure everyone had. Where existing is too much, where thinking hurts, and emotions are battling a weakened sense of self. Where all you want to do is go to sleep and hope the next day is better.

It wasn't so much about not being human and being a cat, but about escaping the humanness of human life. That's what I wanted.

I nodded and sighed again. "Yes," I replied simply.

He nodded. "You suffered as a human."

Charlie, who was sitting next to him, closed his laptop gently and added, "We have a theory that you are the center of all of this, but we can't pin down how."

"What do you mean?" I asked as Daithi closed his book and leaned in to listen to Charlie.

"It's all very coincidental the way this has happened. I

don't believe in coincidences. We think the answers lie in your past."

"My past?" I scrunched my face up. "Why do you think that?"

"Are you Norse, by any chance?"

I shook my head. "No."

"There is a connection. I can feel it," Charlie mumbled.

Zaide whispered, "We would like to hear your story, if you would tell it to us."

My story? My breath stuttered at the thought of telling them.

I glanced at Charlie's curious brown eyes and Zaide's kind purple orbs. Being vulnerable in front of them would be hard but not impossible. They'd shared parts of their stories with me. They had their own trauma and understood mine.

Daithi hearing anything he could use against me sent my heart racing with fear.

But if it helped them figure out how I fit into this mess …

I took a deep breath and traveled a hundred years into the past.

CHAPTER 22

MARGARET CLAUDIA

FRIDAY 8TH JULY 1921

*M*y mother pulled a gown over my head, and my shoulder ached as she pulled my hands through. I didn't have the strength to stop her, my voice raw from screaming and pleading. Nor did I have the strength to dress myself. My head swam every time I lifted it, and my body felt so heavy that I could drop through the cracks in my wooden floor.

She dragged a comb through my hair like she used to when I was a child. The reminder of our past relationship caused a pang of sorrow to hit the walls of numbness surrounding my heart. A tear slipped from my eye.

But just one. They hadn't given me water for two days, so I couldn't afford to waste what little I had on tears.

Ribbon wrapped around my hair, and Mother tied a bow. I was gift-wrapped. A prized mare. A pig, seasoned and cooked, placed in the middle of a banquet table with an apple in its mouth.

Yet I could do nothing.

"Is she ready?" my father asked from outside the room.

"She is," my mother replied.

She fluffed my hair once more before my father pushed the door open and stomped inside. I didn't look up. I stared at my lap, my head too pained, too fuzzy, and too heavy to lift.

He clapped his hands. With a joyous tone to his voice, he said, "Well, let's get going, then. There's a car outside waiting." When I didn't stand from the dressing table, he snapped, "Claudia, you will not disobey me today. Get up. Now."

"I-I can't." My words were a stuttered, slurred whisper, which made me cringe.

"You can't?" he asked, then screamed, "You can't?"

If I could think clearly, I would have been terrified. Some small part of me was. But my mind was slow, and I couldn't hear that small part. I could barely hold my eyes open.

"My love, perhaps we should give her something to eat and drink before the wedding," I heard my mother implore.

"She hasn't said 'I do.'"

"She can barely walk or talk. She's so weak. It will be humiliating for us if she isn't able to go through with this."

I whimpered, and my eyes blurred with tears that didn't fall. I knew food and water would make me feel better, but I couldn't feel the urge for either anymore. And if they delayed the wedding because I was too weak to stand, I would spend more time locked in this room, screaming, starving, slowly dying and praying for escape.

My father huffed. "She can eat and drink in the car. Prepare her something now."

I heard my mother's shoes tapping quickly out of the room and down the stairs.

A hand grabbed my hair and pulled my head back. I gasped at the pain and opened my eyes. My father stared down at me, snarling. "I don't care how weak you are. You will walk down that aisle, you will say 'I do,' and you will lie in your marriage bed with your legs spread and please your husband. If you do not please him, he will have no reason not to share you with his friends." He let go of my hair and pushed my head forward. I stopped it from hitting the dressing table. "It's your choice, Claudia."

I don't remember much about the journey to the courthouse. Father dragged me down the stairs and into the car. Mother handed me a sandwich and water, which I gulped down. My stomach felt sore, but the throbbing in my head lessened ever so slightly.

Unfortunately, a clearer head meant that the fear I couldn't think about slipped into my mind like a snake and poisoned everything.

Like a lamb going to slaughter, they had set me free of my room and could beat and abuse me no longer, but I was trading one cage for an even worse prison.

While the journey was a blur, I remember walking into the courthouse in vivid detail. My mother shoving a bouquet in my hand and pulling my arm to wrap through my father's. She walked down the aisle to take her seat at the front.

I remember my father's tight grip on my hand, which was sweating and trembling.

I remember the white empty chairs and the smell of the roses in my hand. My dress itched and scratched over my skin and bones as though ants covered me instead of white lace. There was a roaring silence in the room, yet my heartbeat sounded like drums in my ears. My breathing was shallow. I counted down my steps as I walked toward the man standing by the officiant.

He was well dressed, well-groomed, and looked to be the perfect gentleman, but his black eyes and twisted smile were cruel. I swallowed thickly, looked away, and held back a shudder.

I was glad we weren't at a church. I didn't want God to see this, although I was sure He had abandoned me a long time ago. Praying in my bedroom was a habit rather than a cry for help. I didn't expect Him to help. After all, if my father could treat me so poorly, why wouldn't my Heavenly Father?

My father transferred my hands from his to my soon-to-be husband's, and at their icy touch, I gritted my teeth and tried not to flinch.

His smile widened, and my heart cried as that horrible pulling sensation started. My legs, already weak, wobbled and gave Mr. Jenkins an excuse to pull me into his arms with a laugh and whisper, "So much fun."

Bile rose in my throat as he righted me, and I spent the rest of the ceremony concentrating on not vomiting. I repeated words with a cracked voice. I signed a paper with a trembling hand. Two other people signed it too, although I did not know who they were. All the while, I convinced myself to keep breathing steadily. I didn't look up. I blocked out the sound of his voice. If it weren't for the fact he held my hands captured in his tight grip, I could ignore him entirely.

It will all be over soon. Just keep standing, keep breathing.

"You may now kiss the bride." The words seemed to boom around the room and echo.

My eyes flickered up from the floor to his lips immediately and saw them approaching as he tugged me closer. I flinched as his lips pressed against mine. My first kiss.

And it was revolting.

His lips were as cold as his hands. They parted, and his tongue forced entry into my mouth, jabbing and swirling. I almost choked. His hand moved to my hair and pulled my head back sharply. His teeth bit hard on my lips, making me whimper. He chuckled.

While my mouth was assaulted, the pulling sensation that usually followed his touch intensified. Something inside me traveled up to my mouth and met him. And he took it with the rough kiss. I felt a loss. A loss like he was taking my very soul from my body.

I pushed against his chest, and with another painful bite, which I was sure drew blood, he moved away. He looked satisfied. The smug smile chilled me, and I dropped my gaze, my lips stinging.

I walked out of that room as Mrs. Margaret Claudia Jenkins.

So much had been taken from me. My career, my money, my freedom, and now my name. I knew there was more to take. That my new husband would take as his right. I feared it more than a fist, more than starving, more than death.

If that kiss proved anything, it was that the worst was yet to come.

My parents didn't say goodbye. They walked away without a backward glance. My last memory of them is the back of my mother's blue dress and jacket, her hat flapping in the wind, and my father opening the car door for her to get in.

Their complete and total abandonment of me was the final nail in my coffin.

I'd long since learned that a heart could break many times. Broken parts continued to crack and shatter, leaving holes that got bigger with each painful puncture. But in that moment, it didn't shatter; it disintegrated. It died in my chest, fell to pieces, and now I was nothing.

Between them, my parents and Mr. Darren Jenkins would make me a doll. A person with nothing inside. An empty shell.

I couldn't even cry because I was still so dehydrated.

With another blurring journey, I found myself in my new home. If I cared at all for the man, if this were what I wanted, and if I had any ambition to marry, I would think the home was nice. It had a large front garden full of plants and a back garden that had plenty of room for children to play. The rooms were tall and spacious, and the kitchen was fully equipped.

But I didn't care.

As he dragged me through the house, pulling at my still-healing shoulder and showing off all his possessions, his disgusting touch tugged at me, drawing all my strength until my legs were wobbling so much I was struggling to walk.

Finally, he showed me to the bedroom. I gulped as I crossed the threshold and looked around. Not out of interest for the room, but to look for things he could use to hurt me. The unassuming weapons were always the most painful and betraying.

"And this, dear wife, is where you'll stay for the next couple of hours." He threw me onto the bed, and my whole body stiffened as fear rushed through me.

Hours? Hours? It would take hours?

I thought sex lasted minutes, not hours, and the thought of him being with me ... on me ... in me ... for that length of time made me nauseous.

It will be all right. You will survive this. Just pretend you are somewhere else.

But a louder voice in my mind swallowed that voice. *Why would you want to survive? What do you have to live for? A life of servitude, abuse? Children you couldn't protect, or worse, who were like their father? Is that what you want?*

No, of course not, I argued.

You aren't doing anything to prevent that future right now.

The voice was right. I lay prostrate on the bed, awaiting

whatever god-awful act my husband wished to inflict upon me. I was a willing, broken victim.

I turned quickly and shuffled away until I fell to the other side of the bed.

Mr. Jenkins laughed in a way that reminded me he was evil, that even the slightest touch from him was unexplainably painful. As though his touch was poison.

Coming to the side of the bed, he grabbed my ankle and yanked me forward. I yelped and kicked out uselessly, clinging to the foot of the bed, but he only laughed and dodged my foot while pulling the other.

"I don't have time to play with you, my jewel. I've been waiting for this for a long time," he growled, becoming impatient with my struggling.

His fist grabbed my dress, and he tore it as he pulled it away from my legs, baring my undergarments to him.

My heartbeat stuttered, and I screamed.

No. Please. God, don't let this happen. Please. Save me.

He slapped his large hand over my mouth and muffled my scream. Tears pricked at my eyes, and my head swam with panic, but I continued to fight. I needed to fight.

I heard the clink of his belt as his other hand pulled it free of his trousers. I whimpered, and his hand over my mouth moved down to my throat and gripped tightly.

"You are mine to use, jewel. In any way I please. You need to resign yourself to that fate now. It will hurt less." His belt dropped to the floor, and his hand cupped my mons. Everything inside me clenched as his finger sought entrance.

No.

My fear turned to anger. Despite my weakness from weeks of neglect, my mind used the last of my strength to focus, to ignore the bone-aching sensation from his touch, to push energy into getting away. I spat at him.

My saliva hit his cheek, and the world seemed to slow

down. The black of his iris swallowed the white of his eye, which flashed yellow. He sat back on his heels and wiped his cheek with the cuff of his white shirt sleeve. Anger flushed his cheeks, and he bared his teeth in a snarl. His hand wrapped around the belt.

"I'll have to teach you how to respect your husband first."

In seconds, he rolled me onto my stomach, ripped open the back of my dress, and pinned me, kneeling painfully and heavily on my thighs. My arms were useless. I couldn't reach anything to help me. I couldn't reach back to push him.

The pain that ripped through me at the first slash of his belt across my bare back was unbearable. Black spots appeared in front of my eyes. My hands clenched so hard my fingernails dug into my palms. A scream ripped out from me, loud and shrill and full of the pain that rattled through every tiny part of my body.

Father had used a belt to beat me once before, but it didn't feel like this. This felt like fire and lightning. I heard it whip before the strike lashed my skin. And I realized on the third hit that I was being beaten by the metal side of the belt. It gouged out skin and tissue and caused blood to pour down my sides.

At some point, I stopped feeling. I stopped counting. I lay motionless, staring at a crack in the floor under the bed.

He lifted off my thighs and then parted them.

I stayed still. A broken doll just praying for the suffering to be over with.

A loud knock at the door stopped him as his manhood poised at my entrance. The banging sounded again, louder and more urgent. Mr. Jenkins huffed and gritted his teeth. He pushed my head harder against the wooden floor as he used it to get up.

"Don't move. I'll be back," he snapped as he left the room.

I didn't move. I listened.

I heard raised voices, and then he was storming up the stairs again.

Just stay still. It will be over soon.

The door swung open, but he didn't touch me. He collected his shoes, coat, and belt, then said, "I'll be back later, and we'll continue where we left off."

There was a click after the door closed. He'd locked me in.

I dozed for a while, face down on the floor, my back exposed, bleeding, and raw. The pain and the stress of it all required my body to have more sleep, but I couldn't completely let my guard down knowing I wasn't safe. Any moment, that monster, my husband, would come back and ruin me.

As the sun set outside and cast long shadows in the bedroom, I decided it was time to move. If I were going to suffer, I would rather suffer comfortably, or as comfortably as one can suffer, in bed.

I got up on my hands and knees, my back throbbing and my arms shaking with the effort, and something caught my eye. The crack I'd been staring at was twice as big as the other gaps in the wooden floor, and through it, I could see something glinting as the setting sun hit it.

A hidden compartment in the floor?

Adrenaline numbed me as I reached under the bed, pulling myself toward the square cut in the wood. It jigged like a poorly fitting lid on a box, and I lifted it up to find a book, an envelope, and a small bottle.

Shuffling back out from under the bed, I pulled myself and my treasures up to sit gingerly on the bedspread.

I opened the envelope to find four pieces of paper inside. They read:

"If you are reading this, I'm dead, and you are next. Darren Jenkins is a monster. My diary will document all the ways I know this, and I will leave it for you. Save yourself if you can. If you can't, add something so the next wife can remember you. And maybe she can be the one to escape. - Jennifer Jenkins."

"You have something he wants, and so he steals it. But you are not nothing without it. You can still be strong. There was no escape for me, but I pray there is for you. - Violet Jenkins."

"It may not be now, but soon he will kill me. His frustrations grow. My punishments are daily, and my power diminishes too quickly. I'm going to be expendable, and he probably already has his eye on his next victim. You. - Lucia Jenkins."

"Break the cycle. Stop your suffering. Drink the bottle and die."

My shaking hand dropped the note, and I stared at the bottle sitting innocently on the bedside table. The handwriting was a messy scrawl, unlike the other notes with differing ladylike penmanship. I was also the fourth wife.

Who was telling me to take my life? Was this him trying to trick me? Test me? Punish me somehow?

For the next hour, I flicked through the diary of his past three wives until tears saturated the tattered remains of my bloodied dress.

He was evil. Truly evil. They suffered horrors and were only concerned that when they passed, someone else would take their place and suffer, too.

I pulled the pen from the diary's ribbon and wrote on the back of the fourth note:

I don't want to suffer as they have. I want to choose my ending, and this is it. I'm a coward, but I leave half for you. Take it. Unless you can make him take it.

Sinking back down to the floor, I placed the envelope full of notes and the diary back in the compartment.

I stared at the bottle in my hand. The liquid looked clear and unassuming. I lifted the small glass stopper and smelled it, but I couldn't recognize it.

Running a dry tongue over parched lips, I lifted the cool glass to sit poised while my mind went to war.

Am I really going to do this? Take my own life? It's a sin.

But why should I live only to suffer? God has abandoned me.

What if this is a trick? What if I wake and my suffering truly begins?

It is a risk, but either way, I suffer. Do you not want to choose your ending?

I do.

I tipped the glass back and swallowed half the liquid before cramming the stopper back in and returning it to the compartment and covering everything.

Dizziness struck me as I stood to sit on the bed. I lay back and closed my eyes, listening to the quiet stirrings of the house.

The sound of a key in the lock was the last thing I heard before I died. A grin was etched on my face, because I took what he wanted before he could. I won.

CHAPTER 23

CLAWDIA

The room seemed to pulse with tension. I didn't look up at them. I stared at my hands and picked at the skin around my nails.

Everyone seemed to speak at once.

"Clawdia."

"Clawdicat."

"Little Cat."

They stopped. Charlie rested a hand on my thigh. "I'm so sorry that happened to you. You deserved a better life than that."

I nodded and blinked back tears.

Don't cry! I shouted at myself. *I'm done being so emotional!*

Zaide's eyes were full of pain as he stared at me. "You are safe now, Little Cat. I understand your fear and hurt."

I sniffled, "You do?"

"I was a slave without hope for a long time. There were days I often thought about taking the route you did. Perhaps I knew help was on the way."

A tear slipped free, and I cursed myself, wiping it away aggressively. But I wasn't just crying for myself; I was crying for the Zaide, who almost lost hope. "I'm sorry. I must seem so pathetic to you. You suffered worse for much longer than I did, and I'm crying about it."

He shook his head sternly. "There is no one way to deal with trauma, Little Cat. We have both suffered. We have both done our best to escape it. Now we must allow ourselves to heal."

My eyes were sore, and my head was fuzzy as I nodded. I resigned myself to living a life of inescapable and over-whelming emotion. A human life, with all the bad and the good that comes with it.

I stood from the table. Charlie and Zaide reached out for me as if I was going to run or disappear or leave. "I'm just going to the bathroom." I chuckled and hiccupped.

Washing my face, I noted purple bags under my eyes and my red, puffy face. I sighed at the ugly sight, but I no longer hated my image. I didn't cringe at the memories of my past self, because I was a new Clawdia who was a mix of Margaret Claudia and Clawdicat.

Maybe being human won't be as painful as I thought it would be. Maybe I won't always be reminded of my past. Maybe I can move past it all. Heal like Zaide did instead of running away from my feelings by being a cat.

In my mind, a door opened, and possibility and hope came flooding in.

I could go back to nursing school if Winnie let me. I could earn money, buy things, and live as I once did. I could date, maybe fall in love.

A small smile on my face and hope in my heart, I left the bathroom, only to find Daithi waiting outside for me. I froze.

His face showed nothing but sympathy. "I can try to turn you back."

My heart raced. "What?"

"Being a cat was your protection from the memories

which haunt you. I took that from you and have not been understanding. I would like to make it up to you." Emotions were clear on his face, and his words were everything I wanted to hear. But it made me suspicious.

"By trying to turn me back?" I asked slowly.

He nodded solemnly. "If that is what you want."

"The witches don't think it is possible." I shrugged and tried to move past him.

"I have far more power than them," he scoffed and blocked me.

I frowned, not sure why he was being so insistent. "I haven't saved Savida yet, and I promised you I would."

"You have done enough." A flash of something passed over his face before I could identify it.

The fact that I hesitated to take his offer told me all I needed to know. I didn't want to be a cat again. I might miss the simple life, but ultimately, I needed to stop running from my past, my fears, my pain.

My relationship with Winnie and even Charlie had changed too much for things to go back as they were. I enjoyed talking and eating human food, and although the emotions were turbulent, I knew they'd eventually be more positive than negative. I loved bantering with Charlie. I loved the adoration in Zaide's eyes. And I wanted to meet Savida properly and tell him the story of how we saved him.

I sighed, knowing it would be a challenge to rescue him without Winnie dying because of her sworn promise and me dying with her.

I rubbed my head, the ache becoming more pronounced. *Bed. I need to go to bed.* I nodded to myself.

"Very well," Daithi said.

I forgot he was waiting for an answer. Looking up, my eyes widened to the size of saucers as I opened my mouth to tell him no. He inhaled, and then his body glowed, and magic swirled out from his palms.

My protest caught in my throat as magic brushed against my skin, following my arm to my mouth and forcing entry into my body. I was choking on it. I had forgotten how much it hurt to change shapes. My body contorted, and I screamed.

Charlie and Zaide ran from the kitchen to find me lying on the floor, panting.

"Daithi, what have you done?" Zaide roared.

"It was her wish," Daithi said.

Charlie sounded hesitant. "Daithi, she's screaming."

I heard Zaide's growl. "She is in pain, Daithi. Stop it."

"It's too late."

Charlie interrupted, "I thought we weren't using magic in case we needed you at full strength."

"This feels like the right thing to do. Savida would want me to do this, and I have some making up to do."

Poisonous fire ran through my veins, and just as I thought I wouldn't survive the pain, it eased. My scream morphed into a yowl.

As I panted, my eyes closed, and I took a moment to compose myself. When I opened my eyes, I couldn't see the different shades and my emotions felt duller.

I looked down and saw a blurry mess of blond fur. My paws. I flexed them, feeling my sharp claws pierce the carpet beneath me as I stood up. Looking around, I swished my tail.

Everything looked so big. I'd forgotten about that.

I ran to the sofa and jumped onto the cushions to get higher, able to see Charlie's confused expression and Zaide's devastated purple eyes.

Back in this body, I felt comfortable, unburdened, and familiar. I was Clawdia the fierce. A furred beauty. The brave and mischievous Clawdia. Everything I wasn't when I was human.

But comfortable things don't grow.

Becoming human again had changed me. Reminded me of the good feelings, the hopes and dreams I had and the simple pleasures in life. It reminded me how challenging life was supposed to be, and I couldn't go back to comfortable now.

It was time to heal and change for the better.

Just as soon as I could tell Daithi to turn me back.

Charlie sighed and rubbed my head. "Nice to have you back, Clawdicat." I licked his fingers, and he sighed again.

I meowed, wanting to tell him this was an accident. I wanted to stay with him and Zaide.

Could I type on Charlie's laptop?

"We need some dinner because I am absolutely starving, and then we need to get to bed and get back to finding Savida's fire." He rubbed his belly and walked to the phone on the desk. He flicked through a pamphlet on the desk, and when the person on the other end of the phone picked up, he began telling them exactly what he wanted to eat.

Jealously had me huffing. I wanted to eat with them. I imagined a lasagna with garlic bread or a steak pie with lots of gravy and mash or a chicken casserole with lots of black pepper ...

And then my nostrils tingled.

I breathed out sharply to prevent the coming sneeze. But it was too late. As if reacting to the thought of pepper, my body curled in on itself, and I sneezed so hard it was like being struck by lightning.

My foggy head and running eyes momentarily stopped me from processing what I saw when I looked down— human hands. I gasped and squealed as I saw the rest of my human body. I touched my now naked skin, shocked and confused, then looked up, tears edging into my eyes, and saw the shocked face of Charlie. His blond eyebrows launched into his hairline.

He looked at Zaide and Daithi, who were in the middle of an argument.

"Guys—" Charlie started.

Daithi continued lecturing, "You cannot expect that someone so emotionally damaged—"

"Guys—" Charlie tried to interrupt again.

"—would want to be mated to you. We also don't know the effects of mating on either of you."

"For fuck's sake," he muttered and marched toward their towering bodies.

"A soul pair bond of your race hasn't been—"

Before I could try to understand how I was suddenly human again or what they were arguing about, my nostrils tingled once more. The same lightning strike hit me again as I sneezed. This time, with the brutal pain and the aching head, I turned back into a cat.

I can be both. Human and cat. I just need to know how to control it. Do I have to sneeze?

Excitement bubbled up inside me. I didn't have to choose. I could have my cake and eat it.

"Shut the fuck up!" Charlie shouted. To make them notice me, he pushed them away from each other. Since they hadn't been paying attention to him, they fell back onto the sofas with ease despite their size. "Look!" He pointed at me.

I did the cat version of a smirk and then innocently licked my paw when Zaide and Daithi looked at me.

Charlie rubbed his eyes and dragged a hand through his hair. "What the fuck?" He looked tired, and a glimmer of guilt twinged my conscience for messing with him until I remembered it wasn't my fault.

Daithi answered, "Yes, Charlie, she is a cat again."

"No, she isn't. Wasn't," he growled. "She was human just a second ago."

Zaide responded slowly. "She was human, and then Daithi turned her back."

I giggled in my mind.

"Don't talk to me like I'm fucking delusional. I know what I saw." He pointed at me again. "She was a cat, and then she sneezed and turned back into a human, and then I tried to interrupt your fighting to show you, and then she was a cat again." He glared and yelled, "Turn back right now and tell them!"

Zaide put a comforting hand on his shoulder. "Charlie, it has been a long week for us all, and you are overworked. You have barely slept the past few nights. Perhaps you need to retire for the evening and when your food arrives, I will bring it to you."

"I'm not overtired." He shrugged Zaide's hand off him and glared at me again. "You're making me look stupid, Clawdicat."

I love when he calls me Clawdicat. Especially in an angry tone. I licked my paw innocently again.

I didn't care if it was weird. It was us and I'd missed it.

"She is a cat, Charlie, as you can clearly see. Perhaps you are just seeing what you wish to be true," Daithi added.

"We will all wish she were human, but she is happier now." Zaide said, getting a little choked up and teary-eyed.

My heart ached at the sight. *He really cares about me. He'd rather I'd be happy than make him happy by being human. He is so selfless. Handsome. Amazing.*

I was taken out of my reverie when Charlie shouted, "I'm not crazy, and yes, you're right. She is happy because she's making me look like a fucking doughnut." I chuckled to myself. He wasn't wrong. "I swear to you, she can turn into a human when she sneezes."

Daithi rolled his eyes. "A sneeze does not hold any magical properties in which it could change a shape."

"No, but it's a shock," he muttered, clearly up to something.

There was a knock at the door, and I almost cried at the thought of food. I ran toward it, and Charlie thanked the man profusely as he pushed a trolley of food into the room. By the time the door had shut with the man's exit, Charlie was already sitting back down, plate in hand, and shoveling piping hot food into his mouth. He had finished his plate by the time Daithi and Zaide had sat down with plates.

I hopped next to Zaide and sat on his braid, biting at the stone on his hair tie until he gave me his attention. I gave him my best pleading eyes to convince him to feed me his food.

"Can cats eat this?" he asked Charlie.

"No. The tomato in the Bolognese is not good for them." Charlie smirked at me. "But if you just turned back into a human, you could eat delicious human food again."

I glared.

Zaide's face twitched. "Charlie, I really don't think—"

"You didn't see it because you were arguing over how you wanted to tell Clawdia a secret before she turned human."

My ears perked up.

Charlie watched me and waited, and I watched him to see if he would say anymore. When I realized his ploy, I narrowed my eyes and continued to bite and lick at Zaide's hair. He stroked my fur, and I leaned into the attention.

Charlie screamed.

We were all startled. I attempted to scramble over the back of the sofa to hide, but the lightning feeling struck me again, and I fell onto the floor behind the sofa in my human form.

With my breath knocked out of me, I paused for a

moment before peering over the sofa. Daithi and Zaide had jumped up, Daithi with his magical hand at the ready and Zaide with raised fists. When they had looked around and saw no danger, they lowered their weapons and addressed Charlie.

"Charlie, what in the world—" Daithi started.

"You are not well." Zaide shook his head. "It is time to go to bed."

Charlie met my eyes and smirked. "Welcome back."

"You are a horrible person," I retorted.

Daithi and Zaide turned to see me and gasped.

"Don't be a sourpuss," Charlie joked. "I was just testing a theory."

Zaide pulled me over the sofa and into his arms. "Little Cat, you are human! Charlie was not mad? You can be both?"

"It certainly seems that way." I covered the little dignity I had left, aware that I was very naked and very close to him. "Now I just need to make sure I can do it when I want to and not when Charlie has a screaming fit or when I sneeze."

Zaide leaned back and pulled his t-shirt over his head. For a brief second, my bare back touched his bare chest, and blood rushed to my cheeks. He handed the shirt to me. "Put that on for the moment. No one will look." Both Daithi and Charlie looked away as I let go of my private parts to pull the warm shirt over me.

It smelled like Zaide, and I couldn't resist sniffing it as I cuddled into the fabric.

His arms wrapped around me and pulled me more securely onto his lap. "We will practice how to change form, Little Cat," Zaide promised. "You are clever. I'm sure you'll learn quickly."

My heart warmed at his faith in me.

"How is it you keep manipulating the effects of my

magic?" Daithi asked, looking emotionless as ever. I lifted my shoulders in a shrug but thought it was odd of him to ask.

"Perhaps it isn't magic at all. Perhaps it is fate," Zaide told him softly. I turned to see his gaze locked on the skin of my shoulder. He nuzzled it, and I stiffened in surprise.

He'd always been affectionate and kind, but sitting partially naked on his lap with him nuzzling my shoulder made me realize, *He likes me. Cares about me. Wants me.*

I wasn't sure what to do with that. I cared about him, loved his attention and affection, but knew nothing about relationships or love or sex. I had a lot of trauma to work through, and with how handsome he was, he could get anyone in any realm. He didn't need me.

Charlie frowned and then yawned dramatically. "Well, this has been exciting. But I'm actually exhausted, so I'm going to get to bed." He looked pointedly at Zaide and me and added, "I think you two should talk about that secret he was keeping."

CHAPTER 24

ZAIDE

"*Y*ou don't have to tell me the secret if you don't want to," Clawdia began as Charlie and Daithi shut their doors, leaving me alone with my soul pair.

A soul pair I'd lost twice yesterday, first to kidnappers and then to her witch, and then lost her again today when she chose to be a cat again.

After hearing her story, I knew how traumatic her past was. I understood why she didn't want to be human, but I regretted not telling her about our connection. Perhaps it would have given her something to hold on to.

I hugged her closer to my chest and pressed another kiss to her bare, soft skin. She shuddered. "I do have to tell you."

"Is it ... bad?"

I shook my head. "No, Little Cat. I don't think so. But you may have a different opinion."

She looked up at me, her head tilted back against my chest to stare into my eyes. "What is it?"

I took a deep breath. "We came to the human realm for a reason. Do you know what that reason is?"

"You were looking for a person called Margaret." She frowned, confused, but then I saw the moment her light behind her eyes switched on. "Me?"

I chuckled. "You."

She twisted so her legs sat tucked across my lap and her cheek rested on my chest. I could see her frown when she said, "I was a cat."

I shrugged. "You were not always, and you are not now."

She nodded, and the tendrils of her soft hair brushed my bare chest. I restrained a shudder. "Why were you looking for me?"

I sighed, brushing a hand over the soft skin of her leg, and told her of our past. "My race were once powerful beings. But greater powers punished us for our power and arrogance by tearing our souls in half and tossing them across the dimensions, never to find each other again. We have no power of old, only our strength. We live as half beings with a hole where our other half should be. You are that other half. My soul pair."

She digested that for a long moment as my heart raced and my stomach jumped.

She is not screaming or running from me. That is a good start.

"What does that mean, exactly?" she asked slowly.

My tongue felt thick in my mouth, and I swallowed nervously. "Many millennia ago, our souls were one. We were a titan living in Tartarus, with the power to alter the fabric of the universe."

"But titans don't have that power any longer?"

I nodded. "Because our souls were split, our power was split too. Daithi thinks you hold the titan powers but can't use them."

"The power won't come back now that we are together?"

Together. I knew she didn't mean it in the same sense that I heard it, but it gave me hope.

"Daithi believes we may both regain the powers of old—"
I cut short the rest of the sentence.

She raised a golden brow. "When? How?"

"As far as we are aware, you and I are the first to find
their other halves. Everything is theoretical."

"And this theory is?" Her eyes were wide with curiosity. I
hesitated, and she prompted, "You can tell me."

"He believes we need to consummate the bond," I blurted.

The silence that followed made my palms sweat, but I
said nothing, allowing her time to consider it.

*Hedri, my god of love, please reassure her of my honest inten-
tions. My desire for not just her body, but her heart and soul, too.
Please help her understand and not be fearful.*

She looked at her hands when she asked, "A soul pair is a
romantic bond?"

My stomach dropped. "Is romance objectionable to you?"

She blushed, a dark pink color I watched rush upward
from her chest to her face. I wanted to know where it
started. Where else it spread.

She stuttered as she replied, "No. Erm. No. It's just ... I
don't know anything about romance."

"Neither do I." I smiled. "But I'd like to learn."

"You would?"

"I am enchanted by you, Clawdia. I have been since I met
you as a cat, and I continue to find reason to care for you.
You turned human, which reminded you of your traumatic
past, but you wanted to help save my friend. This journey has
been difficult for you, but you've been brave and faced it all.
Even being a cat again—"

She pressed her small fingers against my lips and interrupted, "I didn't want to be a cat again. It was an accident."

I frowned, and her fingers fell from my face. "What?"

The words poured out of her in a rush, "I've been feeling
more settled in myself, and today I looked at myself and real-

ized that I'm not Margaret Claudia anymore. I'm Clawdia, and my past is past. My parents and Darren Jenkins are long dead, and I won't let my memories hold me hostage and ruin my future."

Pride rose in me, and I beamed down at her. "This is fantastic news, Little Cat."

"Then Daithi caught me on the way out of the bathroom and said he wanted to make up for his poor behavior to me, but I didn't want to be a cat. I wanted to stay with you and Charlie. I enjoy being with you. Daithi thought I was saying yes to him, but I was nodding to something I was thinking about. It was an accident."

I thought it was strange that Daithi wanted to apologize for his actions by taking her away from me but concentrated on the most important information that her rambling revealed.

She likes being with me. She wanted to stay with me.

"I'm glad to know you like being with me." I asked hesitantly, "Does this mean you aren't objecting to romance?"

She bit her lip. "I don't know how to feel about this, Zaide."

Her stomach growled, and I smiled. "Why don't I feed you while you think?"

"Yes, please."

I nodded and placed her on the sofa gently before gathering a plate of something Charlie ordered and walking to the kitchenette to warm it.

She watched me with a puzzled expression as I came back to her, placed her food on the coffee table, and moved her back into my arms.

I needed to touch her, hold her. Now that she knew she was mine, and after the events of the last couple days where I almost lost her, everything inside me wanted to stay as close to her as possible. She didn't protest.

She ate like she'd never had food before and groaned in pleasure. The sound had an arousing effect on me, but I ignored it.

When she finished, the plate clinked onto the coffee table, and she rearranged herself more comfortably in my lap again. We sat in companionable silence. I twirled the soft strands of her hair around my fingers—the gold of her hair and the gold of my skin only shades apart. They were similar yet complimentary. So right.

"I'm glad I'm your soul pair," she announced to the silence.

My heart soared. "You are?"

She didn't look at me when she replied, her gaze directed at her hands in her lap. "I've always thought you were handsome. Like a fantasy warrior. You're so big and fierce looking, but you've treated me with nothing but adoration and kindness. You've defended me, saved me, cared about me, and given me your hair to hold on to. I feel stronger with you."

I heard the unspoken "but" in her tone and tense body. "There is something you aren't saying." I ran my hand down her leg to assure her I wasn't upset by this. "I always want your honesty, no matter how much it might hurt."

She sighed and looked up at me. There was fear in her eyes, but also a glimmer of hope. "I have a lot of other emotions, too. I'm scared this is too good to be true, that you will turn out like everyone else who has been bound to me. My parents and Winnie claimed to care for me but ultimately hurt me."

My poor Little Cat. She wants to trust, to love, so much, but she is so traumatized by her past she can't believe in her own soul.

"I cannot make promises about our connection when I know so little about it. And I can't understand the minds of those I don't know. But, Little Cat, I am a very pious male. A miracle occurred to give me my freedom. I prayed for it every day since I was taken. I don't take that for granted.

When I couldn't find my family, Daithi had a vision that gave me another reason to continue searching the realms. A soul pair. You. A chance at a future full of adventure, power, and love. All things every creature should have. Having found you, I know I will never betray you, hurt you, or give you reason to feel you aren't enough. I want to love you and be loved in return," I finished in a whisper.

She stared at me, tears filling her eyes, and whispered, "This power is unimportant to you, isn't it?"

It wasn't quite the response I was looking for, so I frowned in confusion and shrugged. "I am curious about what we could have been, but family, love, connection are why I want you."

She bit her lip, and I waited for her to continue with her doubts. "Charlie—" she began.

I cut her off, knowing what she was about to say. "You like Charlie, and you are upset our connection may prevent anything happening with him?" She looked startled but nodded slowly. "Our connection is theoretical. All I know is that I want you with everything in me, but I understand if that is not mutual. More than anything, I want you to be happy. However you chose to do that."

She spluttered, "I-I—you don't … He isn't—and it's not a —" she huffed, "He doesn't want me, so it doesn't even matter. I don't want to be unfaithful to you. You shouldn't accept anyone who is."

The outrage in her voice made me smile. "Unfaithful suggests that we've made commitments to each other."

"You wanted to be … romantic to see if we get our powers back. I'm not romantic with just anyone." She crossed her arms, looked away, and pouted in a show of anger I found both thrilling and arousing.

I gripped her chin gently and turned her to face me. My lips inches from hers, I whispered, "Let me make this very clear, Little Cat. I don't want to be romantic because Daithi thinks it's the way we get our powers. No, I want you because you are beautiful and it's all I'm able to think about when I'm alone at night. Or in the shower. My desire for you is beyond all reason."

Her pupils swallowed the whites of her eyes. She blinked, blushed, and then smiled shyly. "You've answered all my fears, so I suppose I'm saying that I'm not opposed to you wooing me. Consider us committed."

"You will not regret this." I pressed a kiss to her forehead and just sat quietly for a moment. We breathed each other in, memorizing the moment. Her fingers brushed my chest. The purple glow emanating from my scared skin illuminated her hand as she tracked the scars up to my neck.

"Can I ask a question?" she asked softly.

"Of course, Little Cat."

"Why do your scars glow?"

"Daithi believes it shows that titan blood holds the last remnants of power. I'm inclined to believe him since blood is how I was born."

"Daithi has a lot of theories about titans." She raised a curious brow. "How are you born from blood?"

"Since the Fall—the separation of our souls—we could not procreate the normal way. We became impotent. That's why I knew you were Margaret when you first became human."

A blush darkened on her cheeks as she remembered that morning in all its glory. "Oh. That ... makes sense."

I chuckled and picked up the hand resting on my chest to kiss it. "I apologize if I startled you."

She coughed uncomfortably, and I laughed again as she squirmed. "No. No problem."

I rubbed my thumb over her knuckles as I continued to tell her about my home realm. "Because we couldn't procreate, our gods created a life pool in which prospective parents only needed to mix their blood with some water of the pool and then drink it to become pregnant."

She froze. "Your gods are real?"

"As real as you and I. They were once titans with the strongest powers. They escaped the Fall and are now gods among us broken ones." I reached behind me and pulled my braid to sit in our lap. I showed her the stone attached to my hair tie. "This stone is for prayer. It's engraved with the names of my gods. Charos, god of death. Hedri, god of love. And Riseir, god of life."

"I wondered what it was." She stroked her thumb over the white lines in the black stone.

"Now you know. There are no more secrets between us. You can ask me anything you want."

She rested her head on my shoulder and looked up at me. "Will you tell me about it? Your life?"

I wrapped my arms around her, hugging her to me, my hands resting at her hip where my shirt had ridden up. I tucked it down to stop from being tempted by her soft skin.

"I was the firstborn of my parents. They didn't love each other, but they had children together since they were from strong family lines. I had four siblings, a brother and three sisters. Thos, Maderes, Efari, and Kadeia. Only hours after giving birth, my mother would place my new sibling in my arms so I could meet them. It became a tradition. Each one of them stole a piece of my heart the moment I looked into their eyes. They were my favorite people of all the realms."

Clawdia's fingertip on my downturned lips made me jolt out of the memories that resurfaced at the thought of my siblings.

"What happened to them?" she whispered, a sympathetic,

sad expression on her face.

Unable to give her detail of the horror, I summarized. "Slavers started portaling to Tartarus accompanied by faei. We would wake up to find titans missing from their beds. Eventually, portals appeared in the middle of the day, but we were so few we could do nothing to fight them. We were all taken. All of us."

"I'm so sorry." She tucked her face into my neck, and her hand reached around to the back of my neck in a half-hug. I nuzzled into her hair and squeezed my thanks.

My voice was gruff with emotion when I spoke. "It was a long time ago, but I still hear their screams for me to save them. It haunts me." I swallowed and tried to banish the memories. "We were all so young. Kadeia had only just started school. I don't even know if she'd remember me."

"You have no idea where any of them are?"

I shook my head. "When Daithi and Savida saved me, I told them about my family. We searched many dimensions, hoping to find them. We were never successful. Daithi's visions didn't show him anything about them. It was a fruitless search but one we all enjoyed despite the disappointment. Savida especially loved traveling."

"When we've saved him, we can keep looking for them all."

"You'd come with me?"

"Of course. Maybe Winnie can come with us, too. As an apology, she can use her magic to track them. And maybe if we have powers, we can help."

I didn't imagine Daithi would be so forgiving as to allow Winnie to join our search. And I didn't know what the effect of taking a familiar that far away from its witch would be. Despite that, I loved how she was already planning our life together.

I must have been quiet too long as I thought, because

Clawdia rambled nervously, "You know, if we are going to be … romantic … eventually … not right now, but maybe someday—"

I chuckled and placed a finger on her lip to stop her. "You don't know how much it means to me that you would leave the human realm and rescue my siblings with me."

She beamed at me, pleased with herself. "Maybe they've already been rescued like you were. Maybe that's why you couldn't find them."

"That would be a miracle indeed, and one I will pray for."

"You need something new to pray for now that you have me." Her sly grin grew until she burst into soft giggles.

I threw my head back and laughed at her cheeky response. It told me she was getting more comfortable with me and with the idea of being mine. My heart felt fit to burst, and I hugged her tightly. "You are right."

"How *did* Daithi and Savida save you?"

It was another topic that I avoided since it reminded me of where they took me from, but she was mine and needed to know all of me. To distract myself, I pulled her hair over her shoulder, started braiding.

"It was five years into my captivity. I was a fighter slave, and one day, I lost a fight. I had done it on purpose since my opponent was unwell and fighting for his captured family. I didn't want to be the reason a child lost its father.

Daithi and Savida saw me taking my punishment in the alleyway leading to my cage. Daithi had seen it happen in a vision and knew where to look for me. I was in too much pain to focus. The next thing I recall is waking up to sunlight —something I hadn't woken up with in years—and lying on a comfortable sofa rather than a cold stone floor."

Clawdia stopped my hand mid braid and forced my attention back to her. "I'm glad they saved you from that," she whispered.

I nodded silently.

"How did Daithi have a vision about you when he didn't know you?" Her brow crinkled, and I smoothed it with my thumb.

I cupped her face and brushed her cheekbone. I could see her eyes getting tired, her blinks becoming slower. "Fate leads Daithi's visions. If he is meant to know something, his vision will show him. I believe my gods sent him to rescue me, and I'm grateful to them and to Savida and Daithi for doing their work," I explained.

She nuzzled into my hand but then turned to rest her head on my chest, and my hand fell down her neck to her collar. With her eyes closed, she mumbled, "The way you feel about Daithi and Savida is how I feel about Winnie. She gave me a new life and rescued me from my past. I'm so disappointed in her for doing this, but I love her and want to stop her, save her."

"I understand that, Little Cat. I don't blame you for continuing to care for her," I assured her.

"I'm just sorry my savior hurt yours."

"There was nothing you could do to prevent it, Little Cat. Fate has been meddling and Savida, it seems, was always entangled in the witches' plot."

"It's not fair." She yawned. "He's hunted just because of his fire. It's wrong."

I nodded, not that she could see me. "It is. Just like hunting titans for slaves is wrong. The realms have never claimed to be kind, but we must capture as much of our own happiness as we can."

She was clearly drifting off to sleep, her breaths deepening, evening out. Unable to help myself, I stared at her in wonder and gently stroked her hair.

Suddenly, her eyes flashed open, and she jolted to alertness. "Little Cat, what's wrong?"

"Zaide, someone tried to kidnap me yesterday. They were taking me into a portal. People have been going missing. You don't think ..."

I finished her thought. "That the human realm is now faced with the same plague of slavers the titans had?" I had briefly thought about the possibility when we were in the car after her abduction and Charlie mentioned humans were going missing, but I was so focused on Clawdia, so glad she was well and with me, I thought little more about it.

"It's more than possible." I agreed, and my stomach dropped at the thought of what could have been. "I could have lost you to the same fate I suffered, that my siblings suffered." I closed my eyes tightly as guilt and powerlessness overtook me for a moment.

"I'm here. I'm fine." She sat up and placed her hands on my cheeks. When I opened my eyes, she stroked my face with a light, reassuring touch. "We should tell someone. Maybe Daithi knows how to stop them from coming here."

I held her wrists and shook my head once. "It is late, Little Cat. There is nothing anyone can do until morning. We should say our prayers and get to bed." She bit her lip, a sign she was holding words back from me again. "What is it?" I prompted.

She pouted. "I don't want to go to bed." But I heard the unsaid request, and it made my heart soar.

She doesn't want to leave me yet. She enjoys being in my arms.

With a calm facade, I said, "Let us gather a blanket and sleep here instead. I will tell you tales until you fall into slumber."

Lying on the sofa and wrapped in a thick quilt, Clawdia cuddled at my side, her body and legs sprawled half on top of me. I whispered a story about three titans who became gods until I, too, succumbed to the call of my dreams.

CHAPTER 25

CHARLIE

*T*he sun peeking through the cracks of the blinds was enough to wake me. I wandered through the room, scratching at my stomach unconsciously, wearing only my boxer shorts, and as I opened the door to the lounge and kitchenette, the sight of Clawdia and Zaide fast asleep and cuddled up on the sofa together greeted me.

Hot jealousy burned through me, and my fists clenched.

She was mine first. I wanted to yell and stomp my feet like a child. I didn't because I was a grown-ass adult and life isn't always fair.

It didn't take a therapist to figure out why I was feeling so possessive. I might have unofficially shared Clawdicat with Winnie, but when she was with me, at my house, scratching my toilet rolls up, she was mine. The only thing that had ever been mine. She seemed as lonely as me and played hard to get with her affections. Her antics made me laugh and cry, and she was a great cuddler in the cold winter nights when we'd binge a Netflix series.

And now Zaide had her. She was his soul pair. He deserved her. No one would love and cherish like a man who'd had nothing. But I knew now that I wouldn't get Clawdicat back, and I wouldn't ever get a chance with Clawdia.

I sighed, jealousy and disappointment warring with the happiness I felt for my friend getting what he deserved. I was a mess of soppy, pathetic emotion. So, I did what I did best and compartmentalized. I said, "Not today, weird emotions," and put them in a storage box in the back of my brain.

Ignoring the happy, sleeping couple, I padded into the bathroom, had a shit, showered, and shaved. I got changed and walked my jean-clad arse into the kitchenette for a cup of tea and some shitty Swedish cereal that we found in the nearest supermarket. After a spoon or two and a scroll through Facebook, I was less irritable.

I'm not me when I'm hungry.

I saw Zaide's head peep up over the sofa. He spent the next three minutes trying to detach himself from Clawdia without waking her up.

"The bathroom is free," I told him when he finally walked toward me.

"Thank you. I will wash after I have eaten. My stomach woke me." I chuckled and passed him the cereal box. He poured himself a bowl. "I told her she was my soul pair last night."

I looked back at my phone and breakfast. In a totally normal voice, I said, "It went well, I take it?"

"She said she was glad, that she liked me and will let me woo her, but doesn't want to rush into ... romance relations." He opened the fridge. "We are both ... nervous for multiple reasons."

I swallowed cereal, which now rolled heavily like cement in my mouth. "Understandable."

"Have I upset you?" he asked after a moment of silence as he poured milk into his bowl and threw in the spoon.

You stole my cat. But I said, "No. What makes you think that?"

"You haven't looked me in the eye at all."

"I'm just not a good morning person," I told him, looking him in the eye. "I'm not mad at you."

He gave me a pointed look. "Charlie, do not lie to me. You enjoy the morning."

Damn him for knowing me. I sighed. "I'm just figuring some things out in my head."

He was quiet. "You will come to me if you need help with this figuring." It wasn't a question, so I just smiled at him in agreement. He grunted, picked up his bowl, and wandered into the bathroom.

"That isn't sanitary!" I called after him.

"Why only do one when you can do both at the same time?"

"That is beyond disgusting."

"What are you shouting about so early?" Clawdia's soft, sleepy voice asked as a pair of beautiful violet eyes peaked over the top of the sofa to glare at me.

"Ah, sleeping beauty, you have arisen! A celebration in your honor," I exclaimed with false cheer.

She raised her eyes brows. "You're unusually chipper this morning."

"There is a lot of sugar in this cereal." I took the last bite and threw the bowl in the sink.

"Keep your celebration for another time. I want more sleep."

She looked adorable, all rumpled and surrounded in blankets. There were lines from the pattern of the sofa etched into her reddened cheeks, and the corners of her eyes were full of sleep. It wasn't a look I thought I'd be attracted to, but on her, it was making it hard to hide my arousal.

I sat on the arm of the sofa, where she had snuggled down again. "Tell me, Clawdicat, what or who kept you up so late?"

She blushed a deep red on her pale skin. "You already know the answer to that. Otherwise, you wouldn't be so annoying."

I chuckled. "Look at that color! Why, it would almost make me think that you two did something … unseemly. Do I need to chaperone you now that the secret is out? Protect your virtue?"

She glared, then sat up and shoved me so hard I almost fell off the side. I barked a laugh.

"No, you don't need to do any such thing. You're such a tease."

"Oh, I don't know about that. From where I'm sitting, it seems like you're the tease."

I'd clearly touched a sensitive spot, because she sat up straight and asked, "What do you mean?"

Warning lights flashed in my brain, and I tried to back myself out again by making fun. "Poor Zaide. A golden otherworlder who thought he'd die a slave meets his soul pair, something that hasn't happened ever, and she wants to go slow."

"He said he was okay with that," her voice trembled, and my playfulness vanished.

"Hey, I was only joking. Zaide wants you any way he can have you. Fast, slow, big or little, cat or human." I wrapped my arms around her, and she snuggled into my shoulder.

"I don't know how to do this," she whispered. "I've only seen this in films and books. I don't know what to do."

"This? You mean love? Relationships?" She nodded. "Well, that's easy. You just take it one day at a time and do what feels natural. You're in control of it. He won't take more than you offer."

"I just don't feel like I have a lot to offer."

"Get that out of your head right now. For fuck's sake, Clawdicat, you have half the man's soul. You're offering him everything. And beyond that, you're smart and witty and stunningly beautiful. Why is it you only believe all that when you're a cat?"

She looked up at me, awed. "I've never thought of it like that. I do feel amazing as a cat. Powerful even though I'm small and fluffy."

"Delusions of grandeur." I laughed.

"I think it's because I feel safe. I wasn't safe as a human. I was safe as a cat. Maybe that's why being human again makes me doubt myself."

"You need to switch your brains. Human Clawdia needs more confidence, and cat Clawdia needs less."

"While we're doing that, why don't we go to Oz and ask the wizard for courage, too?" She laughed sadly, self-pityingly.

"A pop culture reference from a 100-year-old lady. Why, miracles will never cease with you! You're a wonder!" I exclaimed and tickled her.

She giggled, pushing my hands away. "Charlie, stop!"

"Admit that you are a wonder."

"That's a stupid thing … to admit," she said breathlessly, still fighting me off and laughing.

"Admit it. I'll hear no more of this self-flagellation."

"Wow. A big word. Was that on your calendar today?"

I choked out a laugh. "You cheeky little—" I threw my hands up, being dramatic. "I give up. I'll just let you wallow in your pit of despair. Let me know when cool Clawdia wants to hang out." I turned myself away from her and moved to get up.

She giggled and grabbed my hand. "Thanks, Charlie." I smiled and settled back into the sofa, letting her cuddle up to me again.

I don't know why I was letting her. She was Zaide's, and getting closer to her would only hurt me, but it felt right. We were quiet for a while, listening to the sound of the shower. Zaide was taking so long, and then I thought about his Rapunzel-style hair and knew exactly why we went through so much shampoo.

Clawdia interrupted my thoughts. "Were you in love with Lydia?"

I made a face. "Well, no, not exactly."

"What do you mean, not exactly?"

"I cared about her and thought it was something like love, but not exactly. My experience with love has been limited, so I could be wrong, but I always got the feeling she was hiding something from me, and that made it difficult for me to trust her."

Clawdia nodded her understanding and then said, "Winnie and I couldn't work out what you saw in her. And Winnie was her friend—"

"Wait. Lydia and Winnie were friends." My mind buzzed.

Clawdia frowned. "Yes, you know that. Why is that important?"

"Does Winnie have many human friends?"

Clawdia sat up. "No, they are all witches."

"She knew what you were, right?" Clawdia nodded. "She's a witch too? Shit. How did I miss that?"

"Maybe because you didn't know that witches existed until a group of otherworlders came for a visit?"

"Now is not the time to be funny."

"Just practicing being the cool Clawdia you wanted to hang out with."

"Keep practicing." She laughed, and I ran a hand through my hair.

Zaide finally made an appearance from the bathroom. He was wearing a towel around his waist, and his golden body glistened. I noted the color creeping up Clawdia's neck as she looked at her soul pair.

"What were you doing in there? We've found the reason for life on Earth out here."

He was unimpressed. "What did you find?"

"Well, that would be telling."

"Keep your secrets, human. They are probably very dull." He smirked and then looked at Clawdia. His face softened. "How are you this morning, Little Cat?"

Clawdia's eyes were enormous, and she squeaked when she said, "Well." Then she cleared her throat and tried again. "I'm well, thank you. Are ... are you well?"

He nodded and, with a small grin on his face, walked into his bedroom. When his door shut, her wide eyes turned to me.

"You really don't know how to do this, do you?" I remarked with a laugh. She covered her face with her hands. I rescued her from the box of shame she was about to sit in. "Look, enough about you. I'm having a crisis over here. Let's figure this shit out."

She lifted her head from her hands with a sigh. "You're very dramatic, Charlie. It's not a crisis. Your ex-girlfriend was a witch. So what?"

"It's a problem because I don't believe in coincidences." I stood up and started pacing. It helped me think. "What are the odds that we discover Lydia is a witch when we need a witch to tell us what and where this witch event is taking place?"

Daithi walked into the room, having heard the question, and answered it for me, "Very unlikely. However, fate seems to have a hand in this. Perhaps you should reach, tentatively, for the bait."

"You think I should contact her?"

"I think you should see what she knows. If she knows

CHARLIE

anything."

I sighed. "No one said anything about contacting exes when I signed up for this."

"You signed up for a trip across the Earth."

"We're in Sweden, remember. We traveled somewhere." I looked at Clawdia and rolled my eyes. "No pleasing some fuckers."

"I would like my lover to be conscious for the rest of our journey around the world, Charlie. Talk to the witch." And all the fun drained from the room as he wandered to the bathroom.

"It's hard to remember that he wasn't always an arsehole," I commented.

Clawdia grimaced. "He is grieving."

I knew she struggled with his attitude too, since he almost always aimed at her, and her kindness made me smile. But I also wanted to know why he was suddenly so remorseful last night and offered to turn her back into a cat.

Shaking my head free of distracting thoughts, I called out the plan. "Okay, Clawdia, eat some of that sugary cereal—I can hear your stomach from here—and I'll call Lydia." She smiled, saluted, and walked to the kitchenette.

I gave myself five seconds to appreciate her legs before I called Lydia's number.

When I'd broken up with her, she wasn't happy about it. She'd told me if I ever regretted it, to call. I knew she would think this was a "let's get back together" call and not a "give me inside witch information" one. I was already cringing at what I'd have to say.

She answered, as I knew she would, in a husky tone that threw me off for a second. "Charlie, this is unexpected."

"By unexpected, do you mean unexpectedly joyful?" I quipped.

"I mean, I didn't think you'd be calling so soon."

"You've been expecting my call, then?" I cringed. We'd been broken up for three months. She still expected us to get back together after all that time?

"Well, yeah. You know, don't you?" she stated.

Didn't see that coming. She hoped I'd find out she was a witch and call her about it? Why?

I played coy. "Yeah, but why don't you spell it out for me?"

She huffed in frustration. "It's too early in the morning to be dealing with your mind games. You know I'm a witch, and you've found out about your own witch blood and want help."

I was silent for a beat.

What. The. Fuck?

Clawdia was watching me as she ate her cereal. She mouthed "Everything okay?" and I gave her a wide-eyed funny look she couldn't interpret.

Lydia sounded in my ear again. "Charlie?"

"How … how did you know?" I recovered poorly, my mind reeling.

Is she being serious?

She breathed a relieved laugh. "Oh, thank God. For a moment there, I thought I'd let the cat out of the bag."

I mimicked her laugh robotically. "No, no, I've known for a little while now. And, um, I wanted to know, how come you didn't say anything about it to me?"

She sighed. "It wasn't easy for me, Charlie, believe me. I wanted to tell you, but I wasn't sure at the beginning, and by the time I'd tested you and was sure you'd come from a witch line, you'd broken up with me."

"So, you kept it from me as punishment?" I blinked as anger started boiling inside me.

Clawdia audibly gasped and mouthed "A baby?" I shook my head and turned away from her so I could focus on the problem at hand.

I'm a witch?

"No, I just—" she stumbled and started again. "I know you liked your life the way it was. I didn't think you needed to know that."

I scoffed, and bitterness tinged my words. "You knew I was a foster child and didn't know who my parents were, and you didn't think I'd want information about where I came from?"

"I'm sorry. You're right, I shouldn't have kept it from you." She sounded genuinely apologetic, but I was still too angry to accept that.

Forgetting the reason I called, I continued my interrogation. "How did you test me?"

"What?"

"How did you test me for being a witch?" I said slowly, trying to calm myself.

Clawdia touched my elbow, and I turned to look at her. "A witch?" she mouthed. I closed my eyes and nodded once. She hugged me and stayed close as Lydia continued. I wasn't sure if she was trying to comfort me or just listen in on the conversation.

"I just took a strand of your hair and asked for it to search for likeness in hairs of other UK witch lines. It went to the Bradbury line. One or both of your parents came from there. It's a powerful line. You have a lot of their physical and magical features."

"Explain that. How did you know I had magical features? What are they?"

"A magical feature is like a personality trait in witch lines. Some are better at foresight, others at seeking, brewing, spellcasting, et cetera. You always know exactly how to find things, Charlie. You did it so often and so unassumingly that I knew it had to be magical, but you didn't recognize that because to you, it was normal."

"What do you mean?"

"I'd always leave something somewhere in your house, and without even looking for it, you'd know where it was."

"That's not magical. That's organized."

"No, you have a gift. You find things. If something is missing, you find it. Haven't you always felt it was too easy?"

I knew she was right. I called it my superpower, but I didn't actually believe it was a superpower.

This is crazy.

"Okay, so I'm a seeker, and my Bradbury line are also seekers?"

"Yes. They breed seekers."

"What do you fall under?"

"Well, the Blacks are good at potions."

"Right." I was a little speechless.

Information about my birth parents was the one thing I could never find. And now I knew why. They didn't want me to find them.

Lydia was hesitant now. "How did you find out, if you don't mind my asking?"

I couldn't think quickly when my mind was so over-whelmed with new information. "Winnie told me."

"Oh, Winnie told you. That's great."

I rushed to explain my lack of knowledge. "She didn't explain a lot. We were having an argument. Over her cat."

"What about her cat?"

"Well, Clawdia spends a lot of time at my house. She was angry, thinking I wanted to steal her."

"Oh," Lydia sounded so surprised that I knew for sure that I'd fucked up. I was cursing myself internally when she laughed and said, "Well, no wonder she was so angry. That cat is her familiar."

I feigned shock. "What? She seems like such a normal cat." Clawdia glared at me, and I stuck my tongue out at her.

"Not normal at all. You know what one is, right?"

"Only what I've heard from films."

"Yeah, they are a little more special than that. Hardly anyone can call a familiar. It takes a lot of practice and a lot of luck. Winnie attracted loads of attention when she got Clawdia, and familiars gravitate to strong witches. No wonder she was angry with her familiar for being with you all the time. You've clearly got a lot of strength."

"Yeah, that explains it. So, I won't get a familiar?"

Clawdia glared again. I pressed my lips together to stop a laugh escaping. Jealous Clawdicat.

"Not unless you work for one. I can send you a book on it if you like."

"Yeah, that would be great. Hey, listen, I've known about this for a little while now, and I've been hearing whispers about something happening, some kind of event. I thought it might be good to meet some people, get a few more answers. Do you know what that's about?"

It was a left field question, and I wasn't expecting her to immediately respond, but Lydia was full of surprises. "I don't know what you've been hearing, but this event isn't like a charity ball. It's a serious event for serious witches."

"Well, maybe I want to be a serious witch."

She sighed. "It starts this evening, so unless you can get a flight to Sweden this afternoon and meet me in Eskilstuna, then you are going to miss it."

"So, here's the thing … I'm already in Sweden. I sort of knew something was happening here. I just didn't know when or where."

"Wow! Okay, that's awesome. I can meet you now and introduce you to some people before tonight."

CHAPTER 26

CHARLIE

*O*n the drive to the coffeehouse, I felt numb. I hadn't processed what Lydia had told me properly yet. Even telling Clawdia, Zaide, and Daithi was like someone else was speaking.

The sat nav took me to the center of Eskilstuna, close to the hotel where Winnie and Mary were staying. A bell rang as I pushed the door into the small, dimly lit shop. I was immediately hit with the smell of coffee as I looked around at the bookcase wallpaper and dark, comfy-looking chairs.

At a table in the back of the shop, I saw familiar brown hair worn loose in curls. When I reached her, she jumped up excitedly and pulled me into a hug. "Charlie! It's so nice to see you. You look great."

I didn't look great. My only good sleep was last night's, and the purple bags under my eyes still told the story of the previous nights. Either she was being polite, or she still liked me. Neither option was appealing since, one, she was about to commit a kind of magical genocide, which included my demon friend.

And two, my attraction to her had definitely died. Her

green eyes, which used to look so fresh and clear, now looked like a filthy pond. Her skin wasn't smooth anymore. Even her teeth looked yellow. I couldn't tell if she had always looked that way and I had just been blind for months or if our break-up hadn't been as kind to her as it had to me.

To be polite, because I'm a fucking gent, I said, "Thanks. So do you."

"Oh, no. I've put on a bit of weight."

"I can't tell." I could tell.

She laughed shyly. "Thanks. I ordered you a coffee. You still have it with oat milk?"

"Yes. Thanks, Lyds, that's great." There was an awkward pause, which I tried to fill with a slurp of my coffee.

She chewed her lip and said, "Okay, well, I'm sure you're curious about all of this, Charlie. I promise to explain. Most people are setting up at the site, so now is a good time to chat."

"Well, as long as I'm not the virgin sacrifice for whatever you guys are up to, I'm good."

"We both know you aren't a virgin." She laughed, and I repressed a shudder at the memory of sleeping with her. I couldn't figure out why she was so repugnant to me now. "It's nothing that sinister. Witches are the good guys."

"Oh, really?" I tried to hide the cynicism in my voice, but it seeped through. Thankfully, she knew I was always a cynical bastard and suspected everything.

"Of course. We are the only ones on the planet with powers beyond the imagination of most people. We can save the world."

I rolled my eyes. "Save the world from what? There's a lot that needs saving right now. Global warming, wars, people starving, meat markets. Haven't heard about witches stepping in there."

"Those are important issues, but mankind can fix all that. They just need more money motivation. Witches can't help there. But this, this is something we have been planning for centuries. Something big and important, and if we do it right, then no one will ever know that witches were involved."

I leaned forward, glad we were finally getting some useful information. "So, what is this thing?"

"Well, it's hard to explain. We are trying to bring back a defender, something that could win when a magical problem occurs."

"A defender?"

"Have you heard of the Norse myth of Sigurd?"

I smirked slightly. "I've heard about it vaguely. Didn't he kill a dragon?"

"He did!" She was shocked. "Charlie, I didn't know you were so cultured."

I laughed. "Hey, don't be so surprised. I'm a man of the world."

"Well, anyway," Lydia began when she recovered from my wit, "Sigurd was a legendary hero. But there are untold parts to every story, and witches have done their best to hide the truth from the world."

"I feel a story coming on."

She smiled and continued, "The dragon, Fafnir, was a greedy, power-hungry monster. He killed his brothers for money and then killed witches for their magic. Consuming magic your body isn't built for is like eating McDonald's every day and every meal for the rest of your life."

"You'd explode?"

"No, you'd get ridiculously fat. You'd have so much fat that your body wouldn't know what to do with it, where to put it. It's the same with magic. His body changed into something it wasn't in order to cope: a dragon."

"I think he got lucky there. I'd rather eat too much and be a dragon than a fat bastard."

"Eating too much magic means slaughtering lots of witches," she said dryly. "I think you have more potential to be a fat bastard."

"Wow. That's rude."

"Will you shut up and let me tell the story?"

"I'm sorry. The dude ate magic, turned into a dragon … continue."

She took a fortifying breath and went on. "Other witches tried and failed to kill him, their magic adding another spelled scale to his skin. He was indestructible. Or so they thought. In a vision, a witch saw his grieving nephew promising revenge and knew he would be the one to save them.

She visited him, told him she was looking for a defender, someone who could be called upon to rescue witches, humans, and the world alike. This included getting the revenge he desired. He was young and excited by the task and agreed without listening to the terms. The witches set to making him the best defender the world had ever seen. They spelled his armor, gave him potions, and every day for a year, they gave him a touch of magic."

"Wouldn't that make him a dragon like the other guy?"

"Fafnir was doing it at an uncontrolled rate. He wasn't giving his body time to process the magic. With just a touch a day, Sigurd could internalize the magic, become faster and stronger without changing his form. The time eventually came to put their plan into action.

The witches created a trap, which Fafnir flew straight into. Stupid with the size of his ego, he saw his nephew and thought it would be an easy kill. It was a long and tiring battle, but Sigurd did the impossible and killed his uncle. As the winged body fell flat against the ground, the witches celebrated the defeat of a monster.

With everyone thinking the day was done, they were unprepared when, with his last breath, Fafnir took a giant claw and stabbed it into Sigurd's body. The witches flew into a panic to save him. They bathed his body in the dragon's blood and fed him parts of the dragon's heart, tried to heal him with spells and potions. But it was too late. He died there as a hero to all witches.

The witch with foresight knew Sigurd would be needed again, and so she wrote the truth of the story, including her vision of the future, when witches would be threatened again, and a plan to save us. The ceremony tonight is the first part of the plan."

I processed the information as I sipped my coffee. "I have a lot of issues and questions with this story, and I'm not sure where to start."

She sighed. "You wouldn't be you if you didn't interrogate everything."

"How do you know all of this?"

"Because she wrote it." She looked at me defiantly, daring me to find the untruth in her words.

"How can you trust it?"

"Because she had the Sight. People with the Sight are bound to tell the truth."

"Bound?"

"Yes, with magic. It punishes you if you don't do as you promised."

"Okay." I took a breath. "So, the ceremony tonight. What does it entail? What's the end goal?"

"The end goal is to raise Sigurd again."

"Raise him from the dead."

"Yes." She said it so matter of fact, so calmly, as though it would be so easy, I had to freeze for a moment.

What the hell have I gotten myself into? Raising the dead? Protection from something threatening witches?

Fuck my life.

I shook my thoughts away and got back to business. "Okay, how?"

There was a fire in her eyes that freaked me out as she gesticulated. "Well, the first step is to raise the body. The problem they had the first time they tried to heal him was that there weren't enough witches. Not enough magic. This time, we have witches from all over the world here. Everyone is so excited to be part of this event. We have enough now—more than enough."

"Yes, but you aren't just trying to heal him. You're trying to raise him from the dead."

"Correct, and so that involves another part. Raising the soul. This would usually present as a challenge. However, witches have been using demon fire for lots of things in spells and potions. It can do almost anything. Obviously, this is a big ask of any ingredient, so we needed more. Lots and lots. The foreseeing witch said that until this day, every witch that could should summon a demon and bury them in the earth."

I swallowed thickly before asking, "What does burying it do?"

"It forces its fire to keep healing the body of the demon. When buried and trapped, its body responds like any other being and suffocates and panics. Their fire keeps them alive."

Knowing that Savida suffered like that for God knows how long, made me sick to my stomach. "I thought you wanted the fire. Why wouldn't you just take it? Why the torture?"

She rolled her eyes. "If we take the fire too early, then it might not be as strong as we need. You never know what you're going to get when you summon. It could be old or young, powerful or weak; burying them makes sure that the fire grows more powerful and is ready when we need it to be."

"Okay. So the fires you have been collecting for years are going to bring back Sigurd's soul?"

"That's the plan, yes."

"Wouldn't it have been simpler to spend a year collectively making a new defender? This seems so unnecessary."

She glared, and it reminded me of every argument we had when we were together. Oh, the good old days. "It isn't unnecessary. If there were any other option, we wouldn't be doing this. And clearly, there isn't another option, because no one has seen one."

My body tingled. Something more was going on here. I just didn't know what.

I continued, "I think someone's telling lies, Lydia. If the story said it took a year for Sigurd to be ready, it only makes sense to find someone to do that again. No need for all this pomp and ceremony to raise a guy that is over a thousand years old. Leave the bloke alone to his afterlife in Valhalla. Poor bastard."

"You are so cynical. Look, he promised he would be our defender and that he would come when he was called upon."

I sat back in disbelief. "He can't escape that promise in death? Fuck me, remind me never to make a promise to you lot."

"Charlie, stop being flippant."

"Lydia, stop being blind." I replied quickly, feeling more and more like I was talking to a cult member rather than my ex. "You're following the word of an ages-old text, doing something dangerous and unnecessary."

"Look, Charlie, you've been a witch for all of a few months, so don't come to me and announce that you have all the answers, because you don't."

I let out a frustrated huff and then admitted defeat. Arguing with her was not productive. "You're right. I'm sorry. You're doing me a huge favor, and I shouldn't be having a go at you."

She deflated. "I don't want to fight with you. Let me introduce you to some people. Maybe you'll understand a bit more after spending time with us."

"Yeah, okay."

She stood up and smiled. "Come with me."

She walked to the back of the store with the bookcase wallpaper, and I watched as she twisted a doorknob I hadn't seen, disguised by the books, and opened a door into another room.

Fucking witches and their secret rooms.

I made sure she entered first so I wouldn't get another bad luck curse and followed her into a room similar to the small cafe. It had the same dim lighting and the same bookcase wallpaper but was bigger and had far more people sitting at tables and standing up, chatting.

"Simon!" Lydia called and dragged me across the room to a ginger bloke casually dressed in t-shirt and jeans, eating a sandwich and reading a book at a table in the corner of the room. He looked up at the sound of his name, and I noticed his oversized glasses covering his brown eyes. They seemed familiar somehow.

He smiled politely, but I could tell he wasn't pleased to see us. Or maybe it was just Lydia. "Hi, Lydia. How can I help you?"

"Hi, Simon. I wanted to introduce you to Charlie. He's new, found out about his witch heritage a few months ago."

"Oh yeah? What line?" His polite smile turned to one of genuine interest and welcome.

I shrugged. "Apparently Bradbury."

His eyebrows raised, and his smile widened. "No way. I'm

a Bradbury. We'll have to find out where you fell out of the family tree."

Lydia turned to me and said, "Simon will help you figure out where you came from. He's a pretty prominent figure in the Bradbury line. I'll leave you in his capable hands. Bye, Charlie. Maybe I'll see you around." She flashed a seductive smile, which I repressed a shudder at, and walked away, leaving me with Simon.

"You mind?" I asked him since he didn't get a choice and she'd left him to babysit me.

He chuckled. "Not at all. Sit down. Let's see if we can find your family."

I made myself comfortable on the leather chair and said dryly, "So is it like a normal DNA blood test or some magic spell that lets me find that shit out?"

"That would be the magic spell blood test." He smirked, and I warmed to him.

I made an "aw darn" movement with my hand. "Ah, a combination. I should have seen that coming."

He smiled and then whispered, "I can do it now if you like. I shouldn't since we are supposed to be reserving our magic for later, but family helps family, and I know I wouldn't want to wait."

Confused by the whispering, I replied hesitantly, "I mean, if you can, that would be great."

"Hand please." I reached out my hand, and he pricked my index finger with a needle he magicked out of nowhere. And it fucking hurt, but I didn't make a sound because I didn't want him to think I was a wuss. "Sorry."

He released my hand, and I looked at the drop of blood on the needle. "Now what?" I asked.

He shook the needle so the drop of blood hit the palm of his hand. "Watch." Then rays of light emerged from around the drop, and as they grew longer, some also grew thicker.

"What's happening?" I wasn't sure if I should ask because he needed to concentrate, but since I was a witch too now, I was interested to know how this was done.

"You're aware that Bradburys find things?"

"That's what I was told."

"I'm finding your closest living relatives and asking them to call me." The strings of light now resembled tentacles, and they danced as they continued to get larger and longer. One of them suckered itself to Simon. He laughed in a kind of startled but pleased way.

"What does that mean?" I pointed to the string attached to him.

"Means I'm your cousin. Welcome to the family."

I blinked. "No way."

"Way."

I was officially mind-blown. I had a family. Real blood relatives. One was right in front of me. "Fuck."

He nodded, seeming to understand how I was feeling. "I'm just searching for your other parental line. And hopefully we'll hear from them soon."

I frowned. "What if they are normal humans? They won't see the tentacles and the message, will they? That would definitely fuck them up."

"No. If they are human, they won't see anything, but they'll find you. They won't feel better until they do. It won't happen immediately, but eventually, you'll find out who they are."

I sat, mouth agape and dazed. "I can't believe it. I knew I could find almost anything for anyone. But I couldn't find my family. It drove me fucking mad. You just did that in seconds."

He considered that. "Maybe they are witches, then. They could cloak themselves from your search. Not much else can withstand the hunt of a Bradbury."

The light dimmed, and the blood dried. Simon smiled widely at me. "Is it weird if I hug you?"

"A little. I'll accept it, though."

He laughed and pulled me out of my seat and in for a manly hug, including the essential three back slaps. It made me feel better. Welcomed. I chuckled. "This is so strange. My mother was an only child, so Grandma is definitely keeping secrets."

"The name goes through the mother's line?"

He nodded and took a bite of his sandwich that he'd set aside to do the seeking spell. "Witches are matriarchal. I'm lucky not to be married off to a witch of higher status, but my sisters are still too young to be the head of the family, so I'm safe for the moment."

"Rough." I grimaced.

He shrugged. "It's a male witch's life. I can't wait to introduce you to them all and see the look on Grandma's face."

I made a face. "That won't be fun. Maybe she had a reason for giving my parent away. Maybe she was raped and didn't want to be reminded. Maybe she had them outside of wedlock and was ashamed. Maybe she had a vision that the baby was going to be a mass murderer, so she sent it away to a baby prison."

He was silent. "You know, the first two actually made me feel bad. The last made me admire your creativity. Nice job."

"I try." I smiled innocently.

"I wouldn't give up my day job or anything, but hey, you'll be able to tell some cracking bedtime stories." He looked me up and down. "If you aren't already?"

I paused for a moment, not understanding. Until I did. "Er. No. No sprogs."

"That you are aware of." He wiggled his eyebrows.

I frowned, slightly insulted. "What does that mean?"

He waved his hand in a "oh, stop being silly, I'm joking"

way and said, "It means, cousin, you are a pretty boy and probably get a lot of action."

"Not nearly enough," I scoffed, thinking about how Clawdia stared at Zaide this morning.

He laughed. "I feel that." He nodded in the direction that Lydia had disappeared. "You and Lydia were a thing?"

"Yeah." And the shudders I had been repressing overcame me. "Why?"

He continued with a cheeky grin, "You know she uses beauty potions, right?"

My grin fell straight off my face. "You're fucking joking."

"Nope."

I stared open-mouthed. "I knew she looked ugly today. I just thought it was the not sleeping with her thing."

"I mean, that makes it worse, but yeah, we can't use magic until tonight."

"You rule breaker, you."

"That was important. Anyway, this whole ceremony gives me the creeps."

I let out a huge sigh.

Yes! He's not a soulless prick!

"Thank fuck. When Lydia explained, I was like, 'That is the worst thing I've ever heard.' She thinks talking to you might help me understand."

He nodded and whispered, "Don't get me wrong, I know why it needs to be done, and I understand the privilege of getting chosen to be part of history, but it's still a bit fucked. I'm not going to lie to you about that."

"I'm still not clear on that part. Why does it need to be done?"

"The people going missing at the moment are being taken by otherworlders through a portal. The protector can stop portals being opened to our realm."

They really think they are going to help save people. I didn't know if it was true or not, whether the protector could do what they thought, but they believed in it so wholeheartedly that there wouldn't be any reasoning with them. To them, we were the baddies.

Simon wasn't soulless, but he was still agreeing that destroying one race of people to save another was right. That human lives were more important. I didn't want to think that made him a bad person, and so I tried not to judge my new family too harshly.

Changing the subject, I said, "So, when are you going tonight?"

"The ceremony starts this evening at about eight o'clock when it gets dark. It'll last until the moon reaches its highest peak, and then he will rise," he finished in a Frankenstein voice that made me laugh.

"Gross." I shuddered.

He nodded. "Super gross."

"And where is this happening?" I could hear Daithi in the back of my head, demanding I ask more questions, but I needed to play this casually so I didn't raise suspicion.

Simon frowned, and he pushed his glasses back up his nose. "Charlie, I like you, dude. For my new cousin, you're all right. But you don't know anything about being a witch. I don't think you should be there tonight."

I nodded calmly, but my heart beat like a drum. "This is my opportunity to know more about being a witch. I want to learn, Simon." I made sure I was earnest about what I was telling him, because if his gifts were anything like mine, he'd know if I was only telling half-truths.

He looked torn. His eyes glanced around the room. Then he leaned over the table to whisper, "Look, I don't want to scare you, but our leader has warned us that there are other-worlders who might interrupt the ceremony. It's dangerous."

"I laugh in the face of danger." I leaned back and crossed my arms.

"I'm being serious, Charlie," he hissed.

I relaxed and sighed. "I know. I'm sorry. Look, I haven't had an easy life. Trust me to take care of myself."

"You don't understand—"

"I'm not going to let my new family face dangerous other-worlders without me," I said in a no-nonsense tone.

"All right, but you have to promise not to get involved."

My grin was the size of his plate. "I swear."

"Okay. Give me your number. I'll text you the coordinates. It's about a ten-minute trek from the main road."

CHAPTER 27

CLAWDIA

The door slammed shut behind Charlie, who was off to meet his ex-girlfriend to talk about his witch heritage. While I was glad he had a clue to his past, I was jealous it came from Lydia. And anxious that he'd see her and remember his feelings for her. But I didn't want to analyze that too closely.

Unsure what to do with ourselves, Daithi, Zaide, and I turned to stare at each other.

"I will be resting and reading. Try not to have any emergencies which need magical attention." Daithi sighed.

He glided to his room, too beautiful for such an angry demeanor, with his green hair curled up from his neck and his skin shining. He looked better today. Less stricken with panic and tiredness.

Moving from the kitchenette to the living room, I sank into the cushions next to Zaide with a sigh. On the television, a news presenter named those who had gone missing this week. It was so depressing I turned it off.

Zaide put his arm around me and pulled me into his chest. Staring down at me with an indulgent smile, he said,

"It is just you and me, Little Cat. What shall we do to be useful?"

Still feeling slightly shy about everything, I didn't want to invite more conversation about last night's revelation.

"We could read books too?" I smiled half-heartedly and pulled out of his grasp to reach for the pile of books on the side table.

"No!" he shouted and pulled me back into his arms. I hit his strong, hard chest at an uncomfortable angle, and with a cricked neck, I glared up at him.

He could have just said no without restraining me. I harrumphed as I rearranged myself.

Panic lit his expression, and I tilted my head curiously. "Why not?"

"Well ... I ... It's ... No ... We ..." He tripped over his words, and his cheeks turned to a lovely rose gold color, which I took to be an embarrassed blush.

"Zaide?" I questioned again.

He coughed. "I'm ... conducting some ... personal research."

"You don't need help?" I asked slowly.

He looked away from me as the rose color in his cheeks deepened. "No," he croaked.

If he doesn't want to tell me, I'll just look at the books when he isn't around. I thought mischievously.

I stared at him, assessing his reaction. He was so big and fierce looking with his purple scars and eyes, but he was a gentle giant. It was one of my favorite things about him, that I felt so safe in his large hands. He blushed again as his eyes met mine, and I smiled. He was so sweet. And although I was horribly curious, as my cat side demanded I be, I knew it wasn't a vindictive secret. He wouldn't hurt me.

"All right," I said softly, agreeing to more than just leaving his secret alone, but also to giving us a chance, to trust him not to break my heart. To loving him. Building a life with him.

My heart felt as though it grew with how full and warm and happy I was. I smiled so big and so wide that my cheeks ached.

Zaide didn't reply with words, seeming as lost in my eyes and I was in his, but his answering smile was soft and wistful. I lifted my left hand to run down his face, my thumb tracking the thin purple scar under his eye, down to his neck.

Cupping his jaw, I brushed my thumb over his lips. Plump, dusk-colored lips that were suddenly the most interesting things. His lips parted, and mine instinctively followed suit. I pulled my gaze back to his and saw the desire, the passion, the affection glittering, pulsing in a color so familiar, so like my own.

Leaning close, I tilted my head up, pulled his face down to me, and gently pressed my lips against his. But I stopped, suddenly unsure. Sensing my unease, Zaide ran his hands over my arms, down my back, and to my face in slow, soothing movements.

With our lips barely touching, we breathed each other in. The rough pads of his fingers grazed my skin, causing both comfort and arousal to sweep over me. I could smell the minty toothpaste on his breath and the fruity scent of his long, drying hair. The heat of his body warmed me, and I heard his unsteady breaths.

Realizing I wasn't alone in my nervousness, I offered him the same comfort, running my right hand over his chiseled chest and broad shoulder while my left hand still cupped his face and gently moved him closer.

At the first brush of soft lips, I moaned, and my tongue peeked out to stroke his lips. Then I was no longer in control of the kiss. Zaide growled, a sound which made me clench my legs together as arousal flooded me.

He pulled me tightly against him, leaving no room between our bodies. His hands were firm and strong as he held me in place against him. He tilted my head and deepened the kiss, our tongues gliding past each other, with each other, in a dance that set my body on fire. I knew I wasn't the only one affected; his arousal was a hard bulge against my hip. I whimpered.

He smiled at the sound, his warm breath tickling my skin, and gentled his lips. His kisses becoming pecks that worked their way from the edge of my lips, to my cheeks, both sides, my nose, and finally, my forehead. With our eyes still closed, I snuggled back into his chest, and he nuzzled my hair. We stopped that way for a few more peaceful moments together before he broke the silence.

"Come, Little Cat, we must do something productive with our time, or Charlie will scold us when he returns. He can't be the only one working hard."

I sighed and nuzzled his chest. It was safe there. I could pretend everything was right with the world. "But I really like doing this," I whined.

"I think we should practice changing your shape."

I furrowed my brow and pouted. "That doesn't sound like a good idea."

"Why not? You need to practice."

"What if I get stuck?"

"Then I will have Charlie scream until you turn back."

I laughed. "You don't need to say that as threatening as you do. He'd scream without incentive."

"Ah, but that wouldn't be as much fun, Little Cat." He chuckled, and I loved to hear the sound vibrating in his chest.

"Okay." I heaved myself off his lap and stood in front of him. "How are we going to practice when I don't know how to do it?"

He smiled and tapped the sofa. "Lie down on here and close your eyes." I did so, wiggling to get comfortable. "I want you to focus on your breath—"

My eyes popped open. "I'm going to meditate into a cat?"

He waved his hand over my eyes, shutting them. "Don't interrupt, Little Cat. But yes, you have magic, probably some of the magic from when we were a whole titan. You just need to access it. You stirred it with your anger yesterday, but perhaps in focusing, you will find the magic within and bring your cat form forth. With practice, you'll be able to do it faster."

I opened my eyes again to look at him. "How do you know how to do this?"

He shrugged. "Many other realms practice this in some way or another, and I enjoy spiritual pursuits. Now, close your eyes and start again."

I took a deep breath and then focused on my breathing. I concentrated on how the air pulled in through my nose and out through my mouth, the brush of the wind tickling my lips. I followed its journey to my lungs, where I could feel them inflating and deflating, moving my ribs, removing the carbon dioxide and adding oxygen to the blood that circulated throughout my whole body.

"Within you, there is magic. It will help you transform. Find it, Clawdia." Zaide's voice was distant and hypnotic.

I traveled along the veins and vessels and lines, searching, until I saw something glinting in the darkness. I moved closer to the sparkly thing and realized it was magic, purple and shimmering. I watched, entranced, as it unfurled in front of me, as though my presence affected it. Following the same vessels that I did, it spread across my body, and I felt its power and strength flood my sensations.

I gasped, unsettled.

"It's okay, Clawdia. It's yours. It knows what you want."

And with another flash of pain, I was a cat.

"You did it!" Zaide crooned, and he untangled me from my human clothes and stroked my glorious fur. "You are a wonder, Clawdia."

I meowed, agreeing.

"Now you just need to practice turning back." I bit his finger, and he chuckled. "Yes, I will give you time to rest first."

* * *

THE FRONT DOOR beeped open in the late afternoon, and Charlie walked in. He collapsed on the sofa and lay his head on my lap. Instinctively, I stroked his forehead and hair.

I took in his handsome face, his eyes pinched closed. "How did it go?" I asked softly.

"Big news. I've got a cousin." I heard the confusion he felt in his voice, the contradicting emotions that were battering him, as well as the stress of saving Savida.

Still speaking softly, I said, "That is big news. How do you feel about it?" I continued to stroke his hair, letting him know I was there for him. Despite having a soul pair in Zaide, I still liked Charlie. I found him attractive, and I cared for him. More so now that this had shown a less grumpy side to him.

I was battling my own contradicting emotions and knew how draining it could be.

He sighed. "I think we need to save Savida and get us to a remote beach before I process my feelings. Preferably with a cold beer in hand."

Zaide and Daithi emerged from different rooms, having heard that Charlie had arrived, and came to join us in the living area. Charlie opened his eyes and watched as they sank into other chairs. He glared at Zaide and pointed. "What the fuck is that?"

Zaide was taken aback and looked down himself, searching for whatever had affronted Charlie. "I don't know what you are referring to, Charlie."

"You're wearing a red t-shirt." We all stared at him in confusion.

"Yes," Zaide drawled. "Is that wrong?"

"Zaide, you don't wear red when going to the boss battle. Anyone who has watched *Star Trek* knows that."

Zaide frowned. "I haven't watched *Star Trek*."

"Zaide, take off the shirt. It's tempting fate too much. We've had enough bad luck without that." Charlie sighed. "It's not your color anyway. Red and gold makes me think of a phoenix or a dragon."

"I don't have any other clean ones," Zaide pouted.

Charlie rolled his eyes. "Do the sniff test. I'm sure one of them won't kill us."

I frowned. "Charlie, that's disgusting."

"Ah, there's the 100-year-old lady I've been waiting to meet."

I glared at him and saw Daithi twitching out of the corner of my eye. He had been patiently letting us banter, but he was ready to burst with the need to know what Charlie had learned. "You are stalling. Tell us what happened," I said.

He sighed and sat up, explaining everything Lydia had told him and then how he met his cousin, Simon.

"So basically, we need to get our shit together, make a plan, and find Savida's fire before they start the ceremony," he finished.

Daithi shook his head. "You said they were setting up this afternoon, so there is no chance of going early and being undetected."

I added, "And Debbie has set Winnie and Mary on us.

They are going to be ready for us. They know what you all are. If Winnie doesn't fulfill her sworn promise to Debbie by stopping us all when she sees us, she dies, and so do I."

Charlie nodded, then stood and clapped his hands. "Okay, so the plan is everyone goes. Clawdia will tell us how close or far Winnie is, and with her, is Mary. Hopefully, we can just scoot past them. If she can't see us, she can't find us and stop us. Loophole. Daithi will have us disguised. We all run in the direction of the ceremony since they'll have to have the fires close, ready for the ceremony. Daithi will distract the witches while we cause hell, grab fires, and run."

We were quiet, knowing the plan had a lot of flaws, variables, and difficulties. But it was the only chance we had. We were all going to take this last chance to save the demon, who was light and happiness. To save the person who'd placed me on his head and played with me. Who was outraged when I was hurt and betrayed by Winnie. Savida didn't know me as a human, but he was still my friend.

"We won't save that many demons," Zaide muttered into the quiet.

"Hopefully we can grab enough that they can't do the ceremony," Charlie replied somberly.

* * *

AT HALF SEVEN, we bundled into the car on the way to sabotage the ceremony. I was in the back, snuggled next to Zaide and holding his braid, playing with the black stone and the white ends of his hair.

I was nervous and trying to keep calm. There was a tension in the air. We all knew this would be hard, maybe even impossible, but we were jumping off the cliff and into the unknown anyway.

My mind flashed back to Winnie explaining her reasons

for this, how she only wanted to belong, and guilt poisoned my thoughts. I was about to ruin something important to her, my witch, who'd saved me, but she was wrong.

I'm doing the right thing. I nodded to myself. *But will she ever forgive me for betraying her?*

My stomach sank. I was tired of thinking about everyone else. I was tired of trying to be perfect so people would love me. It's part of why I loved being a cat—no matter what I did, people loved me.

She betrayed me first. If she can't forgive me, then I'll leave with my soul pair, and Charlie.

As we traveled down the winding road, large woodland areas on either side, I felt Winnie getting closer. "She's nearby," I told them.

Charlie shrugged. "We were expecting them to try and stop us."

"They won't be able to recognize us, Clawdia. I have us disguised. No puny witch magic will see through our glamor," Daithi scoffed.

"What about the car?" Charlie asked hurriedly.

"What about it?"

"They might recognize the car!" Charlie roared. "Fuck!" He banged the steering wheel and made us all jump. Zaide's hand came to rest on my thigh and reassured me.

"They may not." Daithi's voice quivered slightly. "There is still time to hide it."

"This is the only road to the clearing. They will have people watching. We are screwed." Charlie cursed and shook his head clear of his frustrations.

I shuddered. If Winnie saw us, then she would have to stop them, or she would die. And therefore, I would die.

But if she stopped them, she'd kill my soul pair and erase Charlie's mind, and I couldn't allow that. I wouldn't let them die. I'd stop her myself if I had to.

I hoped the disguise would be enough, but I wasn't sure how much influence word choice had on a vow. If she didn't recognize the group that left the car but knew the car belonged to us and that we were likely disguised, would the vow activate?

Charlie parked alongside the tree line a little distance from where other cars started. The tension was palpable. My mouth was dry. My heart thumped painfully in my chest, and fear swirled in my stomach. I felt sick.

"Come on," Charlie whispered.

We all moved silently as we got out of the car and closed the doors quietly, holding our breath and looking out into the tree line, waiting for an attack.

Charlie didn't look at us as he whispered, "Stick together." He creeped to the front of the car, moving soundlessly over the gravel. I tried to emulate him as best I could as I met him there. The four of us formed a tight box as we moved together toward the tree line.

I gasped as fear suddenly flooded through me, making my knees unsteady. But it wasn't coming from me.

"Winnie?" I turned, looking for her. I felt the jolt of fear and hope at the sound of my call. I knew she was close. I knew she could hear me. I just couldn't see her.

"Little Cat, you must be quiet." Zaide's voice was low but soft, and he placed a hand on my shoulder to keep me from moving away from them.

"Something is wrong—"

From the tree line, a female voice shouted. "Take another step, and I kill her!"

Mary.

"Winnie!" I called as Mary revealed herself. On her knees next to her and caged was my witch. My gaze met hers. Fear and sadness were etched into her lovely dark skin.

I moved toward them, the urge to save her driving my

body forward. Mary turned her cruel stare to me and stopped me in my tracks as she brandished a large knife. "I'm serious. I will kill her. And that will kill you, familiar."

I whimpered. "You wouldn't kill your girlfriend."

Mary growled. Reaching between the magical shimmering bars, she grabbed Winnie's hair. I felt her fear spike.

This wasn't a trick. Winnie was scared. She feared for her life.

"You don't know what I've had to sacrifice to get this far," Mary replied and pointed her knife at Winnie. "Do not underestimate me. Do not overestimate my affection for my girlfriend."

With my heart racing and my mind whirling, adrenaline flooded me. I looked for something, anything, that could help me save her.

Winnie shouted, "Please listen to her! Don't let Clawdia suffer for this."

Mary laughed. "Still so concerned for the cat." Her eyes moved to the others. "None of you are getting out of this alive."

"You're crazy!" Charlie shouted. He went to take a step back.

"Don't move!" Mary screamed.

Winnie cried, "Mary, please!"

Daithi tried to bargain. "All we want is Savida's fire. We don't care about anything else. Give it to me, and we will leave."

"He is a necessary sacrifice for mankind, and I won't feel guilty for using a ball of fire to save the world."

"I'm not going to stand here and wait for you to try and kill me," Charlie challenged. He moved to sprint away, Daithi ready to follow his lead.

Mary was quicker. I recognized the signs and knew she was about to cast. I also knew all this stalling meant that with

CLAWDIA

every second, the chance of saving Savida grew smaller and smaller. I couldn't let this all be for nothing. I threw myself in front of her spell, which was aimed at Charlie and Daithi.

Thrown to the ground, I was trapped in a cage just like Winnie. Zaide ran over to me, and I knew I wouldn't be able to convince him to leave me.

"Charlie, Daithi, go find Savida's fire. We will be okay," I shouted.

Daithi immediately ran into the forest, but Charlie hesitated for a moment. Long enough for Winnie to scream, "Charlie, run!"

The next spell aimed at him was red. Deadly. Thankfully, he got running and dodged the spell before it hit him.

Watching their figures fade into the blackness, I sent a small prayer to God. The first in a long time. I hoped they'd find Savida's fire and save him. I hoped they stayed safe.

"You fucking bitch!" Mary screeched, and I turned to see that our cages had vanished and Mary held the knife against Winnie's neck. With an emotionless face, she slit Winnie's throat.

And I felt it.

I screamed for both of us because Winnie was gargling blood, unable to make any noise. Mary dropped her and ran after Daithi and Charlie.

God, the pain. It made me dizzy. My eyes clouded as I collapsed to the ground. I felt Zaide touching me. I heard him denying, praying, pleading for help. My heart broke for him.

He just found me. And now I'm dying.

I just found him. And now I'm dying.

My eyesight, although blurred, returned, and I saw Winnie. On her own. In a pool of blood.

We are dying.

My witch, my friend, my sister was dying.

Tears streamed down my face as I crawled with one hand and held my neck with the other. As I reached her, I saw the panic, the fear, and the sorrow in her eyes. She was suffocating on her blood, inhaling it and gurgling it out. I struggled to catch my breath the same way. I moaned low in my throat, nuzzled into her check, and lay flat against her. Her fingers dug into my skin, and as we lay dying together, struggling for breath, I heard her in my mind for the first time since this all began.

I'm sorry.

And then, for the second time in my life … I died.

CHAPTER 28

ZAIDE

*I*t all happened so quickly.

One moment, my soul pair was alive and bravely throwing herself in front of Mary's spell; the next, she and her witch were dying.

As Winnie dropped to the ground, blood gushing from her throat and gurgling in her mouth, Clawdia screamed, also feeling the pain, the death of her witch. It was going to be her death, too. Mary vanished.

"No. No. Little Cat, it's going to be all right," I tried to reassure her through my panic. She was gasping as she stared at Winnie. I was powerless, and like I had in so many other helpless situations, I prayed. "Hedri, Riseir, Charos, gods, please make this all right. Please. She is my soul pair."

I continued my steady repetition of prayer with my eyes closed. A low moan made me open them to find that Clawdia had crawled to her witch and laid down next to her, intending to die with her, holding her. The sight was like a harpoon in the gut.

My heart cried out in denial, and I surged toward them, determined and scared but desperate not to lose her. Winnie was no longer gurgling. My soul pair was still as I placed my hands on her arm. She didn't react.

I whimpered.

I screamed.

I cried.

When my sobbing had calmed to a steady stream of tears, I saw I was no longer where I once was.

Clawdia was gone. Tiny rocks did not assault my knees. My ears were no longer cold from the wind. My hands were not covered in the blood of my soul pair's witch. I was not in the human realm any longer.

Instead, my hands touched a marble floor. Smooth and polished, it was something I hadn't seen for a long time. It reminded me of home. Faint scents of incense hung in the air as I inhaled between gasping sobs.

She's gone.

The life we would have had together flashed through my mind. I imagined meals together, birthday celebrations, a bonding ceremony with Charlie, Savida, and Daithi once he finally forgave us. We would travel the realms until we settled somewhere with our friends, and eventually, her stomach would grow round with a child. We would have another soul join our mismatched family.

And there would be so much love. So much love that we would be the envy of every relationship. Whatever power we gained in our joining would pale compared to how we loved.

But she is gone.

Tears continued to fall, and my heart continued to break. I was so lost in my grief that I couldn't be scared or shocked at my arrival in a strange place.

"Please, pause your grief, broken one." The voice was booming. Powerful. I shuddered at the sound of it.

My heart skipped a beat, and I gasped, my mind unable to

understand how I was suddenly standing in front of the gods to whom I prayed.

I pushed away from them, my body sliding across the floor with a squeak, and panted, trying to take in the scene.

The marble floors were not the only impressive item in the large room. Gold decorated the walls, forming patterns which swirled, leading the eye to a particular destination—three large thrones on a marble platform. The seat cushions were all gold, and the outside of each chair had a unique design.

The one on the left was black, the edges of the chair jutting out like thorns and brambles. The middle chair was white with the frame decorated with the same swirling pattern that decorated the walls. The chair on the right was red and didn't have any embellishments on its wood frame. Simple and beautiful.

I took in the sight of the gods. Charos, god of death and the one who first spoke, leered down over me. He was titanic in every sense of the word. His skin was a pale gold, but his eyes, hair, and scars were all as black as his throne. Dressed in the traditional black robe I had read in our scriptures and seen in the statues in the temples and gravesites, he was terrifying.

"You are too severe, brother," spoke a figure next to him, this one soft-spoken with none of the sharp features that made Charos so scary. He had an amused smile and a face which appeared unblemished by stress or strain. His shorn hair hid the color, but his skin and eyes were a luminous brown. Not as dark as Savida's, but darker than Winnie's. His robe was red and also mirrored his throne in its simplicity. "Hello, young one. Cry no longer."

"Hedri," I gasped again, unable to comprehend that the god of love was smiling at me kindly. I'd forgotten to bow and threw myself into the motion, my hands slapping the marble as I pressed into the floor.

The final god spoke, drawing my attention, "You have prayed to us many times over the years, Zaide." Riseir, god of life, was the largest of his fellow god-brothers. He towered over me in his golden robe, which matched his golden skin. His hair was like mine, long and white.

"Yes, my lords," I answered quietly. I stared at my hands that were only moments ago covered in blood. Panic started rising in my chest. Clawdia was dying, maybe already gone, passed into her new life, and I wasn't with her.

Riseir raised one eyebrow and shrugged, his golden robe glimmered with the small movement. "Your prayers are not remarkable as many of the broken ones are also in dire need of our assistance."

He stared at me as though he wanted me to say something. "Yes, my lord. Many are slaves."

"So, you see our problem?"

"I'm sorry." I took a breath and tried to calm myself. "I am most honored by your presence, my gods. I am at your service. However, right now, my soul pair—"

Charos waved his hand impatiently. "Yes, yes. Your soul pair is dying."

I swallowed at his indifference. "I know—I know others are suffering worse ... but she is—" I stuttered as I tried to hold back more tears.

I wanted to tell them how her smile set my heart alight. How I couldn't imagine a realm without her light. How she was scared but still so brave. How she made me proud. How she was strong and fierce and beautiful. She is my everything.

Charos paced. The smell of incense hit me again as he stirred the air with his movements. "The slavers purging the

327

realms are making our lives much more difficult by torturing and killing our worshipers."

"We have brought you to us to consult with you." Hedri continued to smile down at me.

Had this happened before, I would have been elated. I would have shouted and screamed and danced knowing that the gods chose me. I was special. My mother would have been so proud to see this, to hear about this. I would have offered the gods all of me. Become a willing slave to their desires.

But Clawdia lay still on a gravel road, and I would sacrifice anything to be with her, to save her.

I promised her I'd always save her.

I shook my head and said, "My soul pair—"

Riseir huffed out a frustrated breath. "Broken one, we have the power to save her. You should appeal to us to do so."

I held my breath as hope surged through me like a flash of lightning, and I stared up at my god. "You would save her?"

He smiled. "We would."

His smile was unnerving, but his words were a promise. He would, but there was going to be a price.

It doesn't matter the price. Save her.

"What do you need me to do?"

Charos seemed pleased that I acknowledged the bargain and continued, "We find ourselves with people who are slaves, growing weaker and fewer each day."

"You are free. You have found your soul pair. You are our hope." Hedri smiled.

I shook my head. "I don't understand."

"Hope. For your people and for your gods," Hedri clarified slowly with his soft smile still on his face.

I change my mind. Hedri is the scariest.

"I am your hope for what?"

328

"For the survival of your race. For the survival of your gods."

I gasped. "You're dying?"

"Gods are only such if they have people who worship them," Riseir said.

Charos added, "Slaves have nothing. Only some call our names from the pit of despair."

"We have already lost so many to their next life," Hedri continued. "And the life pool was destroyed in a raid."

"There are no new births," Charos said.

"Your people are dying, and your gods along with them," Riseir finished.

No.

"But what can I do?" I asked, my body trembling with the great sadness of knowing I was one of the few who were left.

Hedri lowered himself to the floor and sat at eye level with me. I tried not to breathe too loudly as, with his terrifying soft smile still in place, he explained, "When you bond with your soul pair, you will regain the powers of old. It will be weaker than before since it is divided with another body, but power, you will have. You will see a thread of the universe and be able to manipulate it." He patted the marble floors. "It is quite nice down here." He looked at his god-brothers and said, "You should join us."

Charos scoffed, crossed his arms, and changed his stance.

Riseir closed his eyes for a second and then said, "We will save your soul pair and allow you to bond with her without the required intercourse, although that will be necessary to keep the bond strong."

I gasped. "You honor me with such a gift."

"It is not for free," Charos growled.

I nodded understanding. I would do anything to save her.

"It is also not simple," Riseir warned, and my heart sank to my stomach. "I'm afraid your soul pair was born into

Earth's laws of magic, and those require a familiar, which she is, to have a witch. Her witch is dying. She needs a new one to bond with to stabilize her. That is something out of our control."

A witch. A new witch. Who—

"Charlie! He's a witch!" I exclaimed, almost bouncing from the floor. Then I added in a more subdued tone, "But he doesn't know how to do any magic. How does he bond with her?"

Hedri was lying down now, and he spoke as though he were just about to fall asleep. "He need only touch her, find her life thread, and attach it to his own."

I had a feeling it would be infinitely more complicated than that, but who was I to argue with a god? My soul pair, my Little Cat, my Clawdia had a chance now, and I would not ruin it.

I took a deep breath, tried to calm my racing heart, and asked, "What is it you would like in return for my help?"

"With your soul pair, your new powers and your ... questionable choice in friends, you will free your kind and reestablish our society and religion."

It was a lifetime's work. It would be hard and terrifying, but we could do it. My mismatched family could do it. I could do it with their support.

A question, a blasphemous question, appeared in my mind. I tried to shake it away, but it wouldn't leave me. After a few moments of debate, I asked, "Why don't you help? You are the gods."

"How dare you—" Charos eyes lit up like black flame, and I stiffened, wondering why anyone listened to the little voice inside their head.

Hedri waved a hand in the air. "It is natural that he questions." He opened one eye to look at me. "We may not interfere personally in the lives of our subjects. It would be cheating."

"You are helping me. Is that not cheating?"

Hedri smiled. "We are only interfering with the fate of a poor familiar who is the soul pair to a titan."

Riseir explained further, "You will still have to make all the right choices when you go back to ensure you all survive. We are only allowing you to bond with your soul pair without intercourse in order to save her. We are priming you both to be our hands."

The gods' hands. Charlie will not believe this.

I nodded. "I will do whatever you want."

Charos scoffed. "Of course you will."

"Excellent." Hedri clapped and stood in one fluid motion. "In order for you to master your gifts quickly, we are sending our son to train you all. Only when he deems you ready will you be allowed to save your people."

"And to ensure that you hurry with your training, we offer you some incentive." Charos's smile was cruel, and it seemed to become all-encompassing as my world faded to black.

My eyes adjusted slowly to the bright light that seemed to beam down on me from all angles. Squinting, I could make out that the floor was no longer marble. Instead, it was dusty and dry and grainy.

Sand.

My body temperature was quickly rising, sweat gathering on my forehead as the sun, or suns, as I noticed when I looked around, were blazing, burning me.

I stood slowly and looked around for my gods or a familiar face or place. I couldn't see anything I recognized. However, I could see the disgust on the faces of the populace, people with shimmering skin, like scales, yellow, and they all stared at me.

A different realm.

Someone yelled in the distance. That was something I recognized. The sound of a slave getting a beating.

I ran toward it, and the crowd parted as though I were diseased. It unsettled me, but I was also grateful, as it made my sprint to the voices much easier.

In the distance, I saw a human female cowering beneath the whip of her owner.

Humans don't travel the dimensions. How is there one here? Is this one of those missing people?

"Leave her alone, Creath." The booming voice drew my attention, and there he was—Thos.

He was bigger than I remembered, as scarred as I was, and his voice was deeper. But there was no mistaking the chip in his front tooth—my fault for playing too rough with him—and the same golden skin, the same white hair as I had, marking us from the same family. His was shorter and had a curl to it as he raced toward the human to protect her.

He's alive.

"Thos!" I called out, and when his eyes met mine, I smiled. I was so thankful he was alive and well, so glad to see him grown, that I hadn't thought about the consequences of my actions.

He was distracted and therefore open to attack. I opened my mouth to warn him as Creath moved to strike him with a collection of thin wires, but I was suddenly jerked away and back to see the gods in front of me.

"No! Thos! Is he all right?" I demanded.

"He has suffered worse." Charos shrugged.

My poor little brother. My heart cried out for him, but I needed to save my soul pair before I added anyone else to the list, even if doing so would mark my spirit.

I tried to reorganize my thoughts. "There was a human. Why was there a human?"

Charos shrugged again. "Weak people from all dimensions are being picked off and sold for slavery."

"We showed you your brother so that you will train quickly and save your people, your brother included." Riseir narrowed his eyes at me as though expecting me to refuse. But I could only see how this would benefit me. I would save all the people I loved, be a hero, have power, and be the hands of the gods.

I couldn't see a trap or trick or any repercussions.

They are alive? All of them? I can save them.

Hope and happiness filled my heart and lifted me to my feet. "I will. I'll do anything and everything in my power to save them," I swore.

"Then we have a deal," they said unanimously. Ominously. I shuddered.

With a flash of light, I was back in the human realm in the pool of blood, which now surrounded my soul pair and her witch.

Clawdia was cold when I touched her. I tried not to let that panic me.

"Charlie!" I screamed.

I focused my attention back on Clawdia.

"Little Cat, don't worry. We are going to save you. Just hold on to me."

CHAPTER 29

CHARLIE

"*C*harlie, run!" Winnie shouted.

I hesitated. Mary had Clawdia and Winnie in separate magical cages, and there was a crazed glint in her eye, one I'd seen in a few men when I was younger, which told me she was prepared to kill.

Mary's free hand glowed with the start of a new spell. The deep red light pulsated sinisterly. And I fucking knew what red meant. Debs might have told them not to kill the human, but I bet she didn't approve of the plan to use a witch as a hostage, either. Mary was a wild card.

I caught Clawdia's eye as I turned to run, the fear and desperation palpable. She wasn't scared for herself. She was scared for me. I could see how much she cared in her heaving chest and outstretched hand, and at any other time, I would have been elated.

But now wasn't the time.

I spun and ran into the forest, following the green hair bobbing ahead of me. The spell flew past me like a red firework and crashed into a tree, spraying bark and shards of broken spell into my path. I cringed away, covering my face, but kept running to catch up with Daithi.

A blood-curdling scream echoed out into the woods, and I almost stopped. I wanted to turn back. "Shit," I breathed as I tried not to think about what was happening on the road.

Zaide is with her. He'll protect her. She's fine.

But Zaide couldn't protect her if her familiar bond was broken by the death of her witch.

"Charlie, hurry!" Daithi whisper shouted, now only a few feet ahead. My feet picked up their pace again, or he slowed his, because I caught up to him, and he hissed, "Where are the fires?"

I scanned the trees, trying to concentrate on the feeling that always told me where things were. But it didn't tell me anything. I jogged in a slow circle and still felt nothing. I huffed a frustrated breath and shook my head.

"They have to be around here somewhere. Just keep a lookout." I set off running again, now looking for the witches since they would eventually reveal the whereabouts of their demon sacrifices. Although the wind whipped around me and burned my lungs with every gasp, I was really pleased my gym sessions were coming in handy.

Daithi's incredulous stare burned holes in my back. "You don't know?"

"I'm not omni-fucking-potent, Daithi. I think they're moving, so I can't pin them down. Let's just head toward the witches." I panted. "Remember to be invisible to them."

"I am."

"Great."

As I followed the tug leading me to the witches, I began hearing the voices of people laughing and chatting and slowed to a jog. We came to a clearing beautifully decorated with flowers and lights, but it gave me the creeps, and I rubbed the goosebumps that appeared on my arms. In the center was a large hole that had been dug out—the dirt distributed at the edge of the clearing and turned into benches for the hordes of witches present.

We are fucked.

"Are you seeing this shit?" I whispered to Daithi, and I saw him nod out of the corner of my eye.

"Charlie! You made it!" Simon called out. I don't know how he saw me with so many people milling around, but he also had the Seeker gift.

"Hi, Simon. Great to see you again." I gave him a manly handshake and my firm I'm-not-panicking voice.

He laughed. "Did you run here? You're out of breath."

"Yeah. I didn't want to miss anything. I thought I was late."

"Not late. Just doing some last-minute preparations and waiting for Debbie to arrive. She's the leader of this event."

"Well, I can't wait to see it all get started." I nodded at the hole in the ground. "You building a pool?"

"That's the reservoir. It'll be where we pour our magic tonight."

Daithi whispered from behind me, "Charlie, ask him about the fires."

That's not an easy segue, Daithi. I thought frustratedly.

I took a breath and activated spy mode. "So, where are all the candles, the wands, the terrified sacrifices? I mean, I'm a little disappointed."

He laughed again, "No candles needed since we've got the place covered in battery-powered lights. Wands also do nothing except maybe stir cauldrons. And there are definitely no terrified sacrifices. Sorry to not live up to the horror movie trends, but this is it. Witches, fairy lights, and little balls of magic."

Got you.

"Balls of magic?" I asked innocently.

"Yeah, you know, the fire we are going to use to raise him?"

I nodded like I only just remembered that he mentioned them earlier. "Oh yeah. Where are they?"

"They are being transported here as we speak. We had a bit of a delay earlier doing an extra security spell, but it shouldn't be long until we start the ceremony."

"Awesome. I'm super excited." I did a little excited two-step, which Simon grinned at, as I thought up my next move. If Debs was coming soon, I didn't have much time. I needed to lose Simon, find the fires, and free them. With a new plan, I grimaced and said, "I don't suppose you guys set up a little men's room around here? All that running did not help."

"We did actually. We're expecting the ceremony will leave a lot of us feeling a bit rough, so we got some Portaloos. I'll walk you to them." He turned toward the east side of the clearing, and I cursed in my head as I followed him help-lessly, looking for a way to escape.

To Daithi, I whispered, "Go look around. Find them." And he moved silently away from me, going in search of his love.

I continued trudging through crunchy undergrowth as I followed Simon. He'd mentioned something interesting, and my curiosity wouldn't let it go unanswered. "The ceremony will leave you feeling rough?"

He shrugged and turned to face me. I realized there were blue toilet blocks behind him. "Well, draining our magic is going to take a lot out of us. If we give too much, then we'll die. Thankfully, we have the fire to prevent that from happening."

Jesus Christ. Why is nothing simple? Shit.

I didn't want to kill the only family I'd ever found. I had to think of something, and quickly.

"Witches!" a voice boomed.

Fuck! It's starting!

337

Simon glanced over my shoulder to the clearing where the voices had quietened to an excited buzz. "Charlie, it's starting. You'll need to pee quick if you don't want to miss anything." He had a gleam in his eyes that made me uncomfortable as he moved to walk past me and join the ceremony. Even so, he was family. You don't let family die. At least, that's what I assumed was one rule of family. But maybe it was different if that person was an evil witch.

I grabbed his arm and pulled him back. "Earlier, you said that you didn't agree with the demon's fire thing," I whispered.

He jerked back like I slapped him. Then he narrowed his eyes and leaned close to whisper back, "Keep your voice down. Fuck, do you want me to lose all standing in the community?"

"Sorry." I wasn't, and I waited for him to prove to me he didn't deserve to die.

"I don't agree with it, but it's necessary," he hissed and then stared at me curiously. Probably getting another Seeker clue that something more was happening here. "Why are you bringing it up?"

His answer didn't assure me that I could convince him to not take part, but if his morals told him it was bad, then at least he wasn't a complete monster. I told him the truth. "What if I told you that my friend, a demon, had his fire taken and I'm here to take it back?"

Debs started her speech, and her voice spilled out across the woods like a river of poison. I cringed when it reached us. "Welcome to this joyous event. Tonight, we make history. Tonight, we ensure our survival."

Distracted by the start of the ceremony, Simon listened, half turned to the sound of her voice. When cheers went up, he blinked. Then he glared. "Are you being serious?" he hissed.

"Deadly."

He shook his head. "I'm sorry, Charlie, but you can't take it back."

I gave him a mocking, sympathetic smile. "I'm sorry, Simon, but you can't stop me. This is a warning because I don't want you to die for something stupid."

He scoffed. "This isn't stupid."

"Well, so far, you've said that you're going to kill tortured demons to raise a protector that died centuries ago instead of just making a new one. That is fucked up, Simon."

Debs's voice boomed. "Otherworlders. Beings from different dimensions. More and more, there are portals opened to the human realm. And more and more people are going missing. But we can stop the otherworlders. We can block the portals. The protector's life force protects this realm, and so we must raise him."

Simon looked at me pointedly, and I raised my eyebrow. "Have you thought maybe summoning them from places might attract attention to the human realm?"

"Well, no. But—"

"The point is, those beings are intelligent and kind, and this is no different from chopping a human up for parts. So, I am taking my friend's fire home and as many others as I can carry. You need to decide whether you are going to die in that ceremony, because when it saps you of all your magic, there won't be enough fire left to save everyone," I growled.

"Charlie, there's no way you can get past all of us."

"See, that's the thing. You've caused your own doom because you've been summoning the demons and burying them. That's attracted other, more powerful races to find and uncover them. I'm not afraid that you have more witches because I have a very vengeful faei who would level this place in a heartbeat to get his love's fire back."

"If you'll join me in coming together and casting a quick

protection spell, we will be safe to perform our ceremony," Debs said. From the corner of my eye, I saw the witches forming a circle, holding hands.

Daithi raced toward me. But he didn't hold a ball of fire. His face was the picture of desperation.

Shit. New plan.

"I don't understand—" Simon began.

I cut him off. "Forgive me for this, cousin."

I punched him in the face, knocking him out completely. I shook out the pain lancing in my hand as Daithi reached me. He didn't even look down at the unconscious witch in front of me. As the witches in the clearing started chanting, he glanced toward them in panic. "Charlie, I've found the fires," he panted.

I looked at him incredulously. "Why didn't you grab them?"

"I could not. The witches knew I'd be coming. They've found a spell that repels me. I can't get close, and I can't undo it in time. Charlie, please, we must hurry. They are—"

"I know. Where are the fires from here?"

"On the other side of the clearing. Behind the leader." He pointed, and I could barely make out the tiny glimmers of lights that danced behind her.

"We can't let them finish their spell. We don't know what it will do to us." I took a deep breath. "It's the 'raise hell' part of the plan, Daithi. You do whatever faei can do and cover me. I'm going to play whack-a-mole."

I ran toward them. Forget the sprint I did earlier. This one was pure adrenaline, refined athleticism, like I had been training since I could walk and this was for the Olympic title.

Instead of jumping obstacles, I was dodging witches as they tried to stop me from reaching the jars. I imagined I was a human Sonic the Hedgehog and no one could touch me. I threw punches and elbows but never took my eyes off my goal.

Piled high, there must have been at least fifty jars, each with a glowing ember inside. A fire which once lived inside a demon. A demon who was probably loved by someone that was praying they found their way home. I couldn't tell the ages of these fires. I couldn't know their history, but more importantly, I couldn't tell which one was Savida's in order to save him first.

Thinking fast, I stopped to pick up a branch by my feet ... I charged. Armed with my wooden weapon, I swung and knocked a dozen jars over.

They smashed to the ground, glass exploding everywhere, and the fire that had been contained was released and flew back to its host—who I hoped wasn't still underground. I didn't stop swinging. Dodged a witch. Smashed some jars. Smashed a witch. Dodged shards of glass. No holds barred. No fucks given. I released all my frustration and rage.

Fucking Sweden!

Swing.

Fucking witches fucking shit up! Giving me a bad luck curse! Stealing my friend!

Crash.

Fucking Zaide and his unnecessary muscles!

Shatter.

Fucking Clawdicat fucking up my toilet rolls!

Smash.

Fucking Clawdia fucking up my head!

"Stop!" a voice shouted. A voice that sounded above all the other screams and yells. Authoritative and calm. So caught up in my rampage, I only recognized it when I looked up and saw Debs staring furiously at me.

I continued to bat witches away and smash jars, but I

noted that many of them were attacking Daithi's magic-made dragon illusion.

"That's not a real dragon, you fools! You're being tricked by the faei! Attack the human smashing the jars!" Deb ordered.

Too bad for Debs that I only had a few more jars left. "Fuck you, Debs," I shouted and swung my bat around. As the last jar smashed to the ground, I was already running, leaving the devastated witches in my dust.

"Daithi, get home!" I shouted. I wanted him to be there when Savida awoke, and I needed to get Clawdia and Zaide so we could meet him back at the apartment. He turned and nodded before darting into the treeline, leaving the illusion to distract the witches.

After two minutes of pegging it, I realized my findy powers had kicked in and I was actually heading in the right direction to the car.

I stopped dead when I heard a scream. "Charlie!"

Zaide.

I raced out of the tree line and onto the road until I saw the silver glint of the rental car.

As I approached, I knew it was bad. Blood had trickled a foot away and dried on the asphalt in thin red lines. Peeking around the car, I let out a pained moan at the sight. Winnie was lying with her throat cut wide open, Clawdia curled up next to her, and Zaide was holding Clawdia's hand like it was the only thing he had left. Their clothes and skin dripped with blood.

I dropped next to them as adrenaline kept me powering through this latest life-fuck. "What happened?"

Zaide was unnaturally calm. "She is holding on to our bond, but her witch has already passed. She is a familiar, and despite my bond with her, she needs a new witch."

My mind raced. "Fuck. Okay. I can run—"

He turned to look at me. His purple eyes pulsed, and I was trapped in his gaze. "Charlie, you are a witch."

"Not a pissing practicing one," I hissed.

"No. But you can do this. You can save her."

I shook my head. I wanted to help her more than life itself. I looked down at her and saw death coloring her already pale skin gray. Her lips, usually red raw from her biting them, were blue. Blood drenched her hair, her clothes.

Tears welled in my eyes. I whispered, "How the hell do I make her my familiar? I don't know the first thing about being a witch."

"Charlie, just touch her," he growled, losing his patience.

I touched her.

"She's cold. Should she be cold?" I was panicking.

"Charlie, concentrate."

"I'm trying. Nothing is happening." But I wasn't trying anything. I wasn't concentrating on anything except that Clawdia was dying. I was failing. My heart raced, and thoughts bounced around my head too quickly for me to catch a look.

"Close your eyes," Zaide growled, and I did as he said. I heard him take a calming breath before continuing, "Imagine you can see a thread coming from her heart. It is gold, like the color of her hair, and is moving toward you."

Like being hypnotized, I followed his every word, every instruction. I pictured the scene as it was in my head; Clawdia covered in blood, cold, dead. I imagined that from her chest, a gold strand emerged. It shimmered and waved and danced and glinted in the sunlight. I could feel its power; its innocent display didn't fool me.

I glared at it. It unsettled me. I wanted to open my eyes so I couldn't see it again.

Zaide said, "I don't want you to be afraid of it. It is the bond. I want you to reach for it and allow it to reach for you."

343

I understood why it scared me. Permanency. It was something I had never had before. I didn't believe in it. I didn't look for it. I lived with as few deep connections to the world as I could get away with.

But I wanted to be a permanent part of Clawdia's life.

I reached for it, and it shimmed away. Frowning, I went still and willed it closer instead. After three breaths—each one becoming filled with more urgency and more panic as the strand didn't edge closer to me—finally, it shivered and lay itself flat on my open hand. I let out a breath I didn't know I was holding and closed my hand around the bond, already feeling stronger.

"I have it," I told Zaide in a trance-like voice I didn't recognize.

"Pull it to your heart. Gently. Imagine that the strand ties itself around you."

Again, I did as he said, not opening my eyes, but using my mind like the muscle it was supposed to be. When my hand hit my chest and I imagined my heart with a little gold bow wrapped around it, I froze. Power enveloped me. And then cold flooded me. I shivered as if I'd just gone skinny dipping in the arctic.

I curled in on myself, trying to conserve heat, eyes still shut. "Zaide, I can't breathe. I'm cold. What's going on?"

I thought I'd fucked up, that I'd done something wrong, and pinched my eyes tighter, physically pained by the thought that I hadn't saved her.

With the hard thump of a large, warm hand on my back, my eyes popped open, and Zaide whispered, "It's okay, Charlie. It worked. You've tethered Clawdia to yourself. You are a witch with a powerful familiar."

I sighed; my relief was so great I thought I'd lose all the air in my lungs. I unclenched my body and peered at him. "Then why do I feel like death?"

"Because you feel what she feels, and she feels what you feel. She is recovering from a near-death experience."

I looked back at her and noticed that all the previous signs of death were fading. Color was coming back to her skin, her chest rising and falling. I realized that if I felt everything she felt, then I'd better learn to be a decent fucking witch to protect her and myself, to make sure this didn't happen again. "Fuck. Well, she's not allowed outside again."

Zaide laughed. "I'm sure she will have something to say about that when she wakes up."

I raised my hand to stroke her cheek. I knew she was alive. But I felt so horrible. I couldn't imagine anyone surviving this feeling. "You're sure she'll wake up?"

"She'll wake when she's healed. I know it." Zaide stroked her hair and sighed happily. It didn't seem weird that we both sat around her, stroking her. We were both bonded to her. We both wanted to reassure ourselves she was all right. "Thank you, my friend."

I choked out a laugh. "Not going to say it was my pleasure, because it wasn't, but ... you know I care about her, too. I'm just glad I got here in time."

He nodded and then asked, "You and Daithi were successful?"

I perked up at the memory. "Mate, you should have seen me with my tree branch taking out those jars of fire."

He chuckled. "I'm sure I would have been very proud of your puny human strength."

I grinned. "Let's get back. Savida might already be awake, and I want to tell him the story. You guys won't add the proper embellishments."

And of course, because it was all too easy, as I moved to stand, I felt myself get pushed back down to the gravel. Gritting my teeth and hissing from the pain, I looked over my shoulder to see another magical cage surrounding us. A figure emerged from the trees.

An unfamiliar voice echoed into the night, the smirk evident in their tone, "You aren't going anywhere."

Fuck.

CHAPTER 30

CLAWDIA

*F*ire laced my throat. With every small breath, pain rippled across my body until it was all I knew, all I felt. While my body instinctively fought for me to live, I counted down my heartbeats. As it became hard to breathe, air see-sawed in and out of my mouth but left my lungs untouched. I was gasping and desperate. I tried not to think about what I was leaving behind as I died.

My first death was not like this. My first death was a relief, freedom and peace. I'd wanted it. I'd needed to escape. I'd had no painless options. Death was welcome.

This death was anger and sadness and pain. It was wrong.

How could Mary kill Winnie? Winnie loved her. Why would she do that? Why couldn't they just give Savida's fire back and then we'd all still be alive? Why do I have to die too? It's so unfair! I just found Zaide. I wanted more time with Charlie. I wanted to save Savida. I wanted Daithi to like me. I wanted ... another chance.

Do cats really have nine lives? I wondered, my head feeling disjointed, separate from the searing pain of my body. I hoped they did. As my eyelids closed and I heeded the call of death, I felt a pop and opened my eyes to find I was staring down at myself.

I, or my body, lay still on the gravel, curled next to Winnie. The blood that continued to pour from Winnie's neck drenched my hair. I watched from outside of my body as Zaide crawled toward me and touched me, his large, golden body heaving sobs as his hands came away bloody.

"He's devastated," a familiar voice remarked next to me. I gasped and swung my head to see Winnie. Or what I assumed to be her spirit. She looked ... exactly as she did on the day that Zaide, Savida and Daithi arrived.

Her red hair was curled and bouncy. Her clothes were the same orange blouse and pencil skirt. Her dark skin was glowing, and the killing gash to her throat was gone as though it never happened. I looked at her body and then back at her ghost.

I blinked and remembered that she had spoken. "He's my soul pair." I looked back at the scene to see Zaide, motionless, bent over me in a prayer. "Was my soul pair," I corrected with tear-filled eyes and trembling lips.

"Like a soul mate?" she asked.

I shrugged, unsure since Zaide said we were the only ones that he knew of.

Now there were none again.

All the possibilities, what we could have done, what we could have been, were all gone now.

"What a mess," Winnie muttered as she assessed the scene. "I'm sorry, Clawdia."

I nodded and whispered, "I'm sorry, too."

That surprised her, because she turned to face me fully, and I found it so strange to see her eyes level to mine. "What? Why?"

I shrugged and tried to blink back tears. "I'm sorry you're

dead. I'm sorry I couldn't save you. You didn't deserve what Mary did to you. You loved her, and she betrayed you."

"Oh, Clawds. You don't need to apologize for any of that." She opened her arms and pulled me into her embrace. The tears I had been holding back flowed quietly out of me. She pulled back and held my face so she could stare earnestly into my eyes, wiping away tears with her thumbs. "It wasn't your responsibility to save me when I didn't want to be saved. I should have been looking after you. You were a gift. You had your own power and strength, and I didn't cherish you like I should have. I used you. And I've killed you. I'm so sorry."

It was everything I wanted to hear from her since this mess began, but I didn't want to hear it when we were ghosts standing over our bodies. It was too late to change anything. Another tear fell, and I squeezed my eyes shut.

"Do you think all ghosts cry when they die, or is it just us?" She gave a watery chuckle, trying to lighten the mood, and I flashed a small smile.

"I wasn't a ghost last time." I told her and looked away at the trees. "Something about this feels more final."

We were both quiet for a little while, just taking in the scenery, until I said, "I forgive you."

"For everything?" I could feel her gaze on me, but I didn't look at her.

"For everything," I agreed.

"Thank you," she said, her voice quivering.

I turned to her and took her hand. "You shouted for Charlie to run. You wanted to protect him, knowing he would try to stop the ceremony. You didn't do that for him. You did it for me. Because you know I care about him."

"I knew I was dead when Mary captured me." Her face collapsed, and tears welled in her eyes. "She hoped to distract you all long enough to have the ceremony happen before you could get there, but I wanted to spite her, even if it meant we didn't save the world. Why would I care about that when I was going to die?"

"Well, thank you. I know you thought you were saving the world, but the world isn't worth saving if we are killing innocent beings for it." She shrugged and gave me a smile. "Why did Mary do that to you?"

Her face fell. "Your guess is as good as mine."

"Aren't you angry?"

"Angry?"

"Mary killed you. Your girlfriend murdered you in cold blood. You aren't upset?"

Her lips tightened, and her eyes narrowed. "I'm not angry. I'm livid." She huffed out a big breath and shook her head. "But she'll get what's coming to her."

I nodded. Karma would come for her. It could be at any time, this life or the next, but it disappointed me that I wouldn't be there to see the end of her. "I always hated her."

"You did?" Winnie seemed surprised. Maybe I'd done a better job of being impartial than I believed.

"She wasn't kind to you."

"You didn't say anything."

I shrugged. "You loved her. I wanted what you wanted."

"I would like to say that I would have listened if you had told me how you felt about her, but I don't think I would have. I was so in love with her I didn't see the signs." A tear leaked from her eye, and my heart clenched.

"I'm so sorry." I understood how it felt to have someone who you loved turn on you, and I wouldn't have wished it on my worst enemy.

She kicked the gravel and sighed. "I was always afraid I would die alone. You know my parents don't talk to me, and the only person close to me was Mary. Maybe that's why I got attached to her. Loneliness."

"But she killed me. You crawled into my arms. I held your hand as I took my last breath, and I'm with you now, waiting for what happens next, and that means the world to me." She took my hand again, and I saw the gratitude and love she felt shining in her eyes.

"I remember when I first called you." She chuckled. "You were so scared that you were screaming in my head and talking yourself into believing it was a dream. You hid under the lounge chair for days, not eating. I would sit with you and explain about me, about witches, about this time. It was the opposite of your upbringing.

It was so hard for you in a new body, in a new time. But you accepted your circumstances. You adapted. And you loved me, a black lesbian witch, despite everything. I didn't tell you how proud I was of you. You learned so quickly. You could scroll Netflix with your paws and had your first unrequited crush. You were, are, an amazing soul, Clawdia. I hope your next life treats you better."

"I hope we meet again and that you find the love you were missing." My lips quivered.

She looked into the tree line at something I couldn't see. "I think it's time for me to go. Blessed be. Until we meet again, little sister."

I pulled her into a hug and whispered, "Goodbye, Winnie. Thank you for calling me to be your familiar. I'll miss you."

I was reluctant to let her go, but she moved out of my arms and slowly walked away before vanishing.

I gasped as it hit me that she'd gone, and I collapsed to the ground, sobbing.

She's gone. She's gone.

My anchor to the world was gone, and I felt adrift, more so than I believed other ghosts did.

In the corner of my eye, something glinted in the bright light from where Winnie had just disappeared.

I turned my head slowly to see two figures emerging, and I gasped and backed away. The gentleman was wearing a white dress shirt with a blue tie and brown waistcoat and trousers. The lady wore a long blue dress, matching the man's tie, that sat just above her ankles. The color complimented the strawberry blond hair that rolled in neat waves around her shoulders. The same color as my own.

"Mother? Father?"

They walked toward me, their clothes moving as though the wind affected them. Old fears rose inside me, and although I knew they weren't alive and that they weren't walking with physical feet, I could hear their footsteps like beats on wooden floors which tapped in time with my racing heart.

I scooted further back but stopped myself.

I'm dead. I'm a ghost. They can't hurt me.

I forced myself to stand up and meet their gaze head-on. Their expressions surprised me. Mother had tears in her eyes, and Father ... looked sad. Aggrieved.

"What are you doing here?" I croaked.

Honestly, I wanted to know. Because Father had abused me. Mother had let him. As far as I was concerned, they should have been in Hell. Not staring at me through the warm, golden glow of a peaceful afterlife.

Fury bubbled up inside me; poison they planted inside me came spewing out. "How dare you? How can you even show your face? I might have taken my own life, but you forced me to do it! It was your fault! You broke me and then gave me to a monster."

"Claudia. We are so sorry. You don't know how much," my father said, and even his voice sounded different. Like it had before the war. Before he hated me.

"I don't want your apologies." I spat. But I did. I wanted apologies and explanations and hugs and kisses like any child who just wanted their parents to care about them.

My mother bowed her head. "No. And you don't need them. But you do need our warning."

Dread filled me. I was dead. Why did I need a warning? "Warning?" I repeated.

"He is coming, Claudia. Be careful. He will want you again. Just as he did before." My father's eyes pleaded for me to understand, to be careful, to listen. He was concerned. It sent my pulse thumping madly.

I didn't understand. "Who?"

My mother looked over her shoulder before whispering, "You will know the truth soon, daughter. The questions about us and your last days as a human will be answered. You will know the reason for your familiar calling. None of it was a coincidence."

I shook my head. "I'm dead. This is the end of my story."

They stepped back into the golden glow, and my mother replied, "No. You were just the catalyst."

And with a snap, everything went black. Everything was painful and sore and heavy. I realized I was back in my body. My body was breathing. Something had happened. Something had saved me.

"Just remember, we always loved you," a voice whispered.

My head was too full and fluid to make any sense of it all. I was a slave to the sensations that battered me. I drifted, unaware for a little while.

When I came to, I tried to open my eyes. They were streaming and sore, but they fluttered open to see only blurred light.

When my eyes focused, familiar brown eyes filled my vision. I croaked, "Charlie. Where are we?"

The end

Excited for the next installment in the Tales of a Witch's Familiar series? CATATONIC is up next!

FOLLOW FOR MORE FUN

Need to share your frustration at the cliffhanger?
We're here for you!

Confused by Charlie's English slang?
Explanations await!

Want to share pictures of your familiar?
Give me those cute pics!

Come and join the reader group The Familiar Forest Facebook page to talk about The Tales of a Witch's Familiar series.

You can also sign up to my newsletter and receive a short story called Catty which reveals more of Clawdia and Charlie's hilarious relationship before the start of this story!

THANK YOU!

Yes, you!

This is my first ever book baby released into the wild and despite it being the most nerve-wracking and stressful experience, you've just made it all worthwhile by picking up a book from someone new and unknown.

Thank you so much!

I hope your pillow always feels like the cold side, that your favorite book gets made into a movie with your dream cast and that your hot drink never burns you.

Whether you loved or hated Catalyst, please take a moment to leave a review and hopefully other wonderful readers will be able to find, read and love/hate with you.

Thank you to my family and friends who have supported and believed in me throughout this whole process. I am so lucky to have you. Love you all to the moon and back.

I've also been lucky enough to have the mentorship of Katie May, and the friendship of Eliza Raine. You are both huge inspirations to me and it's meant so much that you've answered my annoying questions, given advice and encouragement.

Fellow readers and book enthusiasts that I've met at reader events, on social media, or in the wild, thank you so much for the genuine support and excitement when I've sheepishly admitted to writing a book.

To my editor Heather, my proofreader Victoria, and my cover designer Christian, this book wouldn't look half as good as it does now without you. You've helped make my dreams come true.

Until next time!

ABOUT THE AUTHOR

Alba Lockwood is a debut author who writes reverse harem, paranormal romance and fantasy. When she isn't writing about cats, witches, Gods and other realms, you can find her losing sleep reading books from other amazing authors such as Katie May, Raven Kennedy, Tate James and Jaymin Eve.

Alba is from and currently resides in Birmingham, England with her parents, her brothers, and her precious black and white cat, Daisy who inspired this series.

Printed in Great Britain
by Amazon

18204926R00212